LISA HELEN GRAY
CHARLOTTE

A NEXT GENERATION CARTER BROTHER NOVEL
BOOK SIX

Copyright ©
Copyrights reserved
2020
Lisa Helen Gray
Edited by Stephanie Farrant at Farrant Editing
Cover Design by Cassy Roop at Pink Ink Designs
No part of this publication may be reproduced or transmitted in any form or by any means, electronic or mechanical, including photocopy, recording, or any information storage and retrieval system without the prior written consent from the publisher, except in the instance of quotes for reviews. No part of this book may be scanned, uploaded, or distributed via the Internet without the publisher's permission and is a violation of the international copyright law, which subjects the violator to severe fines and imprisonment.

This book is licensed for your enjoyment. E-book copies may not be resold or given away to other people. If you would like to share with a friend, please buy an extra copy. Thank you for respecting the author's work.

This is a work of fiction. Names, characters, places and events are all products of the author's imagination. Any resemblance to actual persons, living or dead, businesses or establishments is purely coincidental.

CHARLOTTE

FAMILY TREE
(AGES ARE SUBJECT TO CHANGE THROUGHOUT BOOKS)

Maverick & Teagan
- Faith (engaged to Beau)
- Lily (married to Jaxon)
- Mark
- Aiden (with Bailey)

Mason & Denny
- Hope
- Ciara
- Ashton

Malik & Harlow
- Madison (Twin 1)
- Maddox (Twin 2 – with Amelia)
- Trent

Max & Lake
- Landon (Triplet 1 – with Paisley)
- Hayden (Triplet 2 – with Clayton)
- Liam (Triplet 3)

Myles & Kayla
- Charlotte (with Drew)
- Jacob

Evan (Denny's brother) & Kennedy
- Imogen
- Joshua

PROLOGUE

M USIC BLARES THROUGH THE CLUB, vibrating through the back of the booth I'm sitting in. The stench of sweat and beer lingers in the air as bodies mill around the busy hot spot. Tease is a popular strip club and has all kinds of clientele.

Bored, single chicks being one of them.

I swirl the paper umbrella in my cocktail, staring at the orange liquid as it makes a tiny tornado.

Sighing, I sit back in the booth whilst people-watching those in the club and immediately spot Candy. I send her a wave and smile as she approaches me, her tiny sequined thong the only thing on her toned body. Candy isn't her real name— it's Harriet— but she likes to keep her anonymity working here. I guess she doesn't want her other job or the university she attends to find out she's a stripper—not that there's anything wrong with it.

She sits down next to me, placing a shot next to my cocktail that's still full. "What's up tonight, Charlie? You don't seem yourself. Misty is worried too."

Misty is Olivia's stripper name. All my friends have one, and it's always how they are addressed in the club, no matter who they are talking to.

Over the past year, these guys have become good friends of mine. I only see them on the odd occasion outside the strip club, but our time together is spent having fun. I love them. They're outgoing, confident, and full of life. There are times when I wish I could be just like them. They even loaned me and Lily some outfits once, to wear to Faith's engagement party, but it was a miss. I'm not cut out for high heels and tight dresses.

I shouldn't be surprised they would read my mood. They're very intuitional.

I turn to look at her. "I'm fine," I lie, leaning into her so she can hear me. Her sweet perfume masks the smell of sweat coming from the men in the room and I relax a little.

She nudges my shoulder. "Want a lap dance?"

I pick up my drink, turning the umbrella once again as I think about her offer. "Not tonight, Harriet."

She pulls the drink out of my hand and I glance up at her, startled. "C'mon. Tell me what's going on."

"Why do you think there's anything going on?"

"Because in all the time I've known you, I've never seen you upset." She pauses for a minute, arching an eyebrow. "And you never turn down a lap dance."

She has a point. I do make it my mission not to get sad. As for the lap dance, they're for research.

"What do you want from life?" I ask, taking her off guard.

"Apart from money, I want to buy a holiday home in Spain and own my own business someday."

I shake my head. "No, I mean, what do you want aside from that? Do you want kids? A husband?"

She shrugs. "I've never really thought past getting my degree."

I fiddle with my umbrella again. "See, I want kids. I want a husband. I want to make someone dinner ready for when they come home. I want to read bedtime stories to my kids."

Her gaze softens. "But what about other things?"

I shrug. "I have everything. I have a great family. I have a business I love. And I write. Books are a huge part of my life, but I want my happily ever after."

"You're so young," she states.

"I'm twenty-one this year."

"Like I said, still young. You've got plenty of time to have all of that."

She's right, I do. I just don't want to wait anymore. All my generation in my family are pairing off. Faith is engaged. Aiden has a daughter and a girlfriend. Landon, who I miss terribly, is even living with Paisley, who I'm sure will want to start a family soon. Lily *is* married and I'm sure it won't be long until she's pregnant. And now Hayden has found someone. I'm alone for the first time in my life, and as they're all moving forward, I'm stuck.

"I guess."

"Want to go and see if Dave will let you make some cocktails?" she asks, her bare breasts rubbing against my arm.

I grab my bag. "No. He's still mad about me setting the counter and Jen's wig on fire."

She laughs, throwing her head back. "The bitch had it coming. He's over it. You know he loves you."

"I'm going to get back, but I'll see you next week."

She stands and wraps her arms around me, pulling me in for a hug. "Don't be a stranger."

I smile and it's genuine this time. "Never. Now the book is finished, I'm good."

"You going to do a part two?"

I shrug. "Maybe."

"I hope so. I've loved helping you on it," she tells me before glancing over my shoulder. "I need to go but I'll see you soon."

"Yes, you will," I promise, waving goodbye as she's called over to another table. I begin my journey through the crowd of tables, weaving in and out until I find my way to the stairs leading down to the exit.

"Leaving already?" Woods asks.

I tilt my head all the way back to look at the doorman, then nod. "Yeah. It's a bit crowded tonight."

He grins, showing his dimples. "Didn't get into trouble this time?"

I chuckle. "No. But it is getting rowdy in there."

As I finish my sentence, the sound of glass breaking reaches us, and Woods is called over the radio. "Go, before it's brought down here."

I nod, clutching my bag as I make my way down the stairs. I turn back as I hit the bottom, seeing one of the other doormen pinning a guy to the wall. I rush out, knowing not to get in the way again, but smash into a hard body. My bag hits the pavement, the contents spilling out all over the place.

"I'm so sorry," I rush out, reaching down for my bag. I glance up into the most beautiful round blue eyes I have ever seen.

My lips part as I stare at him, unable to move.

"It's okay," he assures me and bends down, helping me pick up my stuff. He lifts up the bullet vibrator Misty gifted me.

"I've not used it yet. It's clean," I assure him, and shove it into my bag.

He clears his throat as we stand and rubs the back of his neck. "I'm sorry, I didn't see you there."

"Completely my fault," I tell him, smiling.

He glances up at the strip club, then back down at me, his brows pinched together. "Do you work here?"

I blush at the compliment. Does he think I have the body to work on a stage like that? "No. I'm just heading home."

He smiles, and it's such a charming smile that I melt, wrapping my arms around my stomach. "Me too."

"Were you going in there?" I ask, pointing back to the strip club.

He shakes his head. "No, I've just finished work and was about to get a drink and something to eat before heading home."

I tilt my head, pressing my lips together. "It's a bit late to finish work."

He shrugs. "It comes with my job. Long hours."

Unsure of what to say, I fiddle with the strap of my bag.

"I'm just about to get some food. Care to join me?" he asks, and I look up in surprise.

I think about it for a moment. Any other time I get put in this situation, either my family intervene or I say no.

But I'm done with saying no.

If I'm ever going to find my future husband, or have any children, I need to put myself out there.

And what better way to do it than with a beautiful stranger, one that helps a klutzy female pick up her belongings.

I paste on a bright smile, my stomach rolling with nerves. "I'd love to."

ONE

CHARLOTTE

A YAWN SLIPS FREE AS I PUSH THE heavy oak doors to the library open. The smell of books immediately hits me, and I begin to relax. Books are life, and this place is my dream. Being here soothes a restlessness inside of me.

Tonight, I'm not meant to be here, but Marlene—my newest member of staff—called me as I was leaving the family to say she had locked up and I had a parcel waiting for me on my desk. I had to come to see what it was since I knew we weren't expecting deliveries, and I hadn't ordered anything.

I flick on the office lights, my lips parting at the bouquet of Hyacinths in a square glass vase placed on my desk. A smile lights up my face as I reach for the card attached.

Maybe this is Scott's way of saying he's sorry he couldn't make it to another family gathering. I desperately want them to meet him, and he them.

It's the first time he has bought me flowers though, and I can't keep the smile off my face. If he wants to be forgiven, it has worked—not that I can begrudge him for long.

However, I'm unsure why he bought hyacinths. They represent a lot of things: death, sorrow. But this particular colour—yellow—means jealously.

I unfold the note, my brows pinching together as I read over the words.

Beauty wilts at every hour.
Once plucked, the countdown begins.
Neglect will rot such delicate petals without their sturdy roots.
But love and care can slow the clock down and allow beauty its time in the sun.

Does it mean, I'm the flower and I've been plucked? Does he mean, our countdown, our life, has just begun?

Or is the note telling I'm going to rot without his love or *because* of his love?

Whatever the meaning, the thought was still there. I lift the vase up, bringing my nose down to breathe in the flowery scent. I savour the moment, warmth blossoming inside of me as I clutch the vase to my chest.

My first ever flowers from a guy who isn't family.

Maybe not attending the family gathering earlier had upset him more than I realised. He did say he felt bad but it couldn't be helped. I had been so consumed with feeling let down once again that I hadn't stopped to think about how he would feel.

He told me he isn't in a rush to meet my family, he likes having me to himself, and that family complicates things. And my family really do tend to complicate things. It isn't just about that though; his job keeps him from making his personal life public. He's a guy working his way up into politics, so I can understand that. It's just hard because I hate feeling like my world is split.

With that in mind, I flick the office light off, needing to get back. He hasn't messaged me but I'm hoping, at some point, he will, or that he will show up at mine. I make my way back out of the library, locking the large double doors behind me.

Today might not have been the best start, but it's most certainly looking up. Flowers. He got me flowers. Beautiful ones too. The green glitter bow sparkles under the streetlamp as I walk around the corner, heading up the path—mindful of the potholes—to my home.

I love this house. It's different from all the modern homes, which is what made it stand out to me. The only thing I'd change is the driveaway. There's a cul-de-sac of houses further up, and although most own their homes, the driveway isn't owned by any one of us. The council explained that we need planning permission, but refused to pay for the funding, and paving a road this big isn't something I can do. I am planning to fight and appeal their decision. The road is only wide enough to fit one car up at a time, and it's hard when you need to get through or avoid a pothole.

Clutching the vase in one arm, I use the other to search my pocket for my keys. I begin to hum a tune I heard earlier on the radio, wishing I knew what the song was called and who the artist was.

Fingers clasping around the cold metal, a triumphant smile lights up my face.

"You're back then," Scott declares, and the vase and keys slip free from my grip, both dropping to my feet.

I clutch my chest, staring down at the broken mess of the flowers. It's shattered. "Scott. I didn't see you there."

"Where did you get those flowers from?" he asks, his tone aggrieved.

I bend down, picking up the large chunks of glass and moving them to the side until I can come out with a broom. Tears gather in my eyes as I clean up the broken present. "They're from you, aren't they?"

He snorts as I pick up the flowers and keys. I put the key into the lock and push open the door.

"They most certainly aren't. For one thing, they are tacky as hell."

I flinch and my chest constricts. *They aren't from him?* "But I thought—"

"You thought you could lie to me?" he rumbles, shutting the door behind me. I place the flowers on the side table and turn to him.

"Scott, I thought they were from you. They were delivered to the library."

His gaze scans over my body, and I nervously tug at the hem of my jumper. It's cold out, and this is the thickest one I have. It has a pink kitten on the front.

15   CHARLOTTE

I know he doesn't like it when I wear things like this. I duck my head, feeling embarrassed and ashamed.

His lip curls. "What are you wearing?"

"I'm washing my… my other clothes," I admit. I want to impress him, to feel sexy and grown up, but every time he looks at me like that, I feel anything but. And I only have so many of my other clothes; clothes that make me feel stiff and uncomfortable. But for him, I wear them.

He runs his fingers through his hair, his blue eyes boring into me. "What are we doing, Charlotte?"

"What do you mean?"

He points to his chest, then to me. "Us. Is this going anywhere?"

"I—"

"Because I want more than this. I've been more than a gentleman in giving you time, but now this…" he states, pointing at the flowers.

"I'm not sure I understand what you're saying," I tell him, my voice low.

"We've been seeing each other for a while, and although the foreplay has been okay, I want more. And now I come back after spending all day in the office and you've received flowers," he spits out.

I rush forward, placing my hand on his chest, but he smacks it away, averting his gaze.

Tears gather in my eyes. "Scott, no. I don't know who these flowers came from. I swear. You know how I feel about you."

He pushes my hand away again when I go to reach for him, and my heart begins to crack. I'm losing him.

"Then why won't you let me fuck you? Why do you constantly push me away if there isn't anyone else in the picture? I'm trying here, Charlotte. I really am. I've been patient."

Tears leak down my cheeks. "You know why."

"Do I?" he barks, and I flinch back. His eyes soften and he steps forward, bending down to kiss my forehead. "I'm sorry."

"Please, you have to believe me."

"I can't, I'm sorry," he tells me, stepping back. "I think it's time I go. It's clear you don't want me."

My stomach rolls as he walks toward the door, and for a moment, I think I might let him go. Then his hand touches the handle and something inside of me snaps. I rush forward, slamming the door shut. My pulse races as panic claws at my chest.

I can't lose him.

He's my chance at a happily ever after, even if we do have to work at it. He isn't what I expected, I'll admit it, but that could be fear talking. Fear of taking the next step.

"Don't go," I plead, my voice hoarse.

He lets out a heavy sigh. "Give me a reason to stay."

I rise to my tiptoes and press my lips to his, then grip the back of his neck and deepen the kiss, like he taught me.

He's been my first in so many things. And he has been patient.

"Charlotte," he groans, pushing me away at arm's-length. "I'm not doing foreplay again."

With a nervous flutter in my stomach and a ball in my throat, I reply. "I want more too."

He arches an eyebrow. "You aren't going to pull back?"

Biting my lip, I shake my head. "No," I answer. "Please don't leave."

He grins, and suddenly his mood changes and I'm being swung into the air. I wrap my arms around him, laughter spilling from my lips.

This is the right thing.

Love takes work.

And we are going to work on it.

The floorboards creak under him, and with each step he takes toward my bedroom, the harder my heart hammers.

This is what I want.

It is.

The words are a chant in my mind, and as we reach the bedroom, everything becomes a blur. I no longer feel like I'm in my body, or in control of what is going on. It's like I'm not present, just going through the motions.

He strips me of my clothes, his lip curling as he throws the jumper to the side.

17 CHARLOTTE

Once I'm down to my underwear, I begin to feel self-conscious and curl my arms over my stomach. When we did stuff before, we were under the sheets and I always left one or the other on when it came to my knickers and bra.

But this is what I want.

I close my eyes, chanting it inside my head as he lies me down on the bed, ridding me of my underwear. My lashes flutter open when I feel him shift off the bed, and I watch as he begins to strip out of his own clothes, his eyes hooded as he gazes down at me.

This is what I want.

I've read about a woman's first time in romance books. It hurts at first, but the guy is always gentle, always takes care of them.

Scott will take care of me.

He's always saying he will take care of me.

A flush covers my entire body as he looms over me, manoeuvring between my thighs. He rolls a condom on, grinning at me.

"This wasn't so hard, was it?"

My pulse races as he kisses me, and when he pulls back, I smile. "I love you."

He doesn't say it back. He never does. He says he doesn't need to tell me because he shows me.

This is what I want.

The sharp sting from the penetration has my back bowing off the bed. I squeeze my eyes shut, crying out as he rams inside of me again.

There was no warning.

There was no foreplay.

No gentleness.

No love.

This is what I want.

"Slow down," I croak out.

He shoves his face into my neck, panting heavily. "I can't. You've driven me crazy for months. Now it's finally done, just enjoy it."

"Please," I cry out, the pain becoming unbearable. It's more than a tear. I feel like I have been ripped open.

The books didn't describe this, none of it.

Maybe you're doing it wrong.

I reach for him, but he moves away, leaning up to look down at where we are joined.

"So fucking tight."

He thrusts inside me harder, and each time he fills me to the hilt, he grunts, the sound like a knife to my soul.

This is what I want.

Tears gather in my eyes and the fight to make this special, to make this once in a lifetime milestone the best it can be, leaves me.

This isn't how it was meant to be.

This *isn't* what I want.

"Stop!" I croak out, trying to push him off. He grips my wrists, pinning them above my head, using them as leverage to slam harder inside me.

I cry out, and not with pleasure, but with pain. Each thrust feels like shards of glass entering me. There's no lubricant, nothing.

Because this *isn't* what I want.

"God, I've been dying to fuck you," he growls. "A virgin. All the best girls are virgins."

"Please, stop."

His gaze meets mine, and his eyes harden. "The hard part is over. You'll love it, you'll see."

I don't love it.

"You're hurting me, Scott. Please, please stop," I plead, unable to keep the tremor from my voice.

"So close," he rasps, ignoring me.

My head bangs against the bedframe and I stare at the tiny crack in the ceiling, imagining the love Amelia told me about, the love she found with Maddox.

I imagine a love like that and my heart tears in two.

This is never going to be like that.

Scott grunts before shifting his weight off me. He kisses my cheek and I feel him move off the bed. "Just going to have a shower to get the blood off me."

19 CHARLOTTE

Once I hear the bathroom door shut, I sit up, clutching the sheet to my chest, but not before catching sight of the blood between my thighs, the bed stained like I've started a period.

A sob catches in my throat. "That wasn't what I wanted."

I'm stupid. Naïve to believe. Gullible to love. I'm everything those school bullies said I was.

He didn't stop.

A phone chimes from somewhere close by and I startle, my entire body shaking. Numbly, I slide my legs off the bed and glance around the floor, trying to find where the sound is coming from.

It's Scott's phone. He's a private person and normally doesn't let the thing out of his sight. Maybe if it's important, he'll leave.

I need him to leave.

Or at least, I think I do.

Is there any going back now? Do I want to go back?

Another sob catches in my throat.

What have I done?

As I reach for his jacket, the answer comes to me. I love him, or love the idea of loving him, but he doesn't love me. No one in love could have treated someone like that. Something cold and metal falls to the floor as I pull his phone out and I bend down, picking up the gold-plated ring, before numbly turning to the phone in my other hand. The call ends, but the message on the screen has my heart stopping.

Sophia: Love you too. Will you be back home to put the kids to—

I don't need to read the rest to know what it says.

He's married.

I sit down on the edge of the bed, my vision blurring. I slept with a married man. A *married* man.

I love—*loved* a married man.

It was all a lie.

God, I'm so stupid.

"Hey, do you have—" I glance up, meeting his eyes, and in that moment, he knows I know. It's like the mask he's been wearing has finally fallen. In only a towel, he snarls at me. "What the fuck are you doing?"

Tears blur my vision. "You're married?"

"Why the fuck are you going through my things?" he snaps, snatching the phone out of my hand.

I get up and move over to my drawers, grabbing the first T-shirt and joggers I find. My skin crawls at being naked in front of him.

My thighs ache, almost bruised, and that isn't anything compared to the throbbing of my wrists, or the stinging sensation down below.

"Answer me!" he barks.

I whimper and face him. "I-I didn't want you to miss something," I numbly reply. Why I'm answering after everything that's happened, I don't know. I still don't feel present. This is a dream. It has to be. "You're married."

"No, I'm not."

I point to his phone, my lip trembling. "I saw the message."

He switches his phone off before throwing it on the bed. "It's not what you think it is."

Yes, it is.

It all makes sense: why he only took me out when it was dark and always away from town. Why he only ever came to mine. Why I never met his family, or his friends. Why I don't even know where he works or lives.

Because he lied to me.

He told me things I wanted to hear and I fell for it.

"You liar," I cry out, clutching my chest.

His eyes harden and his lip curls. "You go through my belongings and then try to turn it around on me?"

I flinch. "What? No. I was—"

"Being dramatic, as always."

I shake my head, wondering why I'm arguing with him. This isn't about that. It's about him. He always does this; he always turns it around and makes me feel like I'm the one who has the problem, or I'm the one in the wrong.

"You have kids together."

"I have kids. And?"

"You… We—We've been together months. You never said anything." He laughs and I inhale sharply. "We—" I pause, catching my breath. "You cheated on your wife. You made me believe we were a couple."

"Charlotte, you're hot but you aren't that bright. Did I ever say we were a couple?"

I pause, thinking back on it. He hadn't said those words but he implied them. He said I was his. "But—"

"No. You were lucky you gave okay head, otherwise you wouldn't have lasted this long."

"Why are you doing this?" I cry out.

He looks to the bed, his jaw clenching. "Charlotte, nothing has to change."

My eyes widen. "Not change? Not change?" I screech. "You let my first time be with someone who is already spoken for."

"Don't act like you didn't want to be fucked," he snarls, stepping forward. "You wanted me. You always want me."

"I asked you to stop," I whisper, feeling my chest tear open. He knew what my virginity meant to me. "I *begged* you to stop. And you are married. You have kids."

"What are you saying?" he grits out, stepping toward me.

I'm unaware of him, of my surroundings, too busy trying to compartmentalise my thoughts. "I trusted you. I loved you. And you lied to me. You have a wife and kids. I have just broken up a marriage. Your children's parents' marriage. You—"

I cry out when a sharp sting vibrates across my face. I knock into the drawers, banging my head. I press my hand to my cheek, staring at him through tears.

"Shit! I didn't mean that but you kept talking."

"Don't touch me," I cry out when he takes a step forward.

"Don't," he demands. "Don't romanticise this. Whatever you are thinking, you made up in that head of yours. Like everything. I'm still willing to be here, to be with you, but you have to keep your mouth shut, Charlotte. That's the only way this can work."

Chest heaving, I clutch at the drawers. *He hit me.*

"Don't touch me," I hiss out, trying to step around him.

I need to get out of here.

I need Landon.

My mum and dad.

"It was barely a slap," he snarls. "Grow up."

My back goes ramrod straight. "Get out," I demand.

"All because of a message that doesn't mean anything?"

"Not only because of that," I yell. "I asked you to stop. I told you it was hurting and you didn't listen. No one who cares about someone would do that. You knew I wanted to make it special and you…y-you did that." He takes a step forward and I hold my hand up. "Don't touch me."

"Don't worry, I'm not going to touch you again, so you can stop making shit up in your head."

"No. I didn't. You said—"

"I didn't say anything," he yells. "I expect this bullshit from her, but not from you. I don't need this crap."

"Does your wife know? You stayed here so many times," I whisper, hating that I've done this to another woman. I back up toward the door, ready to make an exit.

Scott can be rude at times, but he's never been like this.

His eyes widen and fear flashes in them before he rushes at me. He grips my chin, pushing me until my back hits the door. I cry out, gripping his wrists.

"Don't bring her into it. And now that you know about her, this is done. She doesn't need to know. If you breathe a word of this to anyone, I will end you," he snaps. "Not that anyone will believe someone like you. You hang out in strip clubs. You'll be lucky if they continue letting children into your library after I'm done with you."

I push him back, using the last of my strength, but he doesn't budge. "Leave and don't come back."

In utter disgust, he runs his gaze over my face. "You wanted it. Don't lie."

"Leave," I scream, my breath heaving with exhaustion. "If you don't go, I'll phone the police and ask them to come and remove you."

"You little—"

A squeak passes through my lips and I weakly try to push him away, needing to escape. "Stop!"

"I'm not letting you call the police," he snarls, reaching for me. I cry out when he spins me around, rearing his fist back. Knowing I have nowhere to go, I clench my eyes shut, just in time to feel the punch across my jaw. "I'm sick of little bitches like you thinking they can run their mouths and tell me what to do. You need to learn your fucking place."

Disorientated, I reach for the closest thing. I lift the book, the *Kama Sutra*, and swing my arm out. Aiming it toward him, I whack him around the head.

"I'm sorry," I cry out, rushing for the door.

He roars out in pain and I hear him following behind. He catches me at the door, shoving me until I face plant on the wood.

"You aren't going anywhere until we get a few things straight," he yells.

I cry out when he tugs me back by my hair, but turn and grip his balls, twisting until he crumples to the floor. He tries to take me with him, but I pull back at the last minute, and do what I've always been told to do: I swing my leg back, aiming it between his legs.

He howls as he reaches for me. His fingers grip my ankle and I trip once again, landing on top of him. I dig my nails into his face, scraping down until I feel skin breaking beneath my fingers.

"Leave me alone!" I cry out.

Crawling away from him, I grab my bag and keys from the side before getting to my feet. He's still on the floor, now pressing his hands to his face. I pull open the door and although my thoughts are a mess, I manage to get into my car.

Switching the engine on, I sob, clutching the steering wheel with both hands.

He hit me.

He's married.

He has kids.

The lights from my car shine inside the front door. Scott is standing in the doorway, one hand gripping the doorframe, the other keeping the towel together at his waist. His gaze narrows on me and a shiver slivers down my spine.

"Lose my number! And if you think of telling anyone about me, I'll end you," he yells. "You crazy bitch."

TWO

DREW

I'VE JUST FINISHED SANITIZING THE last of the equipment when my phone rings. I exhale heavily, reaching for it.

Mum.

I pinch the bridge of my nose, knowing this isn't avoidable anymore. She has been calling off-and-on all week, and I ignored it every time. I know what she wants. I got the invitation at the beginning of the week— the same time the phone calls started. My sister, Alice, is getting married at the end of the month, and she wants to make sure I'm there. Our relationship is strained at best. And ever since she last tried setting me up with one of her friend's daughters, I've avoided her all together. I can't remember the last time I actually spoke to her in person.

"Hey, Mum."

"*Hello*, Andrew."

I sigh. I should have known this wouldn't be easy. "*Hello*, Mum."

"That's better. I raised you right," she snarks. "Now, I've been trying to get hold of you all week. Did you get the invite to your sister's wedding?"

"Yes, I did."

"Well, are you coming?"

"Of course I'm coming. She's my sister," I growl, hating that she thinks otherwise.

"Good, I'll have a room set up for you."

I nearly drop my phone. "I'm not staying with you, Mum."

She huffs out a breath. "Andrew, this is your sister's wedding. She has her engagement party, her rehearsal dinner, and I know they are determined to do that tacky—"

"Hen party?" I answer, my lips twitching.

Only my mother could find a night of fun tacky. I think the only night of fun she's ever had is the one she spent with my father that resulted with me. It's why I'm the black sheep of the family. No matter what my mum did to try and cut my dad out of my life, he fought to stay. He isn't from money, from a wealthy neighbourhood, but he's the best dad a kid could ask for.

The scandal nearly ruined my mother's reputation, one she worked hard to rebuild and did so successfully. She didn't want to go through that kind of humiliation again, so she forced her rules and her morals onto me since long before I can remember. She hated me for not following them. She wanted me to be a doctor or a lawyer, but all I wanted to do was run my gym.

I am a huge disappointment where she is concerned.

"Yes. You have to be there."

"I'm sorry, Mum, but I can't. I have a business to run. I'll come to the rehearsal dinner, and I'll come to the wedding, but I'm not staying."

"I do not believe you," she snaps. "Alice is getting married and she wants you there. I'm sure that job will survive for a week or two. The least you could do is stay for a few nights. You've got plenty of time to find someone to cover for you."

I groan, wishing I hadn't answered the call. It's always the same. She doesn't see this as a successful business, not even an occupation. She sees it as a hobby. "Mum, I'll think about it."

"Well, that's kind of you," she mutters dryly. "I've also told Eloise that you'll be her plus one."

I straighten, gritting my teeth. "No. I'll bring my own date."

"No, I've—"

"I'll bring my own date, Mum."

"You aren't even seeing anyone. Eloise is a good girl. She comes from a—"

"We are not having this conversation," I warn.

"We are. We—"

"Bye, Mum."

I end the call and throw my phone on the bench. I'm going to get shit for cutting her off, but I don't care. I love my mum. She's hard work and at times, outright rude, but she's my mum and I love her. But I draw the line when it comes to Eloise—to setting me up with anyone.

Eloise is a family friend's daughter. The family are very prestigious and set in their ways. I think the only reason I'm a good fit for their precious daughter is because of who my step-dad is. They would do anything to get shares in his company or get him to put shares into theirs. Wesley has a name for himself, more so since he married my mum and used her family connections to get further ahead. To me, it's all boring politics. I hated every minute of it growing up and couldn't wait for the weekends or weeks I got to be with my dad, Silas. I hate it even more now as an adult.

Eloise, in all her designer clothes and uptight appearance, used to be sweet. But she was always off limits to me. She's the same age as my sister, Natalie, and the two are close. Both are bitches and think the world owes them.

But one day, after having a fall out with my mum about going to college to get a degree in sports and fitness, I went out and got shit-faced. She happened to be there when I got back and snuck into my room. And in a drunk stupor, I fucked her. I'm not even sure how or when it started. The night was a complete blur. It was the biggest mistake of my life and it should never have happened. When I woke up the next day, with her naked and lying in my arms, I made sure she knew that. I was still drunk and said things that would have made any other girl hate me.

Not Eloise.

She grew more determined for us to be together and was a fool to believe our parents when they said we had a connection.

Not a chance.

Glass rattling in its frame at the front of the building pulls my attention away from my family drama and I move through the gym into the reception area. My forehead creases at the sight of the troubled woman banging the hell out of the glass door. I race over, pulling it open, and she collapses into me.

I bring her inside, closing and locking the door behind me, glancing over her shoulder for any signs of trouble. The only thing I see is a car with the front end smashed where she's crashed into the bin.

I glance down. "Are you okay? What's happened? Were you in a crash?"

"I need Landon," she cries out, tilting her head up to me. "I need him."

I scan over the bruises on her face and my jaw clenches. They are not marks from a crash. They're from a fist.

"Landon isn't here but I'm going to call the police for you."

"No!" she cries out, reaching for me. "I just need… I need…" She drops to her knees and I catch her before she hits the marble, sitting down in front of her.

"We need to get you medical help," I inform her.

Her round, emerald-green eyes stare up at me, so much pain and turmoil shining in them. Her hands tremble as she reaches up, pulling her thick red locks away from her face. I have never seen anyone with so much hair. It's in thick waves down her back, but right now, it's a mess, the tangled knots clearly indicating a struggle.

"I-I can't," she sobs out. "I need Landon, or my mum, or dad."

"Who did this?"

"I have to go," she tells me and suddenly gets to her feet, giving me the perfect view of the blood seeping between her legs.

"Fuck," I growl, getting up.

This isn't just someone hitting her. I swallow past the lump in my throat, glancing away. I try to control the storm brewing inside of me.

She squeaks and tilts her head all the way back to get a look at me. "You're huge."

She's in shock.

Her eyes dart around the room and I take a slow, steady step forward, bending down a little. I've been told before that my height can intimidate people. "Is there somewhere I can take you if I can't get you help?"

Her lower lip trembles. "I can't go home."

"You said you came here for Landon?"

"He's my cousin, my best friend," she explains. "But you can't call him. He will be with Paisley if he's not here."

Fuck!

Landon already has a short fuse. I feel sorry for the guy who did this to her because I know that once he gets his hands on him, he's as good as dead.

The poor fucker doesn't even know he's already dead.

But if I don't get her help or get her to him, he's going to kill me. Or try to.

"What about your mum and dad? Can I take you there?"

"Yes. I needed to feel safe and I thought… I thought he would be here. But he's not, and I can't go back home, and I left my cat," she rambles. "My cat is alone and I didn't lock up."

"I'm sure someone will go and check on your cat."

"He's not a nice cat to other people," she admits. I pull my hoodie over my head, and drop it over hers. She cries out.

"I'm sorry. But you are shivering."

Once I have it fully on her, her eyes fill with tears. "Are you sure he's not here?"

"I let him go early," I explain softly. I just don't know what to say. She's breaking my heart.

She nods yet doesn't speak, and I decide to take matters into my own hands. "Why don't you tell me where your parents live and I can call Landon for you."

She nods once again. "I didn't think about my cat," she whispers. "I'm such a terrible cat mum."

"I think your cat is the least of your problems right now."

Her lashes flutter and the look she gives me makes me feel like a sick fuck. Because she's beautiful. Stunning. Even covered in bruises.

"But if I think about anything else, it makes it real and it can't be real. None of it can be real. I'm a terrible person. Terrible."

I steer her back over to the chairs by the large windows and lower her down. "You aren't a terrible person. The person who did this is."

"You don't know what happened. What I've done," she whispers brokenly.

"I don't need to. I can see all I need to see to tell you who is in the wrong here."

She nods. "I don't think I can drive my car anymore. I crashed it into your bin."

I rub her arm before standing. "Let me just go and get my things and I'll grab you a pair of socks," I tell her. "Are you sure I can't take you to the hospital?"

"I'm not wearing shoes," she whispers, staring down at her feet.

"Stay there," I gently warn and race out of the room.

She's definitely in shock. None of it is making sense. I grab my things off the bench and then head into my office to pick up a pair of spare socks from my drawer.

She's still sitting there, staring at the floor but not really seeing. It's like she isn't present. I slowly approach so I don't scare her and drop to my knees. She jerks, her tear-filled gaze pleading with me to help her.

"I'm going to put these socks on you, okay?"

"Okay," she whispers.

I lift her foot up to my knee and roll the sock over her foot. I tense, pausing when I spot finger marks around her ankle.

"What happened?" I ask hoarsely.

"I-I don't know," she chokes out.

I quickly roll the other sock on before reaching for her, helping her to her feet. "Let's get you home."

31 CHARLOTTE

I help her outside, keeping her close so I can lock up. I wrap my arm around her, and head toward my car. Once there, I let her go and she visibly shivers. I pull open the car door and she climbs inside, her eyes void of anything but a deep wave of sadness.

"I'm just going to shut your car off," I tell her, and when she doesn't reply, I close the door.

I take a minute to gather my bearings. I never expected tonight to end like this. Just seeing her, tears streaming down her cheeks, and I want to go back into the gym and take my anger out on the punching bag. I know better than to think the Carter's will let me beat the shit out of the person responsible. They'll only turn their anger on me.

Taking a deep breath, I do what I said I was going to do and turn the engine off. I'm about to get out when I spot her bag thrown over the passenger seat. I put everything back inside, my brows pulling together when I spot a black butt plug. The only reason I know what it is, is because my ex won one at a lingerie party. I clear my throat and shove it in the bag before getting out.

I lock the car up and pocket the keys. Someone will have to move it before the police come.

Glancing at my car, I watch as she leans her head against the glass, her shoulders shaking. I pull my phone out and dial Landon, knowing I need to call him now.

After a few rings, he answers, his voice gruff. "I'm not opening tomorrow," he greets.

"Um, Landon, I have a girl in my car who came to the gym looking for you. She's wearing a 'My cat is better than yours' T-shirt. I'm taking her to her mum and dad's 'cause she won't let me take her to the hospital or phone the police."

"Does she have red hair?" he growls.

"Landon, what's wrong?" I hear his missus call out.

"Yeah, man. I'm taking her to her parents now."

"It's Charlotte. Bring her here," he snaps, and my shoulders slump. He has spoken about Charlotte plenty of times before and I know she means a lot to him. "Is she okay? What's happened?"

I clear my throat, and rub the back of my neck. "It's bad. I don't know what I can or can't say to you. She wants me to take her to her parents which is what I'm going to do. Right now, I think she needs to be in control so I'm giving that to her."

"Tell me!" he roars.

"Fuck," I yell, clenching my eyes shut. I have been in his position. I know what it's like to feel helpless. "She's been beaten, but, mate—"

"What?" he snaps, and I hear shuffling on the other side of the phone.

"Landon, what's happening? You're scaring me."

"Tell me," he grits out.

"She's got blood between her legs."

The phone goes dead and I clench my hand around it, breathing heavily. He's either thrown it, or crushed it in his hand.

I need to get her to her parents before he gets there, because if he goes to her in a state, I can see her being scared, and she doesn't need that right now.

Her feet drag up the path and I watch as she struggles to keep her composure the closer we get to the house. I bang on the door, stepping to her side as we wait for it to open.

A beautiful redhead opens the door, her smile bright until she spots her daughter. She scans her body, a hitched sob tearing from her throat. "No. No. Not my baby."

Charlotte jerks and looks up, her face breaking as she crumbles, flying forward into her mum's arms. "Mum!"

"Baby," her mum whispers, tears falling down her cheeks.

"I-I did s-something so stupid. S-so stupid and it hurts. It really hurts," she heaves out, her sobs tearing my insides up.

A man comes barging around the corner. "Babe, who's— I am going to fucking kill him," he roars, reaching for his wife and daughter, pulling them both into his arms.

"I-I," Charlotte chokes out, right before she collapses to the floor, out like a light. I guess she's crashed from the adrenaline, which isn't surprising after something so traumatic.

"Charlotte!" her mum cries, bending down to her daughter. She pulls her into her arms and rocks her. "My sweet girl."

"Who the fuck are you?"

I look to her dad, jerking my chin down in greeting. "I own the gym with Landon. She came looking for him but he wasn't… She wouldn't let me take her to the hospital or phone the police."

His wife reaches for his sleeve when he goes to leave, her eyes filled with tears. "Myles, she… she has—" She closes her eyes, unable to speak the words.

He glances down at his daughter, and when he sees what she's trying to say, he loses it, punching the door over and over. I step in, pushing him back before he can do any damage.

"Stop! She needs you right now."

"What happened?" he rasps.

"I don't know. Landon is on his way. I'm going to wait outside for him. Okay?"

He nods. "Thank you."

He pulls his daughter into his arms and she whimpers, but remains asleep.

"Myles," his wife calls out, gasping for breath, her face pale.

"It's going to be fine," he declares, and they share a look between them, like they have been in this situation before.

"Mum? Dad?" a young boy calls out, standing on the bottom step of the stairs. His eyes widen and his face pales at the sight of Charlotte. He shakes his head, gripping the banister. "No. No."

I step back, giving them their privacy, and head back down the path, waiting near the gate for Landon. It isn't long until a car comes speeding down the road, skidding to a stop outside.

He gets out of the car, slamming the door behind him. I block his path when I see his face tight with anger, his bulging veins pulsing in his temple.

"Landon," I warn.

He swings his fist, catching me across the jaw. Before I can even register the tightness, the ache, I move, restraining him before he does something he regrets. "Where is she?"

I heave out a breath as I keep his arms pinned behind his back. It isn't easy, not with his strength, but I think at this point, he isn't really trying. I have seen him get out of this move plenty of times. "She's inside with her parents. She passed out," I reply.

"I'll fucking kill him."

"You know who did this?" I ask, stepping back once I'm sure he's not going to take his anger out on me further.

Breathing heavily, he grips the ends of his hair. "It doesn't take a wild guess to know it's her waste of a boyfriend."

I pull out the keys from my pocket and hand them to him. "These are her car keys. You'll need to get someone to move it from the gym. She hit the bin and has damaged the front light."

"I should have been there for her," he rasps, staring up at the house.

"Hey, man, I'm not sure what's going on, but I do know you aren't to blame for this. She's in shock and didn't say much. But I know it was you she wanted."

"And I wasn't there," he grits out.

I sigh. "Just be there for her now. She's going to need the hospital," I tell him, and head for my car. "Oh, and she kept going on about a cat and that she didn't lock up her house."

He nods, before meeting my gaze. "Thank you. Thank you for getting her here," he tells me, his voice breaking. "Charlotte, she's… she's special. She won't get over this."

"Take a few days, man. I'll get cover for the gym. With you and her parents, she will get through this."

With that, I get into my car. I sit there for a moment, watching as Landon lets himself into the house. My mind flickers back to Charlotte and the injuries she suffered.

She might not know it yet, but she will get through it. My sister was attacked a few years ago, and fortunately, a passer-by intervened before he could do any worse. She still has nightmares and has issues with leaving the house, but she got through it.

And Charlotte will too. She has a loving, supportive family to help.

With that in mind, I know I have to step up my game with our new self-defence classes. I've let it slide, what with the extra workload.

But I can't stand by anymore and do nothing. Too many women are being assaulted every day, and although I know I can't stop them all, I may be able to help at least one get away from her attacker/s.

If I could, I'd make sure not a single woman from here on out, questioned what it is she did.

It's never about what you're wearing.

Never about how late it is.

Or if you are alone or not.

And in Charlotte's case, whether you are with your attacker or not.

This isn't acceptable, and women should never live to believe these are primary factors in what happened to them.

People need to be held accountable for their actions.

Although I can't change what the world thinks, I can do something. I can teach women *and* men self-defence.

Everyone has a right to defend themselves.

With that, I pull away from the curb, my thoughts with Landon and his family.

THREE

CHARLOTTE

My eyelids flutter open but the minute my surroundings sink in, I clench them shut, trying to block out the images flittering through my mind. My head pounds and my throat feels raw as I choke back a sob.

"Charlotte."

I startle for a minute, and the strong arms wrapped around me register. "Landon?"

"I'm here, Charlotte. I'm here."

All of it comes rushing back and I curl into myself, my stomach and chest heaving with each sob that tears through my body.

It feels like my insides are being ripped out of me. I trusted him. I loved him. And he hurt me. He hurt me in ways I'll never be the same again. I can feel that hole inside my heart and it's gaping, everything seeping out and leaving me feeling empty inside.

37 CHARLOTTE

It was all my fault.

"I am so stupid," I cry out.

"No, baby, you aren't," my mum whispers.

"Mum," I call out, and it comes out almost like a plea. "It hurts."

"Open your eyes, honey."

My dad's voice does nothing to settle me, not like it did as a girl growing up.

"I don't want you to be disappointed in me."

A choked sound comes from him, and I feel the bed dip by my side.

"I could never be disappointed in you," he tells me.

"We need to call the police and get you examined, sweetheart," Mum advises.

I shake my head, my fingers digging into Landon's arm. "I-I can't."

"Guys, will you give us a minute?" Mum lightly demands.

"No," I cry out, my eyes flying open as I clutch Landon tighter.

Mum's face is tear-streaked, her eyes bloodshot and skin pale. "You're safe, Charlotte. You're safe."

"I-I'm such a fool. I did everything right. I was kind, I was polite, and I got good grades, even though I was bullied. The girls hated me and the boys laughed at me when they thought I wasn't looking," I tell her, watching her face crumble. Landon's arms tighten around me. "I bought a house, and I own a business. I did it right."

"Baby," she whispers.

Tears cloud my vision. "I did *everything* right," I choke out, my voice breaking. "There's something wrong with me."

"There is nothing fucking wrong with you," Landon bites out.

I wince as I shift out of his arms, and sit up in my childhood bed. "Yes, there is. I know what people think of me. I'm not that stupid," I tell them, slamming my hand against my chest. "I can hear all the names I was called growing up in my head. I'm a joke to people. I was a joke to him."

"No, baby, you aren't," Dad tells me, tears spilling down his cheeks.

I clutch my chest as I struggle for breath. "All I wanted was to be loved, to have a husband and children. I was doing it right."

"Honey, what happened?" Mum pleads, grabbing my hand.

"He was going to leave me," I whisper, clutching the blanket pooled at my waist. "He said I wasn't serious about him, that if I loved him I would have had sex with him. He thought there was someone else."

Landon tenses, a feral noise coming from him. He clears his throat when he notices I've stopped. "He's a prick."

More tears spill down my cheeks. "I was stupid. So stupid. He's married. He has children. I-I slept with a married man," I choke out.

"What?"

"Is that why he's done this to you?" Landon grits out.

Mum glares at him and I duck my head. "Honey, you're badly hurt. We saw… we saw blood on your trousers. Was it—was it consensual?"

"Of course it fucking wasn't. Look at her!" Landon snaps, and I flinch.

"I said yes."

"What?" Dad asks, his fingers on my thigh tensing.

I glance at Mum, and she moves forward, pulling me into her arms. I know about her past. I know what she went through, but this isn't that. I said yes. Another sob hitches from my chest. "I said yes because I didn't want him to leave. I thought if I could take that step, we would be like everyone else. He would love me the way Landon loves Paisley, the way Aiden loves Bailey et cetera. But it was nothing like I expected it to be."

"What do you mean?" she whispers, pulling back.

I stare into her eyes, blocking my dad and Landon out. "It hurt so much, Mum. It still does. I asked him to slow down, but he didn't, then I asked him to stop," I tell her, my throat raw with each sob. "He wouldn't stop, and I tried to push him away, but he pinned my arms down. It hurt. He wouldn't stop. He wouldn't listen to me, Mum. He wouldn't. It was hurting so much I had to slip into my head to ignore it, to ignore…" I gulp, trying to push away those memories of the pain. "Then it was over. It wasn't what I wanted. None of it was what I wanted." I inhale, tears clouding my vision. "It wasn't what I wanted."

Mum's face crumbles as she reaches for me. "Oh, honey."

"He's married and I slept with him. I didn't know it when I slept with him. He has children. Children. Innocent children. He got mad at me and he hit me. And I've left my cat with a monster and she's all alone and I didn't lock the door because I had to race out of there."

Mum grips my shoulders. "Calm down, Charlotte. You're safe," she declares. "Say it with me: you're safe."

"I'm safe," I whisper, taking deep breaths.

When I open my eyes, Mum's expression is filled with heartache and pain. "Charlotte, honey, you were sexually assaulted and we need to get you to the hospital."

I shake my head, tensing. "No. I said yes."

"You asked him to stop," she declares.

"No means no. It doesn't matter *when* it's said. You say stop, they fucking stop," Dad states, rubbing the palms of his hands down his legs.

I pull away when Landon goes to touch me. "I wasn't sexually assaulted," I snap, the pounding in my head getting louder. "I was stupid. I said yes. I did this. Me."

Mum shakes her head and reaches for me, cupping my jaw. "It's still assault, honey. Did he hear you say no?"

I grip the bedsheet and watch as my fingers tense into the cotton.

"Yes," I answer hoarsely.

"It's sexual assault," she rasps. "For one, he manipulated you into having sex. That's sexual coercion. It's a tactic a perpetrator uses to get what they want. And two, you said no. It doesn't matter if you revoked your consent at the start, or in the middle. No means no."

"But he was my boyfriend—or I thought he was," I whisper. "I let him into my bed. I said yes. It was my idea."

She clutches my hand. "Why was it your idea?"

My nose twitches. "He was going to leave me. He had been patient with me because I wasn't ready," I answer on a hiccup. I don't want to remember tonight, and it's hard to tell them what happened when I can feel the evidence between my legs. But I wasn't sexually assaulted. *Was I?* "I did it to make him stay, so I could prove he's what I wanted. I was so stupid."

"No, baby, you weren't. He was."

"Really fucking stupid," Landon announces, a deadly edge to his voice.

"Honey, we need to get you to the hospital. We need to make sure there isn't any internal damage, and we need to get your other injuries seen to."

"I can't," I choke out.

"You can't seriously want to protect him?" Landon barks, then grimaces, glancing away. "Sorry."

"I'm not protecting him," I admit before turning to Mum. "I'm so ashamed. I said yes. They'll know I slept with a married man."

"You have nothing to be ashamed of. *Ever*," Mum declares fiercely. "Please, let us do this. Don't make the same mistake I made. Don't keep silent, Charlotte."

"Kayla," Dad whispers, reaching for her.

She shoves him away, glaring. "No. He sexually assaulted her. It's rape," she screeches. "My baby girl. Just because they were together, that she said yes, it doesn't matter. She said no; she told him to stop. And look at her, Myles. Look at your daughter."

"I am looking," he yells.

"Stop!" I choke out.

"I am not letting her suffer through this alone. I am not my mother. She has me. I promised myself to never let this happen to my kids."

"I know you aren't. I never said that," he tells her, trying to keep his voice calm.

"She has us to help her," she tells him, before turning to me. "Please don't make the same mistake I made. You have a choice; I'll never take that away from you. It's always your choice, but please, please don't let him get away with this. He knew exactly what he was doing."

"But I said yes."

She pushes away from the bed, her face turning red. "But you told him to stop!" she screams. "You tried to push him off and he pinned you to the bed."

I flinch at her tone, my entire body trembling.

"It's okay," Landon whispers, pulling me into his arms.

She whirls on my dad. "We were supposed to protect them. We failed them."

"Stop!" Jacob screams, pushing through the door, his eyes wild as he stares at our mum. "Stop. Please, just stop."

"Jacob," I whisper.

He turns to me, his tears spilling down his cheeks.

"I knew he was a bad guy. I went to Landon and Maddox. I knew it," he tells me, banging his chest. "I could have stopped this. I could have stopped this."

"Son," Dad rasps, stepping toward him.

He pushes Dad away and locks his gaze on me. "Please, let them help you. Just let them. You don't need to do it alone because you aren't. We are here. We want you to be happy and safe."

"Jacob," I call out, clutching my chest.

He wipes his tears with the sleeve of his shirt. "Just listen to them. I miss my sister. You haven't been the same for a while now and it's because of him. Now we have you back, let us make it better."

"Listen to him," Landon whispers.

I grasp his hand and turn to him, feeling the breath in my lungs get stuck. "I just want it to stop hurting."

He shifts on the bed, facing me fully. "And we'll make it stop, Charlie."

"Okay."

He jerks for a moment. "Okay, you'll go to the hospital?"

I nod. "Yes," I rasp.

"You'll talk to the police?"

Fear snakes down my spine. "Yes."

"I'll go call the police now," Dad informs us, before meeting my gaze. "It's going to be okay."

"I'll call the hospital, so they know to expect us," Mum whispers.

"I'm sorry for disappointing you," I croak.

She walks over, leaning down to press a kiss to my head. "You've never been anything but a blessing, sweet girl."

I begin to sob once again, and Landon pulls me into his chest.

A throat clears and Jacob shuffles in the doorway. "I'm going to call Lily to get Jaxon to sort your cat out."

He leaves, and once he's gone, Landon bends down, kissing my forehead. "I'm so fucking sorry, Charlotte. So fucking sorry."

"You didn't do anything," I whisper, gripping his T-shirt. I glance at the sleeves of the large hoodie I'm wearing, my brows bunching together. *Where did that come from?*

"Yes, I did," he declares, his voice raw. "I wasn't there for you. I haven't been for a while. I've been a bad friend. I—"

"Stop, this is no one's fault but my own."

"No, it's not," he states fiercely. "I'll make this better, Charlotte. You'll see."

"None of this seems real. He was married, Landon. He was making a fool out of me this entire time and I didn't know," I tell him, and inhale. "How could something that was meant to be special, turn out like this? It doesn't feel like I was sexually assaulted, but I feel... I feel..."

"Feel what?" he rasps when I don't continue.

I blink my lashes up at him, feeling them soaked with tears. "I feel dirty. Unclean."

"Because you were sexually assaulted," he tells me.

I close my eyes, pain washing over me as my stomach cramps. "It wasn't meant to be like this."

He presses a kiss to my head. "Charlotte, you are special and one day, you'll meet someone who sees that and cherishes it."

I wipe my wet cheeks with the sleeve of the hoodie, breathing in the spicy cologne. "No one will ever want me. I thought he was it. The one to change my life."

He tenses beneath me and I pull back, finding his jaw clenched. "Charlotte, can you remember when we made a promise to let you guys date and find love on your own terms and we wouldn't get involved?"

My heart hurts because it doesn't matter anymore. I don't want love if that's what it ends up like. "Yeah," I croak out.

"The deal's off. When I find him, I'm going to kill him."

My breath hitches. Not in fear of him hurting Scott, but of him getting into trouble for hurting Scott. "Landon, you—"

"Sweetie, we are going to get you to the hospital. I have a spare set of clothes here," Mum announces, and I turn, finding smudged mascara under her eyes.

"Go with your mum," Landon orders, getting up from the bed.

I slowly get to my feet and watch him leave, worried about our future. I glance at Mum, my lower lip trembling. "Everything is happening too quickly. It doesn't feel real."

She hesitates for a moment before stepping back. "I don't want to force this decision onto you, or make you feel something that isn't true to you. But I need you to understand, rape isn't just being dragged into a dark corner by a stranger. You could ask a strange man back to your hotel room, initiate the entire thing and still say no and mean no. You could go to bed with your husband and if you say no, you mean no. If they don't stop, if they force you to continue, it's sexual assault."

"But I said yes," I whisper pathetically, the empty feeling spreading in my chest.

"Because you were manipulated into it, whether you believe it or not right now. Narcissistic people do it in a way that will make it seem like it was your idea. I bet he put you down often, made you feel small or even commented on the way you dressed. I bet he turned disagreements you had around on you, made himself superior to you." She pauses, her expression grimacing in pain. "He should have stopped when you told him to. He never should have laid a hand on you."

My head flops forward on her shoulder and I clutch her top between my fingers. "It hurts."

"What does, honey?"

"Everything. Everywhere. My heart," I choke out. "I'm so stupid. I live in a world where fairy tales don't exist. I was naïve to believe I could have that."

She pulls back and lifts my chin until we lock gazes. "Fairy tales may not exist, but love does. Our family is proof of that. It's filled with love and one day, sweet girl, you'll find your love."

"I don't think I want to."

She leans down, kissing my forehead. "You will, because with a heart like yours, there's no other possibility. You will get through this. You will forget about that man and what he has done. If you push the physical stuff he has done aside, he still hurt you. He broke your heart and for that, it will take time to heal. But I'm here."

I nod, trying to keep the tremors at bay, but it's so hard when she looks at me with so much love and heartache. I burst into tears and her expression crumbles as she pulls me into her arms. "It's going to be okay."

One part of me wants to believe her, but the other part has given up hope.

FOUR

DREW
FOUR WEEKS LATER

The noise of the gym echoes around the walls of my office, causing the pounding in my head to feel like it's going to explode. And looking at these email replies isn't helping.

I contacted local women aid groups, amongst other groups, to offer my services free of charge here at the gym. But the women were too scared to come to a place where grown-arse men work out, and I can't blame them.

We still had a few women who turned up, and it was great. Donations were given at the door and it was working out fine.

But I don't feel like I'm making a difference. Not yet. Not until more women are comfortable attending.

The door to my office slams into the wall and I look up, finding a red-faced Landon. He looks tired, haggard and aged. The past few weeks have taken a toll on him.

He's looking for the guy who attacked his cousin but has had no luck. "Nothing?"

He throws his cap on the desk before dropping down in his chair. "How the fuck someone can just disappear is beyond me."

"Did they find out his name?" I ask, sitting up. The last we spoke, the last name he had given her wasn't even real.

And she knows nothing about where he lives, who his friends are or where he works. It sucks, and I hate that she has been played like that.

"No. And we're reaching the end of leads now."

"I thought you said the strip club owner remembered him."

"Their security footage deletes after a few months and it seems he hasn't been back there since the night Charlotte met him."

"Doesn't mean he hasn't been to another," I remind him.

He pauses, and I give him a minute to mull over it. "I'm gonna get on that."

"Are you getting any help? Or should I ask, are you letting anyone help?"

"I should have been there for her," he growls.

I shake my head. This is where society is fucked up.

"It's not about someone being there for her, mate. It should never have happened."

"We live in a world with fucked up people."

"Yeah, we do."

"I just wish the police would do fucking more. Every lead they've had so far is what we've given them. No one just disappears. Someone has to know him."

"Just give them time. She's safe now," I remind him. "Is she still at her mum and dad's?"

"No, the stubborn woman wanted to go back home last week. She's doing okay. She has a way of bouncing back from anything, but I can still see her pain. It's like a light has gone out inside of her."

I know that look. It's the same one I see on my sister's face every time I see her. Thinking about Nora reminds me that I haven't seen her in a few weeks. "I really hope you find the fucker, and if you need any help, I'm there."

He glances from the keys to my face. "Going out?"

"Yeah, I need to go see my sister," I tell him as I grab my leather jacket off the back of my chair. "Can you lock up?"

"Of course," he replies. "And Drew?"

"Yeah?"

"Thank you for what you did for her that night."

I shrug. "Any time."

I leave him to stew over his thoughts and head toward the exit for my car, since I still haven't gotten my bike fixed.

"See you tomorrow," Helena, our receptionist, calls out.

"See ya," I call back, and pull open the door.

Paisley runs into me, jerking back with wide eyes. "Wow, I keep forgetting how big you are."

I chuckle. "He's in his office."

She hesitates to move and runs her palms down her coat. "Is he, um—is he okay?"

My brows pull together. "Um, yeah."

"He's only been home a few times. He's worried about Charlotte. But Jaxon has been watching the house too. Everyone has. I'm really worried he blames me for it. Because I pull his attention away from her."

I rub the back of my neck. "Um, he's in the office."

She forces out a laugh. "Guess you aren't into heart-to-hearts."

No, I'm not, but I'm also not into seeing women upset. It's a weakness of mine.

"He doesn't blame you," I tell her when she reaches for the door. She stops, turning to face me. "He blames himself. That night, it was bad. She was in a bad state."

Her lower lip trembles. "I hate that this has happened to her."

"He does too," I remind her. "Go to him. Talk to him. And get him to stop yelling at the staff. I can't afford to lose any more."

She nods, and pushes through the door. I wasn't joking about the staff. He's snapped at anyone who has even looked at him, which ended up with two people quitting.

I have been in his position, blaming myself, and no words from other people are going to help that.

My leather jacket squeaks as I head to my car, my gaze flicking briefly to the spot where Charlotte crashed. I've thought about her a lot over the past few weeks and I'm glad to hear she's getting better.

Getting into the car, I fire off a message, letting Nora know I'm on my way.

NORA IS WAITING for me when I arrive in the yard. I'm kind of glad my bike is still being fixed because the entrance hasn't been tarmacked and my tyres are sinking into the mud puddles.

The scrapyard is my dad's love. He's worked here for his dad for as long as he can remember and took over it when he passed. Now, there isn't just scrap, but he does body paintwork on vehicles inside. He has a pretty good thing going.

The house built on the lot isn't the biggest but it's more of a home than what it feels like at my mum's. There, it just feels cold, like I'm a guest in someone else's home.

Nora gets up from the seat swing, grinning when I get out of the car. "I was beginning to feel like you had forgotten about me."

I pull her into my arms, laughing. "Never."

"Dad's in the shed, working and talking to Uncle Malcom."

"Never mind them. How are you doing?" I ask, picking up the work she left on the seat before sitting down. She squeezes in next to me and takes the work from me, putting it on the table.

"I'm okay. School sucks."

"That wasn't what I meant," I tell her, arching an eyebrow. Her mum isn't the best mum. She comes and goes as she pleases. She mostly turns up drunk, begging Dad to let her stay.

"He's done with her," she admits. "I'm surprised it took him this long. She's crazy."

"He did it for you," I explain.

Her eyes widen. "Why?"

"Because he knows what it was like for me when Mum used me in her games. It made me resent her in a way. He didn't want to be the parent that made you feel like that's what he was doing by keeping her from you."

"Yeah, but your mum isn't a raging bitch. She doesn't get hammered and accidently leave you in the car. She never forgot to feed you or take you to school. She never forgot to pick you up."

I clench my fists together. Her mum is the reason she was walking alone in the dark. She had an afterschool commitment and Dad, thinking he was doing the right thing, gave Nicola the money to pick up her daughter and take her out for dinner.

Nicola saw that as an opportunity to spend the money on alcohol, leaving her daughter stranded.

How he wasn't done with her then is a mystery.

"I'm sorry."

She shrugs. "It is what it is."

I tug on a strand of blue hair, arching my eyebrow. "And this?"

"Self-expression. The school have locked down on the uniform code and now on hair, makeup, and nails."

"But you don't wear any of that," I point out, and gesture to her nails that are chewed off and have dirt beneath them.

She shrugs. "It doesn't matter. It goes against everything I believe in. They can't make us sheep. We have different personalities and should be able to express them in whatever way we can, especially if we already have to agree to wear their stupid uniform."

"But a uniform stops people from judging others. Not everyone can afford stylish clothes or the latest trend. It's like a bullseye for some kids."

She holds up her finger and her nose twitches. "No. This isn't about the uniform. I completely agree with that. But to be told what we can do to our own bodies is what I'm fighting against. If I want to dye my hair blue, I should be able to. If I want a manicure and to have pretty patterns on my nails, I should be able to. And hell, if you saw how zombified some of those girls look in the morning, you'd stand with me on the makeup too. We are going through a hormonal stage. It's not pretty. Yet, they try to dictate what we can wear."

"Nora," I begin.

"She going on about expressing herself?" Dad asks, walking up with Ry, his friend and employee, and Uncle Malcom.

I grin as Nora crosses her arms over her chest. "It's a peaceful protest."

"You got suspended for a week and are being forced to write a letter of apology to your peers."

A sly grin slips over her lips. "Oh, I've written a letter. I've written one stating that today's society is fucked up. Too many women are being told how to dress, how to act, and what they should be doing with life and work. It's one rule for men, and one for us. You don't see teachers criticizing the lads for how short their trousers are. You don't see them being judged for having slicked back hair. No. It's women. We are being conditioned into believing how we dress matters. Read the policy, Dad. It states it's to stop distractions in school. Well, if they can't keep their pervy eyes away from girls, they have no place in being there. But no, it's always the woman's fault."

"Nora," Dad sighs.

She holds up her hand. "I wasn't finished."

"Baby," Dad murmurs, chuckling.

"Nope. I'm not arguing over this. I'm right."

"I know you are," Dad replies, but she's not listening. Not anymore.

"I've also gone into more detail about how women are told what to wear and how to look too much in their lives; that school's condition that way of thinking and it's not fair. Did you know that if a woman is raped, they ask what she was wearing? Yeah. Because being raped in an all in one hazmat suit is different to someone who wore a short skirt and skimpy top. It's ridiculous. Yet, when a man is assaulted, what he wore is not considered. It's stupid.

"I should be allowed to be who I want to be. I should be able to dress how

I want to dress. Stop teaching girls to suppress themselves whilst encouraging males to do the opposite.

"I've ended the letter with this: I'm a strong young woman, and I will continue to fight for my rights and to be heard. And I'll fight for the next generation who has to put up with this sexist bullshit. I'll do it loudly and proudly."

"Preach it," Malcom hoots, holding his fist out for a fist bump. She rolls her eyes but obliges.

I pull her into me when she sags, wearing herself out. "Want me to help you read it over because the bullshit bit might be a little too much?"

"No," she sighs. "I just want them to see that they can't force me to conform. They can't take my personality away. I know I went off topic but it all matters. It's all the same meaning."

"I'm proud of you," I tell her.

"Me too, kid," Dad tells her, kissing her head. He bends over, clapping me on the shoulder. "Want a drink?"

"Not tonight."

"Coming in?"

I shake my head. "There's something I wanted to ask Nora and get her opinion on."

"Are you sure?" Ry asks, biting his lip. "She gets angry a lot."

"You're just mad because Becky took my side and you got put in the dog house."

Dad howls with laughter. "She had you there."

Malcom turns to me. "Will I be seeing you up at the cliff top soon?"

I shrug. "I'm still getting my bike looked at but yeah, soon."

He knocks my chin with his fist. "See you soon, lad."

My uncle owns food trucks that are tucked away up some cliff top. It has one of the best views around and is a place I love to go for solace and peace. It's my favourite place to visit.

They head inside, leaving us alone. "If you're about to give me a lecture, don't."

"I'm not," I tell her. "I really do need your help."

She watches me warily. "What with?"

"Actually, about what you were just talking about," I admit, surprising her. "You know Landon, who now runs the gym with me?"

"The hot one?"

I snort. "That one. His, um, his cousin, who he's really close with, turned up late at the gym a month ago. She was in a bad way." I stop when she grips the edge of the chair, her knuckles turning white. "Forget it. I shouldn't have brought this up."

"Was she okay?" she whispers.

I relax back. "No. It's a long story but she was hurt and I took her back to her family. Ever since, I've been trying to start up the self-defence classes again. Now we have more staff, I can concentrate on it more, but we aren't getting many there, and although I don't know all their stories, I've heard more than one say they were told it was the best fitness class to take. I want to make a difference, not make a woman stay in shape."

Her grip loosens and she looks up at me. "Because you need a leader."

"What?"

"You need someone who speaks from experience, who can speak for all of them. That girl, you said it's Landon's cousin?"

"Yeah."

"Then get her to help with those classes. If people see one person in their position going, they'll follow because they'll feel safe to."

"You're saying they don't feel safe?"

When she looks at me, my breath stills in my throat. "Because *I* wouldn't be able to do it, not unless I knew someone I could trust was in there. And for a lot of victims, they connect better with other people who have been in their shoes, who understand and are patient."

"I don't think she's in the best place," I admit, mulling it over.

"But you have Landon there and she trusted you enough to take her back to her family. Get to know her, let her warm up to you."

"I'm not sure trust is something she's capable of right now. The person who hurt her wasn't who she thought he was."

53 CHARLOTTE

Nora leans into me, resting her head on my shoulder. "You might look scary, but you aren't. She'll see that."

"What makes you so sure?" I ask, curious to know.

She tilts her head up. "Because you saved me from myself."

I kiss her forehead, not saying another word. There isn't anything else to say. After her attack, she was in a bad place. I gave her an outlet, not only to build up her strength, but to let out her anger. Once she was calm of that anger, we moved on to the next step and together, we worked on her self-defence.

If she kept that anger inside, she would have gone down the wrong path, and Nora is the best of us. She's kind-hearted, loving, and cares about everything.

"Love you, little sis."

"Love you too."

"I'll let you get back to your, um, letter of apology, but I'll pop by and see you again soon."

"Good luck with it all."

I stand and pop my head through the front door, finding Dad and the guys sat on the sofa, watching a game. "I'll catch you later."

"Bye, son."

I shut the door then wave one last goodbye to Nora before heading back to the car. Getting in, I chuck my phone onto the passenger seat and groan when it slides to the floor. Leaning over, I reach for it, but my fingers come into contact with something fluffy.

My brows pull together as I lift up the fur ball between my thumb and index finger and hold it up in front of me. "What the fuck," I whisper.

Two beady eyes stare back at me and it takes me a moment to catch on to what I'm holding.

Gripping the glittery unicorn horn, I slide the zipper open and I'm immediately greeted with a stripper business card and a driving licence.

Charlotte.

The purse must have fallen out when I took her to her family. I glance at the address, wondering what I should do.

Do I take it to her or do I give it to Landon?

I look through the windshield at my sister studying one of her books and come up with an answer.

I'm going to speak to her.

FIVE

CHARLOTTE

I come to a stop after showing Mum my room via video call. I needed a change after Scott. My room no longer felt like a safe space. There were too many bad memories so it was time for a cleanse.

My dad and uncles did the heavy lifting and got rid of the old furniture. Me, Landon, and Dad did the decorating. The rest I wanted to do myself. It was something I needed to do myself.

And I have finally finished it. It feels great.

Mum grins over the screen. "It looks good."

I sigh, pushing open the window. "I'm loving it."

"But, honey, what about some fluffy pillows, or what about some lights, or hey, we were in the Range earlier and we saw this pineapple lamp that I think you'd adore. It's rose gold so will match the décor."

I bite my lip as I look around the room. All my old knick-knacks are gone.

Every time I looked at them I heard his voice inside of my head telling me they were for little girls, not grown women.

I shake my head. "I think it doesn't need anything else."

She sighs, tilting her head. "But it's not you. It needs your personality."

"I'll have a look."

"Don't change who you are," she tells me after stepping into another room. "Be you, honey."

"But there was something wrong with me before."

"I'm coming over," she tells me.

"No, Mum. Please, I'm okay."

"No, you aren't, but you will be," she assures me softly.

She's worried about me. I know she doesn't like me being back home but it's the best thing for me. I need to get back to my norm and tomorrow, I'm finally going back to work.

"How about we go shopping at the weekend and get some more stuff?"

She visibly relaxes. "I'd love that."

My fire alarm begins to blare and my eyes widen. I turn back to the phone. "My cakes!"

"Go!" she orders. "Call me later."

I nod, and throw my phone onto my new bedcover. It's rose gold with a light gold feather pattern.

I race into the kitchen and pull open the oven door, and the smell of charcoal burns my nostrils. "Oh no."

I grab my oven mitts, pulling out the tray and placing it on the hobs. My shoulders drop as I look around the kitchen at all the other disasters. I thought this batch would be it.

I lean over, pushing the window open a little, then freeze, my heart racing as I run back out of the kitchen and up the stairs.

Katnip.

I forgot to shut my bedroom door and I left my window open. Racing inside, I run to the window, my eyes widening when I spot her on the tree, her yellow eyes glowing as she turns to me and hisses.

"Katnip, come back," I call out softly. She once again hisses in response. "I know you don't like being cooped up in here, but there are cars out there. And you don't want to become a bad meme because you got squished by one."

Another hiss.

Rushing downstairs, I head outside to my back garden. As I glance up into the tree, I groan, placing my hands on my hips.

"Katnip," I whine.

Dragging the mini step ladder—that I keep out here for this very reason—over to the tree, I take a step up. It isn't the first time she has done this to me.

And won't be the last.

I pull myself up, biting my lip when she moves up higher. "No, Katnip."

Hiss.

The bark is rough on my fingertips as I reach the first branch, panting out a breath as my muscles already protest.

"I don't want to do it but I will. I'll take away those treats," I threaten when she moves further out of reach. "I mean, it's not like you'll starve. I won't let that happen. Hey, no, don't go—"

A scream bubbles out of me as I begin to spiral backwards. A branch scrapes down my back, hooking into the back of my lounge bottoms. I tense, my eyes closing, stretching my arms out to prepare for the fall, but I come to a halt, dangling mid-air.

"Oh no," I groan, pushing my T-shirt out of my face.

"Um, do you need some help?" I scream, causing my trousers to tear as I struggle. "I'm sorry. I thought you heard me coming. It's okay, I'm Landon's friend."

I shove my T-shirt back out of my face, blowing out a breath, and tilt my head a little, getting a better look at him.

I remember him.

He's taller than I remembered and he has a lot more hair. I think. I squint into the darkness, making out tattoos. *A lot* of tattoos.

Holy hot damn he's hot.

"Your name is Drew?"

"Yes," he replies, keeping his distance.

Landon told me he was the one to bring me to Mum and Dad's. I only remember small parts, and he's one of them—and it was his smell I remember the most. I have a lot to thank him for.

I give him a small wave. "Hi. I'm Charlotte."

His lips twitch. "I know."

I force my top back out of my face, trying to keep myself covered. "It's my cat, Katnip. She likes to play hide and seek."

He smiles and it makes the angles of his jaw sharper. "Do you want some help getting down?" he asks, just as another tear happens.

I close my eyes as I whimper. "That would be really helpful."

He chuckles as he kicks the step ladder aside. He rests the back of my neck on his shoulder before I feel him reach for my leg, getting it out of the mess I got it in. "Turn a little."

I grip his shoulders for support, and with his help, I manage to turn, facing him. Seconds later, his warm hands are on my hips and he's lifting me before lowering me to the ground.

With my feet steadily on the floor, I straighten my bottoms, my face flaming when I realise I have my 'Must be Tuesday' knickers on and he would have seen them.

I tilt my head up, way up, and say, "Thank you."

"You're welcome," he tells me, his gaze going to my T-shirt, his lips twitching.

I glance down and inwardly groan. I have on my 'Short girls; God only lets things grow until they're perfect. Some of us didn't take as long as others' T-shirt.

It's funny when you're short. I guess not so much when you're seriously tall like him.

"Hey, cutie."

I jerk, inhaling sharply. "Excuse me?" I blurt out, wondering if I heard him correctly.

Does he think I'm cute?

He's not looking at me though. He's no longer even standing in front of me. On his tiptoes, he pulls Katnip out of the tree. My lips part as she begins to purr, rubbing her nose into his hair.

And he has a lot of hair.

And tattoos.

Even his knuckles and fingers have designs on. I bite my lip, wondering if everything is tattooed.

"Cute cat," he comments, and I blush, looking up from his crotch.

"How did you do that?" I whisper.

He freezes. "Do what?"

"She's purring."

"Um…"

I wave him off. "It's okay, we are still bonding."

I take her off of him and immediately, her claws dig into my skin. I ignore the pain, and cling onto her. I can't take her back inside, not while the windows are still open. "You can go and take her inside."

I bite my lip, not wanting to be rude to him, because he saved me and my cat, but I can't invite him inside. It's my space again.

"I'll wait over there," he tells me, pointing to my decking furniture.

"Okay, I'll be a minute," I whisper, and quickly head in through the backdoor, pulling the window closed in there before heading upstairs and doing the same. I watch from my bedroom window as he pulls something out of his back pocket, placing it on the table before taking a seat.

I catch a flicker of movement in Lily's garden and my eyes widen when Jaxon jumps over the small gate and lands in mine.

Sugar.

Drew stands, his fists clenching, and I quickly deposit Katnip on my bed before racing down the stairs, grabbing the hoodie off the kitchen side before pushing out the backdoor.

"Who are you?" Jaxon asks.

"It should be me asking you that since you just snuck into the resident's garden."

I quickly shove the hoodie on. "Jaxon, hi."

"Who is this guy?" he demands.

"It's Drew. He works with Landon. He, um…" My forehead creases as it occurs to me. "I actually don't know why he's here."

Drew smirks as he lifts the fluffy purse off the table. "I came to return this. I found it in my car."

I smile, but it drops when I realise why it was in there.

"Thank you," I whisper, taking it from him.

"Are you okay with him? Do you want me to get Landon?"

I shake my head. "I'm fine thank you, Jaxon."

He nods, giving one last look to Drew before jumping back onto his side of the garden, heading for his house.

"He's friendly."

I laugh. "He can be a little scary."

"Nice hoodie," he comments.

My eyes widen when I realise it's his hoodie from that night. "You can have it back. I'm sorry."

He smiles. "Keep it."

I sag with relief. Because I was lying. I was willing to bribe him for it. It reaches past my knees if I don't roll it up. I love it.

"Thank you."

"I'm sorry I couldn't bring it sooner," he tells me, pointing to the purse. "I only found it twenty minutes ago."

"Thank you. You didn't need to do that," I tell him, before glancing around, not knowing what to say. "I, um, I got everything replaced."

"That's good."

I fiddle with sleeve of the hoodie. I'm not sure why he's still here, but I have a feeling he wants to say something else.

"Did you, um, want a drink or something?"

He smiles. "No, but thank you," he replies. "There's, um, there's actually something I'd like to talk to you about."

Really? "Talk to me about?"

CHARLOTTE

"Yes," he answers and sits back down. I pull out a chair and take a seat, facing him. "My little sister, she was attacked a few years ago after walking home from school. She was saved before things escalated, and ever since then I've been wanting to build up a self-defence class."

My palms clam up and I fight back tears. "I'm sorry about your sister," I whisper. "Is she okay?"

"She has her bad days, but she's a fighter. She's actually fighting for the right to express herself in school."

I smile at that. It reminds me of Hayden. "My cousin Hayden was suspended for a week for trying to express her rights as a woman at school."

He chuckles. "Same as Nora. Now she's writing a letter of apology that's basically a letter telling them where they are going wrong."

"She sounds awesome."

"She is," he replies. "She's the reason I'm here. And you."

"I'm not sure what you want me to do," I admit.

"At the minute, the only women attending are one's who want to keep in shape. That's not what the class is about. My sister thinks I'm not getting the right clients because the women need assurance to attend. They need someone there who has lived through a trauma, someone who will make them feel safe and secure; to let them know it's okay to be there."

"Are you teaching the class?"

He smiles. "Yes. Landon scared the last class off."

My lips twitch at that. "It could be your height."

"My height?"

"I don't know a lot about victim support, but my mum does. She volunteers to help other women. She's also a survivor and recently, she talked more about it to me and she said it wasn't as much men who scared her, or women, but it was their presence and height. If she felt overpowered, she would withdraw into herself."

"Wait, isn't your mum married to a Carter?"

I nod whilst smiling. I knew he would make that leap of logic. Yes, the male Carter's are well-known for their unique 'presence' and can certainly be intimidating when they need to be. They are a force to be reckoned with. And aren't shy. "They healed her."

"I want my gym to be that for other survivors. I want them to be able to defend themselves or feel empowered by knowing that they can."

I fiddle with my sleeve as the backs of my eyes begin to burn. "I want to feel like that."

"Hey, you will again."

I shake my head as I look up. "I've never felt it to begin with. I've walked through life with my head in the clouds. I had a family who would die for me, kill for me. I never had to worry about anything. Until now. And it's made me realise how weak and naive I truly am."

He sits back, crossing his ankle over his thigh. "I'm not going to sit here and tell you it's not your fault. I think deep down you already know that. I'm not going to pretend I know who you are and say you aren't naïve." He pauses when a choked sound rumbles in back of my throat. He leans forward, resting his elbows on his knees. "But the girl I saw drive into the car park of my gym is not weak. I saw someone who was in pain yet didn't want to disturb her cousin because he was with his girlfriend. I saw someone, so scared and in pain, worry more about her cat. I saw someone who had just escaped an assault and managed to get to safety."

I run my hands over my thighs, taking a deep breath. I can't talk about this, not now, not with him. "I guess you are here to ask me to attend these classes?"

"No, I want to train you to help me run them," he declares, and for some reason, he sounds more surprised by his offer than me.

"What?"

He nods, like he's silently agreeing to something in his head. "Yeah. I want to train you in self-defence. The women need to know they can trust me and you said so yourself, my height intimidates people."

"I'm not scared of your height," I whisper.

His lips tug up but he quickly masks it, keeping a straight face. "It's not just about helping them, or helping me. It's going to help you too."

"Landon already offered," I admit, but I had said no.

"And why did you say no?"

"How do you know I said no?"

He grins and it's nice. *He's* nice. "Because he's family and knowing him, he asked too soon."

I tuck my hair behind my ears and his gaze follows the movement before he clears his throat, glancing away.

"Can I think about it?"

"Of course," he tells me, and sits up, pulling out his wallet. He slides out a card and hands it to me. "My number is on that card if you change your mind. Or you can come Thursday at six as the gym closes early."

"Thank you, and for this," I tell him, holding up my purse.

He gets to his feet but pauses, glancing at the purse. "What is it meant to be?"

A giggle slips free. "It's a monster unicorn."

His lips twitch as his gaze locks onto mine. After a moment, he shakes his head and takes a step back. "Take care, Charlotte."

"You too," I whisper, watching him walk away. My pulse picks up as I step forward, then freeze.

You can do this.

I try again, but my feet are glued to the ground.

Just before he reaches the house, I yell, not knowing what else to do. "Wait!"

He pauses and turns. "You okay?"

"Thank you. Thank you for everything you did for me that night."

"Any time," he replies, before heading off.

The card creases in my hand as I take in deep breaths.

I can do this.

With that mantra in my head, I walk inside, ready to start baking the fourteenth batch of cakes.

SIX

CHARLOTTE

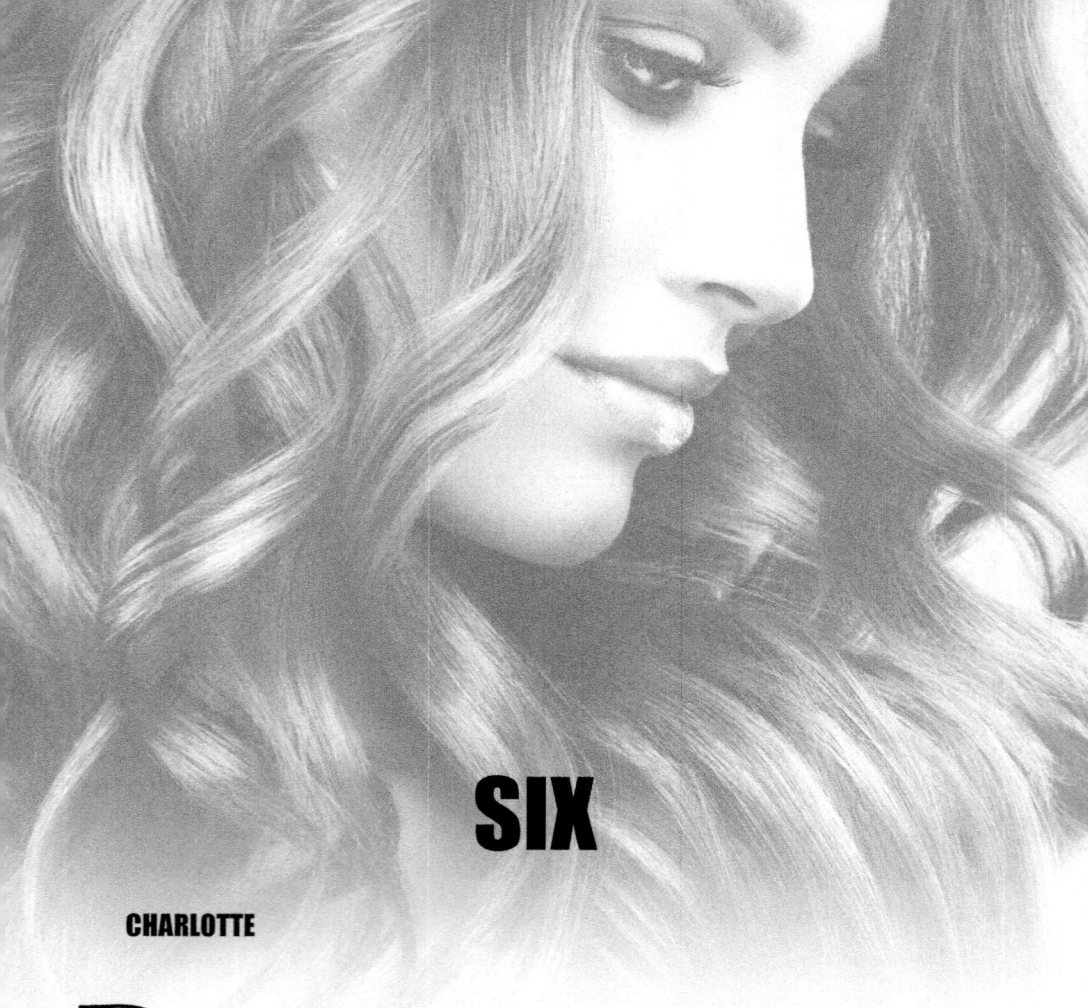

BOOKS ARE LIFE. They are an escape, they are love, they are historic, and sometimes, a teacher without the voice.

Every day I get to surround myself with every type of book and it always makes me feel blessed. Most people don't get to live their dream when it comes to work. In today's society, you can't be choosey if you want to survive and make a decent living. I'm lucky to have a head start. I wouldn't own this place if it weren't for the help of my family, and every day I cherish it that little bit more.

Carter's Library is my favourite place to be.

Being back after such a long period of time feels comforting yet disconcerting at the same time. I'm not sure what I was expecting in coming back, but it's like something has shifted inside of me. It seems to be another thing that thrives without me, just like everything else in my life. I shake those dark thoughts away. I'm not going back there. After the hospital, I had a lot of them, and I didn't like how they made me feel.

I head over to the reception desk. Marlene, a new girl I hired a few months ago, smacks her lips as she chews on her gum whilst filing her nails.

A heavy sigh slips free. "Marlene, did you go over next month's schedule like I asked?"

"Yeah."

"And?"

She looks up with a bored expression. "And what?"

"Marlene," I call out when she goes back to her nails. "How many bookings do we have?"

I rely on those bookings, and although Rita ran things while I was gone, there was only so much she could do.

"It's all on the computer."

She goes back to her nails, leaving me standing there gawking at her. I grab a trolley filled with returns and leave her to it. One day, I'll find someone to work here who will actually love it as much as me. Rita is amazing, but she isn't good with the kids. In fact, I'm pretty sure she despises them.

"Hey, Charlotte, you're back."

I turn at the sound of one of our regulars. "Rose— oh my God, it's so good to see you," I greet, pulling her in for a hug.

We bonded over our love for books. She is obsessed with historical romance novels, just like me.

"And you," she tells me when I pull back. "You've been gone a while."

My expression drops but I force my smile in place. "Yeah, I, um, I had some family stuff going on."

"Nothing serious I hope?"

I shake my head. "No. Nothing serious," I lie.

"Well, I'm so glad you're back. The new chick didn't even know where the historical romance section was, let alone recommend a book."

"I'm sorry." I grimace. "She's still getting used to her new role."

"She didn't even know who you were."

"It's a work in progress," I tell her, then clear my throat. "Follow me. I've actually got the perfect book for you."

"How are you anyway? Still with your boyfriend?" she asks, keeping in step with me.

I nearly trip over my feet. I grip the bookstand, coming to a stop at the end of the aisle. "No, we, um, we broke up."

It hurts. It hurts so much because he was never mine to break up with. None of it was real. It was just a ploy.

And he ruined my first time. My nightmares have been focussed on that night. Not him hitting me, not him yelling, not even him admitting he was married. It was him not stopping, him taking something beautiful away from me.

She reaches out, rubbing my arm. "I'm sorry. I know you really liked him."

"It's okay."

"I've had my fair share of breakups, so if you ever need a lending ear, I'm all yours."

"Thank you, but it's really okay," I whisper, really not wanting to talk about it.

I'm afraid I'll break down and cry. And I hate crying.

"How about your cat? Has he stopped scratching you?"

I relax, happy with the subject change. Then excitedly share the good news. "He purred the other day."

Not because of me but that's okay.

"That's great news."

I beam at her, and reach for the book I was searching for. "It is," I reply, then hand her the book. "Read this one. The author sent us a bunch of copies and it's been a great hit."

She turns the book over, glancing at the back. I'm not a fan of reading blurbs. Not all the time anyway.

"Thank you. This looks awesome."

"It is," I assure her, having already read it.

"Yo, Farley, you've got a visitor."

I force a smile as I turn to Rose. "I've been summoned."

"I guess she forgot your name again."

"It's a work in progress," I repeat, then point to the book. "Enjoy."

"I'm going to finish browsing, but next time, we need to have a coffee and a catch-up."

"Definitely," I tell her, then head out of the stacks. I stroll toward the front, surprised to see Paisley waiting for me. "Hey, is everything okay?"

Her shoulders drop when she sees me. "Can we talk?"

"Of course," I tell her. "We can go into the back. No one sits there."

"I thought you had an office."

I give Marlene a quick glance and shrug. "It's not away from prying ears."

"Ah," she murmurs and then follows me to the back. This is where we have the kids come in and study.

I'm the first to take a seat and Paisley follows, reaching for the cushion and cuddling it to her chest. "I'm sorry to turn up on your first day of work."

"It's fine, it's lovely to see you again. But what has brought you here?"

She ducks her head, playing with some lint on her jeans. "I'm worried about Landon."

I go on alert, sitting up straighter. "Is he okay? Did something happen?"

"No, it's—" she stops, confliction written over her face. I'm about to ask what's going on when she suddenly stands. "It's fine. Forget it. I shouldn't have come."

I grab her wrist, pulling her back down. "No, tell me what's going on."

When I see the tears in her eyes, dread hits my stomach. "Forget it, please. It was wrong of me to come and talk to you about this. You've got a lot going on."

"Please," I plead.

She wrings her fingers together. "He's not himself. He's been staying out late and leaving really early. I barely see him."

"Because of me," I whisper, slumping in my chair.

"No, because of me. I think he blames me for what happened."

"Why on earth would he do that?"

"Because if it weren't for me, he'd have been there for you. He could have prevented this."

I shake my head, reaching for her hand. "No, Paisley. What Scott did is no one's fault but my own. No one could have stopped it from happening."

She wipes under her eyes. "I'm sorry. I had a whole conversation played out in my head but now that I'm here, I feel rude for bringing it up. I know you are still recovering."

"You can always come to me. We are family."

"You don't blame me?"

"Paisley, it had nothing to do with you."

"Not that," she whispers. "But for Landon. For him not being around yours as much."

Over the past month, I've come to realise I had been selfish when it came to Landon. I was acting like a spoilt child who had her favourite toy taken away. Landon doesn't belong to me. He belongs to Paisley and I let my hurt over missing him make him feel guilty.

"I miss him, I'm not going to lie, but I want him to be happy, Paisley, and he's happy with you." I pause, hoping I'm not being rude. "But what has this got to do with what's going on?"

"Because I don't know what to do. I miss him. Rex misses him. And every time I've tried to talk to him, he's pushed me away. And I know it's because he blames me for him not being there for you."

I shake my head. "He can't protect me from everything," I remind her. "You of all people know what the men in your life can get like. He's just taking it hard."

Her eyes glass over. "I know, but this is different. You two were so close before I came into the picture."

"We still are close."

"Not like you were," she denies.

"Yeah, we really are. We just don't see much of each other," I explain. "He's my best friend, always will be, but you're his other half."

She wipes her tears away. "I didn't know who else to come to. I want to help him."

Hearing footsteps approach, I don't reply, waiting to see who it is. When Landon heads out of the stacks, I'm shocked.

"Shit," Paisley whispers.

"Paisley, what are you doing here?"

"She came to see how I was," I tell him. "What are you doing here?"

"I've come to see how your first day was going," he tells me. "And to ask if it's true that you are going to take self-defence classes."

I stand. I'm not sure if he's annoyed or happy about it, because he looks so angry. Paisley was right.

And it's my fault.

"Yes, it's true," I tell him, coming to the decision just then. I hadn't decided, and if I'm honest, I was leaning more toward no. Now, I'm saying yes. Because I don't want my friends and family to continue to worry about me. Self-defence classes might not fix anything, but it will show them I'm doing okay. "Your friend at the gym popped by to return my purse and he—"

"Wait, Drew was there?"

My brows bunch together. "If Drew didn't tell you, how did you know?"

"Jaxon said he heard you talking about it. He didn't mention Drew," he explains. "If you give me a few days to move some stuff around, I can start teaching you."

"Stop," I blurt out. "I love you. You're my best friend, but I'm okay. You don't need to worry about me anymore."

"Of course I'm going to worry about you. You're family."

"So is she," I whisper, pointing to Paisley. "And you're pushing her away."

His forehead creases. "What?"

Paisley stands. "I'm gonna head back."

I grip her wrist, stopping her. "No. He needs to hear this. He needs to stop feeling guilty and worrying about me."

"What is she talking about?" he asks, staring directly at Paisley.

Paisley's lip trembles moments before she bursts into tears. "You blame me."

"Blame you?" he asks, pulling her into his arms. "Babe."

"She thinks you blame her for you not being here for me."

"What? No. Fuck no. I'm mad at myself."

"And you don't need to be. I'm okay."

"Charlotte, you are far from okay. You are still in denial about it all."

I glance away at his pitiful look. "You can't put your life on hold for me, Landon. It's not fair on those who depend on you."

His jaw clenches. "I just hate that there's nothing I can do. I can't even find the fucker."

I step closer and lean up and kiss his cheek. "And I don't need you to. The police will do that, so please, Landon, just be my friend, be my family."

He closes his eyes as he pulls Paisley closer. "I'm not giving up," he tells me.

He's a stubborn arse. "Then at least stop pushing everyone around you away."

"All right," he tells me, then pulls back, glancing down at Paisley. "I've been a dickhead, haven't I?"

She shakes her head. "No. You've just been worried and I get that. But I worry about you. I love you."

"I love you too," he assures her. "And I don't blame you."

I clasp my hands together. "Good. Now, can I get back to work?"

Paisley chuckles, resting her cheek against his chest. "Thank you for listening to me."

"You're more than welcome," I tell her. "I'll give you two a moment."

"I'll speak to you later," Landon tells me, before turning to Paisley.

I smile and head back to where I left my trolley, but as I reach the corner, I bump into Rose. She jumps, glancing up from the book. "Charlotte, you scared me."

"Sorry," I grimace, then realise what aisle we are in. "Are you looking for something specific?"

She glances up and pulls out a book on anatomy. "My sister asked me to pick this up."

"Ah, well, I'll leave you to it."

"Oi, Charlotte, where are ya, babe?"

My eyes widen at the sound of Harriet yelling. I rush back to the front, finding Harriet, Olivia, Emily and Gabby waiting at the reception desk. They are all my friends from Tease. My gaze finds Olivia first, her sleek black hair shining and standing out against the others. She looks different out of her work attire. They all do. None of them dress provocatively unless you count Gabby's cleavage. Gabby is stunning. She wears a light amount of makeup, and her brown hair with highlights is thrown up in a bun. Emily is the only blonde of the group. Harriet's more of a cool brown with highlights. And she preferred her leggings and flowy tops rather than the skimpy outfits she wears at work.

"Guys, what are you doing here?"

Gabby squeals and races over to see me. "You're alive."

I freeze, taking a step back, but she dives on me, knocking me back a step. Had someone leaked the information? Do they know? "W-what?"

"What the fuck is going on?" Olivia asks, rushing over when Gabby pulls back from the hug. "Why do you look like you've seen a ghost?"

"And why haven't you been to the strip club in a month?" Harriet demands.

Marlene begins to choke from the desk. "Strip club?"

Oh no.

"Yeah, we had police there searching for video footage," Emily comments. "And Trixie, she said she heard your name being mentioned."

"Tell us what is going on. When you messaged us you said you were sick."

I wring my fingers together just as I feel a presence behind me. I know it's Landon right away because Emily sighs, hearts in her eyes as she stares up at him.

"Handsome," she breathes out.

My lips tug into a smile when he clears his throat. "Um, ladies."

"Haven't seen you in the strip club for a while either," Harriet murmurs.

Oh no.

I watch as Paisley stiffens, slowly tilting her head up to face Landon.

This isn't going to be good.

SEVEN

CHARLOTTE

L ANDON PALES AT THE PREDICAMENT, holding his hands up. "It's not what you think."

"A strip club?" Paisley grits out. "Really?"

"When I was helping her out with her notes," he rushes out to explain. "You know that."

"A strip club?" she repeats, eyes wide. She turns to the women, her lips parting. "Why did no one ever ask me to go?"

I chuckle when Landon begins to choke.

"I'll invite you next time," I tell her.

"No, you will not," Landon painfully grits out. "No way."

"Um, why not?" Paisley argues.

He arches an eyebrow. "Babe."

She rolls her eyes and turns to me. "I'd love to."

"Good, because this one hasn't been there for a while and we miss her," Harriet blabs.

"Bet it was her boyfriend," Gabby mutters.

"Don't," Landon warns, taking us all by surprise with his harshness.

"What's going on?" Olivia asks, once again noticing more than the others.

"She's been going through shit; back off," Landon warns. "Don't even bring him up."

The girls tense and I sigh, closing my eyes. "Something happened with Scott."

"I told you he was a waster," Gabby comments.

"You think all men are," Olivia argues.

"Which is why I like women," Gabby replies, and a headache begins to form.

"I'm going to go," Landon tells me.

I nod, then force a smile at Paisley. "He didn't get any dances or anything. I promise," I assure her. "He looked pretty uncomfortable the entire time we were there."

She waves me off, laughing lightly. "I know. I just love playing him up."

I lean in, giving her a one-arm hug. "I'll catch you later."

"See you."

I wait for them to go before facing the assembled mob in front of me. Olivia places her hand on her hip, giving me that 'Don't you dare brush me off' kind of look. "Spill."

"Okay, if you want to know, I need cake. And coffee."

"Then lead the way."

I turn to Marlene, rolling my eyes when I see she's actually paying attention for once. "I'll be in the café if you need me."

She shrugs, then goes back to the magazine she had been reading.

The girls follow me to the entrance to the café. This is also owned by me and I love it. It did come with a condition though: I'm not allowed to bake in here. Or *for* here. It's the only way my parents and uncles would help me. Personally, I think it's because my culinary teacher kicked me out of class for being too enthusiastic. I never got my food hygiene certificate.

I wave at Josie as I enter. "Hey, Josie."

Her eyes widen at the entourage behind me. "Everything okay?"

I nod. "These are my friends. When you are ready, we'd like to order."

We take the biggest table at the back of the small café and once seated, Josie takes our order.

Harriet turns to me once she leaves. "What happened?"

"He was married." When none of them say anything, I look up, taking in all their expressions. "What?"

Emily leans over, patting my hand. "Honey, we suspected as much."

My eyes water. "You did?"

Harriet nods. "We couldn't say anything. We never knew for sure and you were so happy."

"At least you didn't lose your virginity to him," Gabby comments.

Olivia snorts. "You're just hoping she'll turn gay."

"And what?" Gabby comments, scrunching her nose up.

Flattered, I force a smile. "I'd be lucky to have you as my girlfriend, but I don't think I'm attracted to girls like that. I mean, they're beautiful and all, but—"

"We don't get your vajayjay flowing," Gabby finishes, sulking into her seat.

Josie drops the tray on the table, her cheeks flaming red. "I'll, um, leave this here. I've given you some extras, but if you need anything else, just yell."

"Thank you," I tell her, reaching for the biggest cupcake on there. It has buttercream icing.

My favourite.

"So, what did you do with him?" Harriet asks.

Tears gather in my eyes as I shove the cake into my mouth. It's Olivia who answers.

"Oh my God, you slept with him."

I nod, unable to meet her gaze. "I didn't know then. He was going to leave me and I got scared."

"Leave you?" Emily asks, ducking her head to meet my gaze.

"He accused me of stringing him along, that I didn't really like him otherwise I'd have slept with him already."

"Oh my fucking God," Emily breathes, eyes wide. "He emotionally manipulated you into it."

"At least tell us it was worth it," Harriet grumbles.

A choked sob escapes and I put the cupcake down. It's probably for the best since I've put on a bit of weight. "It was awful. I thought it was what I wanted but it wasn't. It hurt so much and it was uncomfortable."

"It was your first time," Emily soothes. "It always hurts."

I shake my head. "I asked him to stop. It didn't feel right. But he wouldn't."

"No," Harriet whispers, her eyes glistening with tears.

"It was over quickly and I thought…" I gulp and blink back tears. "I thought it would be okay, that I was exaggerating. It wasn't like I thought it would be. He wasn't gentle and I… I just wanted him to stop."

"I'll fucking rip him a new one," Olivia bites out. "Who the fuck does he think he is, doing this to my girl?"

"Calm down," Gabby orders.

"You calm down. He hurt our girl."

Harriet takes my hand, squeezing it. "He should have stopped."

"It's fine," I assure her.

"It's not okay," she tells me, glancing at the others. "I know you struggle with socialising and understanding some concepts of emotions or acts, but, honey, what he did—"

"Don't," I choke out. "I've had my mum and the hospital say the same thing. I just want to forget it happened."

"The hospital?"

I wipe at my cheeks, pushing the cake toward Emily when she reaches for it. "I, um, I had to go to the hospital."

"It was that bad?" Olivia grits out. "What the fuck did he do to you?"

"I picked up his phone and saw a message from his wife. I confronted him. About it all. And it, um, it got physical."

Oliva pushes back in her chair, getting to her feet. "He fucking hit you?" she yells.

I grimace, scanning the café. There are a few customers, one being Rose, who has just walked in, and their gazes are on us.

I duck my head. "Please, be quiet."

She winces, sitting back down. "When I find him, I'm going to kill him," she hisses.

"It's fine."

"It's not okay," Harriet tells me. "I guess this is the reason for your absence."

I nod, fiddling with my fingers in my lap. "I couldn't come back— not with the bruises. And I needed to recover. This is my first day back at work."

"Why didn't you call us?"

I glance up at the sound of the hurt in Harriet's voice. "Because you all have lives. You are studying and trying to pay your bills." I turn to Olivia. "You're looking after your younger siblings." Emily is next. "You're working two jobs so you can take care of your grandmother and little girl." Gabby is last. "And you're still going through the trauma of what your last boss did."

"That's not how friendship works," Gabby whispers. "You've been there for us."

"Yeah, if it wasn't for you, I'd have never passed my last assignment," Harriet argues.

"I wouldn't have gotten those cupcakes done if it wasn't for you. Nell was already worried her brownies group didn't like her," Olivia explains, talking about her younger sibling.

"Wasn't that the fundraiser where a lot of kids got sick?" Gabby asks.

Olivia shrugs. "Probably the burgers they had on the barbeque."

Gabby leans forward. "And you made me feel safe at Tease."

My forehead creases as I think back. "Wait, I knocked over a tray of drinks and then when Dave came over to investigate what had happened, I ended up kicking him in the face."

Gabby waves me off. "You were a star on that pole, no matter what he says," she tells me. "The point is, he didn't react. He didn't kick you out or yell. He—"

"Offered me a job," I finish, my lips tugging into a smile.

"Landon's face," Olivia teases, and I chuckle. It was such a good night. It was my second time attending and I wanted to get the full experience.

"The point is, you've been there for us but you never let us be there for you," Harriet murmurs.

"That's not true."

Is it?

Emily shakes her head. "No. Remember when your cousin was stabbed?"

My heart hitches at the painful reminder. "Yeah."

"You said you were okay and wouldn't let us come and see you," she answers.

"What? That can't be right."

Olivia nods. "She's right. And then there was the time you stole that duck. Instead of letting us help you, you said you had it covered."

"I didn't want to implicate you in the crime," I whisper, and they laugh, looking at me like I said the funniest joke. "That was serious."

"Charlotte, that isn't the point. We wanted to be there for you. Let us be here now because we aren't going away," Harriet tells me.

"Yeah. We don't want to be the people you only see at Tease. We are your friends, aren't we?"

"Of course you are."

Gabby straightens. "Good. Then operation *Kill Scott* is on the way."

"What?"

She pats my leg. "Don't worry. He's a guy. There's no way he was only at our strip club. We will find out who he is."

"No. Please, don't. I've got it covered. I don't want anyone to get hurt."

"Friends remember?" Olivia states. "We need to toughen you up a little bit. You are too nice for your own good."

"I'm starting self-defence classes at Landon's gym."

"Will other members of your family be there?" Emily asks, sighing dreamily.

I laugh at her expression. "No. Just Drew, the guy who owns it."

"I thought Landon owned it?" Olivia muses.

"They both do now, but it was Drew's before."

"Is he hot?" Harriet asks.

I open my mouth to answer, but the words won't come out. I'm not sure why, but I feel like I can't say the words. Three small letters.

Yes.

"I, um, I guess."

"You're blushing," Olivia teases.

Gabby pouts. "Why couldn't you be gay?"

I chuckle. "You'll find someone."

"Not with the way she acts," Olivia argues.

"What's wrong with the way I act?" Gabby defends.

"You're too bubbly."

"I'm bubbly," I point out.

"Not her kind of bubbly."

Gabby huffs out a breath. "And you are too bitter and argumentative."

"At least I'm getting some," Olivia argues.

"A vibrator doesn't count," Gabby snaps back.

I laugh, pushing a cupcake Gabby's way. "Stop it, you pair."

"Why you two can't just have sex and get it over with is beyond me," Emily declares, pinching the bridge of her nose.

"Take that back," Gabby hisses, and for a moment, I swear I see a flicker of hurt.

Before it can get out of hand, I interrupt. "Want to watch a scary movie one night?"

"Can we bring alcohol?" Olivia asks.

"Yes."

"Will your cat be there?" Harriet murmurs, her gaze flicking to my arms that are covered in scratches.

I chuckle. "She'll be good."

She hums under her breath, not believing me. "Does it have to be scary movies?"

"Yes," we all reply, laughing when she slumps back in her seat.

This is what I've missed.

"Thank you so much for coming," I tell them, my voice filling with emotion. "And I'm sorry I pushed you away."

"Never again," Harriet warns.

"Oh, before we forget, Dave said to tell you you've got free entry for a month and a free drink the next time you come in."

"Really?" I ask, because normally he's tight when it comes to money. I remember watching him yell at a bartender for giving out free shots.

Emily chuckles. "Yeah, don't tell him but I think he misses you."

"It really hasn't been the same without you there on a Friday."

"I miss you guys too," I tell them honestly.

Because I have.

"We can't stay much longer but we will all book the same day off next week and get sitters."

"You're working today?"

Harriet nods, her jaw clenching. "Trixie wants us all to do a new routine."

My eyes widen. "But didn't you guys get a new instructor?"

"Yeah, and that bitch is sucking his dick," Olivia bites out. "I swear she does it knowing it fucks up our routine. We prefer doing our own. We know what the men like."

"Would you like me to help?"

Emily begins to choke on her drink. "No. No offence, Charlotte, but you nearly took my eye out the last time you tried to help."

I grimace. Maybe it's best I don't help. "Unless you know a space in which we can practice, then we'll figure it out. The only reason Trixie is getting away with bossing us around is because she has the studio space."

"My library, but then there's nowhere to put your poles." I know they have some adjustable ones they can put up or down when they like. "If I do think of somewhere, I'll let you know."

Harriet gives me a bright smile. "Cheers, bab."

I lift my hand, grabbing Josie's attention. If we don't have long together before they have to leave, I'm making the most of their company. Because they make me feel like me again. I don't feel broken for the first time in weeks.

I missed them.

EIGHT

DREW

THE LAST OF OUR CLIENTS LEAVE FOR the day just as Az finishes wiping down the last bit of equipment.

"See you tomorrow," he calls out.

"Later," I call back.

I glance over at Landon, who comes out of the changing rooms, and inwardly groan. The guy can hold a grudge without even meaning to.

"Are you going to keep being mad at me?"

"I'm not mad. I'm just pissed you didn't come to me first. I wanted to be the one to teach her."

"You know why you can't," I remind him.

"Fuck that shit," he growls. "You should have said something and you know it."

"Mate, I didn't know I was going to ask until I did. I didn't lie about finding her purse that night. I took it straight to her," I tell him. "Plus, I don't think she's coming so you have nothing to worry about."

I glance at the door once more. There's still no sign of her and she was meant to be here twenty minutes ago. If she's coming, she would have been here. I was stupid to even think she would. It's still too soon, and she's recovering.

"I'm gonna head out. I need to fix some lights at the bed and breakfast," Landon announces, grabbing his bag off the side.

I follow him out to the front, pulling the keys out of my back pocket. I'm going to finish up with a few things then head home myself.

"Well, guess I'm staying."

"What?" I ask, looking up.

Charlotte is pacing outside, her lips moving a mile a minute. My lips tug into a smile as she begins to wave her hands around, like she's arguing with herself.

Landon pushes through the door. "Charlotte?"

She jumps, whirling around to face us. She places her hand over her chest. "You scared me."

"You came?"

She nods. "I said I would."

I get a good look at her and nearly choke on my tongue. Her yoga leggings cling to every inch of her body, showcasing the curve of her round arse. Her top is short, showing her creamy-coloured skin, and it pushes her boobs up and together. Over it, she has on a purple fleece jacket.

And her hair. I'm not sure what the fuck it is with her hair, but I can't pull my gaze away. It's so bright, so full of life, just like her. It's tied up in a messy bun, tiny strands falling down, feathering her face.

"Good, I'll show you where to set up," he tells her, but I put a hand on his shoulder, stopping him.

"I can't have you here whilst I teach her."

"Why the fuck not?"

I look to the sky before meeting his gaze. "Because you have a short temper. Because if you think I'm hurting her or she can't handle it, you'll snap. You'll—"

"I'm not going anywhere."

"Landon," Charlotte calls out, reaching for his hand. "Go. I'll be fine here."

"How did you get here?"

"Harriet dropped me off."

"The stripper?"

"Stripper?" I repeat, gawking at Charlotte. "I thought you owned a library?"

"She's not a stripper," Landon growls.

She shrugs one shoulder. "Yes, that Harriet. And I can walk back. It's fine."

"I'll take you back," I offer when I see Landon go to intervene once again.

He stares at Charlotte for a moment, then briefly at me before I watch him sigh in defeat. "Text me when you're home and you can let me know how it goes."

"I will," she promises, and leans up, kissing him on the cheek.

He gives us a salute before heading to his car. Charlotte whirls around, her big green eyes sparkling up at me.

I gesture toward the door. "Come in." She follows and I close the door behind us. "Have you been here before?"

"No, I haven't. Gyms really aren't my thing."

"What is your thing?"

I close my eyes, inwardly groaning. Did I have to sound like I was coming onto her?

"Books. I like books." She stops in the middle of the gym, staring at all the equipment. "What is this one?" she asks.

"That's a seated lat pulldown. It works your waist and arms, but mostly your back muscles."

"And will I be using these?"

She's nervous. There's a tremble in her voice. "Not today, but you're more than welcome to use them once you've been trained to."

She nods. "So, what *are* we doing?"

"I'm not sure how other instructors work but depending on the client, I use the first session to get to know them, know their limits."

"And how do you do that?" she whispers.

"I watch them. Most survivors of any kind of traumatic event have a lot of pent-up anger. Whether they smother it down or lock it away, it's there. And to move forward with my approach, I need them to come to terms with that feeling. I want them to embrace it and use the techniques I teach as a tool to calm themselves."

"And you've done this before?"

I nod. "I have. I've done it with a few people who have been beaten by a spouse, or randomly while on a night out, and some who were in the wrong place at the wrong time."

"And these women are okay now?"

I shrug. "It's not just women who come here, Charlotte. I have men who have been beaten because of their sexual orientation, because of their spouses or just because they seemed like easy pickings," I explain. "Are they okay? That's a hard question for me to answer, but I know each of them are now stronger and more confident."

"It's so good what you are doing here," she tells me. "But I'm not angry. I don't really get angry. There was this one time but the guy deserved it. He was trying to hurt Faith and the muffins were there and I—" She stops as a blush rises up her cheeks. "I'm not angry. I'm disappointed I let it happen."

"I don't know the details of what happened. Landon has spoken a little about it but not what actually happened. I'm only putting two and two together." I pause when I see her lip begin to tremble. "But no matter what, never be disappointed in yourself."

"So, what do we do now if I'm not angry? Do we move onto the next step?"

I smirk because I get this a lot. It's just adorable coming from Charlotte's lips. I head over to the punching bags and hand her a pair of gloves.

She takes them from me, her nose twitching. "Um…"

"Put them on," I tell her.

She does as I say. "I don't get it. I'm not angry so I really don't need to do this."

"Close your eyes," I demand, coming to stand in front of her as I slide the other glove onto her hand. "We're going to do a little task, bring that hidden anger out."

"Okay," she drawls slowly.

"What do you dislike the most in the world?"

"People who hurt animals," she replies instantly. "And tomato sauce."

I chuckle. "Tomato sauce?"

She shudders. "Tastes like vinegar."

"I'm going to stand behind you. Keep those eyes closed." Her breath hitches as I move. "Trust me."

"Okay."

"What else do you dislike?"

"I-I don't know."

"I want you to bring your right leg forward a little," I order. "Can I touch you to get you into position?"

A squeak passes through her lips. "Position?"

"Yes, to punch the bag when I say ready." She nods and I help her into position before lifting her arm up. "This is the arm I want you to swing. Keep it at this angle and use your hips to put as much force into the punch as you can."

She tenses as I brush my fingers down her arm. I jerk away, stepping back to put distance between us. I hadn't realised I was doing that. I clear my throat. "Think about what makes you angry. What happened. What could have happened. Think about your cat in the hands of someone who is cruel. Think about the person who hurt you, how it felt, how *you* felt."

I don't even get to tell her to swing. She swings her arm out, hitting the bag in the centre.

I walk around, coming to stand at her side. "Take a deep breath and feel it. Really feel it. And let it out. Each time you hit that bag, I want you to tell me what you are angry about, what you dislike."

"I hate that he lied to me."

Smack.

"I hate that he hurt me."

Smack.

"I hate that he took my virginity and tarnished what was meant to be special."

Smack.

My eyes widen at her confession.

Tears gather in her eyes as she hits the bag harder. "I hate that I let my parents and family down."

Smack.

"I hate that I feel weak."

Smack.

"I hate that this happened because I was being selfish."

Smack.

"I hate that my mum can't look at me without being reminded of what she went through."

Smack.

Her chest rises rapidly as she struggles for breath. A sob hitches from her throat as she weakly throws another punch.

"I hate that he's out there and no one knows where."

Smack.

"I hate that he could turn up and I'm too scared to tell my family."

"Charlotte," I softly call out, beginning to worry I've pushed her too far.

"I hate that I've lost a part of myself that I can't find, and that others have noticed."

"Charlotte," I demand, taking a step forward. She's no longer hitting the bag with each admission. She's hitting it with both hands, her voice rising.

"I hate that he did this to me," she screams.

I step forward, but so does she, going for the bag. She's no longer punching but smacking the bag.

"I hate that he took a dream from me and I'll never get it back."

"Charlotte," I whisper, my heart aching as I watch the girl crumble before me.

"But most of all, I hate that I hate myself," she chokes out, right before she falls to her knees on the matt, sobs racking through her body. I follow, bending down to pull her into my arms.

I don't know much about her, but I know this isn't her. I had hoped to gain a lot from this session, but not this. I didn't think it went this deep.

I also noticed she was madder at herself than she was with *him*; the guy who caused this.

"It's okay now. It's okay," I soothe.

"I was so stupid. I feel like such a fool," she cries out. "I gave myself to him and it was all a lie. He knew I wanted children, a husband. He knew all my secrets and desires. He knew what my virginity meant to me."

I don't know what to say, so I continue to hold her, hoping like fuck Landon doesn't come back and find us. He'd kick my arse if he knew.

"I'm never going to have any of it. I'm going to be alone."

"Charlotte, you are young. One bad guy doesn't define them all."

"It does if you're me," she tells me, blinking up at me.

I'm struck by her beauty. "What do you mean?"

"No one wants me. I'm not sure people really like me and I try. I really do try. He was my chance at a happily ever after."

"Fairy tales aren't real," I remind her.

"They are," she whispers. "My family are proof of that."

"Life isn't just about love. It's about living, Charlotte. You can't go on thinking this is it for you. There's more out there."

"Do you really think so?"

I can't explain what I'm feeling. I have been around beautiful women plenty, so it isn't that. It isn't even the subject.

It's her.

There's just something about her.

And I want her to know she can have it all.

I clear my throat. "I really do."

She sits up, and bites her lip when she realises she's sat between my legs. "I'm sorry for that."

I tap her chin. "That is exactly what we wanted. Now I know what I'm working with."

"I thought it was about self-defence classes."

I shake my head. "Self-defence is more than fighting off an attacker. It's a way for those to feel strong again, to take back power. It can be a great healing tool, especially if it's done right."

"Thank you," she chokes out. "I didn't realise I was even thinking some of those things until I said them."

"You've been through a lot," I remind her. "And it hasn't been that long since it happened."

"I know."

"I do think you should talk to your mum though. I can't say for certain, but I think it may be in your head. You have a lot of self-doubt and it could be that you're projecting."

"I just hate seeing the heartbreak on her face whenever I see her."

I duck my head. I had been guilty of that with Nora. "I did that with my sister. I hated that she never had us there to protect her, that her mum let her down once again. I was even mad at my dad for going to another junk yard to pick up some spare parts instead of being at home. I was furious with the guy who attacked her."

"Did they catch him?" she whispers.

I nod. "Someone intervened and scared him off. He ran in front of a bus. And died."

Her eyes widen before she bursts out laughing, taking me off guard. She tries to stop, but more laughter spills free. "Oh God, I– I don't mean to laugh," she chokes out, laughing once again. My lips twitch as she places her hand over her mouth, but suddenly, her expression crumbles and she's bursting into tears. "He's still out there. I'm worried he'll come back because he's mad."

I grip her cheeks, and I know I'm pushing it. I know I shouldn't be touching her. But I can't help it. "He'll never get to you. You have a family who are willing to do what it takes to protect you, and if he does come, I'm going to make you strong enough to fight back and get away."

"Like Hayden?"

I grimace, letting go. I've met Landon's sister and she's scary as fuck. I swear my balls turned blue when she started fighting with Landon over a chicken.

A chicken.

That family is certifiably crazy.

"Maybe not like Hayden," I tell her.

Her lips twitch. "She's feisty and strong."

My brows pull together. "So are you. It's in you, Charlotte. But never forget who you are either. Sometimes the strongest people we know are the quietest."

"I don't know *who I am* anymore," she whispers.

"When you remember, the game changes," I tell her.

She tilts her head up, her lips parting in wonder.

"So, this is why you aren't answering your phone."

I jump, glancing away from Charlotte. "Mum! What are you doing here?"

NINE

CHARLOTTE

Mum?

I get to my feet, and close my jacket when she runs her gaze over me, her lip curling. Or at least, I think it was. Her lips look a little… stiff. There's no movement at all. On any of her face. Yet, she doesn't need to have movement there. Her eyes say it all.

Freaky.

She turns to her son. "I came because you have been ignoring my calls."

He rubs the back of his neck. "I've been busy."

Her gaze runs back over me distastefully. "I can see that."

"Mum, this is Charlotte. Charlotte, this is my mum, Grace Wyatt."

I reach out to shake her hand, giving her my best smile. "It's nice to meet you."

She looks from my hand to her son. "Why haven't you gotten back to me?

This is an important day for your sister and I'll not have you ruining it for her. The least you can do is answer the phone when I call you."

Well, okay.

"Jesus, Mum. I said I was going to be there. Alice knows I'm coming. She isn't worried."

She narrows her eyes into slits. "Alison is too shy to say anything to you. We have important people coming to this wedding."

Drew groans. "And I'll be there."

"Then why did you miss your tux fitting?"

"Because I'm not wearing a tux. I've got a suit."

She gasps, placing her hand on her chest. "You most certainly will not," she hisses.

"Mum, Alice knows and is okay with it. I'm not a best man, I'm not walking her down the aisle, I'm literally like any other guest. She doesn't care."

"We have an image to uphold, young man. I'll not have you prancing around wearing a suit on your sister's wedding day."

Maybe I should go.

"She doesn't care," he bites out, pinching the bridge of his nose.

"Yes, she does," she tells him, before reaching into her bag. She pulls out a card and hands it to him. "The tailor is waiting to hear from you."

He shoves it into his pocket. "I'm wearing a suit."

"You will wear a tux," she orders. "But that isn't the only reason I'm here. You still haven't confirmed your date. We need to know her name." When she turns to me, I shrivel under the look she's sending my way and take a step closer to Drew.

His mum is mean.

"And I guess this is the one," she drawls out, her lip curling. "This won't do."

"Oh, I'm—"

Drew's arm goes around my shoulders and I stiffen. "Yes, she's my date to the wedding, Mum. Now, I'm going to respectfully ask you to leave."

She scoffs. "Because she's here? She's got to meet us if you continue to think you're bringing her to your sister's wedding."

I hold my hand up to interrupt. "I'm—"

"Why do you need to be like this? Next you are going to ask me to take out my gauge," he argues.

I like the gauge in his ear. It isn't much thicker than a regular earring hole, certainly not huge like many I have seen.

Her face reddens. "Andrew Harvey, do not make this day difficult for her."

"For you, you mean?" he snaps back, his arm sliding off my shoulder.

I take a step back, fiddling with my fingers. "I'm going to, um, go."

"No," he tells me, before turning to his mum. "We were talking."

"I'm your mother."

I fiddle with my fingers. "You're busy and I—"

"Just give me a minute," he tells me, and I nod, picking up my bag and stepping away.

"Why must you be difficult all the time?" Grace snaps.

"Mum, I'm an adult now. You can't tell me how to dress, and I won't have you telling me who I can date."

"Eloise is a bright girl. She'll be—"

"A bitch the entire night."

I step into another room at her gasp and marvel at the empty space that has mirrored walls. I twirl around in a circle, watching my reflection do the same.

This is so cool.

I wonder if this is the room he teaches self-defence classes in. I can't speak for everyone, but it would be a little awkward staring at yourself whilst trying to fend off an attacker.

My gaze shoots to the door when their voices begin to rise. I pull my phone out and bite my lip. I can't message my family about what just happened. It would be shared within their next breath and I'm not sure what's going on.

Charlotte: I think I just got asked on a date.

Harriet: I left you, what, forty minutes ago? How did that happen?

Charlotte: I'm not actually sure. His mum came in being all

scary and the next thing I know, he says I'm his date to a wedding. But he's not asked me. Did I give him the wrong impression?

Harriet: I'm lost. So lost. More details.

Charlotte: I think I've given him the wrong impression because he sounded desperate. No one is ever desperate to go on a date with me.

Harriet: DETAILS!!

Hearing footsteps approach and noticing the yelling is no longer happening, I quickly type out a reply.

Charlotte: I'll call later. He's coming back.

I manage to get my phone back into my bag when he finds me. I straighten, my pulse racing.

"Look, I'm flattered and all, but I think you've got the wrong impression. Coming here was for self-defence classes. Not a date," I tell him, giving him a sad smile. "I mean, it's not because you aren't handsome, you are, but I'm not sure if I'm ready to date again. No, I know I'm not. I don't think. I've never been in this situation and meeting your family? Gosh, that is too soon."

He bursts out laughing and my shoulders slump. "Charlotte, calm down. My mum has been on my back about bringing a date to my sister's wedding. I only said it to get rid of her."

That makes a lot more sense. I shuffle on my feet, as my cheeks heat.

"So, you aren't taking a date?"

He rubs the back of his neck. "If I don't want her to try to set me up with the devil then yeah, I'll need to, but I hadn't planned on it."

My eyes widen. "The devil?"

"A family friend," he explains.

He looks revolted at the thought. And I kind of feel bad for going on at him now. Here he is doing this incredibly nice thing and I basically told him he isn't good enough.

"I'll go," I blurt out. "I love weddings."

His eyes widen and he begins to choke. "What?"

I pull on the sleeves of my jacket. "Well, you need a date, and it's the least I can do since you've been helping me."

"Charlotte, it's fine."

"No. I'll go. Plus, you've told her I am now."

He mulls it over then nods. "She might leave me alone if it is you I bring." My nose twitches. "Why?"

"Because I'm not really good with girlfriends. I've only had a few."

I blush. "Well, I can pretend to be your girlfriend. I think." I pause, tapping my chin. "My family do say I'm the worst actress so it might not actually work."

He chuckles. "You'd really do this for me?" he asks, seeming surprised.

I shrug. "Yes. It's not like you're interested in me like that."

He glances away. "Of course not."

"Just let me know when and where and I'll be there."

He clears his throat. "Um, there's not just the wedding. There's the rehearsal dinner. It's something formal my family do, and then there's the engagement party next weekend."

"Um, that's a lot of stuff for a wedding."

He nods. "And she wants me to sleep over for the actual wedding. So, it will be a two-night stay."

I gulp, wondering what I have gotten myself into. "That's okay. I can get a cat sitter."

His lips twitch. "Are you really sure?"

"I am."

He groans and runs a hand over his face. "Fuck! Landon is going to kill me."

I wave him off. "He'll be fine once he hears it's not real. And he's your friend. He doesn't hurt his friends."

He looks at me like I'm crazy. I'm used to that look. "If you say so."

"What is this room?" I blurt out, needing to change the subject.

"I'm not sure yet. I've never filled it."

An idea forms in my head. "What do you think of strippers?"

He begins to choke, and bends forward, banging his chest. "What?"

"My friends, they need somewhere to train and this would be perfect," I tell him, taking a look around. "It just needs a few poles."

"Um."

"And you could keep them in here. A lot of women use pole dancing to exercise. It could bring in more clientele." When he continues to stare, I begin to feel self-conscious. "What? Do I have something on my face?"

"You want me to let strippers come and practice? In here?"

I nod, wondering if I was clear enough. "I'm sure they'll even pay you for the space. Or you could ask if they will teach a few classes for you." I shrug. "It's an idea. It's not my gym."

"And these are your friends?"

I beam. "Yes. You'll like them. They're lovely."

"Let me run it by Landon. I can't see why not and your idea about teaching classes might come in handy. They could do it in exchange for the cost of rent for the room."

I clap my hands together, jumping up and down. His gaze drifts down to my chest. "Thank you. Thank you."

"I've not said yes yet," he warns. "Landon now owns a percentage of the company."

I wave him off. "He's their friend too." Sort of.

"Landon has stripper friends?" he chokes out, his lips twitching in amusement.

"Yeah. Kind of," I tell him, then a thought occurs to me. "Unless you're only saying this because you don't want to say no to my face. It won't upset me. Well, a little, but only because I don't want that Trixie working them into the ground with crappy dance routines. She just wants to keep all the tips. But if you say no— and you can say no— I'll just find them somewhere else."

He chuckles, shaking his head. "Let me talk to Landon. And then we will set a meeting up with your friends."

"This is so exciting. I'd love to be able to learn to dance on the pole," I tell him, then chuckle at the reminder. "I tried once and it ended badly. The manager who owns Tease got my foot in his face and I landed on a bunch of tables. It hurt."

His eyes bug out. "You stripped?"

I shake my head. "Just once. And I kept my clothes on. I just wanted the experience, you know?"

"Can't say I do."

I eye his physique. "I'm not sure if you'd be able to do it. You're so tall."

"Um, I'm good," he tells me, his lips twitching.

"So, where do you want me now?"

"What?"

I gesture to the door. "The class."

"Um, I think we should call it a night, but if you're free this time next week, we can pick up on the next step."

"When will you be doing the group ones?" I ask.

"Let's get you taught first," he tells me. "But if you want to join, they are on a Sunday night."

"I'll come on Thursday and work my way up to Sunday. If you want me to help teach it, then it might be best for me to know what I'm doing first."

"Yeah," he rasps, glancing away.

"And the wedding— I'll message you my number later," I tell him, grabbing my bag. "I guess I should go."

"Charlotte?" he calls out when I take a step to leave.

"Yeah?"

"Don't forget to talk to your mum, and family."

My shoulders slump. "I won't."

"And I want you to stand in front of the mirror each morning and night, and say, 'I'm worth it' three times."

My brows bunch together. "Why?"

His expression softens and his lips pull up into a smile. "Because one day you'll stand in front of that mirror and you won't need to say it. You'll see and feel what everyone else around you knows."

"And what's that?" I whisper, my heart racing.

"That you are worth it. That you're special."

I'm stuck for words, my throat tightening with emotion. I continue to stare at him, my eyes welling with tears.

That's... I don't have any words.

"I should go," I whisper.

His eyes widen. "Shit, let me grab my keys."

"Huh?"

"I'm taking you home, remember?"

I laugh. I forgot about that bit of information. "I'll be fine walking."

He waves me off. "Not a chance. I'm heading home now anyway," he explains.

"Okay," I reply, pushing my bag further up my shoulder.

I wait for him to finish turning everything off and follow him outside. The wind is chilly tonight and I tug my jacket together, warding off the chill.

A blush rises over my cheeks when he holds the door for me. "Thank you."

I take a seat, tucking my bag down by my feet. He folds into the car and turns to me. "I'm sorry about my mum tonight. I know she can be full on."

"Have you met my family?" I tease, not wanting him to feel bad. "They can be a little full on."

"Yeah, but in a crazy good way," he murmurs.

"How come your relationship is strained?"

He pulls out but I see him glance at me briefly. "I'm a disappointment to her."

"I'm sure that's not true."

He chuckles dryly. "No, it really is. She wants me to be something I'm not."

"And who is that?" I ask, watching him closely.

He has really nice lips.

And a deep, husky voice.

"Someone who makes more money than they could ever need in a lifetime. She wants me to be this upstanding citizen and I'm not. I'm not someone who kisses someone's arse to get further in my career. Who she wants me to be is not who I am."

"And who are you?" I whisper, shifting in my seat.

"Someone who swears a lot, likes getting tattoos, and loves running my gym. I prefer a beer at the pub rather than a glass of champagne at a charity or family event. I prefer paving my own way but it's not good enough for her. *I'm* not good enough. She's constantly trying to mould me into the son she always wanted."

"There's nothing wrong with who you are," I tell him as he pulls onto my street. "Don't drive up my street. It's hard to do a turn around."

He pulls up outside Lily's, blocking her driveaway. "Try telling that to my mum."

"Is that why you never answered her calls?"

"Yeah," he admits. "My sister who is getting married is great and is fine with what I want to fucking wear or not wear. Mum is just being difficult."

I'm not sure what to say. I have empathy for him, but I can't relate. My family are nothing like his. I'm not saying none of them can be mean, because they can, but they're never mean to family.

Unless you count the time Hayden shaved off Liam's eyebrows the night before his first date.

"I'm sure it will work out."

"You really don't need to come to the wedding."

"If you don't want me to, I won't, but I honestly do not mind. It will be nice to get away from everyone's concerned stares."

"Okay, thank you."

I push open the door but then stop, turning back to him. "As hard as it is, don't let her change who you are, don't become what she needs. Because there are people who need the real you. She might not see it, but I do."

His brows pull together. "You don't know me."

"I don't need to," I tell him, pushing the door open further. I get out and duck my head back into the car. "If you hadn't been you, I wouldn't have gotten to my family that night. I wouldn't be attending self-defence classes." I pause, hoping he hears the truth in my words. "My uncle is always telling us: 'change the game, don't let the game change you'. And he's right."

"He is?"

I nod, but then frown. "Unless it applies to Monopoly. That game has started wars within our family."

His lips twitch. "Thank you, Charlotte."

"Thank you for tonight and for bringing me home."

"Goodbye."

"See you soon," I tell him, shutting the door.

Maybe self-defence classes really will be good for me. I already feel empowered.

TEN

CHARLOTTE

Warmth trickles down my arm as I quickly rush to the kitchen, grabbing some kitchen roll. I press it to the scratch, biting my lip at the sting.

"It's okay, Katnip. We will get through this," I cry out. "I promise."

She had been asleep in the bathroom sink and I reached for my hairbrush on the side behind her.

I moved too quickly.

So stupid.

By now, I should have learned not to make any sudden movements, catch her off guard, or move my feet under the bedsheet.

Or go anywhere near her.

"It's a work in progress," I mumble to myself, just as the doorbell goes off. I head down the hall, knowing it's Mum waiting to take me shopping.

And to get a new dress now I have an engagement party to attend. I hadn't told anyone about it yet, other than Harriet, but only because I couldn't believe I actually offered to do it.

"Mum, I'll be five minutes. I just need to finish up," I greet.

Mum takes one look at my arm and lets out a pity-filled sigh. "Katnip?"

I nod sadly. "Yeah. I caught her off guard."

"It's fine. I thought we could have a natter first anyway."

I head into the kitchen, and move right over to the kettle and flip it on. "How are you? Jacob still studying?"

"He's working hard," Mum tells me, taking a seat at the breakfast bar. She takes in the room, her lips pinching together. "Honey, I'm worried about you."

"Worried about me?" I ask, busying myself with the cups.

"Stop and look at me."

I exhale, setting the cups on the counter before slowly turning to face her. "I've been wanting to talk to you too."

Her eyebrows shoot up. "You have?"

I swallow, Drew's words floating through my head.

Talk to her.

"Yes, I, um… I was wondering if you know of anywhere we can go to look for dresses."

Her shoulders slump. "Charlotte."

"I'm fine," I lie.

"No, you aren't. A mother knows these things," she tells me, arching an eyebrow. "And a dress?"

"Yeah, I—" The doorbells rings, saving me from answering. "I'd best get that."

I leave Mum in the kitchen and head down the hall. I pull open the door, surprised to find Gabby and Emily on the other side.

"Good, you're in. Your receptionist didn't know where you were. Do you even ask for a CV before you hire people, or references?" Emily rants, pushing inside.

My mouth opens and closes, no words forming.

"Harriet called us," Gabby explains.

I close the door behind them. "Um…"

"What we want to know is why didn't you," Emily scolds. "You get a hot date and don't call your friends? Nuh, uh."

"Date?" Mum chokes out.

My eyes widen as I find her standing at the end of the hallway, gripping the kitchen doorframe. "Mum," I begin.

Emily gapes. "Your mum?"

"My god, you are gorgeous," Gabby breathes out, before turning to me. "Why couldn't you be gay?"

"We would never suit," I tell her absently, more worried about what's going through my mum's head. The girls have taken it all wrong. "And you don't like cats."

"I don't like *your* cat."

"A date?" Mum repeats.

"It's not what you think," I explain, heading back into the kitchen.

She shakes her head. "Honey, you are moving too quickly. You need to slow down. You've been through a major trauma and need time to heal."

"It's with Drew," I blurt out.

"Drew?" Her forehead creases as she follows me back into the kitchen. I grab another couple of mugs down. "Drew who owns the gym?"

"Maybe we should come back," Emily suggests, picking up on the tension.

"It's fine," I rush out, before turning to Mum. "And it's not a date. I said I'd go to his sister's wedding with him because he doesn't want his mum to set him up."

Her shoulders slump as tears gather in her eyes. "Why didn't you tell me? You never tell me anything anymore."

"Mum," I softly whine, sitting down next to her as Emily continues to finish our drinks. "I was going to tell you about it today."

Her expression crumbles. "You've been through so much and you keep pushing me away."

"Because I hate that I remind you of what you went through," I blurt out, grimacing.

"W-what?"

"I'm sorry, I didn't mean that," I whisper. "I, I need to go check on Katnip. She gets upset if I leave her too long after an incident."

She reaches for my hand, stopping me from escaping. "Honey, no. What has made you think that?"

I blink up at her, the bridge of my nose burning from unshed tears. "I see it every time you look at me. I know I remind you of what happened to you."

She shakes her head, and her hand grips mine a little tighter. "No, sweetie, not at all. I'm worried about you, that is all. You keep acting like everything is okay but it's not."

"No, it's not," I whisper in agreement.

"Then why won't you let me help you?"

"Because… I don't know." I run my fingers through my hair and glance away. "I just didn't want to hurt you all more."

"The only thing hurting us is not being able to help you."

"But you do. You always do."

"Promise you will come to me," Mum rasps. "I'm your mother and I want to protect you."

"I promise."

"Well, it's good to see we aren't the only ones you pushed away," Gabby comments, setting a mug of tea in front of me.

Emily places one in front of Mum. "We're here for you. Let us be."

"And you can start by telling me about this Drew," Mum softly scolds. "Honey, I think this might be too soon."

"It's honestly not what you think. He helped me and I want to return the favour."

I give her a pointed look. She opened the door that night; she saw him and knew what he had done for me.

And she knew about the self-defence classes.

"I'm worried you'll be taken advantage of, sweetie."

"Mum, you of all people know not all men are the same," I remind her. "He's nice."

"He's very… um, a little rough around the edges."

"So, he's definitely hot?" Emily swoons.

I snort at the hearts in her eyes. "He's just a… I don't know what he is. I guess we're friends. I'll have to ask."

"I bet he wants to be more than friends," Gabby mutters. "You're hot."

I roll my eyes. "Mum, this is Gabby, and this is Emily. They are friends of mine from Tease."

Mum chokes on her tea, eyes wide as she stares at the girls. "It's so lovely to meet you."

"Not what you expected?" Gabby teases.

Mum wipes her mouth with my dish cloth. "Sorry."

Gabby waves her off. "It's fine."

When the doorbell goes again, I turn to Mum. "You expecting anyone?"

"It's your house, sweetie. Not mine."

I address the girls. "Am I expecting one of the others?"

"No, they are busy today."

I get up and head down the hall, pulling open the door. Dad pushes his way inside. "You are not going on a date with that beast."

"Dad," I yell, barely getting the door shut before Landon storms through. I keep it open when I hear voices heading down the path and rush into the kitchen before Dad blows a fuse. "It's not what you think."

"Drew said that," Landon mutters, not looking happy, but not pissed either.

"Why aren't you pissed?" Dad snaps, glaring at Landon.

"Because he explained what happened. When I hit him—"

"You hit him?" I screech, becoming dizzy all of a sudden.

He waves me off. "It was barely a tap," he explains, turning to my dad. "He even showed me the CCTV of his mum."

"You watched the CCTV?" I whisper, horrified.

Oh my god. He will have seen me beating the crap out of that punching bag and losing it.

"Just the entrance," he admits, watching me closely.

"Do you not think this is too soon?" Dad argues, before turning to the girls. "Sorry. I'm Myles, her dad."

"Wow," Emily whispers. "It's like God shot you all up with beauty and forgot about the rest of us."

Dad grins. "Thank you."

"I'm Gabby."

"I'm Emily."

"They work at Tease," Landon adds, smirking.

Dad wheezes, his eyes widening for a moment before he exhales, slumping down on the chair beside Mum. "It's fine."

"Fine?" Landon asks.

Dad narrows his gaze. "Yes. They seem like bright, intelligent, young women."

"Dad," I call out, knowing he's never this agreeable. I thought he'd have at least said something. They aren't judgemental people— they once owned a strip club— but I'm still his daughter.

"I'm just glad it's not a homeless guy, another wild animal, or your receptionist."

Mum's eyes widen as she slowly turns to Dad. "Remember when she brought that woman home and said she needed a manicure?"

"You mean the drag queen?" Dad muses.

"No, that butch woman who didn't stop swearing and stunk of weed."

"Mum," I scold.

"God, I remember her. She squeezed my balls until I thought they were gonna drop off."

"What did you do?" Gabby asks, leaning forward.

"Told her to fuck off because she was trying to borrow my trainers for a date."

"Stop," I softly scold. "It wasn't that bad."

"No, no, no, no," Uncle Max yells.

"No," I whisper, my eyes widening as I turn toward the kitchen entrance.

"Who is that?" Gabby whispers, eyes wide.

Uncle Max comes barrelling inside, Aunt Lake following close behind. "I tried to stop him. I really did."

He points at me. "No dating. I know we said we wouldn't intervene, but, girl, just no. I'll do anything for you, but I'm man enough to admit that I don't think I'd reach that fucker's head if it came down to a fight."

"Max," I scold, as Lake slaps him upside the head.

"Surely you aren't all okay with this," he yells.

"It was a misunderstanding," Mum blurts out.

Max blows out a breath before rushing to my junk cupboard and pulling out snacks. He shoves half a muffin into his mouth.

"Thank fuck," he mumbles around a mouthful before turning to Lake. "Cancel the step ladder order."

"She's just going to a wedding with him so he doesn't have to go with someone his mum wants to set him up with," Mum finishes, grimacing when Max begins to choke on his Snickers bar.

"I can't do this," he wheezes.

Gabby hands him a glass of water. "Here you go."

"Who the fuck are you?" he chokes out, his eyes tearing as he continues to cough up a lung.

"I'm Gabby. A friend of Charlotte's."

"Works at Tease," Dad adds.

Max begins to choke and Gabby wisely takes a step back when Angel Cake splatters everywhere. "I'm gonna die at a young age."

"What are you all doing here?" I ask, as Hope and Hayden come rushing through the door.

"Who have we got to kill?" Hayden blurts out.

Hope looks up apologetically. "I tried to calm her down."

"She gets it," Max yells, pointing to his daughter.

Emily steps closer to me and leans in. "Your family *really is* scary."

"It's not always like this," I lie.

Her eyes narrow. "Yeah, if you say so."

Suddenly, Max turns to Gabby. "Look, I'm flattered and all, but I'm married."

"What?" Gabby stumbles out, gaping at him.

"You keep staring but I'm sorry, I have a wife who loves and adores me. She needs me. I made vows," he declares.

"I wasn't—"

He holds his hand up. "Please don't make this difficult, she's right there," he whispers, pointing to Lake, who looks bored.

"But I—"

"This is getting kind of embarrassing. I'm flattered, truly, and as hard as it will be, you need to move—"

"You have crap in your teeth!" Gabby blurts out. "And I'm gay. So, so, so gay."

"Well, you aren't getting my wife," he yells, pulling Lake into his arms.

I slap my forehead, groaning. "Please, what are you all doing here?"

"We came for an intervention," Hayden points out. "It's too soon for you to be dating."

"I'm not dating."

She turns to her dad, then back to me. "You aren't?"

"No," I tell her, chuckling. "I'm doing a favour for a friend, *as* a friend."

Hayden slowly turns to her dad. "You worried me fucking sick by telling me she was going out with a beast who would snap her like a twig. You said that if I didn't do anything she'd run away with him."

"And you believed him?" Landon mutters.

"It's Charlotte," she snaps. "She's been through a lot and I didn't want to see her take her cat and run off into the sunset."

"Although Drew is seriously hot," Hope adds. "I like him."

"Don't like him," Max yells. "I know guys like him. They see a vulnerable girl and take advantage."

Landon pinches the bridge of his nose. "Now is not the time to bring up Jaxon."

"I see," Max mutters, before turning to Dad. "And you're okay with this?"

Dad glances up from his plate of pasta. I hadn't even realised he'd gone to the fridge. "She said it's not a date and I believe her. But to be sure, I'm going to make sure this Drew guy knows it too."

"Don't," I blurt out. "His mum wasn't very nice. He doesn't need more parents being mean to him." Landon chuckles and I narrow my gaze. "He helped me."

He sobers. "Yeah."

Mum tilts her head, her smile sad. "Sweetie, we are just worried. You're too nice for your own good."

"He isn't Scott," I choke out, tears pooling in my eyes. "Please, don't make me let him down. Not when he's done a lot already."

"Why don't you ask him to come for dinner tonight and we can get to know him," Mum suggests. "That way, everyone can feel secure enough about this little arrangement."

Dad nods in agreement. "I'm okay with that."

Max finishes off my last packet of Jammie Dodgers and nods. "I fancy spag bol tonight."

"Not you," Mum scolds.

"But—"

"No."

I turn to Landon. "Will you ask him?"

His gaze softens and the tension leaks from the corner of his eyes. "You message him. He'll be okay with this."

"And you won't hit him again?"

His lips twitch. "We work in a gym."

I nod, my shoulders slumping with relief at that. Then they tense again when it occurs to me. "That wasn't an answer."

He scruffs my hair. "It's the only one you're getting. I've got to head back to work but I'll catch you later."

"Me too," Hayden mutters. "If he didn't need me so much, Clay would have fired me by now."

"He loves you," I remind her.

"Of course he does, but when you have a dad that calls you out of work, scaring you half to death, it's gonna get tiresome."

She leaves with Landon, and moments later, Hope follows after giving me a hug goodbye.

"We so need to spend more time together," Gabby whispers.

"I cannot wait to tell the others," Emily murmurs.

When they leave, I slump against the counter. I still haven't told them about the room at the gym.

Mum stands, grabbing her bag off the side. "Let's go shopping."

"Ohh, I need a new rug," Lake announces.

Dad rubs the back of his neck. "I really need to get back to work."

When everyone turns to Max, he rears back. "What? I'm going to get something to eat. I'm starving."

Both brothers rush out and I can't help but shake my head.

I still never got an answer as to how they all knew.

ELEVEN

DREW

When Charlotte messaged to ask me to meet her parents, I wasn't all that surprised. What surprised me was that I said yes. I never met any of my exes' parents.

Landon said it wasn't under debate and that I needed to go if I wanted Charlotte to come with me to the wedding. Although I told her she doesn't need to come, I want her to be there. Having to sit the entire evening without a date would be torture. Just the thought has me shuddering. Mum was determined to set me up with Eloise and I have no doubt she still has something planned.

I sit back in the driver's seat, once more questioning what the fuck I'm doing. And why the fuck I got dressed up. Or as dressed up as I can get. I'm wearing a black button-down shirt and dark jeans, paired with black boots.

I tie my hair back into a low bun, needing it out of my face. I'm still waiting for Charlotte. I offered to pick her up since her car is still getting repaired. It has been ten minutes since she said she was coming and there's no sign of her.

I glance down at my phone. Do I go to the door? She said to park on the main road, but maybe she's waiting for me to meet her at the door.

Fuck it.

Shutting off the engine, I grab my phone from the dashboard and reach for the door handle. Movement from the road catches my attention and my eyes widen when I spot Charlotte racing toward the car like her arse is on fire. I go to get out but she's already moving around the car to the passenger side, pulling open the door.

"I'm so sorry."

I lean over, picking a leaf out of her hair. "Um, did you fall into a bush?"

Red kisses her cheeks, like the petal of a rose. It's cute against the freckles sprinkled across her nose.

She catches her breath before answering. "Kind of."

"Kind of?"

"My cat was meowing at another cat in the garden so I thought, hey, they want to be friends. So I went out to get the cat to introduce her to Katnip, but then Katnip attacked her. Full on attacked this cat. And I dropped the cat in the midst of the chaos." She stops for a minute to take a breath. "Then I went to check if the cat was okay, but it kind of got scared. I tried to crawl into the bush to get it, and then it ran." She bites her lip. "And I got stuck."

This girl is prone to accidents. I have never met anyone as loopy as she is, but it's a good loopy. Amusing.

My lips twitch at the image of her stuck in the bush trying to get to a cat. "Is the cat okay?"

Her shoulders deflate. "I don't know. It was gone by the time I got myself untangled from the bush. I'm so sorry it took me so long. So, so sorry."

"Hey," I call out, waiting for her to take a deep breath. "It's fine. It gave me time to prepare myself," I assure her, my tone teasing as I fire up the engine.

She lets out a breath, relaxing back into her seat. "Prepare?"

"To meet the parents," I reply.

"Ah," she muses.

"So, they want to meet me, huh?"

"They know we aren't really dating," she rushes out. "They're just worried."

I chuckle at her nervousness. "I'm okay with it. I guessed something like this might happen. After knowing Landon so long, I get your family are protective."

"They really are. And you've got nothing to worry about. My dad is, like, the calmest and—"

I reach over, placing my hand on her thigh. "Don't worry about it. I'll be okay."

Her intake of breath makes me realise where my hand is and I quickly pull it away and grip the steering wheel. "He really is the calmest. He was okay that I have stripper friends and everything."

I choke before taking a moment to gather my bearings.

She needs to stop doing this to me. "Um, speaking of, you can set up a meeting to rent out the room. Landon is okay with it."

"He is?" She squeals. "I'm as happy as a pig in mud right now."

I chuckle at her enthusiasm. In fact, I don't think I've ever laughed around a person this much since Hayden kicked Landon's arse in front of the entire gym.

"Just message me a time they are free. The only days I can't do are Monday mornings and Thursday nights, unless they come late on Thursday."

"They are going to be so happy," she tells me, already firing off a message. It pings with a reply and she looks up, biting her lip.

"What?" I ask, when I find her staring at me.

"Um, nothing. She said she's going to speak to the rest of the girls."

My lips twitch. "What did they say?"

She lets out the most adorable sigh ever. "Gabby offered sexual favours as a thank you."

I bang on my chest, my eyes widening as I try to gather myself. "W-what?"

"Don't worry, I've already told her I think women are attractive, but I'm just not sexually attracted to them."

She offered sexual favours to her?

"W-what?"

Jesus Christ.

"You really should get that cough seen to," she tells me, as I pull up outside her parents.

"Um, yeah, I'll get on that."

She beams. "Good."

She unclips her belt as I switch the engine off. "Are you sure it's just us?"

Charlotte bites her lip as she sees Landon and Paisley on the doorstep speaking to another chick. "I thought it was," she murmurs before pushing the door open.

"Charlotte," Landon greets, before turning to me. "Drew."

I lift my chin and lock up the car. "Hey, man."

"Holy crap!" the other chick whispers. "You really are giant."

"A friendly giant," Charlotte rushes out, blushing when she glances at me.

I chuckle and shake my head. "Hey."

She blinks and quickly reaches her hand out. "I'm Hope. Charlotte's cousin."

"It's nice to meet you. I'm Drew."

"Don't you dare," is yelled from inside the house, and instinctively, I move closer to Charlotte, ready to protect her. Landon notices and narrows his gaze.

No one else seems to care about what's going on inside the house, so I begin to relax.

"I swear to God, if you don't move away from the garlic bread I am going to wring your neck," Kayla, Charlotte's mum, yells.

"Oh no," Charlotte whispers.

"Don't you dare go out there," another woman yells.

"I want to know what is taking so long."

"Max, you weren't even invited. You don't get to butt into their conversation and try to intimidate him."

"Intimidate him? Have you *seen* him?"

"Myles, we're Carter's, we can come up with something," the guy snaps. "I should have kept that step ladder on order."

"Max," Kayla yells. "Why are you moving my furniture?"

"Because we will need something to climb on if it comes down to a fight."

"No one is fighting."

"Oh God," Charlotte whimpers. "I'm so sorry."

Landon grins. "Still want to meet the family?"

I shrug. "I've already met most of you, so why not."

Paisley's jaw drops. "You are so going to fit into this family."

The door flies open and a bulkier version of Charlotte's dad comes barrelling outside, his sole focus on me.

My lips twitch. Yeah, he's tall, but I'm taller.

He comes to a stop in front of me, his eyes narrowed into slits. "You make one wrong move and I'll slice that fucking man bun off your scalp."

"Max, that is highly inappropriate and really hard to do," Charlotte announces. "I watched this documentary—"

Landon clears his throat. "Maybe not right now, Charlie."

She ducks her head, her cheeks reddening. "Oh."

I turn back to her uncle. "No offence, but your daughter scares me more. I've seen her fight Landon."

"Who do you think taught her?"

"Me," Landon mutters.

Max points to his chest. "No. I did. And if you don't behave, I'll call her."

"She's not talking to you," Charlotte reminds him.

His jaw clenches. "I'll get her to come."

"She said she was never listening to anything you said again and unless it was a dying emergency, she wasn't coming to your beck and call."

"Are we going to eat or what?" he snaps.

"*We* are. *You* aren't invited," Kayla tells him, before she aims her blinding smile at me. "Hello again."

"Hello, Mrs Carter."

She tucks a strand of hair behind her ear. "Manners. I like it."

"I have manners," Myles grits out before he turns to me. "Just so you know, I can change my opinion quicker than you can blink."

"*So* threatening," Max mutters.

Myles glowers at his brother. "Because threatening to give his hair a trim was frightening."

Max pales. "I was thinking with wax."

Myles shudders. "Wax," he whispers.

Um, okay…

"You are so freaking big," the woman standing next to Max murmurs, staring up at me with round eyes. "I'm Lake."

"My wife," Max bites out.

Lake pats his chest. "But there's always divorce."

Max turns his narrowed gaze to his niece. "Are you trying to take my wife away from me? First the lesbian and now this guy? She's happily married to me."

"Goodbye, Max," Kayla mutters, pinching the bridge of her nose.

"I'm here now and you've cooked enough to feed a small army. There's no point letting it go to waste," he tells her. "Plus, would you really let me starve?"

"Yes, yes I would."

He turns to me, smirking. "She loves to tell tales."

"Max," Kayla groans, heading up the path.

"And none of Charlotte's vegetarian crap. I need my fucking meat, woman."

The rest of the adults follow, and when none of the rest make a move, I don't either.

"I really am sorry about this," Charlotte tells me.

I wave her off. "It's fine. I can handle it."

Landon grins. "Famous last words."

Paisley smacks his chest, her lips twitching. "Stop being mean."

The door is pulled open once more and the young guy that comes out jerks to a stop, his eyes widening for a moment before he begins to turn to red, his temples pulsing. "Fucking hell!"

"Jacob," Charlotte admonishes. "Don't swear."

The anger is palpable, almost choking when he turns to his sister. "Why,

Charlotte? Why go through this again?" he grits out, before he storms over, coming to a stop near me. Landon tries to intervene, but Paisley pulls him back. "I don't give a fuck how big you are or that you can fight. You hurt my sister in *any* way, and I'll kill you."

"Noted," I tell him, giving him the respect he deserves, since this is his sister and I had been him at one point. I'll probably act in the same capacity when Nora gets a boyfriend. "But I'm not going to hurt her."

"And if she wants to wear her fucking jumpers with cats on, have fucking glitter fairies or snow globes, she can. You can't fucking tell her not to."

My brows pull together. "I'm not—"

"Jacob," Charlotte whispers, stepping forward, but Jacob moves his arm back out of reach.

"No. I should have protected you the last time and I didn't. I'm not making that mistake again. I know what Mum said, but that's bullshit. You're a Carter. We all fucking find love in ridiculous times."

Charlotte inhales sharply. "Jacob—"

"Stop!" he yells. "I'm done hearing you tell people you're okay. You're not fucking okay."

"I've been you," I blurt out, keeping my voice calm, even.

He draws back, his expression tight with anger. "What?"

"My sister, she was attacked on her way home from school a few years ago. It only went so far but it left a lasting impression on her soul. It hurt her in a way I'll never understand, and for a while, I blamed myself." His expression relaxes somewhat but now his anger is replaced with confusion. He reminds me of a scared kid in the middle of making a choice on whether to fight or run. "I realised later that my blame, my guilt, was projecting onto Nora and giving her more to stew and stress over."

He looks to his sister, the guilt clear for us all to read. "I, I…"

"I get it; you want to protect her. You want to make sure she isn't hurt again, and that's not a bad thing, but you have nothing to worry about when it comes to me. Even if this was more than we have said, I still wouldn't hurt her."

He glances at his sister, his eyes watering. "I'm sorry. I'm just angry I couldn't be there for you."

She rushes to him, pulling him in for a hug. "It's okay. I love you too."

He clears his throat. "I wouldn't go that far."

She chuckles and pulls back. "Let's go eat."

"Yeah, maybe we can make one of Uncle Max's blood vessels burst," Hope suggests cheerfully.

Landon claps Jacob on the shoulder. "Or we could get our dads to fight again."

Wiping his nose with the sleeve of his shirt, Jacob sniffles. "Nah, that's too easy."

Charlotte turns to me when they head up the path. "Thank you for what you said."

"I meant it. I made her feel worse than she was already feeling and I had no right to do that. It wasn't about me or what I was feeling. And for a moment, I forgot that."

Her green eyes sparkle as they fill with tears. "You really do want to help women defend themselves."

"Yeah, I really do."

Her shoulders straighten. "Then I'm going to do the very best I can to help you. I have books on this kind of stuff and I'll learn as much as I can."

"And you'll have a great teacher," I tease.

"Your sister is really lucky," she declares. "Maybe one day I will get to meet her."

"Yeah," I murmur, then follow her into the house.

This was only meant to be about self-defence, but I have come to realise that you can't just categorise a Carter. They worm their way into your life, and if you're not careful, your heart. And I don't need that kind of drama.

TWELVE

CHARLOTTE

The silence in the car is uncomfortable. I'm not sure if I should bring it up or keep acting like it never happened. With my family, it's always best to pretend it never happened.

"So, um, that was interesting," he comments, and I collapse back into the seat, grateful he's actually talking to me.

"I really am sorry. They are just really protective," I explain, glancing out of the window. "And maybe a *little* crazy."

"I got that when your dad put the wax strips on the table," he rumbles, chuckling under his breath.

"He, um, he likes having smooth skin?"

"And when your uncle got the scissors out and then spent a majority of the time spinning them whilst glaring at me?"

"He was jealous of your hair?" I reply. "I mean, even I'm kind of jealous of your hair."

He laughs and the sound sends a shiver down my spine. "And the incident, during which your mum tackled your dad to the floor so he couldn't attack me?"

"No, she was, um, trying to stop him from entering the room?"

"What about when your dad picked up the knife because my arm grazed yours?"

"He really likes that knife?"

I tense, a part of me waiting for the scolding to come. For him to tell me I'm an embarrassment, that my family are.

But it doesn't come.

Instead, he chuckles, and although a part of me isn't surprised—he isn't Scott—there is a part that is relieved. Relieved I can be myself around him without worrying if I'll do or say something wrong. I relax back into my seat.

"Charlotte," he murmurs.

I let out a breath. "Okay, they are a lot crazy; like, a lot, a lot."

The laughter that spills past his lips is contagious. "It's fine. You have a great family and no one was hurt."

"Except Max," I add.

"How *did* he get that black eye?"

I glance away once more, biting my lip. "Maybe we should change the subject."

"Is it always like that?"

My nose twitches as I try to look back on family meals, wondering if I should answer honestly.

"Kind of," I admit. "What about yours?"

His laugh gets louder, bouncing off the windows of the car. "My mum's home is nothing like that. Even putting your elbow on the table is considered rude. And the topics you guys talked about? My mother would have a hernia."

"What about your dad?" I ask, having already guessed he's closer to his dad. He spoke of him fondly and often, unlike his mother and her side of his family— not including Alison.

He keeps silent for a moment before answering. "His dinners are different.

We don't really sit at the table. He likes listening to the tele, not to people chewing. But there's always a steady flow of conversation."

"That sounds nice; relaxing," I tell him. "I eat my dinners in front of the television when I'm at mine too, but my mum prefers us being sat around the table when we are all together."

"It was so much easier at my dad's. I didn't have to be on edge, wondering if I was doing something wrong."

"I can't imagine having to go through that. My parents have always been nothing but supportive of who we are. They are our biggest cheerleaders."

"What do they think of you learning self-defence?"

"They are relieved. Mum has been really worried about me."

"Did you get a chance to speak to her?"

My shoulders slump. "No," I whisper. "We were interrupted and then we didn't get any alone time afterwards. But I will talk to her."

"It will be good for both of you."

"Are you always this intuitive and sympathetic toward people?" I ask.

He quickly glances at me. "Um, no, I'm kind of an arsehole to most people and I like to keep to myself."

I chuckle at his honesty. "Thank you for coming tonight. I know this isn't what you had planned when I agreed to go to the wedding things with you."

He takes the turning onto mine and Lily's street before answering. "It beat eating a microwave meal. Your mum is a good cook."

I wince at the reminder. "I'm sorry my uncle made you eat a large portion of my spag bol."

Not everyone likes the vegetarian meals, but he didn't leave a thing on his plate. Or maybe he did that to be polite?

"You're kidding, aren't you? I never thought I'd eat a veggie meal, but it was really good."

The tension in my shoulders eases as he pulls up outside Lily's.

"I'm glad," I tell him. "What time are we leaving for the engagement party at the weekend?"

"I'll pick you up at about half six. The party starts at half seven and it takes an hour or so to get there."

"Won't that mean you're late?"

"The more guests that arrive before me, the better chance I have of avoiding my mum."

A giggle slips free. "Okay, just message me if there are any changes."

"You still on for Thursday?"

I nod. "I am."

He pushes open his door and I reach over, stopping him from unclipping his belt. "You don't need to walk me to the door. I'll be fine. Plus, this is my cousin's house. Her and her husband are in so no doubt he'll be keeping an eye out. He's had a camera installed in his garden."

"You sure, because it will literally take two minutes."

"It's fine. I'll see you Thursday."

"See you then."

I push the door open and step out of the car, but there's something niggling at the back of my mind. Instead of closing the door, I lean down and pop my head back inside. "Can I ask you something?"

He gives me his full attention. "Yeah."

"Why are you doing all of this? Is it because you're friends with Landon?"

He doesn't speak for a moment, and I begin to fear I shouldn't have asked. I mean, he could just feel like he has to do these things.

When he doesn't answer, I take a step back. "It's okay, I shouldn't have asked."

"Does there need to be a reason?" he blurts out, and I grip the top of the door as I stare into his warm set of honey-coloured eyes.

"No, I guess not."

I wonder what he looks like with wet hair.

Does he look like Jason Momoa when he walks out of the water in *Justice League*?

"Are you okay?" he asks, pulling me from my thoughts.

I brush my hair forward, hoping to hide the heat in my cheeks. "Y-yeah. Um, I need to go back to my cat. See you Thursday."

His goodbye echoes through the night air as I quickly rush to the path that leads to my house. I slow down once I'm out of sight, taking in a few deep breaths.

Why do I act weird or word vomit when I'm around people?

I groan when I realise I probably always will.

The soft glow of the outdoor wall lantern luminates the area near my door. On the doorstep is a black flowerpot containing a bunch of red petunias.

Bending at the knees, I pick the pot up, along with the note the wind blew over. Tucking it under my arm, I grab my keys and let myself in.

It's like a flashback is playing in the back of my head. The last time I received flowers, it didn't go so well, and I never did find out who bought them for me. After all the counsel my mum has given me, I'm beginning to wonder if she was right, and that Scott sent those flowers as a way to start the fight.

But what purpose do these have? Why would he send these flowers when I haven't heard from him since the night I ran out of this house, hurt and alone?

Why now?

Katnip hisses as soon as I walk through the door, bringing a smile to my face. "Hey, baby. You being a good girl?"

Hiss.

"Okay then."

Hiss.

"One day, Katnip. One day."

I head into the kitchen— my favourite place aside from the library—and place the pot on the side, then flick the main light on.

My heart is already pounding and all I have read is one word.

Charlotte.

"I can do this."

Dread is threatening to pull me under. It has never been like this for me. I refuse to see anything but the good in this world.

And just when it feels like I'm starting to get that part of me back, it's taken away from me again.

Pulling the card out of the envelope, I lean back against the counter, and read:

Rage roils and grief grows,
Heart hammers then suddenly slows.
Dare deny me what is mine,
And rage will have no friend to find.

A tap sounds on the backdoor window, startling me to the point a yelp slips free, and I drop the card. Madison presses her face against the glass, waving at me. Her light brown hair blows across her face, strands getting sucked into her mouth. I chuckle as she begins to choke.

I breathe out, shaking my head at her. "You scared me."

She spits the hair out before answering. "Your dad wouldn't let us come to the meal and I wanted to come over and see if it was true," she calls through the door.

"What was true?" I ask, as I unlock it to let her in.

I step out of the way and she barges inside, hefting her bag over her shoulder. "Is this Drew guy really as tall as they say? Maddox never lets me go to the gym."

I chuckle, closing the door behind her. "He is."

"And he's covered in tattoos?"

"Yes."

"And your dad had a pair of scissors?"

I wave her off as I head over to the kettle and put it on. "No, that was Uncle Max. Dad had a knife."

She jumps up onto the side, swinging her legs. "Do you like him?"

I pause from bringing the cups down. "He's a really good guy. He's helping me through some stuff."

"I meant like him, like him."

I set the cups down on the counter. "We are friends now, I guess. Nothing more. I mean, can we really be friends without claiming each other as friends?"

She laughs. "Charlotte, we aren't in school. You don't need to ask permission. If you spend time like that together, you're friends. Now, if he flirts or tries it on, that's a different story."

"He doesn't flirt or try it on," I argue.

Her brows pull together and she jumps off the side. "Hey, who got you petunias?"

"I'm not sure," I tell her, busying myself with pouring our drinks.

I'm not sure what Mum and Dad told other members of the family, whether it was the short version or not.

And I'm not sure how to bring up my paranoia over them when it may be nothing. But that chill that slithered down my spine while reading that note… I knew it wasn't a love note or any kind romantic declaration.

It wasn't jealousy.

It was anger and resentment. It was anger so far rooted it poured onto the page.

And it was aimed at me.

"Whoever bought them clearly knows fuck all about flowers because these symbolise anger and resentment. Are you sure you don't know who they are from?"

Breathing heavily, I rush over to her, snatching the pot out of her hands. I don't want her asking more questions.

"I'm sure," I tell her, before dropping them into the bin.

"Charlotte, I know they aren't the best but they are still flowers," she cries out.

I bite my lip and quickly grab them out of the bin. My nose stings as I eye the broken petals. "Sorry, I don't know why I did that."

Her blues eyes burn into me. "Charlie, what the heck is going on?"

I brush my fingers through my hair, moving stray strands away from my face. Tears gather in my eyes. "I'm sorry. I really don't know who they are from. Someone sent flowers to me on the same night everything happened with Scott, and now these. I think I'm going crazy. I've stopped seeing joy, stopped feeling it, and I don't know why."

"Charlotte, calm down," she demands, coming to a standstill in front of me.

"I need my joy back, Madison. Why am I constantly thinking of the negatives? Why can't I just receive a pot of flowers and not feel dread in the pit of my stomach?"

"What makes you think the flowers are negative? Maybe someone sent them as a kind gesture."

I pick up the card I dropped when Madison scared the bejesus out of me, and hand it over to her.

Her brows shoot up as she scans the card. "What the actual fuck? Who the fuck sent you this? This is fucked up."

I shrug. "No idea. But this is what caused the argument between Scott and I. He thought some other guy sent them to me," I whisper. "But the poem, it's not like the other one, or at least, I didn't read the first one the same way."

"What Scott did has nothing to do with the flowers unless he sent them himself," she explains, but pauses, hesitating for a moment. "Have you spoken to him?"

"Of course not," I tell her, hurt that she thinks I would after he hurt me.

"I'm sorry. I just don't want you to be pulled in again," she assures me, but it still stings that she even asked that question. "If they aren't from Scott, who do you think did send them?"

"I really don't know. I'm not lying."

"Maybe we should find out because this is some sick shit."

"How?"

She picks up the card, turning it over. "It doesn't have a logo but leave it with me. There are only so many flower shops around here."

"What if it is him?" I ask, biting my bottom lip.

"Then we can hand his arse over to the police," she tells me, pulling me in for a one-armed hug. "We've got you."

"Want to watch *The Conjuring* to cheer me up?"

"Fuck no. The last movie I watched to cheer you up, I had nightmares for months. Let's watch *Who Wants to be a Millionaire* and see how many questions we can get right."

"We would so ace that show," I declare.

"Remember when Uncle Max signed up to enter the show?"

I wince at the reminder. "They arrested Dad, thinking he was Max."

Her eyes widen. "That's right. They wanted him done for harassment."

I nod and lean forward, grabbing a liquorice off the side. "Dad never forgave him. He lost his chance of being on *Deal or No Deal*."

She laughs. "Didn't Uncle Max start a protest to make it right, only it ended up becoming a riot?"

I grimace when I think of how that day ended. "Yeah, then he left before anyone could put the blame on him."

"Come on. We can send him video clips to make him mad."

I grin. "I'll bring snacks."

"I'll finish the tea."

THIRTEEN

DREW

I wince as Charlotte's back hits the mat for what feels like the millionth time tonight. I keep my weight off her, yet the need to press against her is high.

It's coming to the end of our session and although I'd like to say she's doing good, she is too tense and hesitant to pick it up. It's going to take time for her to get used to the moves and then gain the confidence to use them.

And I'm tense because every time she falls, I have to watch the bounce of her tits as she hits the ground. And the small sports bra she's wearing leaves nothing to the imagination.

She's driving me crazy.

More than once tonight I've had to remind myself of who she is and what she went through. She doesn't need to feel the hard-on I've struggled to hide all fucking night after the crap her ex pulled.

She's the sweetest temptation.

I get up off the floor, needing to get away from the delicate scent of vanilla. She reminds me so much of cupcakes. The impulse to taste, to savour, capture…

"Maybe you need to be, like, skilled at this," she huffs out. I chuckle as I reach down and give her a hand up. She breathes out and runs a hand down her stomach, grimacing. "Eww, I look gross."

She really doesn't.

If anything, the sweat shimmering across her stomach and along her spine just makes her that more appealing.

I'm a sick, sick man and I'm going to hell.

I clear my throat, taking a step out of her space. "You're doing great."

She shakes her head at me. "And you lie," she breathes out. "I should have known this was a bad idea. I tried to play Gladiator at the fair once, the game where you have to knock your opponent off the post, and I was knocked down before I even got my footing on the board."

I lean forward, placing my hands on her shoulders. Her breath catches and she lets out the most adorable shiver. "You're too tense."

"I don't mean to be."

"Is it because you're scared I'll hurt you?" I ask. Nine times out of ten, that's normally the reason, but Charlotte can be hard to read. She seems comfortable with me but it could all be an act.

"Of course not."

"Okay, then what do you think the issue is? Why are you so hesitant?"

She bites her lip. "I don't want to hurt you."

I try to keep my expression neutral but it's hard when she says something as adorable as that. "You aren't going to hurt me. I promise. I'd stop before you really reached me."

"I've been known to hurt people. I'm stronger than I look. Just ask Faith. I got arrested."

My lips twitch. "I don't doubt that," I tell her, then pause when her words register. "Why did you get arrested?"

She waves me off, getting her feet back into the position I taught her. "It involved a bad guy, a batch of my muffins and a lot of yelling," she tells me before exhaling. "Let me tell you, he was scared."

I can't imagine it, yet I believe every word. "I bet."

"Now, where do you want me?"

I'd like her lying on her back on the mat, but the image alone could get me killed— if not by her dad, then by Landon.

"Why don't we call it a night, and when we meet up next week, we'll go over some more of the moves from today?"

She pouts. "But I was so close."

I duck my head. She really wasn't. "It's coming to an end now anyway and your friends should be arriving soon."

"Oh yeah," she murmurs, grabbing the towel from the floor to wipe the sweat off the back of her neck.

The front door jingles and I turn, glancing over my shoulder. A group of four girls step inside, admiring the equipment around them.

The blonde catches sight of us first and her eyes light up.

"Charlie," she screams, rushing over. Charlotte gets knocked back a step from the hug she gives her.

"Hey, Emily, you made it."

"Duh, you had us at 'space away from Trixie'. Of course we'd be here."

"How could we refuse," another chick murmurs, then gapes when she turns to me.

They're gorgeous, don't get me wrong, but the stares are becoming unnerving.

"I think I just orgasmed."

"Harriet," Charlotte admonishes.

"Me too," Emily whispers.

"I don't think I'm gay anymore," the brunette whispers, still gawking up at me.

"This is why I'm bi. I like to keep my options open," Olivia comments.

"Girls, he's standing right there," Charlotte declares, her lips twitching.

I shift awkwardly on my feet as I give them a small smile. "I'm Drew."

They sigh dreamily, and I begin to wonder if this was a good idea.

Emily runs her finger up and down in the air, gesturing toward my body. "Do you have tattoos all over?"

"Emily," Charlotte cries, her cheeks flaming. But when she turns to me, curiosity sparks in her eyes. "Do you?"

I chuckle, shaking my head. "Wouldn't you like to know," I tease.

"She really would."

"I really would," the girl who claimed she isn't gay anymore states.

"Why don't I show you guys the room?" I gesture.

"That would be fantastic," Charlotte announces rather loudly. The sound echoes around the empty gym and she winces. "That was loud."

"Does he work out without a top?" Harriet whispers when I continue to the room with them following behind.

"Not yet," Charlotte whispers back.

"Will you take a picture when he does?"

Charlotte doesn't answer at first and I can't help but wonder why she's hesitating. Is it because she doesn't want to share or because she doesn't want to take the photo?

"Okay, I wouldn't mind one," she answers, surprising me.

"Just send it to the group chat," Harriet adds.

"It can go in my spank bank," Emily announces, nearly causing me to trip over my own feet.

I never lack confidence. Haven't my whole life. I can stand up to bullies, even my mother, and pick up girls like it's second nature.

Now, I don't know where to put myself or what to say.

And it's because of her.

She's scrambling my head.

"Speaking of spank bank, did you try the nipple tassels?"

I begin to choke on my own air, and I whack my chest to clear it.

"Gabby, don't kill him," Harriet scolds.

"Fucking hell," I grumble under my breath.

"I kind of ate them. They were sweet, but not too sweet," Charlotte admits.

"You were supposed to get someone to eat them off you," Gabby declares.

I can't do this anymore. I *can't* hear any more.

"Here we are," I announce rather loudly, causing them all to jump.

Harriet winces. "Sorry. We kind of forgot you were there."

My lips twitch. "I gathered."

She smacks her forehead. "Shit, we've not even introduced ourselves," she gasps. "I'm Harriet, this is Emily, that's Olivia, and the one still gawking at you is Gabby."

"It's nice to meet you all."

"I am not gawking. You don't gawk at fine art," Gabby snaps.

"She's right. And you are a piece of art," Charlotte adds, nodding.

"Um, I… thank you?" I choke out, wondering if it would have been better to have Landon do this. I'm better with people, but even I'm fucking this up.

"Charlotte said you want one of us to teach here?" Harriet comments.

"Landon and I spoke. If we're going to invest in this equipment, we need assurances it will be profited from. It's good business sense. However, we can't teach this class if you decide to drop out. We are doing this in good faith and we hope you'll work with us."

Harriet nods. "We appreciate this so much. You have no idea. And as much as each of us love dancing, stripping is not what we would like to do full time. I can't speak for everyone here, but I for one, wouldn't mind teaching the class."

I jerk my chin in a nod. I'm glad they're on board with the idea. It makes things easier for Landon and me. "One or more will need to do a short course. Teaching this lesson won't just be about teaching girls to dance. It's fitness and like any other fitness, you need to be qualified."

"I can't take on any more work," Harriet explains, before chewing on her thumbnail.

"It's not that kind of course. It's a pole fitness qualification. Although, you don't technically need a qualification to teach it. But for insurance, it's best to have this."

"That's fine with me," Emily tells me.

"Me too," Gabby announces.

The other two girls nod too. "So how would payments work?"

"I'm not going to take anything from you. We're hoping that in time, the class itself will pay for the equipment."

"And you want to pay us to teach it and let us use the room for free?" Gabby asks, her lips pinching together.

She watches me for a moment, her expression saying it all. She's trying to work out if she's being conned or not. It does sound too good to be true, but long-term, this is a good business move.

"I'll start paying wages once I see the class is going to be successful," I explain, before moving on to her next concern. "As for the room space being free, I have staff that use the gym after closing time. This will just be four more members of staff using the equipment after hours."

She relaxes. "When would you like us to start?"

"If you come in Monday, I'll have some paperwork for you to fill out. Landon will have a team in straight away to fit the correct equipment. Then it will be a case of having a health and safety guy come in and check it's all okay. Once that's done, we're clear to start. Have a think about how much you want to charge for your classes and try to come up with some promotional material to bring in on Monday. Then we can start advertising the class. You're free to use the space as much as you like once it's all set up, as long as you make sure you teach two nights a week."

Harriet steps forward. "We ran the idea by a few friends of ours and they are all up for attending too. I don't think filling the class will be an issue. It's going to be us finding the time to teach more classes so everyone can book in."

"If it's something you want to do, then I'm open to any ideas."

Gabby tucks a strand of hair behind her ear. "There is one thing I'd like to mention."

"Go on," I encourage.

"Privacy. We understand this is a unisex gym, and you have men come and go. If any of the lessons are taught in the day, we ask that men are kept away from the room."

My brows pull together. "I'm not following."

Harriet rubs Gabby's arm. "We'd prefer it if people didn't know we were actually strippers. At the club, we have anonymity. No one has ever recognised us outside of the club because they don't see past our disguises but that could change once they know we are strippers. They'll notice things they didn't see before."

Understanding hits me, and I quickly rush to reassure them. "No one here will ever know, and neither Landon nor I will never refer to you as strippers. You have my word."

She relaxes. "Then we have a deal. We'll come by Monday and fill out the forms. I've also got some promotional ideas I can put together by then."

"If there are any expenses, let me know and I'll reimburse you."

Gabby grins suddenly. "I'm really looking forward to this."

"Let me see you out then," I tell them, heading back into the gym.

We come to a stop where Charlotte's belongings are in a pile. "Thank you for doing this, Charlotte."

"I didn't do anything," she replies.

"Yes, you did. We would never have found this place had it not been for you."

Charlotte waves her off. "I only asked for rent space. He came up with the rest."

Harriet addresses me next. "We really are grateful."

"You're welcome," I reply. Emily quickly grabs Harriet's arm, the blood draining from her face as she stares over my shoulder. "Everything okay?"

She gulps, pulling her gaze away from whatever has her attention. "Who baked you the cake?"

I grin. "Charlotte."

"Oh God," she whispers.

"Fuck! But we liked him," Gabby whines.

"What?" I ask, feeling out of the loop.

Charlotte chews on her thumbnail, turning to the gorgeous cake she baked for me. "What's wrong with it?"

"Hey, Charlotte, can you come look at this butt plug for me?" Gabby asks, and I heave out a breath at the blunt question.

"Of course," Charlotte replies nonchalantly, heading over to her and gazing down at the phone.

Harriet rushes to my side. "Normally I don't warn people because sometimes it's best to just let them experience it, but we like you. We're grateful you helped us."

Olivia nods. "Don't eat the fucking cake."

"Why? There's nothing wrong with it."

I'm kind of offended on Charlotte's behalf. These are meant to be her friends.

"That's what makes them so deadly," she whispers, checking that Gabby is keeping Charlotte distracted,

"Just trust us. Don't eat it," Harriet warns.

I nod, but I have no plans to listen to them. The cake smells phenomenal and it looks to die for. And I don't normally binge on snacks.

Charlotte takes a step away from Emily. "Hey, guys, do one of you mind dropping me back home? It'll save Drew the trip."

"I don't mind taking you," I rush out.

She smiles sweetly at me. "I don't want to keep putting you out."

"I'm good to drive you," Harriet assures her. "We can drop you off first, then Emily."

"Thank you," Charlotte tells her before reaching down for her hoodie—well, my hoodie.

From the corner of my eye, I watch as Harriet stops scanning the hoodie to eye me once more, putting two and two together. She ducks her head as a sly smile tugs at her lips.

"Six thirty Saturday?" I remind her.

"It's a date," she tells me, and pink rises in her cheeks. This time, it isn't from exhaustion. "I mean, not a date, date, but a non-date."

I chuckle. "I know what you mean."

"You two are so cute together," Emily announces out of nowhere.

"We aren't together," Charlotte rushes out.

"Wow, talk about friendzone a guy," Harriet mumbles, glancing away.

"I mean, we're together now, but in a few minutes, we won't be. We're friends. Of course we are. I mean, I've not specifically asked if he's—"

"Charlotte, we're friends," I assure her.

She groans, closing her eyes. "I'm going to go now. I need to feed my pussy. She probably wants to be played with too."

Emily, who was taking a swig of her Pepsi, sprays it everywhere, her eyes wide as she stares in horror.

"I bet," Harriet teases, struggling to hold back her laughter.

Olivia, on the other hand, isn't shy and bends at the waist, loud guffaws echoing around the room. I'm sure she just snorted.

My shoulders shake as I wait for Charlotte to click on, but she's too busy stuffing her towel back into her bag.

"What's so funny?" Charlotte asks, biting her lip. "Are my leggings ripped? It wouldn't be the first time."

"Your leggings are fine."

"Are you all ready or is there anything you need to go over?" Charlotte asks, glancing at the girls.

"No, we're good."

"See you all Monday and thank you for coming."

"Thank you for helping us."

"See you Saturday."

"See you then," I tell Charlotte, walking them all to the door. I let them out and lock up behind them.

Once they are gone, I head back into the main section of the gym to grab my stuff, only the cake on the bench distracts me.

What the hell, it isn't like I won't burn it off by tomorrow. I grab my pocket knife out of my bag, flip the blade out, and slice down the cake, cutting out a piece.

Fucking hell, it smells amazing.

I bring it up to my nose, taking in the rich vanilla sponge with jam and butter cream in the centre.

I take a bite, savouring the taste, before something turns sour in my mouth. It feels like acid is burning away my tastebuds.

I spit it out, reaching for my bottle of water as I try not to bring up my food from earlier.

"Fuck," I groan when the taste doesn't go. I grab my towel, wiping furiously at my tongue.

At least I know the girls weren't wrong.

Fuck, that was terrible.

I eye the cake, wondering if she made it by mistake or if she really is trying to kill me.

FOURTEEN

DREW

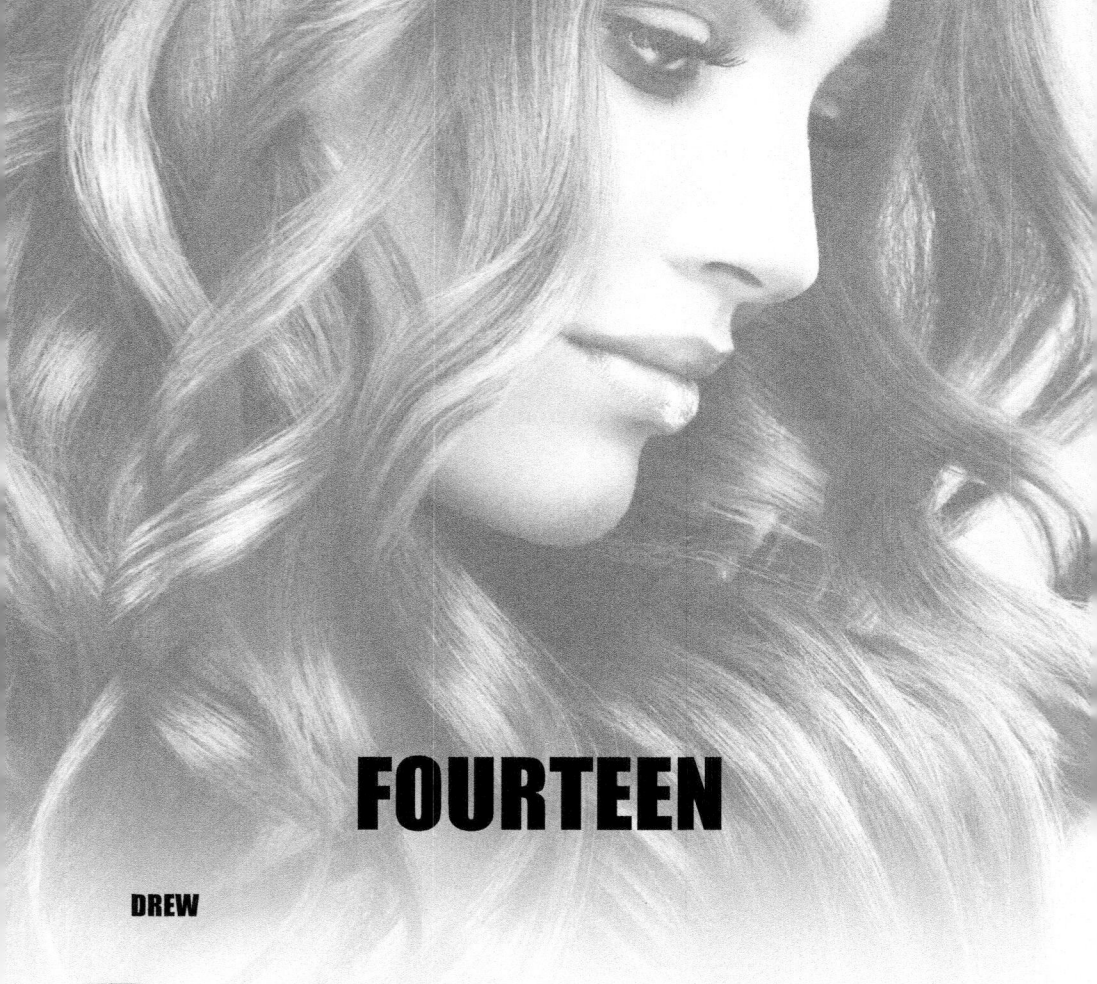

Rain pelts down on my window screen, the sound so loud I can't even hear my own thoughts.

Of course it would rain on the night my sister is having a party. Luckily, she decided to book a room at the hotel, otherwise she'd be cursing the world for ruining her perfect hair and makeup.

Growing up with two sisters, I'm somewhat in tune to a woman's way of thinking, which is why I decided to drive up the dirt lane that leads to Charlotte's. I don't want her to get soaked while rushing to the car.

They really need to work on getting this tarmacked.

I pull into her empty drive, honking my horn once before shutting the car off. I grab the umbrella I remembered to pick up before getting out.

Rain splatters soak through my jacket before I even manage to get the umbrella up. I've only taken a step when the door opens, and I come to a halt. I run my eyes over her black sparkling dress, with gold flowers embroidered onto it. The thin gold/beige belt showcases her hourglass figure.

Our gazes lock and once again, I'm struck by her beauty. She's never worn makeup before. Her skin is smooth and silky, and apart from a few freckles over her nose, she has no blemishes. But tonight, she has gone all out. Her eyes are thick with eyeliner, and her eyeshadow has a smoky effect on her lids that makes the emerald-green pop out. Her lips are painted a nude colour, yet it emphasizes their bow shape. It makes me want to kiss them. Her hair is half up, half down. The volume and thickness of the curls only make her that much more stunning.

She's beautiful without dressing up, but when she does... she could knock a man to his knees.

She turns and reveals the back of her dress, which is lower, showing the silky-smooth skin of her back.

I adjust my dick, unable to control my desire as she locks up behind her.

"Thank you for coming to the door," she calls out, and I snap out of my lust-filled thoughts to rush around to the passenger door and pull it open for her.

After closing the door behind her, I slowly walk around the front of the car, needing to gather myself before getting inside. She's taken my breath away.

Getting back inside, the first thing to hit me is her perfume. It has a vanilla aroma to it and it's a struggle not to lean over, run my nose along the slender angle of her neck, and breathe her in.

Fuck, it's going to be a struggle to keep my hands away from her tonight.

"Are you okay?" she asks, as my knuckles whiten from their grip on the steering wheel.

"Yeah," I croak out. I clear my throat, paste on a smile, and turn to her. "You look really beautiful."

She runs a hand down her dress as a pink tinge blossoms on her cheeks. "Thank you. You look handsome yourself."

As I pull out, I catch sight of a soft pink and white gift bag at her feet. "What's in the bag?"

"It's a crystal stone for your sister and her husband."

"A what now?"

She chuckles under her breath. "It's Rose Quartz. It cultivates love. I wasn't sure what gift to bring your sister as we don't know each other, so I got something she could place in their home."

She continues to surprise me. "Wait, we have to bring a gift?"

Her sharp intake of breath tells me that yes, we do in fact need to bring a gift. "You haven't gotten her an engagement gift?"

I take my eyes off the road for a second. Shit, she really is serious about this. "No. I had planned on getting her some new appliances for when she moves in. She never mentioned anything about engagement gifts."

"Well, you can't go empty-handed."

"I'll stop off and get some flowers."

"No," she yells, nearly making me swerve the car.

"Why not?"

"Because it's a party, and at a hotel no less. They'll be crushed or dead by the time she can get them into a vase."

"What the hell am I supposed to do?"

"Do you have a pen in the car?"

A pen?

"In the glove box, why?"

She opens it up and rummages through the mess I shoved in there. "Aha, got one."

"Why a pen?"

"I'm going to add your name to this gift and to the card."

"Charlotte, you don't need to do that."

"It's fine. You don't want to give your mum more ammunition to be upset, do you."

"Are you sure?"

"Yes, of course. In fact, I was feeling a little weird about giving her a present from myself when she doesn't even know me."

"Let me know how much it cost and I'll repay you."

"Nope. That's not why I offered. Now pay attention to the road. One of my biggest fears is getting into a car crash while wearing a dress."

What?

"Just wearing a dress?"

She finishes sealing the envelope before leaning back, shuddering. "Yes. There's no telling how they'll find you. Will your dress be up by your boobs? Will your vajayjay get less protection being in the open like that? I mean, it freaks me out."

My shoulders shake with silent laughter. "What else freaks you out?"

"A house fire during the night. I've never met a fireman and I don't want my first time to be in my pyjamas," she admits, and I chuckle under my breath. "What about you? What's your biggest fear?"

"Mine?" I muse, thinking about it. "I'd have to say being blind."

"Are you scared of the dark?"

"No, not that, but for social reasons. A majority of the time you can read a person best by just looking at them, and I don't mean appearance wise. I mean their expression. Not being able to read people like that… it scares the shit out of me."

"I never thought about that," she muses quietly. "If I had to choose which of my senses I had to lose, I'd pick taste."

"Taste?"

"Yeah. I've had things in my mouth that looked really good but tasted crap."

I heave out a breath, gripping the steering wheel tightly to make sure I don't steer us into a tree.

"Can't say the same," I choke out.

It isn't an act she's putting on. She truly says these things without realising the significance or how they might be interpreted.

"There's still time," she mutters.

This woman. This beautiful, kind-hearted soul, fascinates me. She has the most outrageous stories to share, and if it wasn't for knowing Landon and their family's reputation, I'd think it was all made up.

But it isn't.

And for that, I want to know everything about her. I want to know what drives her, what got her to this point and where she's going. I want to know it all.

Which is what we do for the rest of the car drive. We spend time getting to know each other, laughing and joking, and sometimes, she'll drift off, humming along to a song on the radio.

She more than fascinates me. She captivates me in a way no other has.

And I can't wait to get to know her more.

I PLACE MY hand on the centre of Charlotte's back, guiding her to the lavish, marble reception area. "Hi, we are here for the Wyatt and Simmons' engagement party."

The dark-haired, middle-aged receptionist pastes on a kind smile and points to a corridor. "If you follow the hallway down, you'll come to a lobby. The party is being held in the banquet hall. There are signs leading to it, so you won't get lost."

"Thank you."

"This is really posh," Charlotte comments, glancing up at the high ceilings.

"My mother wouldn't have it any other way," I admit, frowning at the awful gold sculpture of a guy holding an apple.

To me, it seems a bit much. What happened to a good old piss up and a DJ?

I nod in greeting to a few guests I recognise as family friends, our exchanges never moving past acknowledgements.

Once we hit the lobby, I notice my mother straight away. She's speaking to one of Wesley's investors.

"This way," I whisper, quickly bypassing more guests to get inside the main room. I spot my sister straight away. She's stunning in her cream dress, her hair and makeup done to perfection. She stands elegantly and regal, born for crowds like this. She knows when to nod, when to smile, and when to laugh. It's her expression that gives everything away though. There's a tightness around her eyes, a forcefulness to her laugh, and if you know her and pay close attention like me, it's the way she leans against her fiancé, Joseph. She's paying no real attention to the couple in front of them. Joseph, however, is, and every now and then, he squeezes the top of her arm subtly.

I grin when she pastes on a fake smile. "That's Alison, my sister who is getting married," I point out to Charlotte.

When she leans in closer, I almost stiffen. "Is she being forced to marry? Because she looks like she'd rather be anywhere but here."

I chuckle. "She just needs saving," I explain. I absently reach for her hand and feel her stiffen beside me. "Is this okay?"

She opens and closes her mouth for a moment before nodding. "I mean, I am supposed to be your girlfriend-slash-date."

"That you are," I whisper.

"Did you say something?"

"Nah," I lie, as we make our way to my sister.

Her entire face lights up when she spots me, and she quickly says something to the couple in front of her. She steps away elegantly but the minute she's out of their space, she dashes through the crowded tables.

I let go of Charlotte when she nears, and reach for my sister, swinging her up in my arms. "You having a good night?"

"It would be the best if Mum and Dad hadn't invited all of their colleagues."

"Did you expect anything else?" I ask, as I place her on her feet.

She lets out a sigh. "No."

"Come and meet my date, Charlotte," I tell her, stepping back so she has a clear view of her.

She steps forward, her eyes wide. "Hi, I'm Alison, it's lovely to meet you."

"I'm Charlotte, and it's lovely to meet you too. This is a lovely party."

Alison waves her off. "This isn't my normal style but I don't care as long as I'm with Joseph."

"That is so romantic," Charlotte breathes out before shaking herself out of it. "We bought this for you. It's Rose Quartz. It cultivates love and will bring it to your home and relationship."

Alison takes the bag from her hand, her lips parted. "Thank you so much. This is so kind of you."

"It wasn't all me. Drew helped too," Charlotte lies, and it's easily read.

Alison laughs. "No, he didn't, but thank you," she tells her, before lightly punching me in the arm. "You didn't get me a gift?"

I rub the back of my neck. "I didn't know I had to," I admit, before I notice Joseph walking past. I grab him by his suit jacket, pulling him beside me. I grin at Alison as she rolls her eyes. "I got you him."

"No, I got him myself, but nice save," she comments, before I notice her stiffen, a change coming over her that she only gets around one person.

Our sister. Her twin.

I turn, pasting on a fake smile. "Natalie," I greet, before moving beside Charlotte.

Her gaze runs over Charlotte, her lip curling. "This is your date?"

I narrow my gaze. "Don't start."

"I'm not; I just didn't think you'd actually find someone off the street."

"We actually met at his gym," Charlotte interrupts. "I'm Charlotte, by the way."

When Natalie ignores her outstretched hand and runs her gaze once more over Charlotte's attire, I grit my teeth.

"*Really?*" she says.

Charlotte nods, the passive-aggressive comment going over her head. "Yes. My cousin is co-owner now."

Natalie looks to me. "So, this is a pity date?"

"Natalie, not tonight," Alison snaps.

"Are you angry with me?" Charlotte blurts out. "I can't tell. But if I've offended you, I'm sorry."

I burst out laughing, pulling Charlotte against me. She fits so easily, her head resting over my heart.

Alison ducks her head, struggling to keep her laughter at bay.

Natalie steps forward, her hands balled into fists. "Excuse me?"

Charlotte points to her face. "Your face isn't moving, so I can't tell what you're feeling. Your tone says angry, but your face… there's not a lot going on."

"What?" Natalie gawks, her face reddening.

"Oh my God," I murmur, struggling to keep the laughter inside.

"Your expression— You don't have one."

Natalie takes a step forward, her hand rising. I quickly spin, pulling Charlotte away before Natalie causes a fight she will definitely lose. Charlotte might look timid and shy, but I have seen her punch the punching bag, and it was not pretty. Natalie has none of that inside her. All she has is hate and self-loathing, which she tries to dress up with plastic surgery and fillers and a lot of vulgar behaviour.

Charlotte waves over her shoulder. "It was nice to meet you."

I begin to laugh. Bringing Charlotte was the best decision I made. Until I spot Eloise coming our way. I quickly steer Charlotte to the left.

"Where are we going?" she asks.

"Let's dance."

"I love dancing," she gushes.

I swing her around, pulling her into my arms. Now we're away from the family, from Natalie's rude behaviour, and it's just us, everything from before comes rushing back and I'm back in the moment.

As she presses her body against mine, my cock twitches.

"I love this song," she whispers as she places her hands on my shoulders.

My arms lay limply at my sides because I don't know what to do with them, but then she closes her eyes and her expression… it pulls at my heart strings. I can't think of anything more beautiful in this moment.

I find myself reaching for her, placing my hands at her waist. At first, my touch is light, almost hesitant, but the longer I watch her savour the music, I forget about it all, pulling her in closer.

It's Ed Sheeran's, *Thinking Out Loud* playing. It's not something I normally listen to, yet with Charlotte in my arms, my feet are already moving, and we slowly begin to move to the beat.

"I'm sorry about Natalie. I promise she isn't always like this," I tell her.

She smiles gently up at me. "I'm sorry too. It wasn't until we moved away that I realised she has had fillers. They freak me out."

My lips tug up at the corners. "Another thing that freaks you out?"

She nods solemnly. "Yes. It's like your fear of being blind. You said you go on people's expressions. This is just the same. We're blind to them. *And...* it really just freaks me out. It's not attractive at all. Not when they go too far with them." She groans, dropping her head forward, banging her forehead against my chest. "I'm being judgemental."

I laugh, swaying us to the right. "Then I think they injected my mum's face to be permanently set in a resting bitch face."

Her hair falls back as she tilts her head up, laughing. "Don't be mean."

"It's true," I declare, chuckling as the song comes to an end. "Why don't we get you a drink?"

When an acoustic song comes on, her grip tightens. "This is a favourite song of mine. Let's have one more dance."

I smile, pulling her closer until her head is resting against my chest. "Who is it?"

"It's *Lover* by Taylor Swift," she whispers, before I feel her humming along to the song.

I rest my head on the top of hers, soaking in her vanilla scent. "One more song," I whisper back.

FIFTEEN

CHARLOTTE

I BUSY MYSELF NEAR THE EDGE of the dance floor as I wait for Drew to come back with our drinks. I spot him at the bar and give him a small wave and a smile.

He's a good dancer. A great date. And if this was real, it would be the best first date of my life. Not that I have had many.

Many think a first date is successful because of the food they ate, the place they went to, or the activity they took part in. They're mere contributions. It's the person you spend time with, the connection you feel, that matters. It's in the way they touch you, look at you, hold you.

And he's done it the opposite to how he looks. He's been gentle, respectful, and I've had tingles in all the right places.

I was hesitant to leave the dance floor when the last song ended. I could have stayed in his arms all night and been content because in that fraction of a moment, it was us and it felt real. Not just some favour to a friend.

He was treating me the way I've always dreamed of being treated. The only thing missing was the stolen kisses. And there had been moments tonight when I wanted to lean up and steal a kiss.

I immediately put those thoughts to the side when a tall, slender woman comes to stand in front of me. I have no right in thinking them anyway, not when Scott still haunts my dreams. I was a fool then, and I'd be a fool now if I thought it would be any different. He's just being a gentleman. It means nothing.

The woman with upturned eyes continues to stare down at me.

"Can I help you?"

Her lip curls—or at least I think it does. It's hard to tell since that area of her face has more fillers than cheeks. "You are here with Andrew?"

My brows pull together. "Andrew?"

She flicks her perfect, honey-blonde curls over her shoulder. "I guess *you* would call him Drew."

I smile, wondering if this is another relative. "Yes, I'm here with Andrew."

"I'm surprised he brought a girl."

"Why? Does he normally bring a guy?"

She looks at me like I've grown two heads, a look I'm accustomed to. "No. I meant I'm surprised he brought you. Any date really, but mostly you." Her eyes run over my attire again, and she grimaces.

I shake my head, unable to fathom what she's trying to get at. "I'm sorry, I'm not sure what you mean. We get on really well, so why wouldn't he bring me? Did he say we were arguing? Because we aren't. We've never argued."

"Oh my gosh, you really are weird," she bites out, her venom coming from nowhere.

"I'm sorry, have we met before?"

"God no," she spits out.

"Then what is it you want?"

"I did feel sorry for you, but now I think I should feel sorry for him."

"Why?"

"Well, he'd never go for anyone like you," she tells me, running her gaze up and down my body. "Too much meat. He's into his fitness— likes them flexible."

"I'll have you know I can do the splits, and I'm not fat. I'm perfectly healthy, thank you."

"You are chubby."

This girl is rude and I'm growing frustrated. If only I could mimic Hayden… I quickly run through everything she would do or say if she were here in my shoes.

And there's only one thing I can come up with.

"Fuck you!"

Her expression drops and she gawks at me. "Excuse me?"

I take a step forward, and she takes one back. "I'm sorry. I'm not sure what came over me."

"Save it for someone who cares. Grace will be hearing of this. I'm sure she'll love to know who her son is loitering with."

"Mother knows exactly who I'm spending my time with, Eloise."

Eloise.

This is the girl his mum was trying to set him up with. I run my gaze over her once more, this time sceptically. She isn't his match. Not at all. For one, he's kind, whereas she's not. He's filled with life, and she seems vapid and shallow.

And she's so skinny he'd probably snap her if he gave her a hug.

"She just told me to—"

"Eloise, why are you here?"

She pastes on a fake smile, sticking her chest out. For the first time I notice her cleavage and wonder if she realises the move isn't attractive.

"Let's start over," she tells him sweetly. "It's so good to see you and I don't want our first time to be clouded by…" Her lip curls when she turns to me. She clears her throat, her expression relaxing somewhat. "Thank you, I'm parched."

His lips part as she takes the drink from his hand. Nuh uh. No way. I smile sweetly, quickly taking the drink from her. "Whoopsie, that's mine."

Drew chuckles as he comes to stand closer to me. "Well, it's been… something, but we're going to find some food."

She places her hand on his arm, stopping him. "Why? We've not seen each other in nearly a year, if not longer. I'm sure…"

At her snide look, I reply. "I'm Charlotte."

Her smile tightens. "I'm sure she wouldn't mind if we go somewhere and catch up."

I wave her off. "Of course not." I choke on my drink when Drew nudges me. "But then who would remind me to take my meds?"

Eloise's eyes widen. "Meds?"

I nod. "Exactly."

Drew chuckles as he pulls me against his chest. I lean against him, loving the scent of his cologne. It's enough to make my vagina tingle. The rich, spicy scent filling my senses.

"Eloise," a replica of Alison greets.

Natalie's back, and although her and Alison are twins, they're nothing alike. And the difference isn't because of all the surgery and Botox Natalie has had; it's their personalities.

"Drew, brother, not trying to run off again, are we?"

He steps away, giving his sister a hug, though not a warm one like he had given Alison. This one is standoffish, tense.

"Be good," he warns, thinking I can't hear him.

She shares a look with Eloise. "I see it didn't take you long to find Eloise."

"She found us," he tells her.

"I was just saying, we should go somewhere a little quieter so we can catch up, but his friend—"

"Girlfriend," I interject, hoping they believe the sweet lie.

"*Girlfriend*, doesn't feel comfortable with us being alone."

"I never said—"

Natalie clucks her tongue. "I'm sure you can bear to be apart for just a short while. After all, they were very good friends once upon a time."

I gulp the rest of my drink, already feeling the effects of the alcohol running through my system.

"Charlotte and I have other plans."

"Really?"

"Natalie, it might have escaped you but you can't pull the wool over my eyes like you do everyone around you. I'm here with my girlfriend and I'd like for you to respect that."

"Of course I respect that. Why don't I keep her company while you and Eloise catch up?"

"No," he tells her sharply, before taking my hand. He pulls us away from them and I turn a little, waving to them over my shoulder.

"Nice to meet you," I call out, earning death stares in return.

"I'm sorry about that. She can be a little… much."

"It's okay. I'm used to it."

He gently pulls me to a stop, staring so deeply into my eyes it almost feels like he can read my thoughts.

He tucks a strand of hair behind my ear. "Never get used to it."

My lips part as I sway toward him. "It's fine. Sometimes people just don't get me."

"Because they've never seen a star shine so brightly," he tells me, his eyes widening slightly at his own words. "Let's dance."

He goes to take my drink and for a moment, I nearly let him.

"One minute." I gulp the rest of the drink down before leaving the empty glass on the table.

"Drew, dear. Drew."

I see his mum walking as steadily and as fast as she can toward us without actually running. Drew's fingers tighten around mine as he ignores her calls and swings me around. I'm not sure what song is playing, but it doesn't matter. This one has a faster beat, and I laugh as he twirls me around, causing the edge of my dress to spin around me.

I'm bursting with joy as I slam back into his chest. "Thank you for inviting me."

"Thank you for coming and putting up with my torturous family."

"Alison isn't that bad."

"She's the good twin," he teases, twirling me out and then back in.

I place one hand on his chest, grinning. "We should make this night good for you too."

His eyes darken as he pulls me closer. "And how do you think we are going to manage that with my mum circling like a shark hunting its prey."

I chuckle. "My uncle always says alcohol solves everything."

"Alcohol?"

"Yeah, you can handle anything with alcohol in your system."

He grimaces. "I wish, but I'm driving."

I shrug. "We'll find another way home."

He pauses for a moment, thinking about it. "You know what? Fuck it. Let's go have a drink."

I laugh as he pulls me off the dance floor, but it fades away the minute his mum stands in front of us, her arms crossed over her chest as she frowns disapprovingly. "Really, Andrew? You must have heard me call you."

"Mother, it's so good to see you. How are you?" he asks, leaning down to peck her on the cheek.

She eyes me much the same as her daughter and Eloise had. "I see you brought a date."

"Alison said I could bring a plus one."

"Yes, well, it didn't mean bring just anyone."

"I'm his girlfriend," I announce happily, watching her expression strain like she's constipated.

"I'm sure," she snidely replies before turning to her son. "Have you had a chance to catch up with Eloise? She is looking remarkably beautiful tonight."

"We've seen her," he replies tersely.

An older man with greying hair steps up to Grace, placing a hand on the small of her back much the same way as Drew is doing to me. The reminder only makes me more hyper aware of his hand touching me. A shiver runs down my spine every time his thumb caresses my back.

"Drew, it is so good to see you, son," the man greets happily. "And who is this beautiful young lady?"

"This is my girlfriend, Charlotte," he answers, before sharing a man hug.

They slap each other on the back before putting space between them. Drew comes back to my side, placing his hand lower on my back. I shiver, stepping closer. "Charlotte, this is my step-father, Wesley."

I hold out my hand and give him a bright smile. "It's so lovely to meet you. Drew has said some wonderful things about you."

He hasn't said much but I know from my upbringing it's the polite thing to say.

He shares a look with Drew, giving him a wink.

"I like her," he tells him before shaking my hand. "What a pleasure."

"Really, Wesley. Must you encourage him?" Grace snarks.

Wesley sighs and rolls his eyes heavenward. "Must you make his life hell every time you see him, my love?"

She huffs out a breath. "You could have both made an effort to dress up."

I run a hand over my dress, one that isn't cheap or casual. It's stunning.

"Mum, don't insult me or my guest."

"I'm just saying, dear. Eloise is single. You belong together."

"Why do they belong together?" I blurt out, insulted by her words. It isn't very often I let things get to me, but her bluntness is on another level.

Wesley's lips twitch as he eyes a speechless Grace. "I believe she asked you a question, my love."

"We're going to the bar," Drew announces.

"Just spend time with Eloise, son. She will be a good wife and you can clearly do a lot worse."

"And we're going," Drew snaps, pulling me away.

I give Wesley a wave. He gives me a two-finger wave back, then winks at me. I chuckle to myself as we head to the bar.

"I really am so fucking sorry about them. If I knew they were going to be as rude as they have been, I would never have let you come and be victim to it."

I lean against the bar. "You'd be surprised by what I can handle. I don't suck in the negative energy. It's irrelevant to me. I choose to take in and absorb the positive."

"That's one way of living," he murmurs, mesmerised for a moment.

"It is. Negative energy gets you nowhere and gives you nothing. It doesn't make your life better," I explain. "It's why I choose to only share the positivity in the world."

He opens his mouth, ready to say something, but for some reason, chooses not to and instead turns to the barman, giving him our order.

"What was you going to say?"

"It doesn't matter."

"It does."

He brushes away the loose strands of hair that have fallen out of his bun. "Is that why you're handling what happened to you better than most?"

It's a fair question, one I don't want to answer, but feel like I should. "Honestly, a part of me wants to forget it ever happened, but the other part has learned from it. I choose to keep moving forward because there isn't any other choice for me. Yes, I'm hurt by what he did; yes, I'm heartbroken over the lies and betrayal, but I'm also well-versed enough to know I'm in denial. People can judge what they must about that night. Pick it apart and question every detail. But it doesn't change anything for me. I experienced it differently, *saw* it differently, and what was meant to be beautiful, only turned out to be ugly. I let go of most of that negative energy the night you put me in front of the punching bag."

"Just like that?" he asks, looking doubtful.

"No. I still have a long way to go. I just refuse to dwell on something I can't change. I'll heal in time."

"Charlotte, I—"

The barman chooses that moment to place the drinks between us on the bar. "There you go, mate."

Drew picks up his pint, taking a swig. I take mine, the fruity cocktail already making my taste buds tingle. "Let's get drunk."

He grins, knocking his glass against mine. "To getting drunk."

SIXTEEN

DREW

The party is coming to an end, which means guests are more intoxicated and are getting louder by the minute.

"Do I have a big arse?" Charlotte yells, holding her phone to her head. On the screen is the name of a celebrity she has to guess.

We're in the middle of playing charades since the live band my mother hired are a snooze.

Speaking of, my mother storms over, her expression pinched and red. "Really, Andrew."

I grimace at the scathing look she gives me. "We're playing charades."

"You're acting like a child."

I roll my eyes and turn to Charlotte. "A huge one."

"That's what she said," she teases, ignoring my mum. She has put up with her hostile behaviour all night and in the end opted to pretend she wasn't there whenever she came along.

I wish I had the same strength.

"Guests are watching you, Andrew," Mother scolds and hands over a card. "Take your guest back to this room and stop embarrassing your sister."

I take the card and in the midst of grabbing it, I knock her hand, causing her bag to slide down her arm and drop to the floor. Charlotte quickly rushes to her knees, helping me place everything back.

Mum, however, doesn't even try to pick up her belongings. Charlotte holds up another room card, one similar to mine and grins as she tucks it down her dress. I shake my head, my lips twitching. I hand Mum her bag and take Charlotte's hand. "You're right, Mum. We wouldn't want to embarrass you."

"It's been such a lovely pleasure meeting you, Mrs Wyatt."

Mum looks shaken by her comment. "I wish I could say the same."

Charlotte suddenly spins to face me. "I'm Kim Kardashian, right?"

I chuckle at her change in subject. "Yeah, babe, you were."

"Really," Mum huffs out.

"Goodnight, Mum." Charlotte laughs as we walk away. "You do realise she will just get a replacement card?"

Charlotte grins and takes my hand. "Yes, but we aren't doing it so she doesn't get a room. I'm going to take a leaf out of my uncles' book— if you don't mind me playing a trick on your mum."

"A trick?" I ask, willing to do anything she asks of me right now.

We're both a little pissed, and for the first time I'm really enjoying myself at a family event. It feels good to be free from responsibility and upholding a certain image.

I'm twenty-six years old, and although I've had nights out with mates, it has never been like this. We could have spent the night in a bus stop and I would have enjoyed myself in her company.

Charlotte suddenly stops, her red hair flying as she spins to face me. Her cheeks are a rosy red as she exhales heavily. "Okay, I'm kind of lying. This is something I've wanted to do for a while. I was hoping to do it on our next family holiday."

"Love, you're going to have to fill me in on the details 'cause I have no idea what you are going on about."

"It's all about the details."

I chuckle. "What?"

She rests her hands over my chest, laughing. "We are going to make her room look like a murder just happened."

"Again, what?"

She waves me off. "They'll have extra pillows. Fancy places like this always do."

When she heads toward the lifts, I trail after her. We step inside the lift, and are greeted by an older couple dressed up like they spent the night at the casino.

"Hey," I greet.

Charlotte gives them her megawatt smile. "You guys look so beautiful."

The older lady smiles affectionately. "So do you, my dear. That dress is simply stunning."

"You don't think I look fat?" she blurts out. "I got told I look fat in it."

The couple reprimand me with one scathing look. My balls shrivel up and I take a step back. "Wait," I begin, but Charlotte continues.

"But you two, you look so cute, so beautiful. I hope I find that one day."

"She means—"

The ding announcing we've reached a floor interrupts me and I groan when I realise it must be their stop.

The lady places her hand on Charlotte's arm. "You take care, dear. Don't let anyone tell you that you are anything but beautiful."

Tears gather in Charlotte's eyes. "That is so sweet of you," she blubbers.

She stops next to me and my insides turn at her approach. "You should be ashamed of yourself, young man. If you were a few feet smaller I'd have your hide," she threatens. "Treat her better."

"But I—"

The man steps up next, gently pushing his wife forward. "If you were my boy, I'd have clipped you round the earhole."

"But I…" He walks away, not letting me finish, and my shoulders slump. Great, now they think I'm an abusive arsehole.

Charlotte falls against me, hugging me around the waist. "Weren't they the best people?"

"Yeah," I grumble, wondering if I have time to find them and change their minds about me.

The lift doors shut and moments later, they open again. "Tell me again what we're doing."

"Let's just get it done. The party is nearly over and we don't want your mum catching us in the act."

"You know what, fuck it. She's been difficult all evening."

She nods enthusiastically. "If only we had Eloise's room number. We could scare her into leaving the hotel and we won't need to see her again."

I chuckle. "You were the one who accepted her breakfast invitation."

She groans. "It's a curse. I don't like saying no to people."

"She wasn't asking you."

She smacks me on the shoulder. "I know that, silly, but it was fun watching her reaction."

We head down the next hall, checking the door numbers as we go. "This is it."

She pulls the card from out of her dress and opens the door. The beep echoes and Charlotte freezes, glancing at me over her shoulder. "Shush."

"I didn't make a noise."

"For this to work, it has to be done right. Make sure you get the fridge. They'll have either small ketchup bottles or sachets. I'll get the body ready."

I twist my lips warily. "We aren't actually killing someone?"

She laughs, poking me in the bicep. "Oh, my lord. I'm not a murderer. But my uncle made up a fake dead body with bedsheets one time and put it in bed with my dad. According to my uncles, there were tears, piss, and a lot of screaming, but according to my dad, he just jumped a little."

It smells like my mother's perfume as we head inside the main room. Trust my mum to get a suite that's bigger than my flat.

"Jesus," I hiss out, seeing the champagne bottle on the side.

"They are totally having—"

I place my hand over her mouth before she can traumatise me for life. "No. We do not speak of that."

She giggles and steps away. "It's a natural thing."

"Nope. Lalalalala," I sing as I grab the champagne bottle. There is no way I'm leaving this here. I place it on the side next to the door. "We'll take this with us."

"I'm going to get the bed ready," she tells me, heading into the master bedroom.

My gaze scans the room, finding my mother's things in place like she's making a home for a year instead of the night. If it were me, I wouldn't have bothered unpacking. I'd just grab what I need when I needed it.

The pristine room is triggering. Suddenly I'm having childhood flashbacks of Mum telling me to have my room cleaned in a certain way, and I want to rebel.

A grown-arse man and I'm acting like a child.

Fuck it.

I have years of pent-up anger when it comes to my mum and her strict rules and expectations.

Heading over to the picture on the wall, I look at it before pulling it off and rehanging it upside down, then do the same with the other pictures in the room. By the time I'm done rearranging the room, I have a massive grin on my face. My mother is going to pitch a fit when she walks inside. The room isn't trashed, far from it, but the things out of place are going to have her losing her mind.

Charlotte comes out of the bedroom, bumping into the wall. "All done."

A wider grin spreads across my face as I walk past her, ducking my head into the room. I burst out laughing at the bedsheet she's stuffed with something to form a figure of a body. It's tied in places with the ties from a dressing gown. "She is going to freak."

"Let's go before she gets back."

We rush out of the room and I barely slow down quick enough to grab the bottle off the side.

"Thanks for coming with me tonight," I tell her, as I open the bottle.

"I've had a lot of fun. More fun than I've had since the night we found Cluck."

"Cluck?"

She waves me off. "It was a misunderstanding and not important."

"Okay…"

"What floor is our room on?"

"Two down from this one," I declare, pressing the button to call the elevator. When the door opens moments later, I can't help but touch her. I rest my hand on the bottom of her back, leading her into the elevator. She shivers as we come to a stop inside the door.

I slide my hand across her back before leaning over and pressing the button to our floor.

The champagne tastes sweet on my tongue as I gulp a large amount down.

All night I have been hyperaware of her. Every move, every touch, every brush of her body against mine. However, now we're alone, about to go back to our room, it's like my body is on another frequency and all I can *sense* is her. I'm trying really hard to be a gentleman.

Her fingers brush mine and she inhales sharply. "I wish we could see your mum's face," she tells me as the elevator comes to a stop. There's a yap as the doors slide open. "Puppy!"

My lips twitch as she steps out, bending down to the puppy and giving him a lot of fuss.

"He likes you," the puppy's owner tells her.

She looks up at him, her smile bright, beautiful. It's one of those smiles you can't help but return. "He's friendly. What's his name?"

"Ted."

I clear my throat to cover up my snort. Charlotte looks up, her nose twitching. "I told you to get that looked at."

"She's always bossing me around," I tell the guy, who's eyeing her up like a man after his prey.

Wanker.

His eyes widen when he finally pulls his attention away from Charlotte's legs, probably wondering if he could get a glimpse of what she's wearing under her dress. His mouth opens then closes, and I smirk, enjoying his discomfort.

"You like it," she teases, getting to her feet after patting the dog one more time.

"Sorry, I didn't see you there," he tells me.

I just bet he didn't.

"He's pretty hard to miss," Charlotte blurts out, as I slip my fingers through hers.

I tense a little, wondering what compelled me to do it, but I have no answers. Not even with previous girlfriends had I done any kind of public display of affection.

She isn't your girlfriend.

I take another swig of the champagne, clearing my thoughts. She's fucking with my head. She's the apple the Evil Queen tempted Snow with.

And fuck do I want to take a bite.

The guy steps past us, getting into the lift.

"Bye, puppy," Charlotte sings, before dragging me down the hall.

I tug on her arm, pulling her in the other direction. "It's this way."

We come to a stop when we hear Eloise behind us. "Andrew? Did you come to see me?"

"Oh, sugar," Charlotte whispers. "She totally wants you."

"It's not mutual," I whisper back, before leaning down. "Run!"

"Andrew? Andrew?"

She squeals as I tug her arm, pulling her in the direction of our room. I read the numbers on the door as we head past them.

We nearly topple over when we reach our door. Checking down the hall, I can't see Eloise, but I can hear her calling my name.

"Quick," I demand, as Charlotte shoves the key card into the slot. We both push inside, breathing heavily as we slam the door behind us. I place the bottle on the side before sliding my back down the door, Charlotte doing the same next to me, giggling.

"That was close," she heaves out before bursting into laughter.

"Drew?"

My eyes widen as I gently slap my hand over Charlotte's mouth. She struggles to keep her laughter in and my lips twitch. She has a beautiful laugh. It comes from the soul.

"Hey, do you know what room Drew is staying in?" Eloise says from somewhere outside the door. "He was here but now he's gone. I tried the front desk already and they can't share the information. But he was definitely here and he was with *her*."

Her voice trails off and I begin to relax, until Charlotte falls against me, laughing uproariously. "Oh god, your face."

"It's not funny," I lightly scold.

She sucks her bottom lip into her mouth. "Maybe she doesn't have a room? I mean, we could offer her the floor."

I slide away the hair that has slipped free. "As kind as your offer is, I'm *not* kind. That skank is coming nowhere near our bed."

She giggles once again, getting closer. "Did you see her face?"

No, because right now, all I see is her. *Fuck, she's radiant when she smiles.*

And I can't pull my gaze away. There's a light in her eyes that hasn't been this bright before. It's the same spark Landon spoke about when he mentioned how worried he was for her.

I can understand why people gravitate toward her, why she has stripper friends who are nuts.

Her lips part as our gazes lock, and for a moment, neither of us look away, not until her gaze drops to my lips. I'm not sure who moves first, me or her, but both of us lean in.

Tension chokes the air and I feel my groin tightening at the heated look she's giving me. A tiny puff of air slips past her lips as she leans up. I try to calm my rapid heart, to be rational and list off the reasons for why this isn't a good idea.

But I can't.

Her big green eyes blink back at me as our noses touch. It's like she's waiting for an invitation, for permission.

Finally, her full, soft lips press against mine, and I fight the urge to pull her into my lap.

Fuck, she tastes as good as she smells.

Just as I'm about to reach for her and deepen the kiss, she pulls back, her eyes wide.

"I shouldn't have done that."

SEVENTEEN

CHARLOTTE

*W*HAT AM *I* THINKING? He has been so good to me and I basically pounced on him. But that kiss… That simple kiss. I press my fingers to my lips, still feeling him on me, still tasting him. They tingle with awareness, urging me to go back for more.

I'm not sure what came over me. I'd fought the urge to kiss him all night. It had been something building inside of me all night, something I had never felt before.

"Charlotte," he rasps, his voice smooth like chocolate.

"I'm sorry, you probably didn't want me slobbering all over you," I admit sheepishly.

I close my eyes at the feel of his palm cupping my cheek. His fingers are calloused, rough in places, but they feel good. *His touch* feels good.

Maybe he liked the kiss.

My lids flutter open and I stare up at him, badly wanting to kiss him again. "That was a good kiss."

He leans down, and my heart rate accelerates. "It *was* a good kiss."

Does he want to do it again?

"Can we do it again?" I whisper.

He doesn't answer. Instead, he pulls me closer, capturing my lips with his. I grip his shirt, my fingers tightening in the material. Our breaths mingle together as he deepens the kiss, his taste driving me wild.

I rise to my knees before turning to straddle his thighs. His back thuds against the door as he leans back, sliding his hands up my thighs and under my dress. I shiver as he grips my hips, pulling me closer until I can feel how hard he is beneath me.

Why aren't I freaking out?

Why does it feel this good?

I rock back and forth, an electric sensation running through my core. Our gazes never break, too enthralled with the moment, with each other.

It feels so good, like every fibre of my being feels it too.

It makes me feel like a bigger fool. I fooled myself into thinking what Scott and I had was good, that in time, other things would fall into place. However, it had never been like this. This is on another level, one where I'm *not* kidding myself it means more than it does. Actions truly do mean more than words.

I want to feel this forever. The rush of it all, the desire I feel coursing through my system.

Oh my God, I'm a slut.

He pulls back when I try to kiss him again, glancing away. A sharp stabbing pain hammers in my chest. "W-what? Did I do something wrong?"

"We're both drunk. We shouldn't be doing this."

My brows pull together. "I don't think that's actually a factor in why we can't kiss. People do it all the time. It's not against the law. Its—"

He chuckles, pressing his lips to mine to keep me quiet. "No, but I don't want to take advantage of you."

"I really want you to," I blurt out, before closing my eyes and groaning. "That didn't come out right."

"I hate to bring it up, especially right now," he tells me, sounding in pain. "But you've been through a lot. I don't want to add to it."

"It never felt this way," I whisper. "This feels right. It feels good. My vagina seems happy. *Really* happy."

He groans, rubbing a hand down his face. "You're killing me."

My brows snap together. "I most certainly am not," I tell him. "Does it not feel good for you?"

"Charlotte, I've been dying to rip this pretty little dress off you all night, but I know I can't."

"Then I'll take it off," I tell him, getting up off the floor. He follows as I flick my heels off, at the same time reaching for the zip at the back of my dress.

He sees where my hand goes and steps forward. "Charlotte, no."

I step back. I'm not sure if it's the alcohol, or because I'm chasing the desire of something good, but I feel a confidence I've never had before. For the first time in months, I feel clean.

The zipper echoes in the room as I slowly pull it down. "I think we should."

He groans, his eyes bulging as the dress falls down to my cleavage, showing him I'm not wearing a bra.

Taking a long stride toward me, he places his hands on mine, stopping me. I let go of the dress, so the only thing keeping it up is him and his body. "Charlotte, I'm trying to be the good guy here. Landon will kill me. And are you really ready for this?"

This? I didn't think I'd ever be ready for sex again. But for him? My body is doing all the answering. It feels right.

I run my hand up his chest, the smoothness of his shirt adding to my arousal. He tenses under my touch, and reaches for my hand, holding it gently in his. "Charlotte, think for a moment, please."

I blink up at him, feeling tears gather in my eyes. "I want you; *this*. You've made me feel more alive than I have in months. Give me something beautiful, Drew. Give me something to remember, something that isn't tainted or wrong."

He growls and pulls away, causing my dress to fall to floor in a puddle at my feet. I squeal when he lifts me up, his fingers digging into my arse.

"Fuck, Landon is going to kill me."

I reach down, kissing the corner of his mouth. "He never needs to know."

His eyes darken. "You were never this kind of blunt before," he comments.

I grin. "I should have told you I get horny when I drink wine."

He growls, the sound primal and dark. "You had four glasses."

"I know," I whisper against his lips, feeling brazen all of a sudden. "And I don't have my clit vibrator with me."

"Fuck," he rasps, and kisses me hard, carrying me over to the bed. I slide my fingers into his hair, reaching for his hair tie. I gently pull it out, letting his hair fall free and wild.

He lies me down on the bed, then steps back, staring down at me with a dark promise in his eyes as he rips his jacket it off, letting it fall to the floor. "I need you to be really sure about this."

I sit up, not the least bit embarrassed that I'm bare to him, and help him undo his buttons. "I'm really sure. My vagina is sure. My heart is sure."

And I am. There's no doubt, no hesitation, no obligation. The alcohol has a lot to answer for but only when it comes to the confidence crawling through me. It has nothing to do with me wanting this. I wanted him before I touched a speck of alcohol, even though I never really admitted it. Now I just want him more.

I undo the buttons on his trousers and, tilting my head up, our gazes lock. It's that look. That need. It's blazing down at me. It isn't just my body he wants.

He wants *me*.

I lean forward, unable to look away until I have no choice, and lick from his groin to his belly button.

He has a magnificent body. His tattoos shadow one another, merging so they all become one. I make out a skull on his right ribcage, a weeping angel woven into his bicep, and a set of eyes that remind me of a panther on his other. There isn't an untouched bit of skin. Each design has been carefully woven and etched into his skin, blending from one to the other in wisps of smoke and other markings.

His muscles ripple, like he can physically feel the touch of my gaze. His body isn't the only reason I find myself attracted to him. Although I can't pinpoint exactly what that reason is, I know it's real.

And that alone spurs me on.

He pulls his trousers down and I sit back, my eyes widening. "Holy dick on a stick."

"Babe," he murmurs, his lips twitching as he looms over me.

I eye him once again before meeting his gaze. "Wow. You must be popular."

"Babe, stop talking about my dick."

"Like, really popular. I know strippers who would be scared to ride that pole."

He chuckles, resting on his elbows above me. "Babe, really, stop talking about my dick."

"There's *a lot* to talk about."

"I guess I'll make you stop," he rasps, leaning down. He captures my nipple between his lips, swirling his tongue around the hard tip.

"That should work," I groan out.

I arch off the bed as he clamps down, and a moan slips free. *Oh God, that feels good.*

Really good.

"You are so fucking sexy," he rumbles, running his tongue down my stomach. I lean up, watching as he kneels at the end of the bed. He grips my knickers, slowly sliding them down my thighs. "If you ever want to stop, just say the word."

"What if I want you to go faster?"

His pupils dilate, the muscle in his jaw tensing. "Just let me know."

The minute his intentions are clear, I freeze.

"I don't like that," I tell him.

It grossed me out before Scott tried it. After he did, it put me off ever wanting to do it again.

His brows pull together. "W-what?"

"It's boring, and if I'm honest, my clit had friction burns the last time." I hold my hands up. "I swear."

Books lie. I know they're fiction, but they could at least have the decency to make it realistic.

He chuckles, shaking his head. "He wasn't fucking doing it right."

I have my doubts, but I guess Drew wants to prove me wrong.

The minute his mouth latches onto my clit, my entire body flames like a furnace. Sweat beads at my forehead as I fight to keep in my moans of pleasure.

Maybe books don't lie.

I clench my eyes shut, savouring each moment. Every time his fingers dig into my thighs, I remind myself that he isn't Scott. He's real. *This* is real. I have no room in my head to be thinking about *him* right now. Only Drew.

"Oh, do that again," I ask, running my fingers through his hair. I feel him smile against my thigh before he does that thing with his tongue. "Yes!"

He most certainly knows what he's doing.

His thick fingers probe at my entrance and I tense for a moment. He's gentle, smooth, and when he curls his fingers up inside me, I almost come off the bed. The slight tension ebbs away, and with his skilled fingers and tongue working hard, I know it won't be the same as before, not how it was when Scott did this to me.

I want more.

He slides another finger inside of me and I feel full, stretched. There's no burn though, no sting. It feels like heaven.

"I want more," I rasp as he pumps his fingers inside me, hitting the spot just right.

"Wait," he urges.

"Now," I demand back, a little sharper than intended. "Sorry."

He grins, kissing my pubic bone. His fingers slide out of me and he looms over me, dragging me up the bed by my armpits. "So bossy."

I kiss him, massaging my tongue against his. He tastes so good. Beer, champagne and a minty tang.

Suddenly, I'm no longer on the bed. Drew has me up and is spinning us until I'm straddling his thighs. "W-what? I…" I no longer feel brazen.

He grips my hips, sliding me over his cock.

Or maybe I am.

That feels so good.

"Just go with what you feel comfortable doing."

"I've never done it like this before," I admit.

"It's only until you're comfortable and then, babe, I'm taking over."

The promise in his voice has my thoughts and wants scattered all over the place. My clit pulses, needing more than just a quick flick.

I rise to my knees and grasp his cock, lining it up at my entrance, when suddenly, he knifes up, his eyes wide with horror. "Condom!"

We both move at the same time, tipping over the edge of the bed. He reaches for me, turning so he takes the brunt of the fall.

"Oh fuck," he groans.

"That's what we were trying to do," I tell him, before falling into a fit of giggles. "I have a condom."

I quickly slide off him, and get up, reaching for my bag I dumped near the door. I'm not sure why Gabby put a condom in here when she helped me get ready earlier, but I'm glad she did.

I throw it in his direction and he catches it, unsnapping it with his teeth.

He has it on by the time I reach him. He grabs me around the hips, lifting me up. I circle my legs around his waist, kissing him. I love kissing him. I feel it in all the right places. My vagina most certainly loves it.

"You can still change your mind," he reminds me, his voice raspy.

"Stop talking," I demand softly, brushing my lips against his.

He sits down on the bed and reaches between us, lining his cock up at my entrance.

I want this.

I *really* want this.

I slide down his cock, my lips parting as a gasp slips free. I feel full and yet he isn't all the way in. I take my time, going at my own pace. I feel free to explore, and go down a little further.

His muscles tense beneath my fingers, and a low, primal growl rumbles from the back of his throat.

"Am I hurting you?" I whisper.

"Babe, you are killing me in the right way. You feel fucking good. Smell fucking good."

"It's my lotion," I blurt out.

He chuckles, gripping my hips as he drags me forward, the move causing me to slide down further. "All you."

He leans in, licking from my collarbone up to my neck. My knees and thighs begin to tremble as he rocks me back and forth, each time hitting the right spot inside of me. "Oh gosh!"

"Ride me," he demands, reaching for my hand and placing it on his chest. It looks so tiny against his body, making me feel sexy, girly.

My mind clears and I allow my body's instincts to take over, letting it seek what it craves, what it needs. My heavy breaths, the creak of the bed with each bounce, and the deep groans from Drew fill the air. Combined, they heighten my arousal. It feels naughty, cliché, but so right.

So flipping right.

His finger brushes over my nipple and my eyelids fly open. "Do that again."

Lips twitching, Drew obliges. "Feel good?"

"So good," I tell him, leaning forward to capture his lips. I run my fingers through his hair, grasping it as I bounce up and down on his cock.

It was never like this. It should have always been like this. And not even the act itself, but the intensity, the desire and lust. It should have always been there.

There's something building inside of me that I have never experienced before. I've had orgasms, but this feels more intense, and every time our skin slaps together, it arouses me further.

I'm so fucking turned on.

The roll of my hips begins to speed up, and Drew is no longer holding back. His fingers dig into my hips, forcing the movements to be harder, faster, and it feels so good.

"My turn," he rasps, easily lifting me in his arms. Our connection doesn't break, not even when he turns and lowers me to the bed. He reaches down and lifts my legs until my knees are tucked to my chest and he slides deeper inside of me. It feels different. A little sharper but just as good, if not more so.

He glances down to where we are joined, his hips moving. "Fuck!"

He slams inside me, knocking me further up the bed, and I moan, soaring through agonising pleasure.

Glancing up at him, I can't help but admire his beauty. His hair is curled and fanning around his shoulders. His strong features are tense yet still a thing of beauty. All of him is. Every ripple of muscle is more powerful than the last.

Yet under all that strength, all that power, there's a softness to him. A kindness you don't get to see in most guys.

I was blind when it came to Scott. Blind to who he was. Or maybe I just wanted to fool myself into seeing something that wasn't truly there. Because as mine and Drew's gazes lock, it feels like I'm seeing into his soul.

He may be beautiful on the outside, a work of art, but on the inside, he's even more so.

The bed banging against the wall gets louder, the thuds more frequent as he quickens his pace.

There's no longer just a pleasant hum down there, not just tingles tightening my lower stomach. It's like an electrical current is rolling all over me, making me hyperaware of everything.

And I mean everything.

His fingers dig into my knees. "You are fucking magnificent."

"Kiss me," I whisper.

He drops my knees immediately and they fall to the side as he looms over me, thrusting in and out like his life depends on it.

I run my fingers through his hair, my nails scraping over his scalp, causing him to growl as he slams his lips against mine.

I meet his thrusts, needing that body contact as he slides a hand down my side, and along my thighs. He pushes them apart, spreading me open to him as he continues to slam inside of me.

I'm not sure what to do. I'm letting my body do the answering, following his lead with everything, trusting him to guide me where he needs me, and trusting him to give me what I need.

"Yes," I rasp, as I pull away from the kiss, my head tilting up. He leans down, kissing my neck.

My entire body is covered in a fine sheen of sweat but I don't care. I reach for his lips again, this time kissing him with everything in me.

"Your cunt is fucking greedy for me."

I'm taken aback by his words. Not because they're crude, but because of how turned on they make me. They spur me on, and before I know it, I overpower him, rolling him onto his back once more. My hair drops down, acting like a curtain when I kiss him.

He feels deeper, and I'm getting close.

So fucking close.

"My turn, baby," he orders, and rolls us again.

I stop, locking gazes with him. "Then go harder."

His pupils dilate. "I don't want to hurt you."

"I'm not breakable."

He slams inside me and the picture hanging above the bed shakes before it drops, falling behind the headboard. I laugh, but Drew soon pulls my attention back to him.

Until the banging on the wall starts up.

I guess we're being loud.

We pause, both of us staring at the wall, where the banging came from. "Fuck," he growls.

I grasp his cheeks, pulling his attention back to me. "Fuck me," I demand.

He lifts me up, and my legs tighten around his waist as he carries me over to the other wall, right next to a dresser. My back slams against it and I shiver at the chill running down my spine.

"I've never done it this way before," I admit.

He grins and it's predatory.

"Now I'm definitely in charge," he declares with a promise. "And, babe, by morning, you'll never be able to say that again."

EIGHTEEN

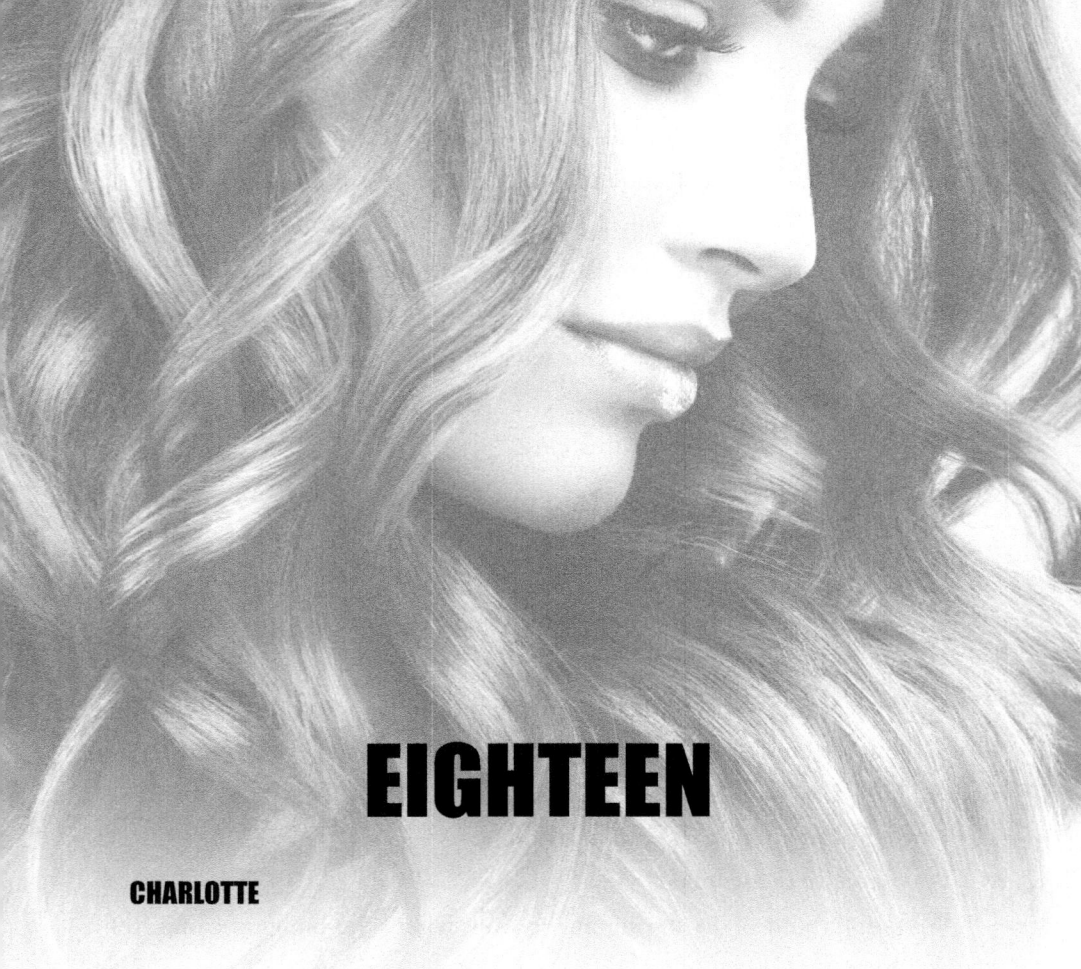

CHARLOTTE

I inwardly groan, rolling onto my stomach and shoving my face into my pillow. My head has a thousand mini hammers swinging at every angle of my brain.

How much did I drink?

I catapult up, rolling off the side of the bed when everything comes rushing back.

I had sex with Drew.

Really good flipping sex with Drew.

"No wonder my vagina feels like it went through a twenty-man orgy last night," I whisper, and it really does feel like it. I don't think there's a position we didn't do, but I'm willing to Google it before boasting about it. My vagina still pulses, twitching like an overused car battery.

I practically threw myself at him. I'm such a hussy.

'My vagina feels happy.'

I slap my forehead, wondering where I come up with this stuff. Half the time I don't even mean to say it, it just comes out. Last night was not sexy at all, not when I consider the shit I blurted out.

He slept with you.

I'm not sure what time it is, but it has to be early. I feel like I've only had an hour's sleep, if that. Every time I thought we were done, he would touch me again, and I'm not sure who pounced on who first, but it always ended the same. Him coming inside of me. He was lucky the hotel catered to everything, so he could have someone purchase condoms for us.

I pull the sheet around me, struggling as I get to my feet. God, my thighs and groin are killing me. I think every muscle in my body aches.

I test that theory when I finally manage to stand without worrying I'll topple over, and stretch my arms up. *Yep, definitely all over.*

My lips feel swollen, still buzzing from kissing him. And boy can he kiss. I smile to myself at the memory. I have never acted like that with anyone and I'm not sure where it came from.

Now I don't have alcohol boosting my confidence, it feels weird, but nonetheless meaningful. It was still the best night I could ever have wished for. Tears gather in my eyes as I think of my mum's words *that night*. She was right. About it all. Scott tarnished what I felt for him. He took so much from me, and he did it without care or remorse. She was right when she told me what it should have been like.

And last night… it was all that and more.

My thighs clench together when I think about what he did with his tongue; what I begged him to do— *loudly*.

My gaze runs over the bed. The sheets are still rumpled from last night's activities, and Drew is nowhere to be seen. I'm not going to lie, it hurts that he isn't here, even if some of the night is a blur.

Maybe I did push him into it.

Tears spill down my cheeks as I reach for my dress near the end of the bed, before pulling it on and zipping it. I sniffle, searching for my knickers, looking everywhere and not spotting them until I bend down to look under the bed.

Just as the door opens.

I freeze, my fingers on the thin scrap of material.

"Fuck!" Drew growls, and I know he's seeing everything.

And I mean *everything*.

I close my eyes, inwardly groaning. He's probably scared I'm throwing myself at him again. And if he didn't think it before, he most certainly does now.

"I can't have any more sex," I blurt out, getting to my feet as I dry my cheeks. I trip when trying to get my foot into the knickers and groan when I fall onto the bed. "My vagina is really sore right now. If it could speak, it would weep. With tears of joy, or tears of fear, I don't know. But it would weep. But not like I've got a transmitted disease, weep."

He rears back, his eyebrows shooting to his hairline. "I was going to remind you that before we left last night you accepted breakfast with my family, so I wanted to give you these," he explains, handing me a bag. "It's some fresh clothes and toiletries."

My shoulders sag. I forgot about the invitation Eloise extended to Drew. When his mum overheard, she demanded his attendance and I agreed, even though it wasn't extended *to me*. "I'm sorry."

He tenses, gazing right into my soul. "Why would you be sorry?"

I drop the bag onto the bed next to me. "I threw myself at you and you were probably scared. I can be a little much when I'm drunk—" He chuckles, and I pause, butt-hurt he'd make fun of this. It's serious. "This isn't funny," I whisper.

He steps forward, sliding my hair over my shoulder. "No, it's not. What it was, was a fantastic fucking night. You didn't force me into anything, I swear it to you," he tells me, before pausing, his gaze running over my face. "Are *you* okay? I know you had a drink and I—"

My cheeks burn as I say, "It was better than I ever imagined."

"You imagined it?"

I shove his chest lightly. "You know what I mean."

"Seriously though, are you okay?"

I nod and busy myself looking anywhere but at him. "I really am."

"Good," he murmurs. "Go get showered. I said we'd be down there in twenty."

My eyes widen. "Crap."

I race to the bathroom but then double back, snatching the bag off the bed. "You could have said that before."

He chuckles, and I feel him watching my arse as I run back to the bathroom. "What fun would that have been?"

I snort, closing the door behind me before taking a breather.

I had sex.

Really great sex.

A massive grin spreads across my face and a giddy feeling swirls in the pit of my stomach. Sex had been something I couldn't wait to experience from the time I really understood what it meant. Romance books made it sound easy, pleasurable, and then Scott happened. With Drew, it was like he sparked my soul. Last night was what I had always dreamed about, what it should have always been.

Now I know what a loving touch feels like, I'll never make the same mistake again.

I'm not even troubled over the fact it was potentially a one-night stand. If anything, it only heightens the experience, makes it more memorable for me. Without Drew, without the connection I felt with him last night, Scott might have been the only touch I knew or remembered, so I'll always be grateful to him.

So will my vagina.

To KEEP UP pretences, Drew holds my hand as we head into the large dining room. This isn't the same room we were in last night, but it's just as big. And instead of purples and blues, it's neutral, white and beige.

As we reach the table where his immediate family are, my fingers clench around his hand and I come to a stop.

Oh no.

Oh, no, no, no.

He stops when our linked hands pull taut and turns back to me, his eyebrow raised. "Everything okay?"

I shake my head. "It's really not."

His forehead creases with worry. "What's wrong?"

I draw closer to him, leaning in. "We played a trick on your mum last night."

Realisation dawns on his expression before he bursts out laughing. "I completely forgot about it."

"Did you see her this morning?"

"No, only my step-dad, who messaged me."

"So, you don't even know if she knows it was us," I ramble. "She already hates me."

"Don't get yourself worked up. She treated you like shit last night. She deserved everything we did."

I whimper. "What *I* did."

He continues to laugh. "Stop worrying."

I can't help it. My heart is already pounding. I'll never understand why I get like that when I've had a drink. My dad blames the red in my hair, and my mum blames it on the fact I'm a Carter.

"I'm never drinking again," I complain.

His lips twitch. "Charlotte."

"No, that's a lie. I'll definitely drink again but I'll limit myself."

"Charlotte—"

"Okay, that was a lie too," I groan. "Once I've had one, I always want another, especially if it's a fruity drink."

"Charlotte, there's someone behind you who wants to get past," Drew blurts out, his lips struggling to stay firm.

I squeal, picturing every horror movie I have ever seen and spin around, clipping the tray the guy is holding in the process. Hot tea spills all down his shirt. "I'm so sorry."

Drew pulls me back when I go to help. The waiter looks annoyed, but not angry. "It's fine. Why don't you take a seat and move out of the way?"

I nod, thinking that's a perfect idea. "I really am sorry."

Drew's body shakes beside me. "You continue to surprise me."

His family spot us, but it's his mother I can't look away from, her expression pinched, displeased. "Good of you two to join us."

"Mother, you're looking a little tired. Not much sleep?" Drew comments as he pulls the chair out for me.

I whimper when I take a seat, Drew following and taking the one beside me. I glance at his mum. She does look really tired. Drew's step-dad sighs. "Please don't get her started again."

"Started again?" Grace squeals. "There was a dead body in our bed, Wesley. A body."

"It wasn't real, just as the manager confirmed. And the police."

His mum turns to her son. "This hotel will not be getting a tip from us."

"What happened?"

"We aren't exactly sure," Wesley replies.

His mother has no qualms about answering. "I'll tell you what happened. This place is haunted, or they hire lowlife's to make the beds. I nearly had a heart attack when I walked into our suite."

"Because of the body?" Drew asks, and I feel more than see him struggling not to laugh.

I inwardly groan, wishing he'd drop the conversation. I already feel bad enough. Or at least, a tiny bit.

A waiter pours me a glass of orange juice and I swear I whimper at the sight of the yummy goodness.

"No, because the pictures were all over the place. The place was haunted, son. Haunted. Can you believe that?"

"Not really, no," he replies, making me choke on the juice I had just taken a sip of.

Grace's eyebrows shoot up. "It is. And that is not even the worse of what happened."

"Is this about the dead body now?"

"No. Whoever they let into our room, stole our champagne. A nine-hundred-pound bottle."

I gape, my eyes watering. Who pays that for a bottle of champagne? It was good, but not *that* good.

"Grace, let's not bore them with the details," Wesley orders.

"Bore them? Bore them?" She screeches. "I nearly died, Wesley."

"Died?" I ask, speaking up for the first time.

Her lip curls at the sound of my voice, but she answers anyway. "My heart stopped when I saw the body. It took the paramedics to bring me back."

"No, she didn't," Wesley comments, letting out an exasperated sigh. "She just had a scare and it brought on a panic attack of sorts."

I whimper, tears gathering in my eyes. "That is awful. Who would do such a thing? I'm so sorry this has happened to you. Are you okay?"

Drew ducks his head, his shoulders shaking as he silently laughs. "Who *would* do such a thing?"

My cheeks heat when the answer hits me. "Oh no," I whisper before kicking him under the table. I completely forgot for a moment. His amusement is not helping. "Grace, I'm so sorry you had a bad experience. Is there anything we can do?"

She's taken off guard by my kindness. I can see it in the way she watches me warily.

It's Wesley who answers. "She's being overdramatic. It was a bunch of pillows wrapped in a spare bedsheet."

Grace's jaw tightens and her hand flies to her chest. "It took years off my life. I thought someone was well and truly dead in our bed, Wesley. How can you not care about that, or about the stress it caused me? I was scared to death. This hotel has a lot to answer for."

My shoulders shake as I duck my head, covering up the tears that are flowing down my cheeks. I hadn't meant for her to react so badly or be that scared. I don't know what I was thinking.

And she nearly died.

"Sweetie, are you okay?" Wesley asks and I look up, wiping away the tears as I struggle to hold back my sobs.

When I notice his question is being addressed to me, my breath hitches. "I'm just so sorry that happened to you."

"Are you making fun of my mother?" Natalie snidely demands, speaking up for the first time.

I sniffle. "No, I'm really not."

Drew wraps his arm around the back of my chair, rubbing my shoulder blades. I freeze, visions of his teeth nipping me there clouding my mind.

He pumps hard inside of me, his teeth grazing my shoulder. "You want it harder?"

"Charlotte," he calls out, shaking me from my thoughts and the dirty things he did to me after I said yes.

"Sorry, what?"

"You okay?" he asks, searching my gaze.

I nod. "Yeah," I lie, then lean in close to him. "She's really going to hate me if she finds out."

"She won't," he whispers back. "It was just a little fun."

For the rest of the breakfast, I stay silent yet watchful, making sure my actions haven't completely traumatised his mother. Pranks aren't for everyone.

By the time breakfast has finished, the manager has come over and assured us our breakfast isn't being charged to our rooms, which is a good thing since the prices are extremely high. I could go shopping for a week's worth of food for the amount they charge for a full English breakfast.

When it's time to leave, it's only Wesley, Alison and her fiancé who offer me a goodbye. I don't take it to heart. I'm used to this kind of treatment.

We're nearly back at my place, and the closer we get, the sicker I feel. There's a heavy pit in my stomach and it rolls, the unease eating away at me.

Neither of us have brought up what happened last night, not what it meant or what it meant between *us*. It's the elephant in the car that no one wants stamping all over them.

I don't think I'll be able to give him answers, even if he does question me.

I'm not sure what it meant, I only know what it meant *to me*, and that was a great deal. He gave me something I never thought I'd get. But I'm not sure where we stand now and that kind of scares me. I like him. I like him a lot. I love our sessions, even if we have only had two, and I love talking to him. For someone larger than life, and for someone so young, he's quite perceptive and has a lot of things to say. Things I enjoy hearing.

After pulling into my road, he drives up to my house and parks on the drive. He switches off the car and I nervously fiddle with the handles of the bag. "Thank you for such a great night," I announce.

His pupils dilate and his eyes darken, smouldering with that intense burn. "It should be me thanking you." He pauses, his lips parting as if he wants to continue, but then decides not to.

My shoulders slump. He isn't going to bring it up and I don't have the courage. Or maybe I just don't want to hear the answer.

I unclip my belt before pushing the door open. I slide my legs out before stopping, turning back to him. "Can I ask you something?"

Interest piqued, he nods. "Anything."

"Last night…" I close my eyes, and then shake the dark thoughts threatening to loom over me. When I open them, his expression is still as intense as ever and a shiver races down my spine.

"What about last night?"

"Can I count that as my first time?" I whisper, my fingers tightening around the handle of the bag.

The look he gives me has my clit pulsing and my heart racing.

"Of course," he hoarsely replies.

I lean over the handbrake and press a kiss to his cheek. "Thank you. And for last night. See you soon, Drew."

"You too," he whispers as I get out, slamming the door behind me. I watch him drive away before heading inside, a big smile on my face.

NINETEEN

CHARLOTTE

FINGERS TIGHTEN AROUND MY WRISTS, pinning them above my head as he pumps inside of me.

The sound of our skin slapping together, our heavy breathing, and the moans and groans… it's thrilling.

"Harder," I beg, sliding my fingers down his broad, muscled back.

His lips, feather light, press against the sensitive area on my neck, and an electrical pulse runs over my body.

"Earth to Charlotte," Rose says, clicking her fingers in my face.

My cheeks immediately heat as I pull myself out of my mind and the dirty images that have been filtering through since Drew dropped me off yesterday morning.

"Sorry," I reply absently, my thoughts drifting back to the night in question once more. I was bent over the end of the bed, and Drew's fingers were digging into my hips while he powered inside of me.

I think I whimper.

"Are you okay?"

I blink, reaching for the coffee mug to distract me, and grimace. "I'm sorry, Rose. I didn't get much sleep last night. It's good to see you."

And I didn't sleep much. Because I was too busy researching sexual positions to see which ones we hadn't done. I fell asleep with a list in one hand and a book in the other. But I wanted to know if Drew was right and that I'd never say, 'I've never done that before' again. He was right and wrong. The positions left were a little unorthodox but I couldn't deny I was curious to see if it was possible to do them. And then there's the argument about location.

Rose pulls a chair out across from me before taking a seat. "It's good to see you. How have you been?"

"I'm doing okay."

"I heard something happened between you and your ex. Was his name Scott?"

My breath hitches at hearing his name. "Who told you about Scott?"

"I overheard the receptionist and another woman."

I blanch at that, uncomfortable with members of staff talking about me, especially with the thought of them talking to a family member of mine. I don't want people knowing.

"He wasn't who I thought he was," I admit.

"They never are."

I force out a laugh. "Yeah, I guess."

I don't think that. With Drew, he is who he is and he gives no fudges. It's one of the things I like about him. He doesn't pretend to be anyone other than who he is.

"You don't have to talk about it with me but I am here if you need to. Sometimes speaking to someone who isn't family does the world of good. I mean, it must not be good to have family members judging you, or have that feeling that you've disappointed them."

Her words hit close to home. I don't think my family are judging me per se. I know they love me too much and they care. But sometimes when one would say, they knew he was wrong for me, or that I have changed, I do feel judged. Their words do impact me and make me feel low.

I duck my head because I do feel like I've disappointed them. It's like she's pushed herself into my thoughts and read my insecurities out loud.

"He hurt me," I admit on a whisper.

"Did that fucker cheat?"

I snort, because it wasn't me he cheated on, it was his wife. "It wasn't me he was cheating on, it was his poor wife. I didn't even know until the night I slept with him for the first time."

Her eyes widen. "You are shitting me. What a fucking arsehole. What did the wife say?" she rants. "And at least it wasn't your virginity. How fucking shitty would that be, having a guy do that to you? I mean, how would you be able to move on and trust after that? And his wife, I wonder how she is." When I don't say anything, her eyebrows shoot up. "You were a virgin?"

I glance around the mostly empty library. "I was, yes," I whisper. "And I don't know anything about his wife. The only reason I found out is because I picked up his phone and saw a message." Tears gather in my eyes. "They had kids. Those poor kids."

"She doesn't need your pity," she tells me. "She needs to be rid of that husband of hers. Does she know?"

I shrug. "I don't know. He hurt me that night, really bad, and the police are looking for him."

"What the heck? He ran away like a coward?"

I lower my eyes to my cup of tea. "He never told me his real name. He lied about that too. Or at least his last name is a lie."

"Oh, honey, I'm so sorry this has happened to you."

Tears gather in my eyes. "I just feel like a fool."

"Be glad you aren't the wife."

"I know. She has it worse than me. I just keep thinking I'm the reason they might have broken up. Or maybe she doesn't know. I have no clue. The police are still looking for him."

"Did he hurt you before then?"

"He didn't just hurt me," I admit, feeling ashamed. But after my night with Drew, I have come to terms with the fact that what he did was wrong. Whether or not I said yes from the start, that I was the one who suggested it, I still said no. My night with Drew opened my eyes. Whenever I asked him to slow down, he did. If I asked him to go faster, he did. Not once during our time together did I ever think he'd take advantage or carry on if I wasn't comfortable. I can't say I would have felt the same if it had been someone else, and it kind of scares me to wonder what that means.

"What did he do?"

"I asked him to stop, and he didn't," I tell her, before straightening in my seat. "It's not something I feel comfortable talking about. I'm still conflicted over the whole thing. On one hand, I know what he did is sexual assault, yet on the other, I feel like I asked for it."

"Did you?" she asks, and my mouth gapes open. She reaches forward, taking my hand. "That came out wrong. I just meant, was you the one who instigated it?"

I nod. "Yes."

"Oh, honey."

I can't meet her gaze. "It's fine. I don't want to think about it. Hopefully the police will figure out who he is."

"Or his wife. I can't believe she didn't have any clue that her husband was cheating. I mean, could you be any dumber?"

I know her dig is at the wife and she's trying to be friendly and supportive, but I feel the dig in my soul, as I too didn't have a clue. I didn't pick up on the red flags, and not just about him being married but all the others. He had a way of putting me down but praising me in the same sentence. Mum said he was gaslighting me, which is how he manipulated me into sex. I have a lot to come to terms with but that… I'm not quite ready to go there.

Seeing Madison racing toward me, I'm glad for the interruption. "Hey, what are you doing here?"

Out of breath, she takes the seat next to me, barely taking notice of Rose. "I've been to or called every florist in this area, even ones further out. Not one has sold those flowers in the past forty days, either that or they are refusing to give me the information we need. But we both know Uncle Liam will get that information eventually."

"What does that mean if it's not one of them?"

"That this person lives further away or is really good at hiding their tracks."

"What's going on?" Rose asks.

It's Madison who answers. "Some creep is sending her flowers with creepy-arse poems and we're trying to figure out who."

"I bet it's your ex," Rose replies, her eyes wide. "What a dickhead."

"I don't know. It doesn't scream male to me. I reckon it's someone else."

"Who?"

Madison shrugs. "Fuck knows, but I'm making it my mission to find out."

"Yo, Charlotte," Gabby yells.

Madison turns, her mouth gaping open. "Holy hotness."

I chuckle at her bluntness. "You've not met Gabby, Harriet, Olivia or Emily before, have you?"

"Not yet but I've heard so much about them," she replies.

"We have news," Harriet announces when she reaches us.

"Big news," Emily adds, her expression animated.

"Dude, you've had sex," Gabby blurts out before turning to Madison. "And you're hot."

"Thank you," Madison answers, before she snaps her attention to me as my cheeks redden.

"No, I haven't," I deny.

"Oh my God, you're lying," Madison blurts out. "What the fuck?"

"I haven't," I lie once more, my hands fidgeting under the table.

Gabby snorts, taking a seat next to Rose. "I can smell it on you."

I sniff my shoulder, smelling nothing but my Jimmy Choo perfume.

"You have that look about you," Olivia comments.

Madison reaches for my hand, clasping it in hers under the table. "Charlotte, why didn't you tell me? Are you sure that was a good idea after…"

A lone tear trickles down my cheek. "It was everything I ever wanted it to be," I whisper.

"Please tell me it was dirty," Emily declares, wiggling her eyebrows.

I chuckle, but don't pull my attention away from Madison. "Please understand and don't think I'm bad or a slut." I close my eyes and take a moment before continuing. "I needed to know it wasn't always going to be like that night. It felt right."

"I'd never slut shame you at all. I just worry about you. I love you, Charlotte, and I say this as respectfully and with as much love as I can; but you let people walk all over you. You're too nice for your own good and I don't want to see that happen again."

"We'll skin him alive if anyone tries," Harriet promises her.

Madison smiles. "Thank you. I'm glad she has good friends."

"And family," I add, giving her a pointed look.

"I'm Madison, her cousin."

"Oh, another family member," Gabby declares excitedly, before running off introductions.

Once done, Madison turns to me, exhaling heavily. "It was special?"

I smile, seeing the resolve in her eyes. "It was the best night of my life."

She screams suddenly, her hands and arms flapping around. "Oh my God, oh my God, oh my God."

"What?" I ask, chuckling at her antics.

"Oh my God," she groans, her expression filled with horror.

"What?" I demand.

"You had sex with the giant and Landon is going to kill him."

"The giant?" Emily asks, leaning forward.

"Holy fuck, the giant," Harriet yells.

"Way to go, Charlotte."

"Not helping," I groan.

"Who's the giant?" Rose asks.

"The hottest guy you'll ever meet. I would turn straight just to ride his pony," Gabby answers, grinning like a cat who got the cream.

"Madison, you can't tell anyone. No one, I mean it."

"You tell your mum everything," she reminds me.

I glance down at our joined hands. "And I'll tell her about this. I want to share how good it was and tell her she was right about everything, and that I should have waited longer. I should have waited for Drew. I'm worried she'll be disappointed in me again."

"Charlie, it's not about waiting. He should never have done that to you," she tells me, her voice soft. "And your mum could never be disappointed in you. She'll be happy for you."

"I hope so."

"When are you next seeing him?" she asks as everyone sits down to listen.

"Thursday."

She grins. "Where's he taking you?"

My brows pull together. "The gym."

"The gym? What a fucking cheapskate. He couldn't take you out for dinner?"

I giggle at her anger. "It's not a date."

"Then when is he taking you out on a date?"

"It's not like that," I tell her, not meeting her gaze. "I don't know what's going on, and before you begin to rant, he never made any promises. I didn't go into it expecting them either. Am I embarrassed I waited to lose my virginity and ended up being with the wrong person, and then in a space of a month and a bit, ended up sleeping with another man so quickly?" I take a lungful of air. "Yes. Am I ashamed? No. Because it meant a lot to me, Madison. If this Scott business has taught me anything, it's that love can sometimes come easy, but having someone who meets your needs and wants, who respects you— it's rare. He was nothing but a gentleman."

She leans forward, pulling me in for a hug. "That's all I care about, but if he hurts you, tall or not, I'll kill him."

"Always so blood thirsty," I tease.

"You know it," she fires back, before glancing down at her watch. "I need to go back to work, but this conversation isn't over. I want all the details."

"Can we be there?" Gabby sulks. "I'd like to hear this too."

"You can tell me why you are here," I warn her, before kissing Madison on the cheek. "I'll call you later."

"I'll message you once I've spoken to Uncle Liam."

"Okay, and thank you for the help and not telling the others."

She gets up, her expression wary. "But you do know you need to tell them. Not all of it, not about you know who— you're a grown woman, after all— but the rest… You know what they're like when we keep things from them."

"I know and I will. I'd just really like to speak to Mum first. She's popping round later."

"It was nice to meet you all," she tells them after giving me a nod.

Once she leaves, I turn to the girls. "What's this big news?"

"Our friend, Amber, who used to work with us, got in touch after we put feelers out about Scott."

I sit up, my gut clenching. "What did she say?"

"She knew him and it was bad. We said we'd wait to hear the rest with you if she was okay with it. We weren't sure if you had questions," Harriet admits.

"I do. A lot," I reply. "Does she know where he is?"

Harriet glances away, grimacing. "No, it was the first thing we asked but she said she might know who does."

"Who would that be?"

"His wife," she answers.

I slump back in the chair and bite my lip. "What if she doesn't know? How do you tell a woman her husband cheated and assaulted another woman?"

"Why should her feelings be worth more than yours? Your cousin is right, you are too nice for your own good. You aren't going there to brag to her but rather going there as another woman wanting justice for what was done to you," Olivia comments.

"When does she want to meet us?" I ask, not expanding on her comment. I can't. I might be gullible, naive, but I'd never let the wrong actions of others dictate who I am. I'll always be kind and give people the benefit of the doubt. If everyone was distrusting, or uncaring, there would be a lot of suffering in the world.

"She has Wednesday off. She has an optician's appointment in the morning but can meet us midday if you're free?"

"I'll make myself free," I assure her. "Did she say anything else?"

"Just that things happened that had her leaving her job and going elsewhere. She lives in Lindal now."

"Oh my gosh," I whisper, hoping it's not as bad as I'm imagining. "Are you sure it's Scott?"

Harriet nods. "Yes. Same name, same MO, and thinking on it after we spoke with her, you kind of look the same too."

"Are you going to come?" Gabby asks. "We can make a road trip out of it."

"You guys have done enough already. You don't need to take time away from home for me."

"We want to be there," Emily assures me. "We want this bastard caught. What he did is sick and morally wrong."

"Thank you," I tell them, giving them a watery smile.

Rose places her hands on the table. "Now you can tell us about this new guy. What's he like?"

I roll my eyes, and give them a run-down of that night, keeping most things private.

They don't get to know everything. Some things are meant to remain between Drew and I.

By the time I'm done, Gabby stands. "I have to go. I've got a date with my clit stimulator."

Harriet bursts out laughing before turning to me. "We do need to go but, Charlotte, I'm seriously fucking happy for you."

"It's my cue to leave too," Rose announces, also smiling. "But the girls are right. You deserve your happy ever after."

"See you Wednesday," Olivia tells me.

As Emily picks her things up, she looks at me. "You doing anything else this afternoon?"

"I'm actually leaving soon. I'm in the mood to make cupcakes."

She busies herself searching through her bag, looking awfully hard for something. "Did you lose something?"

"Just my keys," she squeaks, before straightening. "Well, thank you for a great chat."

I smile. "Thank you for visiting."

"See you soon," Rose tells me.

"See you," I reply, then give the rest of the girls a hug before following them to the front. Once they leave, I turn to Marlene. "If you need me, call me."

With that, I grab my stuff out of the office and head home. I have cupcakes to bake, and I need to rehearse what I'm going to say to Mum that doesn't make me sound like a slut.

TWENTY

CHARLOTTE

Stepping back from the counter, I take in all the yummy goodness covering my worktops. Enveloped in an aura of freshly baked scones, I'm in heaven. Yet, after years of experience, I know they won't taste as good as they look. Even the cupcakes are teasing me. They're made with happiness, that is all that matters. In fact, I don't even remember baking them for the first time in my life. My thoughts were too consumed with Drew, and once I snapped to the present, they were ready to go in the oven. That has never happened to me before. Normally I'm so into my own head, I pick and calculate every detail going into what I'm baking. By the end of it, my muscles are knotted, but right now, I feel relaxed, free.

Katnip swats at my ankle and I bend down, picking her up before hugging her to my chest. "Who's a good kitty."

Hiss.

"But you are so beautiful. Why do you continue to be so grumpy?"

Hiss.

I sigh, heading over to her bowl. "It's okay. One day, Katnip. One day."

The doorbell rings and a broad smile crosses my face.

Mum.

I'm dreading the conversation we need to have but Madison was right earlier. I do tell her everything. She's my best friend, my confidant. And she always knows what to say whether I want to hear it or not. And I miss her.

Gently lowering Katnip to the floor, I leave her to feast on her food as I head to the door.

Unlocking it, I pull it open. "Mum, you had a good day?"

"I have. Did you?" she asks, pulling off her coat.

"It's, um, been eventful."

"Sounds ominous," she mutters as she follows me into the kitchen. "I can't stay long tonight. I'd like to get back to your father."

I turn back to her after flicking the kettle on. My dad has a big heart, but his job as a social worker takes its toll on him. Some days are better than others. "Did he have another bad case?"

She nods as she goes to make a fuss of Katnip, but thinks better of it when she hisses out, going to swat her. "Yeah. He can't go into detail but it's bad. It's getting to him."

"Mum, go home. You don't need to be here. Dad needs you."

She forces a smile and I know it's for my benefit. "I want to speak to my girl without the men in our lives interrupting us."

I hand her a cup of tea before taking a seat next to her. "I've missed you too."

"If you ever want to come home, you and Katnip are welcome."

"Dad put her in a cupboard."

"That was your uncle Max," Mum amends, watching me closely. "Something's different with you."

I blush, ducking my head. "I—"

"And you baked," she states, utterly surprised.

I hadn't told her about the cake I baked Drew. She knew why I had stopped baking. I had shared that knowledge with her. But I baked Drew's without really thinking about it. It was a knee-jerk reaction from years of baking for people. Once I tried to bake after, I couldn't bring myself to do it. And just like before Drew's cake, I didn't find joy in it anymore. My mind reverted back to Scott's cruel words about how disgusting they were and it was like he was standing right next to me, judging me. So, I stopped baking.

"Yeah," I reply, glancing down.

She grabs my hand, squeezing. "I'm glad. I was beginning to worry. I know how much you love doing it. But that's not what's different. I can't quite put my finger on it."

"Are you ashamed of me?" I blurt out.

Her eyebrows shoot up and her eyes widen. "What? No, never. What has brought that on?"

I play with the handle of my mug. "Because I feel like I've let you down. No, I know I have and all this must be bringing up bad memories for you."

"God, Charlotte, no. Not at all. You're my daughter and I love you. You are all that concerns me. What happened was not your fault."

"Mum," I whisper, her distraught expression tearing at my heart.

She wipes away a tear, clearing her throat. "I should have protected you better."

"Mum," I plead, but she isn't listening, pulled under by her own nightmare.

"I shielded you from the world, kept the dangers and all the bad things away from you. Because I wanted you to be a child. I didn't want you to be scared about the simple things in life. But I was wrong. I should have given you the chance to experience life differently."

"Mum, I'm not stupid. I know what is out there; just because I choose to ignore it and only focus on the positive and the good in the world, it doesn't make it your fault. Too many people focus on the negative. They leave negative reviews but never positive. They read bad press but never the good. They comment on negative statuses on Facebook, but never praise the positive. I choose to see the positive, Mum. Me. That has nothing to do with our upbringing."

"But I—"

"If you truly believe that then you believe he hurt me because I didn't have the experience, which in turn means I deserved it," I rush out, needing her to really hear me. This isn't her fault either.

She pales, a sob hitching from her throat. "No. I've never once thought that. Oh God."

I reach for her hand, squeezing it. "I know that, Mum, and I know what you were trying to say to me."

She cups my face, wiping a tear that slides down my cheek with her thumb. "I'm sorry. This happened to you, not me. I just hate that you went through it."

"I know you do," I whisper. I don't like hearing the pain in her voice. "There are some other things I need to talk to you about, and I'd like it if you kept some of it between us."

Her brows pull together. "Please tell me he hasn't contacted you."

"No," I rush out, assuring her. "Can you remember the flowers I received that night?"

Her lips pinch together. "The ones me and your father think Scott sent himself?"

I nod. "I've received more, along with a creepy note, and looking back, I think the first one was the same. I just read it wrong."

"Charlotte, why didn't you say anything before?" she demands, unable to remain calm. "What did it say? Are you okay? Did they threaten you?"

I hold my hands up. "No, they didn't threaten me. I don't think," I explain. "I'm telling you now. I don't know who's sending them or why but Madison is helping me locate the person who purchased them. And please, stop worrying. It's nothing we can't handle."

"Honey, you need to take this to the police. What if he's still around? What if it's someone who wants to hurt you?"

A chill runs down my spine. "Mum."

She sinks back into her chair. "I'm sorry. I shouldn't have said that."

"Madison doesn't believe it's him. She doesn't think they are from *any* male."

"It doesn't make sense."

"I know. We can't make sense of it either."

"You will tell me if anything happens again, won't you? I know you're a grown woman, but please, give your mother peace of mind. I hate that this might guilt trip you, but I don't sleep much during the night. I can't. I'm petrified you'll be hurt again."

I pull her in for a hug because she's seriously the best mum in the world. "I love you and I promise I'll tell you. This was something I couldn't explain over the phone."

"Is there anything else?"

I bite my lip. "Don't go crazy but I think we might have a lead on Scott." I run over everything the girls said to me and our plan. By the time I'm finished, Mum is pale, concern written all over her face.

"I don't like this. I know I can't force you, but I think you should go to the police with this information. Please."

"I'm not convinced it's the same person they are talking about. If it is, I'll go to the police. Pinkie promise."

"I know you said I need to keep this between us, but your father needs to know about this. Charlotte, you can't be lax with your safety."

There's nothing worse than being scolded by your mother. "I'm sorry. I didn't know there was anything to tell until today, otherwise I would have said something sooner."

She sighs, running her fingers through her thick red hair. "I will be telling your father and you can't expect him to keep it quiet."

"That wasn't the part I wanted you to keep to yourself," I tell her, fiddling with the rip in my jeans.

She tilts my chin up. "What did you want to tell me?"

This is harder than I thought it was going to be. I scrape the chair back, getting up. "Just give me a minute."

She gulps. "Oh God."

I want to share what happened. I want her to know. But to put it into words without the worry of her judging me before she knows the full story… yeah, I don't know how to do that.

I begin to pace. "I have something important to share, something that means a lot to me, and I want you to remain unbiased," I ramble.

"Charlotte, I say this with respect, but you're scaring me, so get talking."

I stop at the counter, facing her. "I don't want anyone else to know. I can't have people twisting or cheapening what I'm about to tell you. It wasn't like that. I swear to you, it wasn't like that."

"Honey, calm down."

"I had sex with Drew the giant and I liked it!" I groan, slapping my forehead. "That came out *so* wrong."

Her silence has my heart racing. She continues to watch me, her lips parted.

"I promise I'm not a slut. It just happened. I wanted it to happen and it was the best night of my life," I assure her. "It was how it was always meant to be."

Silence.

I begin to pace once again, continuing to ramble. "It's not that I want to keep it a secret, I just don't want people judging me. What I said earlier? I meant every word. I don't want people to cheapen what happened, or make Drew think he was in the wrong. He wasn't. He understands more than most what it meant to me."

Silence.

"And who knew other positions could be so exciting."

"Stop!" Mum bursts out, her cheeks flaming scarlet. "Charlotte, I—"

"It wasn't a mistake, Mum. It wasn't anything more than it was, but I think something inside of me was seeking that touch, that connection."

"And he didn't hurt you?"

I smile, taking the seat next to her. "No, Mum. He was a gentleman. I know this was something I never wanted to do. I wanted a life partner, a family. But it really meant a lot to me."

"Sweetie."

"He erased it, Mum," I choke out. "He opened my eyes to everything you had been telling me. What Scott did was wrong. It wasn't that he misheard me, or he was carried away. It wasn't a case of terrible sex. *He knew*. He knew the moment I first said no that he should stop and he didn't. Drew…" I sigh, closing my eyes. "He couldn't have made it more special. We experienced something beautiful and I will not be ashamed of that."

"I'm not going to lie and say I'm not surprised. I am. But I'm also going to trust that you know what you want."

"It's what I wanted."

A smile spreads across her face. "Then when are you next seeing him?"

I can tell she means romantically and not platonically. "I'm not sure it was more than it was."

Her lips tighten. "What did he say?"

I reach for a cupcake and tear it in half. "I didn't ask."

"You didn't ask?"

"No."

"Why?"

"Because I'm scared it didn't mean the same for him."

Her expression softens. "It's you, how could it not."

"I'm not going to rush or force anything anymore. I'm going to let things happen naturally."

"The best thing to ever happen to me was your father. You'll get that, Charlie. I promise."

I shove the cupcake into my mouth, utterly surprised by the taste exploding on my tongue. I begin to choke, and Mum's eyes widen.

"Another mistake?"

I finish chewing and hold up the other half. "Try it."

"I had a big dinner. I'm good."

I roll my eyes and shove the cupcake into her mouth. "Good?"

Her eyes widen, her lips straightening as a pleasantly surprised expression washes over her face. "Oh my gosh," she grumbles around the mouthful of food. "This is so good."

I take another in case it's a fluke, and I'm happy to find it's just as good as the first. "So good," I moan.

"Did you make these?"

I nod. "I did."

"What recipe did you use? I'll have to make these for your father."

My lips turn down. "I don't remember."

"You don't remember?"

I shake my head. "No. I was, um, a little inside my head."

She grins, taking another cupcake. "You were thinking about Drew?"

Busted.

I nod. "Take some with you. I'll figure it out again."

Mum hesitates. "Just one. We can snack on the rest," she tells me, making me giggle. Her eyes scan the other counter. "Are those scones?"

"Yep," I answer absently before diving off my chair, wondering if they too are just as good.

And boy are they.

DROPPING DOWN ON my bed, I reach for the cat brush I left on the side last night and pull Katnip onto my lap. I haven't even pulled the brush through her thick fur before she starts moaning like a banshee. It's cute. It's a mix between a banshee and a grumpy old lady.

"You are so adorable," I coo.

Her nails claw into my chest as she tries to escape. I grimace at the sting, feeling my skin tear under my pyjama top. I comb through her hair, ignoring her cries to be free and focus on the new drama series I've got playing on Netflix.

My phone beeps, alerting me of a text message, and I cease brushing Katnip to look at the screen. I drop her to the bed when I see Drew's name.

My stomach rolls over with a nervous flutter.

Drew: So… Alison messaged me. The hotel got back to them with the footage of the room and she knows it was us.

I bite my lip, my heart racing.

Charlotte: Oh no. Has she told your mum? I will take FULL responsibility.

I chew on my thumbnail as I wait for him to reply. Why, oh why, did I have to drink at the engagement party. I'm a different person with alcohol coursing through my system. And I'm never the same person the day after.

Drew: I told her I'd say the worst thing you can say at a wedding while they are in the middle of their vows.

I let out a surprised giggle.

Charlotte: What is the worst thing you can say at a wedding?

Drew: She didn't even ask because she probably imagined the worst. I'd say the worst is: "I object."

Charlotte: Coming from her brother, that would be bad.

Drew: What about you? What would be the worst thing said to you at your wedding?

Charlotte: If someone gives my uncle Max a mic to give a speech.

Drew: What would he say?

Charlotte: What wouldn't he say should be the question. He's kind of, um… eccentric.

Drew: I've met your uncle. That is one way to describe him.

Drew: How is your head today?

I shift, getting more comfortable on the bed. I can't believe he's messaging me outside of our little deal and him teaching me self-defence.

I don't want to get my hopes up, but well… my hopes are up. Does it mean something? I'm not sure.

Charlotte: My head's fantastic. Good even. The best.

There's a huge grin on my face, even if I'm not entirely sure why he's asking about my head.

Was there something wrong with my head the last time we saw each other?

Drew: No lingering hangover?

Charlotte: Oh, hangover… no, I was good once we got coffee. What about you?

Drew: I never get hangovers.

Charlotte: How has your sister taken what we did to your mum?

Drew: She finds it funny. She just messaged me. She said she's told Mum they lost the footage and now Mum thinks it's some conspiracy.

I bite my lip to stop myself from laughing. I feel awful we put his mum through that.

Charlotte: I'll send her flowers as an apology. She won't even know they are from me.

Drew: She deserves to be shaken up once in a while, and no one was actually hurt. She was being dramatic.

Charlotte: I hope so.

When he doesn't reply after a minute or so, I panic about what to say. I'm not ready to end the conversation.

I grab a bag of sweets out of my drawer, and reach for one. The sour tang of Haribo explodes on my tongue.

Charlotte: Are you still okay for Thursday?

I chew my lip as the three dots appear on the right side of the message, and my stomach flutters.

Drew: Can't wait.

Charlotte: Me either.

Drew: See you then, gorgeous.

Gorgeous.

He called me gorgeous.

I flop back against my pillow, letting out a giggle. From years of advice, I know not to message him back. Hayden would kill me if she found out I did.

Instead, I read over the messages again, unable to keep the smile off my face.

TWENTY-ONE

CHARLOTTE

Emily: We are on our way.
Charlotte: See you soon.
Emily: You better not be stressing. It's all going to be okay.

It really isn't. Marlene hadn't shown up for work this morning and she isn't answering her phone. She forgot her work hours once before but she never ignored my phone calls on those days.

I called Rita to come in and fill in for us, but I can't get rid of the sinking feeling in my stomach that something is wrong.

We had a lot of activity in here yesterday. First a birthday party and then my family showed up, demanding to try my cupcakes. But I had already shared them with some of the guests before they arrived.

They got into it with Marlene when she wouldn't stay to cover for me so I could go home and bake more.

Maybe they scared her off and that's why she isn't here. It wouldn't be the first member of staff to leave because of them.

I feel awful because thinking back, that was the first time one of them ever demanded me to bake for them. Usually they are giving me reasons not to bother. They never want to trouble me. And the one time they did, I had to work. But I couldn't just close up to bake them treats, as much as I'd have liked to. I hate that I hurt their feelings by saying no.

They sort of took that out on Marlene as she was leaving to head home. My uncle Max even clung to her ankle like an octopus, begging her not to let an old man starve. The members of the public inside the library started to plead on his behalf and she got so mad she went to kick him. She somehow missed and got the buckle on her boot caught on the desk and it tore off, ruining her favourite boots.

Still, that couldn't be reason enough not to come into work.

Was it?

She did leave screaming they were all psychos and needed to be committed but I thought she was joking because everyone knew Uncle Max was banned from those places. It was public knowledge.

I click on Marlene's contact once again. I tap my foot restlessly on the floor as I listen to it ring and ring, just like it has done since I first started calling this morning.

"Hello?"

I jump, pulling the phone back a little to make sure I dialled the right number. "Um, is Marlene there?"

"She's in the hospital," the girl replies. "Can you believe that?"

"Oh my God, what on earth for? Is she okay?"

"She was poisoned."

"Poisoned?"

"Yeah, by a cupcake."

The blood drains from my face as I stagger backwards. I grip the back of the chair and turn it to face me before my knees threaten to buckle. My arse hits the soft cushion and I grip the phone tighter in my hand.

"Cupcake?" I whisper before bursting into tears.

Did I do this?

Was this my cupcake?

Oh my God, those poor kids ate my cupcakes.

My breath hitches as I fight to stay coherent.

"Hey, don't cry. But yeah, silly cow said she took a box of cupcakes from the library. Apparently, they were for her stuck-up boss. They were tested early this morning and it was them."

"Me, I'm her stuck-up boss," I hiccup, pointing to my chest. "That's me. Did she say where she got the cupcakes? Did they have a buttercream frosting?"

"Look, lady, I have no clue what cupcakes they were but… Hold on," I hear rumbling, like the phone speaker is being wiped with a cloth. "It's your stuck-up boss. Don't sound stuck up to me, love. She's crying like a new-born here."

"What does she want?"

"Wants to know what frosting was on it and where you got them from."

"Really? I nearly die and that's all she has to say?"

"That's not all I have to say," I call out, hoping they can hear me. I wipe my nose, waiting patiently for her to reply.

"Just answer so I can get back to scrolling through Facebook."

"I don't know. I threw the note in the bin after they were delivered."

More rustling and seconds later, the line clears. "I heard everything."

"Well shit."

"I'm really not stuck up," I tell her.

"Hey, it's between you two."

"So, they weren't my cupcakes?"

"Luv, she said they were delivered. Did you deliver cupcakes?"

My breath hitches. "No. I didn't have any delivered."

"Then no, they aren't your cupcakes, but the fact you're worried they are… maybe you shouldn't bake anymore."

Maybe.

"Can you tell her that I wish her a speedy recovery and that I can't wait to see her back at work."

She repeats the message and I hear Marlene yell, "Not unless you tell your family to stay the fuck away from me, the crazy morons."

I bite my bottom lip, grimacing. "Um, I can hear she's upset. I'll let you see to her. Lovely speaking with you. Bye."

Ending the call, I clutch the phone to my chest. *Poisoning.* How did this happen? And what note?

Heading out of my office, I make my way over to her desk and reach for the bin. *Empty.*

Our cleaner, Vicky, had been in yesterday. Which means one thing. They're in our industrial bin at the side of the building.

Letting out a whine, I grab my bag and head out, bumping into Rita on the way. "Hey. I'm sorry to have to call you in on your day off."

"It's fine. But, Charlotte, you really do need to look into hiring someone better. Back in my day, if we acted like that, we were fired on the spot."

"She's in the hospital," I explain before leaning in and whispering, "Poisoning."

"Oh no. Is she okay?"

I suck in my bottom lip. "I think so." I forgot to ask and now guilt eats at me. "She seemed okay. Yeah, I think she's okay. Right?"

Her brows pull together. "I haven't spoken to her."

I wave her off. "It's fine. I do need to go, though. I have to check the bins outside."

"The bins outside?"

"Notes," I tell her in all seriousness before heading out the door.

The wind blows my hair around my face when I get outside. I glance up at the dimming sky, groaning. It's going to rain. Drat.

I rush to the side of the building and stop in front of the bin, lifting the lid. I hold my arm up to my nose, gagging. "I own books and serve coffee," I groan.

Inside, I find household rubbish bags and know I'll have to contact the council once again because of it. This isn't the first time someone has used our bin for their own personal use.

I slide my bag to the floor and hang over the side, shoving away a bin bag I know hasn't come from the library to move on to the next. I pull open the top, finding rubbish from the café.

Come on.

I shuffle further in, my legs dangling in the air.

"Where are you?" I mutter, searching for the blue bag with yellow daisies on that we use for the small bins around the library.

My phone begins to blast Cardi B's *WAP*. It's the ringtone the girls programmed to play if one of them call me.

I try to shuffle back but my shirt gets caught on the clip on the bin. The metal begins to dig into my skin the more I tug backward, so I try to move forward instead.

My phone begins to blare again.

"She's round the back," I hear shouted, just as I catch sight of the daisy bag.

"Yes!" I yell, the tips of my fingers struggling to reach the bag.

"What are you doing?" Emily asks, sounding disgusted.

I scream as I topple over into the bin. *No, no, no.* I gag as I straighten myself, glancing up to see three heads popping over the side of the bin.

"Do we need to ask?" Harriet asks, her fingers pinching her nose.

It really does stink in here.

"It's a long story," I assure them, grabbing the daisy bag. I quickly open it, rifling through the contents.

"We can stop off at a McDonald's drive through. You don't need to go to extremes."

I ignore them, sifting through the papers until I find the card. I hold it up, grinning. "Got it."

My name is written in bold, black writing.

"What is that?" Harriet asks, pointing to the note. "And why are you still sitting there?"

I get up, and together, they help me down.

"Ouch, you'll need to disinfect that," Emily points out.

I glance down to my torn shirt, wincing when I see blood staining it. "I'm okay."

"What was worth going through all of that for?" Olivia asks, scrunching her nose up.

"Something that came with poisonous cupcakes."

Olivia shares a look with Emily before turning back to me, her expression filled with pity. "Did you bake again?"

"Not mine," I whisper, my attention returning to the envelope.

I pull the card out, my heart racing.

Happiness is only a cupcake away.

My brows pull together and I turn it over, my heart stopping when I see the poem.

Your sweetness is a lie.

Deception is your game.

Truth rots your soul.

And only you are to blame.

"What the fuck?" Harriet whispers.

I tuck the card into my back pocket, my eyes burning with unshed tears. "Do we have time for me to get changed?"

Harriet watches me closely before nodding. "Of course."

Olivia's shoulders sag. "Good, because the smell is rotten."

I force a smile. "It really is."

"We'll meet you back at the car."

While they head over to the car, I go back to my place, my mind on the card burning a hole through my pocket. I was *sort of* supporting Madison's notion that this isn't a male, but after this one, I think it may be Scott sending them.

Is he worried I'm telling lies about him? It's something he threatened me about before I left.

I know I should call mum, or someone, but I need a minute to figure out what it means without having them all yell at me. I also know I need to go to the police with the new information.

First, I want to get answers. Hopefully after today, I'll have them.

CHARLOTTE

"Is this the place?" Emily asks from the driver's seat. She leans forward to look up at the flat above the Chinese restaurant.

"It is," Harriet assures her, checking her phone from the passenger seat.

The area looks sketchy. People are in groups hanging outside the shops, and I swear that when we drove down the road, we saw at least two drug deals happening.

The shops don't look better. Most have their silver shutters down, and the rest have paint peeling along their fronts, as well as broken signs and graffiti all over the windows and brick walls.

"Are you sure this is the place?" Olivia asks from next to me. "Doesn't seem like the place Amber would stay. I'm scared to get out."

I'm with Olivia. I don't mean to judge— I feel terrible for it— but I can't help but look around and wonder if some chick is going to steal my shoes. I've read stories about it happening. My uncle Liam had a client who lived around here and they made him search for the culprit who pinched their underwear. I know once I get home, I'll want another shower.

"It's probably all she could afford. Let's not judge her for that," Harriet comments, giving Olivia a pointed look.

Did I say that out loud?

Emily turns to Harriet. "But I can worry the wheels on my car are going to be stolen, right?"

Gabby snorts from the other side of me. "It would be doing the car a favour. At least you could claim on your insurance and get a new one."

"It got us here, didn't it?"

"Let's not argue," I softly warn them. "We're here for Amber."

Harriet's the first to get out of the car. Gabby follows and I slide out behind her. I pull my hood up when a droplet of rain lands on my cheek.

"Hurry, it took me hours to get this hair straight," Olivia calls out, racing toward the building.

Someone is coming out as we reach the door, so we let ourselves in, piling inside to get out of the rain. We turn back at the sound of rain hammering down on the road outside.

"Shit!" Harriet whispers. "I've got fucking clothes out drying."

"Bit late now," Gabby replies.

Emily nudges my shoulder. "You okay? You've been quiet since the bin incident."

I'm processing. I have no idea who could be doing this other than Scott. I have no conflict with any other person. I make it a mission to be kind to everyone, even to those who aren't very nice to me. I'm also scared because I have no idea what any of it means. Were they sent to scare me? Was it in preparation for something? I have no idea, but I've watched enough thrillers and horrors to know it does mean something and I shouldn't keep ignoring it.

"I'm good. I just have a lot on my mind," I assure her softly.

"It's this one," Harriet announces, sharing a wide-eyed look with us when we find the front door is open a little.

Which isn't the safest thing an area like this.

"Hello?" Gabby calls out, pushing open the door.

I groan when she steps inside. "You never go inside," I hiss. "This isn't good."

"Hello?" she calls out again.

Emily takes my arm as we follow Gabby and Harriet. Olivia stays outside and I turn. "You coming?"

"Do I look fucking stupid?"

Emily snorts, but suddenly, Gabby screams. The shriek coming out of nowhere surprises us all, and we end up screaming along with her. I grip Emily as both of us try to shoulder our way out of the door.

There's a new scream added into the mix and my heart begins to race.

Emily pushes me aside, tripping over her own feet and landing in front of Olivia. Harriet and Gabby step over her, still screaming as they dive out of the door.

I'm not sure why I'm panicking, but Olivia's next words get me to stop screaming. I straighten my top, wincing when it catches on the small cut I got from the bins. The blood made it look worse than it was but still, it stings.

"What, what? What's going on?" Olivia asks, rising to her tip toes. Her eyes widen and I spin around to see what she's looking at.

A young girl—I'd guess eighteen or nineteen— stands in the doorway, frozen as she gawks back at her. Her hands shake around the pile of clothes she has in her grip.

Her auburn hair is tied up in a knot, and her eyes are red and swollen, as if she's been crying.

She takes a step back. "Who are you and why are you here?"

"We're not intruders," I blurt out. "We're here to see Amber. I swear. We are not robbers. I mean, would burglars turn up in the middle of the day? Would they—"

"Charlotte, I love you, but shush," Emily whispers after getting up from the floor. She stands next to me, pasting on a wide smile. "We're friends of Amber's."

The girl's shoulders drop. "I'm April, her sister."

"Is your sister here? She invited us. We've come to speak to her," Harriet explains, moving back inside.

April's eyes water and her bottom lip trembles. I step forward, taking the pile of clothes from her and placing them on the little shelf beside her.

"It's okay. I'm sorry we scared you," I assure her softly. "We really were invited."

"It's not okay," she blubbers. "Amber got hit by a car last night on her way home from work. She's in critical condition at the hospital. They aren't sure if she'll wake up."

Harriet inhales sharply. "What?"

I pull the girl into my arms, giving her a hug. She must have needed it because she hugs me back, squeezing me so tight, I wince.

"I'm sorry to hear about your sister."

"I need to be back there in an hour. I can't believe it happened. Witnesses said it was done on purpose, that the car deliberately aimed for her. The police are looking into it, but I don't understand who would do it to her. My sister is amazing."

"She is," Gabby agrees.

The girls share a look with each other, keeping me out of the loop. Harriet nods before turning to April. "Why don't we help you do whatever it is you're doing then go to the hospital with you."

April steps back, wiping her nose with the sleeve of her shirt. "There's no point. She's in ICU and they won't let anyone else in. I'm only allowed in for short periods of time."

"But we can be there for you," I explain, rubbing her arm.

"I'm sorry. I'm a blubbering mess and you don't even know me."

"It's okay," Harriet replies.

She wipes her tears. "Was there anything important you needed her for?"

"No," I reply, not wanting her to worry about it.

"Yes, but it can wait. We wanted to know about her ex, Scott."

Her eyes widen. "You're those friends. She mentioned she talked to you but never said she was meeting up with you."

I rub her arm. "We don't need to talk about this. Why don't I make you a cup of tea and then we can get whatever you were doing done and get you back to the hospital?"

"I'll make the tea," Olivia offers, rushing into the kitchen on the left.

"He dated Charlotte and did some pretty serious fucked-up shit," Harriet reveals and I turn to her, silently warning her to drop it.

"Why don't we sit down," Gabby declares.

April nods and shakily turns to the room behind her. We head into the living area, and take a seat on the beige sofas. April sits between me and Gabby on one sofa and Harriet and Emily take a seat on the other.

Wiping her nose, April turns to me. "You dated him?"

"I'm not even sure what we were. He lied."

She nods. "He lied to my sister too."

"What did he do?" Crap! I had no right to ask that. She has more important things going on right now. It was insensitive and rude. "You don't need to tell me anything." I clamp my lips shut, fiddling with the thread on my jeans.

"I don't know everything. I only ever met him once and it was by accident. He was manipulative, controlling and within the short time I witnessed them together, he was snide with his comments. Amber… she was too nice for her own good."

Spotting a picture of April and another woman with bright red hair, I point to it. "Is that Amber?" She nods. "She's beautiful."

She sniffles, tears forming in her eyes. "She really is."

"Why did they end things?" Harriet asks, her voice soft.

"She wouldn't tell me, but I could tell it was bad. I had my suspicions. She cried a lot. She got depressed and then moved here not long after. It got bad, to the point I tried to get her to see a doctor, but things got better after moving here."

"I'm so sorry she went through that," I tell her sincerely, tears gathering in my own eyes.

She rubs the palms of her hands down her thighs. "She wanted her first time to be special. She spent years having men sleazing over her, acting like they had a right to degrade her at her work, so she wanted that to be a moment she looked back on and cherished. And she thought he was the person to give it to her."

I share a look with Gabby, sucking in my bottom lip. It could just be a coincidence that the two of us were virgins. My stomach rolls at the thought of him doing what he did to me, to her.

"Did he send her anything or try to contact her after they broke up?" Emily asks, as Olivia walks in with a tray of tea.

I take the one she offers me, everyone else doing the same. April blows the steam away before taking a sip.

"It's okay if you don't want to talk about it."

"She didn't get sent anything but some things happened after."

"What things?" I ask, taking her hand when I see it begin to shake. Gabby takes her drink and places it on the wooden coffee table in front of us.

"A woman attacked her at work, accusing her of being a home wrecker and a whore. It's why she had to voluntarily resign from her position and leave.

The boss was fed up of the drama this woman was causing. Amber would never sleep with a married man. Never. Not long after her car was trashed, so was her flat, and then her car again. When she went for a new job, the woman turned up there too and Amber was fired." She takes a deep breath. "It's why I moved to be here with her. She didn't want to be alone anymore. She was being hassled by other women who were also accusing her of sleeping with their husbands. But she wouldn't do that. Whatever Scott told his wife, she believed him."

"Hey, we aren't here to judge. We know exactly what he is like," I assure her.

"I just miss her. She's in a bad condition and I don't know what to do. She's the person I go to when I need advice or if things are bad," she explains, snivelling. "I wish she were here to tell me what to do."

"Were you getting her things ready to take to the hospital?"

She nods. "Yes. She likes having her things around her. She'll want something there for when she wakes up." Her eyes close, a painful expression tightening her features. "*If* she wakes up."

I squeeze her hand. "She will," I assure her. "I'm sorry we've bothered you at such a hard time."

"No, if it's Scott you came to talk about, she'll want to help. She might not have told me everything, but I know he did something bad. And I'm not talking about his wife attacking her either. *He* did something. It happened the night she was going to surprise him."

"Surprise him?"

She nods. "Yeah. She saw an invitation to a party in his pocket the night they finally had sex, and decided she was going to surprise him by going to make up for it not being that good. We went to get her a new outfit, and she was so excited, but after that day, I didn't hear from her for a long time. She shut me out for weeks. I think he hurt her that night. I know he did."

I clench my eyes shut, trying to hold the tears at bay. "He hurt me too."

"Have you contacted the police?"

I nod, glancing down at my lap. "I have, but he gave me a false name— or at least, his last name is fake by the sounds of it. I never went to his house or met any of his friends. He didn't let me take pictures either, so I don't even have that to give to the police."

She tenses. "Amber has one."

"Has what?" I ask, sitting straighter.

"A photo. Someone at her old club was taking photos for the new website, and he caught a photo of them together in a booth. Because he never got written consent to use the image, he gave it to Amber instead. It was before the place was open to the public so he knew they must have been at least friends."

My pulse picks up. "Do you have it? We could give it to the police."

"I'm not sure where she would have kept it but we definitely have it. I remember spotting it when we moved in."

"She didn't chuck it?" Harriet asks.

April shakes her head. "No. She kept it to remind her that she shouldn't trust so easily."

Harriet continues to ask about her sister— how she is; do they know who ran her over— but I can't focus on the answers, not when my mind is reeling over it all. I stare at the picture of Amber's smiling face, and can't help but notice the resemblance between the two of us. It isn't that we have red hair, or even that we were virgins, but from everything the girls are saying, we're similar in personality too.

Do I trust too easily? I believe in trusting until proven otherwise. Is that what I'm doing with Drew? Should I trust him, only to have him hurt me? Am I repeating a cycle I won't get out of?

I want to believe that isn't the case, but I have spent my life being made fun of. Some don't even realise they're doing it. I might give them a smile and a polite nod, but deep down, their patronising, snide comments… it's like nails raking through my soul.

"Charlotte," Gabby calls, poking me in the shoulder.

I shake the thoughts away and paste on a smile for my friend. "Yes?"

"We are going to get her stuff ready to take to the hospital. Do you want to help?"

I nod, and stand. "Point me to what you need."

I have to keep busy, to keep my mind from those thoughts. And helping April, in any way I can, will do that.

TWENTY-TWO

CHARLOTTE

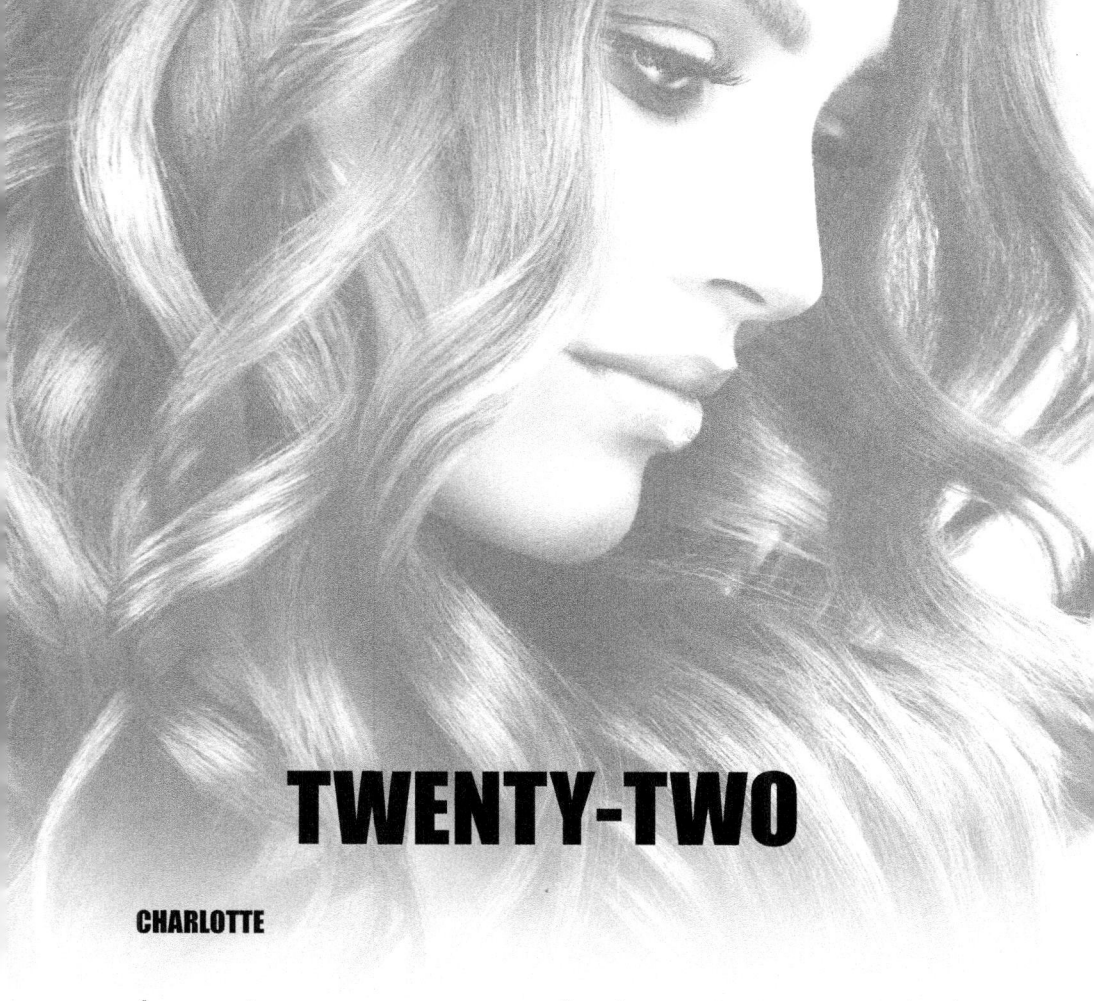

April's arms wrap around me after she programmes my number into her phone.

"Please don't hesitate to call me if you need anything. And I mean anything," I tell her.

This may be our first meeting but I already feel like we're going to be close friends.

We went to the hospital with her to visit Amber and as predicted, no one was allowed in, not even April. They were running some more tests. We decided to stay anyway to give her moral support. She's due to go back to the ward soon to hear what the doctors have to say and if it wasn't for the fact the girls need to get back, I'd stay with her.

"Same," the girls offer.

"And tell Amber we won't lose touch next time," Gabby assures her.

"Thank you all for coming. I know she's not awake to know yet, but she'll appreciate it. She's always saying how much she misses working at Tease."

"I'll come visit you soon," I promise. "I'll text you before to make sure it's a good time though."

I step back, letting her give the girls a hug goodbye, then we head off to find the car. It's a massive car park and none of us were paying attention to which space we parked in.

Before I make it three steps, April is calling me back. I turn, giving her an encouraging smile. "You okay?"

"I'm sorry for what he did to you and I hope they catch him."

My shoulders drop a little and I give her a small smile. She is so darn cute. We told her what Scott did to me, and she felt it, her empathy there for us to witness.

"Me too," I reply. "Take care, April."

She jerks her chin before heading back inside the hospital.

Harriet, sensing my mood, steps up beside me, wrapping her arm around my shoulders. "It's going to be okay, you know."

"Will it though?"

Gabby interrupts. "Did anyone else find it weird that Amber got run over the night before we were coming to see her?"

Harriet inhales. "You think it was done on purpose?"

It's Olivia who answers. "As much as it kills me to agree with her, I think she's right. It seems too coincidental to me."

"Bitch," Gabby mutters.

I chew on my thumbnail, and tense. Harriet tilts her head to the side. "What's wrong?"

"My receptionist is in the hospital too."

"Who did the bitch piss off?" Emily asks. "I still think you should fire her arse."

I hesitate for a moment but if I don't get it off my chest, I'll explode. "You know the cupcakes I was telling you about?"

Emily snorts. "The one's you miraculously think tasted amazing?"

"Not those, though I did take them into work."

Gabby groans. "Oh God, you gave her food poisoning, didn't you?"

"I've never purposely given someone food poisoning. You can't prove it was ever my baking either."

"Tell that to Dave. He still rants about it," Emily teases. "Those muffins were the only thing he ate and he said coming back up, they tasted like acid."

I roll my eyes because that was just a coincidence. "It wasn't my cupcakes. Apparently, someone had a batch sent to the library and they were poisonous."

"How do they know it was from the cupcakes?"

"Because they tested one. She must have taken them home. But they were for *me*. She just never told me."

"Doesn't surprise me," Harriet mutters. "Karma really is a bitch."

"What's stranger is it came with another note addressed to me. At first, I assumed they were from a random person, then I thought Scott, but my cousin seems to think it's a woman. Now I've received this note, I'm more inclined to think it's Scott again."

"You think it's Scott trying to shut people up?"

I stop when we reach the car. "I don't know. I really don't."

And now that I have all these thoughts running through my head, I'm becoming paranoid. I scan the area, for what, I'm not sure. I just can't shake this feeling of dread. It's been there since Marlene's sister or friend answered the phone. Now with Amber in the hospital, that feeling has only grown.

It isn't the feeling of someone watching me, or monitoring me, but like I'm being hunted. Like I have an invisible target on my back and I have no idea why or who put it there. As the feeling grows, the more scared I become, paranoid in my own mind.

Harriet rubs her hands up and down her arms, shivering. "Let's go," she announces, scanning the area, and I want to ask if she feels it too.

"Yeah, it's going to piss it down," Olivia states. "The weather is not appreciating the effort I put into straightening my hair today."

When Emily unlocks the door, I go to get into the back, but Harriet stops me. "Why don't you sit in the front. You can be in charge of the music."

"It does cheer me up," I admit, stepping aside to let her climb into the back. I get in the passenger side and buckle up, and the minute Emily has the car started, I change the radio station to nineties pop music. Britney immediately blares and my lips tug into a wide smile.

As Emily leaves the carpark, I sing along with the girls, laughing when I hear Harriet get the words wrong. I turn in my seat, giggling at the sight of Gabby singing into a make-believe microphone, her eyes closed as she blasts out the lyrics.

I turn to the front, singing along quietly. These are the people I want to share my time with. Even when I'm scared and down, they have a way of boosting my spirits. Just like my family do.

The journey back is pretty much the same. We sing, we laugh, and we reminisce about the songs playing. By the time we're halfway home, I'm feeling a little better. The rain drumming against the window screen has helped lure me into a laxer state.

Sitting back, I enjoy the sounds of laughter from the girls. Emily turns right at the junction and drives down what I know to be the backroads that lead home. They're less busy than the motorway, and it's the quickest route back. I watch as Emily's fingers tighten around the steering wheel, her breath hitching. It's then I notice how quiet she's been.

"Are you okay?"

When her gaze flicks once again to the rear-view mirror, I go to turn, wondering if it's something the girls are doing, but she grabs my arm, stopping me. "Don't!"

I freeze, my entire body tensing. "What's wrong?"

The girls quieten down and I lean forward, turning the radio off. My stomach is tied up in knots as I wait for her to reply.

"Don't look, but I think we're being followed," she announces, her voice shaky.

"We're on a country road. It's probably just going in the same direction as us," I assure her softly.

"No. I saw it behind us when we were pulling out of the hospital. The car's an ugly pea-colour."

"It could be—"

"Oh shit, it's speeding up."

I ignore her earlier warning about not looking and turn around in my seat, staring through the back window. My eyes widen when I see how fast it's approaching.

"Maybe they want to overtake?"

Her breathing heavy, Emily grips the steering wheel. "How? There's nowhere *to* overtake, and if they go any faster, they'll end up in a ditch or wrapped around a tree. These roads are too bendy and narrow."

"Slow down at the next passing point," Harriet orders.

She means the little dips in the side of the road that lets another car pass. Slowing like she was asked, Emily takes a deep breath, her hopeful eyes widening.

The impact of the car hitting us has the seatbelt locking around me. I cough, my panic choking me. The girls scream in the back, whilst Emily freezes, her entire body shaking.

"Oh my God, oh my God."

"Go," I gently order, rubbing her thigh. I want to remain calm for her, even though inside, I'm far from it. She presses her foot down, moving away from the car. I duck my head, seeing in the wingmirror that it's already following, its bumper bent and smashed.

"Drive," Gabby yells.

"I am," Emily screams, putting her foot down on the accelerator. "Can you see who it is? I can't see anything with this fucking rain."

I guess we aren't going to be calm.

"No, they're wearing a hoodie and something across their mouth," Olivia calls out.

"I think it's a face mask," Gabby replies. "Why would they be wearing a face mask?"

"Fucking hell," Olivia snaps. "Why else would they be wearing it. They don't want us to identify them. It's not because we're in a world pandemic or have an airborne disease going on."

"No need to get snappy at me," Gabby argues. "And don't jinx us."

Emily whimpers as her silver, Honda Civic skids around the corner. With the tarmac slick from the rain, I'm shocked the back end doesn't spin out.

"I can't go any faster," she cries out.

The window wipers are going at full speed, the rain heavier and echoing through the car. "Oh my God, we're going to die," I cry out.

"We are not going to die," Harriet barks. "We are going to call the police."

"And do what? Ask them to kindly ask the person trying to kill us to pull over?" Gabby snaps. "I can't die. I haven't tried out all the sexual positions yet."

Tears gather in my eyes. "My cat's going to be an orphan. No one will take him in."

"Pull over so I can deck the fucking prick," Olivia snaps.

"I'm not pulling over so he can make road meat out of us. I'm not going to be on the receiving end of some bad meme," Emily yells.

"No one will take Katnip in. My family are scared of him," I cry, shaking when we reach another tight bend. Emily slows down, giving the car behind chance to hit us again. The car swerves, barely missing a tree before Emily's able to straighten it.

Harriet's idea about the police seems like a good idea right now. I grab my bag from between the seat and search for my phone.

With shaky hands, I panic, reaching inside to take everything out of my bag.

"Is that a vibrator?" Olivia asks, when I throw one toward the back of the car.

I throw the tube of lubricant next. "Girl, I'm impressed," Harriet mutters.

"Where's my damn phone," I cry out, taking out a pack of bird seeds.

"Why the fuck do you have bird seeds in your handbag?"

"I like to feed the birds," I mutter absently, still searching. "It has to be in here."

"You carry underwear in your bag?" Gabby asks.

"Just in case of an emergency."

"Do you pee yourself often?"

"I got it," I yell in triumph. "And no, I don't, but things happen and you never know. I like to be prepared."

"Guys," Emily shakily pushes out.

I dial nine-nine-nine and wait for the call operator to answer.

"We've got this," I promise Emily, trying to hide how scared I truly am.

"Nine-nine-nine, what is your emergency?"

"Police please," I shakily get out, then wait to be put through. A woman answers and asks what my emergency is. I rush out, "We're being chased by a pea green car."

"I need you to slow down. Can I take your name?"

My eyes widen. "It's Charlotte Carter, but why do you need to know it? Are we going to die?"

"We aren't going to die," Gabby snaps.

"Are you alone?"

"I'm in a vehicle with four other friends," I explain, before giving her our location and car registration.

"Can you slow down?"

"The person is trying to kill us," I cry out, wondering why she isn't listening to me.

The phone is suddenly snatched out of my hand.

"Look, we're being run off the road by this car," Olivia snaps. She takes a breath and quickly fires off the registration number. "We can't slow down. We can't pull over. We can't stop. Soon we will be off this God forsaken death trap off a road and then there's no telling what they'll do. I have things I want to do in life. I want to visit Paris. Not very original, but still on my bucket list. So get someone here right now," she yells.

"Oh God," Emily yells and my eyes widen at the sight of a van coming up ahead.

"Oh my God, we are going to die," Gabby cries.

"You said we weren't," I yell back.

"Stop yelling," Emily screeches, holding her hand down on the horn.

The van pays no attention and I feel the car slow down a little. The rain is coming down in torrents, lashing against the windshield.

I close my eyes, humming to myself.

"Are you really humming *Fame: I'm gonna live forever*?"

I turn around to see the pea green car, the full beam lights glaring through our back window, blinding me. I meet Harriet's gaze, whimpering. "It seemed fitting."

"Oh God," Emily whispers.

My stomach is uneasy, rolling as the car jolts from the impact of the car behind. I turn back around, gripping the edges of the seat as I take in the van ahead of us. Trees wall us on either side, giving Emily no room to veer right or left, not unless she wants to end up in a ditch.

This crash is inevitable.

I close my eyes when the car jerks once again. This time, Emily puts her foot on the break and the car swerves, causing the tyres to skid on the tarmac.

We're going too fast.

My eyes clench tighter. Images of Katnip, my family and friends filter through my mind. The last image I see before everything becomes a blur, is Drew, his honey-coloured eyes heated as he stares down at me.

The blow to the car is deafening. The sound of metal scraping and crunching bouncing around my eardrums. I heave at the smell of burnt rubber, the scent burning my nose.

Oh God!

My weight is thrown forward, and my face smashes against the dashboard. Glass explodes, cascading around me.

The last thing I see is the van coming at us from the side, and the trees standing tall and proud behind the bank in front of us.

Oh fuck!

TWENTY-THREE

CHARLOTTE

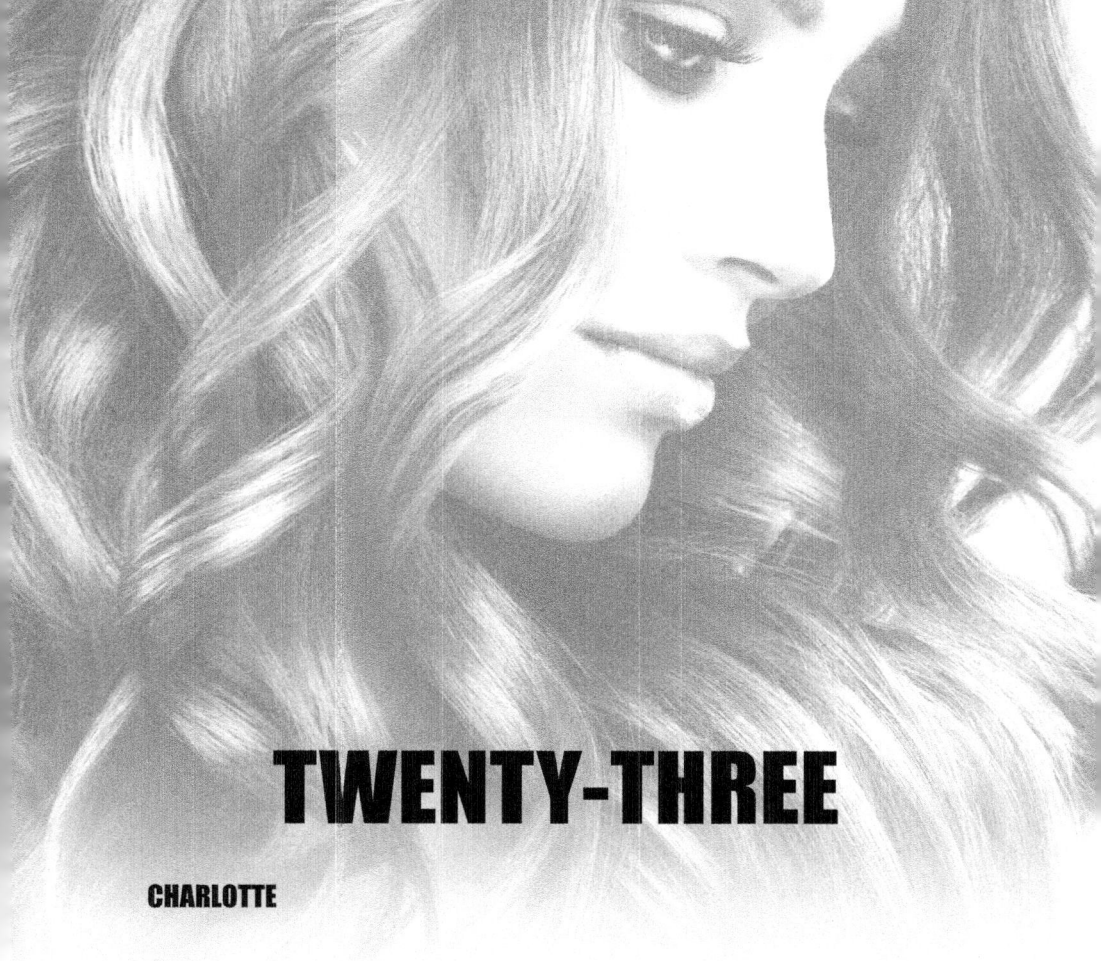

My body falls to the side as the door beside me opens. I let out a giggle as I fall into strong arms before releasing a moan. I guess I keep forgetting I was in an accident and that there's still a lot of pain.

"Charlotte," Dad's panicked voice calls out as he clutches me before I can hit the driveway.

"Dad," I call back, wrapping my arms around his neck. "You have such a strong nose."

"A strong nose?"

My nose scrunches up. "I think I meant arms?"

"What am I going to do with you?" he mutters.

I smile, resting my head against his shoulder. "You could take me to Disneyland." Sitting up, I get in his face until our noses meet. "We should go to Disneyland."

"We aren't going to Disneyland."

"But Dad," I whine. "I want to see Minnie Mouse."

Mum sighs. "How much did they give her?"

"She's so high she probably won't be able to tell you."

"I can tell you," I inform them, jerking my head into a nod. "*If* you take me to Disneyland."

"You've just been in a major accident, Charlotte. The only place you're going is the sofa or bed."

I sniffle as memories of what happened come flooding back. "I thought I was going to die and Katnip was going to be an orphan." I wipe my nose on his T-shirt. "I love you guys so much. You're the best mum and dad. I mean, you're the only mum and dad I have." I eye my mum. "I did come out of your vagina, didn't I?"

She rolls her eyes. "Of course you did."

I lean back against Dad. "I can't imagine coming out of another."

"Maybe we shouldn't give her the next dosage," Mum comments.

I pout. "But they make me feel so good." I giggle to myself before singing. "And I'm feeling good."

"You are lucky you've only got minor injuries," Dad scolds.

But the pain meds are good, so good in fact that I feel like I'm floating with the clouds. *Such pretty clouds*. They help me forget about my injuries.

I have a pulled muscle in my shoulder, a sprained wrist, abrasions, and cuts to my face, arms and chest. I also walked away with bruised ribs and knee, and whiplash. I was seriously lucky.

Emily, however, wasn't as lucky. She has a broken arm in two places and a couple of cracked ribs from where the steering wheel had crushed into her chest. The rest got off with minor injuries, although Olivia seems to be suffering the most with whiplash.

And poor Emily's car. She loved that car. She named it Betty.

"Did they catch the green-pea car?" I ask, struggling to remember as he carries me into the house. "Because I think it should be held accountable for killing Betty."

I hadn't gained consciousness until we reached the hospital. Everything was pretty much a blur. If it wasn't for our phone call to the police, Emily might have been looking at dangerous driving charges.

Mum and Dad turned up as the police were questioning me, but I had been so high on pain meds, I don't remember much of it. I do remember arguing with my dad about staying in, but I didn't want to be there. I couldn't. Hospitals hold too many bad memories for me and I just wanted to get out of there. He tried to compromise and demand I stay with him and Mum, but after arguing for what felt like hours, I agreed to let my mum stay the night with me. I just couldn't leave Katnip on her own. The vicious fur ball might not like me much, but I love her like a child, whether she likes it or not.

"She would have been all alone," I sob out as I hear keys clanging together. "Just like Emily will be now Betty is gone."

We walk inside, and he steers to the right, heading into the living room. He places me gently down on the grey, plush sofa.

"No. You know whoever was in it managed to get out. They are looking at neighbouring towns to see if they can pick up anything on their CCTV. And I've got no idea who the fuck Betty is."

"Stop being mad," I demand, running my thumb over the crease on the bridge of his nose. I giggle when his frown deepens. "So moody."

Mum sniffles and steps back. "I'm going to make you a drink and something to eat."

"I'm not hungry," I groan, the room spinning around me.

Dad takes a seat next to me, covering me with the blanket. "I'm so angry with you right now. You should have told us about the notes and about going there today."

"I didn't know we were going to be chased. And I told Mum on Monday."

He turns to my mum, who pauses at the door. "I didn't know about *this* note."

He sighs, turning back to me. "You're taking years off my life, Charlie."

I burst into tears. "I'm sorry, Dad. I really am. I just wanted to make it better."

"Make what better?"

"All of it. I wanted to prove I'm not a disappointment, that I could handle myself," I explain, ducking my head. I can't say what I want to without giving so much away. But Drew is the reason I want justice. He made me see that what happened wasn't normal or okay. It wasn't just a bad case of sex with Scott.

Sex with Drew really changed my life. My eyes widen as a smile spreads across my face.

It was really good sex.

"Charlotte, you are never a disappointment. We aren't disappointed or angry. You're a grown woman who is capable of making her own choices. We were angry on your behalf, devastated that this happened to our loving, caring daughter."

"I'm scared that he's out there and none of us know where. We don't even know if Scott's his real name."

"Why didn't you tell us this?" he asks, his voice gentle.

I'm not sure why I'm telling them now. "Because I didn't want you to worry."

I already told them about our visit with April and about her sister. I even told them about Marlene. They aren't happy I kept it from them at all.

Mum sniffles as she walks back inside, dropping a sandwich and a drink on the table. "I told you not to go today. I said it was a bad idea."

"We were visiting a friend. I know you want to protect me but none of us could have predicted what happened."

"I'm sorry," Mum whispers. "I was just so scared when we received the phone call."

I force a smile. "It's okay."

Before Dad can go into it again, there's banging at the front door. Dad gets up. "From that bang, it can only be one person."

I nod, cuddling into the fluffy pink pillow Mum hands me. I beam wide, stretching the bruise across my cheek. Ouch. "It's my favourite person. Landon."

Mum comes to sit on the edge of the table in front of me. "You need to try and eat something."

"I think we should go out and eat."

"Honey, you need to rest. Eat the sandwich."

I pout. "I think I feel sick."

She chuckles as she tucks the blanket around me. "At least try."

Landon barges into the front room, sweat beading at his forehead. I wave, giving him a lopsided grin. "Did you run here?"

"Why did you not say anything?" he asks, pacing back and forth. "You knew I was looking for him."

"I wasn't looking for him," I reply, getting dizzy. "We don't even know this was him."

"Of course it was him," he yells, causing my temples to pulse. He grimaces at my wince. "Sorry."

Hayden walks in and following behind is pretty much my entire family, including my brother. Jacob's eyes widen at the sight of me. "Fucking hell."

"Language," Mum scolds.

"You guys," I cry out. "I love you guys."

Hayden eyes her brother. "You better not be giving her shit," she warns.

He spins to face her, glaring. "This fucking sicko has been hurting her and you expect me to wish her well and a speedy recovery? Fuck that shit!"

I giggle, turning to Mum. "He swore."

Hayden, used to this, rolls her eyes. "And what are you going to achieve by acting like this? Do you think you'll find him quicker if you treat her like shit?"

"He's not treating me like shit," I interrupt. "He's taking me to Disneyland."

"Not now," they both warn me.

Hayden pauses, eyeing her brother. "You're taking her to Disneyland? Is that wise after what happened the last time?"

"I'm not taking her to fucking Disneyland," he argues. "And what do you suggest I do? I've been searching everywhere for any leads on this guy and have found none and now she's hurt yet again because of him."

My lip trembles. "Why won't anyone take me to Disneyland?"

"Honey," Mum soothes.

What he said registers. "We don't know this was Scott," I declare.

"Not now," Jacob tells me. "I wouldn't mind knowing why you didn't call me."

I tap my chin. "There wasn't enough room in the car for one, and I didn't think you'd appreciate hanging out with four hot women."

He looks at me like I've pissed in his shoe. "I'm male. And I heard they are dancers. Why wouldn't I want to hang out with them?"

"Well, next time I have a girl's night in, I'll remember to invite you," I offer, smiling. It's been a long time since we hung out. "We could even give you a facemask. Men get them all the time."

Aiden snorts. "Dude!"

Jacob doesn't bother to hide his grimace. "Yeah, I'm good, but anything to do with this and I want to be there."

"You don't want to hang out with me?"

His mouth gapes open and he looks to the others. "Um, we're hanging out now?"

I lean up, patting his cheek. "Yes, yes we are." When I notice everyone staring, I exhale. "I didn't ask for this to happen."

"But you should have told us what was going on," Landon yells.

"Don't yell at her," Hayden snaps.

"I'm going to fucking kill him," he growls, stepping back. "I'm going to find the cupcakes that are meant to be the shit."

"They were so good," Mum compliments.

"So good," I sing, leaning back against the cushions. "Maybe I should make more."

Mum gently pushes me back down. "Rest."

Max, who has been quiet until now, shoves his son into the door before racing out of the room.

"My cupcakes," he argues.

Hayden sits down next to Mum while she fills in the rest of the family on what happened. I'm still surprised everyone fits into my small front room.

"Next time, invite me. I'm your girl, remember. I've got you. And I'll totally cut his dick off and feed it to him."

I force a timid smile. "You say the nicest things to me. I want to be more like you," I gush.

"Maybe keep being like you," she warns. "Just less accidents."

"I nearly died," I tell her, tears falling down my cheeks. "I have so much to do. So much."

"Like what?" Madison asks.

"Go to a nudist beach for starters."

Madison ducks her head. "Maybe make a new list."

"Seriously though, who do we have to kill? I was speaking to Madison on the way over here and she said she doesn't think the notes and flowers are from a man," Hayden blurts out.

I fiddle with the edge of the blanket. "I'm not so sure after the last note. Some things just point to him." I quickly run by everything she's missing or missed Mum explain to the others and by the time I'm finished, her eyes are wide as saucers.

"I'll fucking kill him."

"These are not fucking good," Max cries, holding up my new batch of muffins. I made them yesterday, feeling in the mood, but they don't have the same taste, so I tried to make the cupcakes again, but again, they aren't the same. And came out burnt.

Dad comes in cradling his stomach. "I feel a bit sick!"

"Why eat them then?" Jacob asks, arching an eyebrow at Dad.

Dad points to Uncle Max, who has collapsed by the door, breathing heavily. "Talk to that fucker who rammed a dozen in his trap."

I sniffle. "I'm sorry," I cry. "Would Disneyland make it better because we can go." I turn to Mum, my eyes widening. "Or we could go and see those swans we spotted on the way home."

"Maybe another day," Mum whispers.

Uncle Max turns to Mum, his eyes narrowed into slits. "Why did you lie to me, woman?"

"I didn't lie," Mum tells him, but there's no hiding the amusement in her tone.

I glance behind Aiden, who's standing in the doorway, trying to find Landon. When I don't see him, I turn back to Hayden. "I think he's mad at me. Do you think he's mad at me? I mean, he could be mad at me." My shoulders shake as silent sobs rake through my body. "I think Disneyland would make it better."

"He's mad because he can't control the situation, not because he's mad at you."

"I didn't mean for any of this to happen."

"Stop crying. You know I don't do crying," she warns.

I sniffle, my vision already blurred with tears. "I can't help it. I'm just really sorry for worrying everyone."

"Fuck everyone else. Just do you," she tells me. "And we know you didn't mean for any of this to happen."

"We're just worried about you," Lily explains, sitting down on the pouffe beside me. Her soft touch causes another wave of tears. "You're so kind-hearted."

"And we want it to stay that way," Mum explains softly. "You have a lot of people who love you, sweetie, and we want to protect you."

"I know," I whisper brokenly, shoving the blanket away. "I need to speak with him."

"You need to rest. Your knee is badly bruised and I'm not going to comment on your ribs."

I sit up, ignoring her protests. "It's just for a minute."

"Let her," Dad tells Mum. "Maybe he can talk some sense into her staying with us until they find this guy."

"Dad," I warn, holding onto him when he helps me to my feet. I grit my teeth, breathing through the pain in my leg and chest.

He lifts me easily, carrying me out of the room. I slap his shoulder. "Giddy-up."

We barely get a step outside when I hear Hayden asking about when they are doing a manhunt on 'the fucker'. Her words.

Dad snorts. "Max has his hands full with that one."

"What did he have in his hands?" I ask, my brows pulling together. When Dad ignores me, I press a kiss to his cheek. "I really am sorry."

"You have nothing to be sorry for. Just don't keep stuff from us again. You were lucky today. Next time it might be different."

Everything he said is right. I'm just not going to hold back in life to suit other people. Why should it be the women who feel the need to be careful? Why not teach others to be kind instead?

Landon is pacing the kitchen when we enter. His eyes widen when he sees Dad carrying me. "Charlie, you need to be resting."

"I don't want you to be mad at me," I tell him as Dad puts me down on the stool.

"I'll give you a minute," Dad announces, stepping out of the kitchen.

Landon slowly approaches. "Do you know why you're my favourite?"

"Because I bake you treats?"

His nose scrunches up. "No."

"Then why?"

He takes a seat next to me. "Because you see the world differently than the others. Even Lily, with all her goodness and kindness, isn't blind to the real world. With you, everything is glitter and rainbows. Fuck, you have kitten coasters and fairy lights everywhere in your house."

I giggle, leaning forward. "I really like colours."

He nods. "I know. And just like the glitter and pretty colours and lights around you, you also fill your life with people who bring you the same. You made friends with strippers. And do you know how?"

I try to think back, but I can't recall the moment. "No."

"Because you complimented Harriet's gold, glitter thong," he reminds me. "Hell, you chose a psychotic cat over the cute white one because he went for your glitter globe keyring."

"I'm not sure I understand where you are going with this," I mutter, a little defensive over the Katnip comment.

"My point is, I hate seeing that colour in your life dim. It was worse when you were with Scott, and it was non-existent after he hurt you, but day by day, you're becoming more like yourself. I'm worried that the next time something happens, we won't get you back, and Charlotte, the world is a brighter place with you in it."

I burst into tears, and drop forward, wrapping my arms around his chest. "You say the sweetest things."

"I do fucking not," he snaps.

I tap his nose, my smile watery. "You do. You like that I see colour. So cute."

"That's not why you're my favourite. It's only one of the reasons. The main reason is solely selfish on my part."

"And why's that?"

"I've seen how unkind the world can be, the brutality and unfairness. Seeing things through your eyes… it kept the darkness inside of me from taking over completely."

"You never had that darkness to begin with. You're one of the best people I know."

He smirks. "Duh."

I sigh, grateful I no longer have to worry about him being mad. "I really am sorry though. None of it was intentional."

"I know. I just want to protect you. You're too kind-hearted to tell someone to go fuck themselves."

I giggle, shaking my head. "Unless I'm mad."

"Yeah, but you say it so politely, it doesn't count."

"You have a visitor," Dad announces, stepping into the kitchen. He doesn't look happy, and my body tenses, preparing for the worst.

"A visitor?" I ask. Everyone I know is here or at home resting.

When Drew ducks through the doorway, I fall out of my chair, a dopey grin on my face when I land on the floor. I hiss through the pain. "Drew, you're here."

Dad helps me to my feet. "Charlotte, you need to be careful," he warns.

Drew's eyes widen when I stand, briefly casting a glance at Landon, who's behind me. When our gazes meet, I can't help but teleport back to the night his hands were on me, his gentle yet rough touch. I lick my lips. "You are so pretty."

He clears his throat. "Landon rushed out in a hurry and Paisley explained you were in an accident and were here. I came to see if you were okay."

I step forward, my sore knee causing me to fall forward. Both he and Dad reach for me, but it's Drew who catches me.

"So big," I sigh. I fight back the urge to cry out, too soothed by being in his arms. A throat clears, and we awkwardly pull back from one another.

"Are you okay?"

I tilt my head right back, ignoring the pain in my neck. "I nearly died, Drew. I thought about you and—"

"Honey," Mum interrupts.

"I've never been to a nudist beach. I've never gone to a moustache competition. And today, I nearly missed my chance," I blabber.

"I'm glad you're okay."

I nod solemnly. "Me too. I still have time to be a sex icon now."

Dad begins to wheeze, clutching the back of the chair.

"Maybe you should lie down," Mum suggests.

I grin up at Drew, swaying slightly. "Want to go—"

Mum steps up beside me, trying to pry me away from Drew. "Charlotte, you need to rest. Please, come and lie down or at least sit down."

"I don't want to lie down," I tell her, frowning. "I want to go to Disneyland."

"Why are you here?" Landon asks.

"To check she's okay."

"That doesn't explain what *you're* doing here," Landon grits out.

I narrow my gaze, pointing my finger at Landon. "He's my friend. Leave him alone."

Something flickers over Drew's face before he masks it. "Like I said, I wanted to make sure she's okay."

"You could have messaged me," Landon argues.

"Why?" Drew asks. "I'm capable of coming here to see for myself."

"Drew, it's so good of you to come," Mum steps in, eyeing Landon warily.

Madison's eyes widen as she steps into the kitchen. "Holy fuck!"

"It's nice to see you again, Kayla," he greets.

"Isn't it lovely, dear," Mum asks, giving Dad a pointed look, "that Drew came to check on Charlotte?"

"No, seems a little fucking fishy to me."

I groan when Uncle Max steps into the kitchen, a smug smile on his lips. "Hey, dude."

"Hi," Drew replies, staring blankly back.

Max helps himself to a Snickers bar and points it at Drew. "I found out what giants are most scared of."

Drew crosses his arms over his chest, not in the least bit pissed off. "What's that?"

"Ceiling fans," Uncle Max replies.

While everyone continues to bicker back and forth, I'm stuck staring at him. He's here. He came to check on me.

I'm probably reading too much into it, but I don't care. The gesture alone is incredibly sweet.

And he is so beautiful.

He would take me to Disneyland.

His gaze flicks to me and he gives me a warm smile. "How are you feeling?"

I don't need to see it to know my grin is lopsided. "Like you let me into the ring with three of your best trained fighters," I tease.

His pupils darken. "Who did this? Paisley said it was intentional."

I open my mouth to answer, but Landon gets there first. "Is there something I should know?"

"Yes," I tell him, nodding seriously. "You spelled 'decision' wrong in your last status."

Both ignore me, too fixated on each other. Well, *weird*.

Drew's jaw clenches, his eyes hard on Landon. "No. Is there something you want to ask?"

"Just remember who she is and what I'd do if you even think of going there."

"And I think she's old enough to make her own decisions, and you should know me better than to think I'd ever hurt a woman."

I lift my hand into the air, waving it around. "I'm here. I'm right here."

Mum places my arm down at my side. "Not right now," she whispers.

I lean in, grinning. "Oh. Okay." I wink before going back to watching the showdown.

Landon shuts up at that, but Dad, not one to stay silent, steps in. "What are you not telling us?"

"Honey, why don't we give them some space."

"Fuck that," Max states before turning to Drew. "Why don't you have a muffin?"

I groan and stare up at Drew. "I really wouldn't. But maybe you can take me to get one. We could go dancing, fighting, or to Disneyland, but maybe not take a car. We could bicycle." I turn to Mum. "Do I have my bike still?"

Mum shakes her head, her eyes sparkling. "No, honey."

"Damn," I whisper, before turning back to Drew, my smile slipping. "I'm really sorry. We don't have a bike."

"It's okay. Another time," he muses.

"I'll make it up to you when we go to Disneyland," I tell him, nodding seriously as I think it over. "You could even get us in the parade. I've always wanted to be in one but the last time I tried to take part, it didn't go down so well with Disney. You could be Hercules."

Dad chokes, whilst others struggle to cover up their laughter.

His lips twitch, like he's fighting a smile. "I can see you have a houseful so I'll message you later? We can revisit Disneyland?"

I nod, unable to keep the grin off my face. "We can totally do that."

He chuckles, bending down to kiss my cheek. "Get better."

I nod, and he gives everyone a chin lift before leaving the room, a few of them following.

My heart flutters, my eyes never leaving the door as he leaves.

He came to see me.

"He'll never see me coming being that tall. They are always looking above,"

Uncle Max mutters, before grabbing another chocolate bar and following them out.

"Come on, let's get you to bed," Mum orders, tucking her shoulder under my arm.

"Not until she tells us what's going on," Dad argues.

"It's none of your business," Hayden argues. "This isn't a stranger. Not a random guy we've never met. Landon works with him and he's a good guy. Now drop it."

I giggle at her expression. I hobble over, pulling her in for a hug. She tenses beneath me, but I don't care. "I love you."

She winks when I pull back, but then pauses, taking in the rest of the room. She snorts at their expression. "You guys make me laugh thinking you actually have a say."

"He really is dashing," Mum comments, causing me to laugh.

The laugh turns into a whimper as I become more aware of my injuries. "Mum?"

She rushes to my side, helping me stand. "Are you okay?"

"I think I might need to go rest now."

She sighs softly. "Come on."

TWENTY-FOUR

DREW

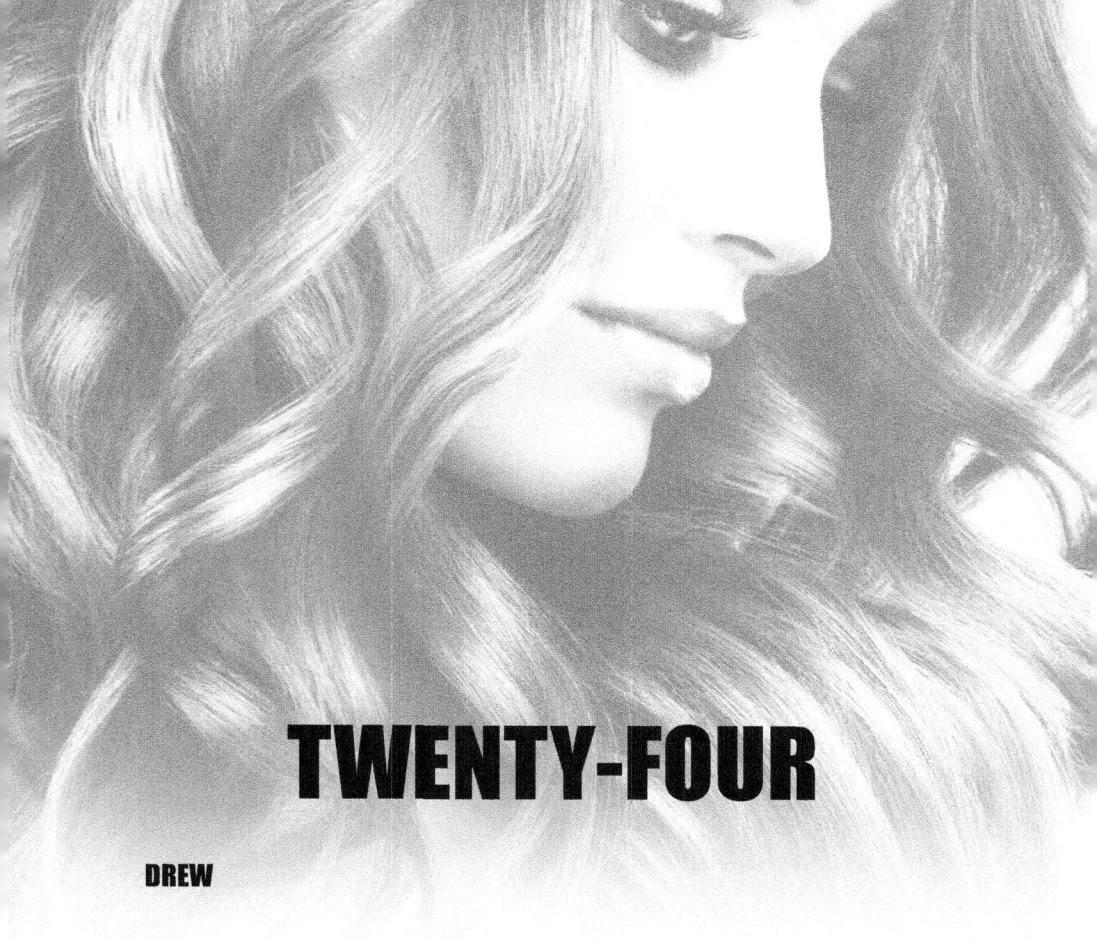

Nora's stare burns into me as I pace the confines of my office. She's giving me a moment to get my thoughts together, but right now, my head is a fucking mess and I can't compartmentalise anything.

"You're making me motion sick."

Coming to a stop, I shove my hair into a bun, needing it off my face. "You should have seen her, Nora. She had bruises everywhere. It must have been a bad crash to cause that many injuries."

"You really like her, don't you?"

I sit down on the edge of the desk, thinking it over. I do like her. I really fucking do. She's quirky, funny and blurts out the most random stuff. It isn't that she's easy to be around it's that I *like* being around her.

She's shy, yet bold. She's innocent, yet carries around an arsenal of sex toys. I can never quite figure her out. I like her view on the world, about focusing on the positive. Giving out what she takes in. I like it about her. Especially when I grew up with two parents who could suck the energy out of you. Mum is bitchy, moans constantly and only ever has something negative to say. Dad, on the other hand, can never take responsibility for the shit that goes wrong in his life. Not all the time, but most of it. It's always someone else's fault.

Charlotte, however, doesn't judge. She has opinions, but she never judges people. She sees the good in everyone.

But her family… they never give her enough credit. Yes, she's delicate, but she's also strong. I'm not going to let them scare me off, not when she has already come to mean a lot to me. I'm just not sure what step to take next. I have been wanting to ask her out without coming on too strong. Although I've had other girlfriends, I never felt like I had to make an effort to get them. It just happened.

"Yeah, I do."

She grins, jumping off the desk opposite mine. She walks over and punches me in the arm. "Then why so glum about it?"

"Because her family are certifiably crazy."

"When has that stopped you?"

I snort. "They're protective of her?"

"They're family. Of course, they're protective. But when has anything like that ever stopped you?"

My lips twitch when I think of her uncles' threat when I was heading out earlier. "Her uncle said he had connections in construction before I left earlier."

Her nose twitches. "Really not sure where you are going with that."

"He wanted me to know he could get a hold of a bulldozer to take me out. He has issues with my height"

She bursts out laughing. "Discrimination. Not new when it comes to your build. I can't wait to meet her." She pauses, watching me. "I will get to meet her, right?"

"I'm not even sure if she sees me that way. She never said anything after Saturday night. But I'm sure you will even if it doesn't go anywhere."

She snorts. "Why is it always down to the girl?"

I feel another woman-empowering speech coming along.

"What are you saying?"

"Look, although not all men do this, there are some who only want the one-night stand. Nothing more. She was probably scared to bring it up in case it meant more to her than you."

I'm insulted by her remark. "*Of course* it meant something to me."

"She's been through a lot. And from what you've said she's naïve when it comes to social cues. She probably couldn't read that you wanted more."

I walk around the desk, dropping down in my chair. "At the moment, I'm more bothered about what's going on with her. They wouldn't tell me what's going on and I want to help. If she's in danger, I want to know so I can up her lessons."

"Is that the only reason?" she asks, arching her eyebrow.

I throw my pen at her. "When did you become so grown up?"

She shrugs. "I can't help that I'm the smart one."

I snort and just as I'm about to reply, the office door is pushed open and Landon steps in. He takes one look at Nora, his eyebrows raising. "Clearly Charlotte's not as special as you made out."

I roll my eyes, not in the least bit intimidated. "Landon, meet my sister, Nora. She's been here before but you missed her."

His eyes widen in surprise. Nora waves. "Hey."

He sighs, running a hand down his face. "Stay away from her."

"No."

I'm not going to argue with him. I don't want to fall out, but I'm not going to let him push me away from her. The only time I will back off is if she asks me to.

His jaw clenches. "She's been through a lot. I'm not saying this because I think you're a bad guy but she needs time to heal. I don't want her to be taken advantage of. Not after what she's been through. It's too soon."

"Why?" Nora asks, surprising me.

"Why what?" he asks, glancing from her to me, then back to her.

"Why shouldn't she move on?"

When it's clear he's not going to answer, I intervene. "Nora, leave it."

"No," she tells me, turning to address Landon. "I know some of what happened to her."

Landon's accusing gaze burns into me. "Really? Did you Tweet it out?" he bites out, advancing on me.

I hold my hand up. "No, I didn't."

"I was assaulted," Nora blurts out, her tone softer than before.

He stops, his jaw clenching. "What?"

"A few years ago, I was walking home and a stranger attacked me. I was in a bad state. He touched me in places I didn't want to be touched, places I had never been touched. Before he could get his trousers down, a passer-by intervened."

His shoulders deflate. "I'm sorry that happened to you."

"Don't be," she tells him flatly. "But your cousin, she doesn't need your pity either. She needs your support."

"This is different," he bites out.

She slides off the desk, sighing. "No, it's not. You're treating her like a victim, not a survivor. Why does her recovery time need a clock? I'd understand if she was making the same mistake but this is Drew. You know him. Have known him for a long time," she reminds him, and even I'm speechless. Landon, however, looks seconds away from arguing. Nora gets there first. "Out of all the men she could have picked to spend her time with, she picked a good one. One who understands more than some about what she's going through. He'll treat her with the care she deserves whilst still treating her like a person and not a broken piece of glass."

"You don't know her."

"I don't need to. I'm talking from experience, and granted, not all survivors will react the same. But from what's he's told me about her, all she wants is her own independence back. She wants to take back the power that was taken from her. And who better than Drew to give it to her."

"So there is something going on with you two?" Landon asks, his gaze burning into mine.

"Something has happened, yes. Not that it's any of your business," I pointedly tell him. "Do I like her? Yes. How could I not? But I'm not going to hurt her or push her into something she doesn't want."

"Does she return those feelings?"

I shrug. "I don't know. I've not broached them with her. But I also won't keep you updated if she ever does. It's hers to share. She's a grown woman."

"I know that."

"Do you? Because all I saw today was you guys trying to control the situation. I understand you all being wary about her spending time with another guy after what Scott did. But I'm not him."

"I know you're not," he tells me, looking defeated. "But you are also not the person she's looking for. She wants a marriage, children. She doesn't want a casual hook up. She'll get hurt and I'm not going to stand back and watch that. Not again."

That doesn't come off as a shock. "You don't know what I want, but I can guarantee I'll never hurt her," I point out. "I'm sorry if you're upset over it. I know it's coming from a good place. But you need to give her some control back. Right now, she feels like she's letting you all down, and I might not know what happened today, but I've got a sinking feeling she did something to try and make it up to you guys."

He glances away and I feel like shit for pointing it out to him. He's a good mate, one of the best, which is why I offered him partnership at the gym.

"She means a lot to us," he croaks out.

"I know she does. Which is why I understand why you are all protective of her and each other."

"Even if it is unjustified," Nora points out.

"I'm being a prick, aren't I?" he asks.

I chuckle. "A little, but it's all coming from a good place and not a toxic one." I give him a minute before I broach the subject I really want to talk to him about. "What happened? Is she doing okay?"

"I thought you could see for yourself?" he tells me, but his tone is light-hearted.

I grunt. "I didn't want to disturb her in case she's resting."

"She is. Aunt Kayla put her to bed not long after you left."

"What happened? I didn't even think she had her car back yet."

"She hasn't. She went to go chase up a lead they had on Scott and on the way back, someone ran them off the road."

I sit forward, and my hands curl into fists. "What the fuck? Why did she go alone?"

"She was with her friends from Tease."

Nora's nose scrunches up. "Isn't that a strip club?"

"Yeah," I reply absently. "She liked hanging out there to get content for a book she was writing."

"I really need to meet her," she murmurs.

I glance to Landon. "Did they catch the person who ran her off the road?"

He grits his teeth, glancing away. "No. They fucking didn't," he admits, before glancing at his watch. "Look, I need to go. If you want to know the rest it's Charlotte's story to tell. Not mine. Her dad managed to get her old phone back from the police and replace it since the screen was smashed to fuck."

Nora's phone goes off and she looks down, reading the message. "Dad's here," she announces before turning to me. "I'll talk to you later."

"See you later."

"I'll be going too," Landon declares, grabbing some files off his desk.

I wait for them to both leave before pulling out my phone.

DREW: How are you doing?

I sit back, waiting for a reply. When I see the three dots, my body tenses, hoping it will be her who replies.

Charlotte: I'm okay. Just a little sore. I feel like I've got the world's worst hangover. Who is this?

My lips twitch. Only Charlotte could reply to a message and have a conversation when she isn't sure who the sender is. I think about playing her up, but until I know for sure she's mentally okay, I don't want to cause her any unnecessary stress.

Drew: It's Drew, and apparently I'm taking you to Disneyland.

Charlotte: * Insert groan * I'm so sorry. I would blame it all on the drugs, but I think it's my inner consciousness wanting to go to Disneyland and be a princess.

I chuckle at her response. I'm not sure what to say, whether to pry or not, so instead of asking what I really want, I decide to keep it light.

Drew: Landon said your dad had to get you a new phone?

Charlotte: Yeah. I'm going to need to replace the vibrator too. It was a mess. It got lodged into the seat and door and bent and cracked in places.

Shaking my head, I can't keep the laughter at bay.

Drew: What was you doing with a vibrator?

Charlotte: It was in my bag and I threw it to one of the girls to hold during the car chase. It ended up as collateral damage. It was my favourite colour too. I'm kind of gutted it never got used.

Drew: That doesn't explain why you had it in your bag.

Charlotte: I was using it for a friend.

I choke on air at her reply. What the heck? A friend. Before I can reply, she messages me back.

Charlotte: Not because she wanted me to. I mean, she did. I try samples for her and review them. She doesn't watch.

Charlotte: I don't record it either.

Charlotte: I think I'm still high.

Drew: Are you alone?

Charlotte: Is this a sexting message because I'm going to tell you upfront, I'm not good at it. I end up going into technicalities, like shower sex. Did you know it's not as easy as people think it is? Me and Harriet tried.

Charlotte: Not actual sex.

Charlotte: It was just to demonstrate. The other girls were there too.

Charlotte: I'm going to shut up now.

Laughter spills out of me as the three dots at the bottom disappear.

Drew: I meant alone at home. Now.

Charlotte: My mum's downstairs sleeping. Everyone else left so I could get some rest.

Drew: Fancy some company?

Charlotte: I don't think I'll be able to make it downstairs to open the door and Mum is moody when she gets woken up.

Drew: Open your bedroom window. Won't be long.

My FINGERS BRUSH against the rough bark as I climb the tree outside Charlotte's window. I texted her a minute ago to say I was outside so hopefully she receives it and I don't scare her. Heaving myself up onto the branch that ends just below her window, I rap my knuckles against the glass before pushing it open.

I dangle off the windowsill, spotting her on her bed. "I bet it's a pain keeping that tree trimmed. Why not cut it down?"

"I like it," she whispers, as I ungracefully climb through her window. I get up, straightening out my clothes.

There is a lot of pink as I take in her room. And glitter. Yet oddly enough, it still seems modern. Glancing back at her tucked into bed, she looks lost. My eyes widen at the size for such a small person. It's a little bigger than a king.

I notice the blush rising on her cheeks when I pull my attention away from the bed. She looks so fragile and unsure and I can't help but admire her beauty.

"How are you feeling?"

"Tired, and a little sore."

"You've not got any pain meds?" I ask, as I second guess my decision to turn up here. "How come you aren't sleeping?"

Maybe she just wants to be alone.

Her lip trembles. "I don't want to feel fuzzy again," she replies, ignoring the other question.

"How are you really feeling?"

Her big doe eyes stare up at me, almost pleadingly. "I'm so scared I can't get to sleep."

I move away from the chest of drawers and take a seat on the bed next to her. I tuck her into my side, rubbing my hand down her arm. "Do you want to talk about it?"

She shivers, yet doesn't pull away and instead, moves closer. "A lot happened before the crash so I hadn't been paying attention. So much of it was running through my head. But Emily had been paying attention. She noticed before any of us realised there was an issue." She shudders, her fingers curling into my hoodie. "It happened so fast."

Hearing the tremble in her voice, I pull her closer. "I'm sorry this has happened to you."

"It kept ramming into the back of us and then the van up ahead was getting closer. I knew we were going to crash but I wasn't prepared. I don't even remember much of the pain, or of what happened. I only remember feeling terrified." Her fingers tighten around the fabric of my hoodie. "I keep hearing the sounds. The metal, the screams, the horn and even the sound of the rain. It keeps replaying in my mind and I don't know how to shut it off."

"It's going to be okay," I assure her, hoping those words are true. "Do they know who was in the car?"

She shakes her head a little. "No. They took our statements at the hospital, and the guy driving the van."

"You said a lot happened before. What was it?" She quickly runs over everything that happened and the more she tells me, the tenser I get. "Charlotte, why did you never say anything?"

"I wasn't sure anything was connected. Not until tonight." She pulls back, tilting her head to look up at me. "I think someone is trying to kill me."

I kiss the top of her head. "We'll find the fucker. I swear. You just need to be careful in the meantime. Once you're better, we can talk about adding more classes to your schedule. I want you to be prepared if anything does happen."

"Do you think it's him? Scott?"

"I don't know, but if I were to guess, I'd say yes."

She yawns, snuggling into me. "I just want to feel safe again. I took so much for granted before. And people have been hurt because of me."

She sniffles and my heart clenches. "Not because of you. You had no hand in it. All you're guilty of is being a good person."

"Please don't tell the others I'm scared. They'll hover," she tells me, her voice breaking out with sleep. "I don't want them getting hurt because of me."

I rise a little, lifting the throw blanket up at the end. I chuckle when I see it has a ragdoll printed on it. I throw it over us and just as we get comfy, her cat dives from somewhere onto my chest.

"Hey," I rumble, chuckling when it immediately crawls up to my neck, snuggling into my hair.

"She likes you," she mutters, another yawning escaping.

"Go to sleep," I whisper.

Her hold on me tightens. "No. I want you to stay."

"I'm not going anywhere," I promise her, content when her eyes flutter closed.

As soon as Landon comes in tomorrow, I'm giving him no choice but to let me help find this wanker. My dad has connections, knows people who can find the impossible.

And once I find him, I'm not handing him over to the police.

TWENTY-FIVE

DREW

Dad is due to arrive at any moment. As promised the night of Charlotte's accident, I'm going to find this fucker who is messing with her. The conversation didn't go down well with Landon. I have no ties or hold on Charlotte and he was worried I was doing it for the wrong reasons. If he thinks for a moment I'm going to use this to get into her knickers, he's wrong on so many levels.

He also tried once again to point out we have nothing in common and want different things. Landon doesn't know me well enough if he thinks I'm shallow enough to only want a woman for a quick fuck. And yes, we might not have anything in common, and we might be two different people, but I think that's what makes me so drawn to her. She isn't some chick from the gym who's into fitness or some chick I picked up from the bar. Charlotte has an air about her that draws people in.

After spending the night with her at her house a few weeks ago, I had found myself missing her, wondering what she was up to or if she was okay.

I'm not searching for this guy because I want her; I'm doing this because a woman was hurt, a woman who, for all intents and purposes, means something to me. I might not be able to categorize those feelings or give it a label, but none of it fucking matters. What matters is helping Charlotte. And I'm going to do that with or without Landon. It just happened to be easier with his assistance as I don't want us looking in the same places he and his family already have.

"I don't get it. We have been looking high and low for this fucker and all of a sudden, your dad has a lead."

I shrug. "Yes. It's that simple. He gets shit done. He didn't say whether or not the lead will be useful, so don't get your hopes up."

"Anything at this point would be great. Even my uncle Liam is struggling because there isn't much to go by. He always used cash at the strip clubs. He never bought Charlotte anything for us to even retrace those steps. The only places we had to go on were strip clubs and none of the women who worked there wanted to talk to us."

That surprises me. "Why?"

"Because they have dickheads in there all the time. They didn't want to give us false information," he explains, rubbing his jaw. "Although this new chick, the one that's in the hospital, she doesn't strip anymore. She's a barmaid at the strip club. We went there and she never said anything. It all seems fishy to me."

"A girl who has been hurt and burnt by a male isn't going to want to talk to one. Let alone bring up bad memories that are better left in the past," I remind him. "I think hearing it was a friend asking about the information is what compelled her to come forward."

"And look where that got her," he bites out.

Dad pushes through the door, Nora beside him. He takes in Landon, sizing him up. "I'm taking it you're the cousin?" Dad greets.

Landon steps forward, reaching for his hand. "I am."

He nods before turning to me, handing me a piece of paper. "Like I said to Drew on the phone, I don't know if this information is worth anything yet."

"What is it?" I ask, running my gaze over a list of names and addresses. There are five in total.

"From what you've told me, it seems this isn't the first time or second time he's hurt a woman. I had my guy look into similar cases. He narrowed the search down with key words and the brief description of this guy from the police report."

"You read her police report?" Landon grits out.

Dad only spares him a glance. "You want answers. I'm getting them."

"Landon," I warn, giving him a pointed look to be quiet.

Dad continues. "These women might not have been hurt by the same guy. But it's worth a look."

"What makes you think it is though?"

"All five women were strippers. All of them were virgins until they met this guy. Three of five of those women were hassled by a woman they claimed was his wife. And none of them ever found the guy, although one swears she sighted him a few years later. My guess: they move a lot."

I glance down at the names once again, gritting my teeth. "Do you know anything about these women?"

He hands me another piece of paper, this one stapled to a few more. "I found out some things about each of them. What helped with the timeline of this guy's behaviour was the seriousness of the crime. Or should I say how far he took it or the level. The first woman on the list met him at work but was accosted by him outside of work. He turned up at cafes, restaurants or clubs. One night at a club, she got drunk and he offered to walk her home. She was raped. Then after, he told her no one would believe her after she had been throwing herself at him all night."

"They didn't get footage of him?" I ask.

He shakes his head, his lips tightening. "No. Any security at that club was ruined that night. There was no other evidence, and the police could never arrest anyone because they didn't have a name."

"For fuck's sake," Landon growls, sitting down on top of the desk.

There's more. I can tell by the way he's gauging Landon's reaction. "What, Dad?"

"I'm not sure it started off with strippers. I think he chooses them now because he thinks it will discredit them."

"Charlotte's not a fucking stripper."

"But doesn't she like hanging out in strip clubs?" Dad comments.

"She did tell me she met him outside the strip club," I admit, ignoring Landon's stare.

"But he was in her life for months. He would have known she wasn't a stripper."

"That, I can't answer you. But one thing they all had in common were that they were virgins. I'm thinking the stripper part of the equation came in after being caught. Somewhere out there is a person who has filed a sexual assault against the right guy. Trying to find that case will be impossible until you know his name. But I'm betting my life savings there is one."

"Were there any arrests with these?" I ask, holding up the stack of papers.

He shakes his head. "No. But that's not saying they don't know something more. One of them might be able to tell you something that helps. I can't get involved with that part. If you want to speak to them, to find out if they are indeed a survivor of his abuse, it's up to you."

Landon stands, taking the piece of paper off me. "I'll go."

I rub the back of my neck. "I don't think that's a good idea, mate. You're... *You.*"

"I'm not going on my own. I'm going to take one my female family members."

My eyes widen. "Not your sister."

He snorts. "No. I'm hoping Charlotte's mum will come with me. If she doesn't, I'm going to take Madison."

I nod. "Good idea."

"I'm going to get on this and sort out times we can go. I'll get their numbers and call them first."

Dad steps forward. "We'll keep digging, but whoever this guy is, he's used to hiding his tracks," he tells him. "It's a good idea taking her mum. It will make these women feel more empathetic toward her, and more than likely get them to talk."

Landon nods, then turns to me. "I'll catch you later. No letting her leave on her own. Her car's back but she's still not comfortable getting into it so Jaxon is dropping her off. Uncle Myles was going to but something happened."

"I'll get her back okay," I promise.

He leaves and I turn to my dad, letting out a weary sigh. "Be honest. What chances do we have of finding this guy?"

"I'm going to be honest, son, it's not good, but nothing is impossible."

"Actually," Nora begins, but Dad gives her a look to stay silent. She huffs, folding her arms across her chest.

I grin. "What have you done now?"

She side-eyes Dad. He sighs. "Tell him."

Letting out a puff, she does just that. "My principle told me I had to re write the letter of apology. I said no."

"And?" I drawl, sensing there's more.

"So I wrote the letter on every whiteboard in the school."

"In?" Dad comments.

Nora rolls her eyes. "Marker pen."

"And?" Dad pushes.

"And the principle didn't like it so I did it to his car. I said if I wasn't allowed to express myself on paper, or by the way I look or dress, then I'll find other ways to do it. He took exception to that."

I chuckle, ruffling her hair. "You're going to get a criminal record before you're eighteen."

She snorts, shoving my hand away. "Not likely. Once I give them the woman rights act, they back off."

"They won't always do that," Dad warns her before turning to me. "Is this girl worth the crap that guy will rain down on you?"

Nora shoves him in the shoulder. "Dad!"

"What? I'm not saying he couldn't take him," he argues, then addresses me. "You could easily take him."

I chuckle. "It would be an even fight. He's stronger than he looks."

"He did look like a scary mother fucker."

"But to answer your question, yes, she is. You'll only have to meet her once to know that."

There's a timid knock on the door before Charlotte walks in, her head bent down while she rummages through her bag. "I think I've left my keys in the door," she tells me, dropping her bag on the desk. "It's my uncle Max's fault. His gun exploded all over me. He scared Katnip, who dived onto the back of my neck. I'm pretty sure her claws went into my head because it's sore back there. My dad tried to help get her off but then the second load of glitter went off and it got into his eye." She looks up. "Who knew glitter could be so deadly."

"Why did he have a gun?" I ask, tensing.

"It's not a real gun," she tells me absently. "His last one was too powerful to use on my mum. He's trying to get payback for my cupcakes. But I swear, they really did taste good. I wasn't lying this time. I swear."

My lips twitch at her ramble. "I want to introduce you to—"

I'm struck for words as she pulls out a pink pair of fluffy handcuffs. She places them down onto the desk next to Landon's mug. "I know they are in here somewhere. They have to be. They are always in here."

Dad's eyes widen at the handcuffs; Nora grins, watching Charlotte closely.

"Why don't I help?" I offer.

Next, she pulls out a long black whip, then it's a bottle of lube. Nora giggles, trying to smother it with her hand.

"It's fine," she tells me, but then begins to shift side to side, her expression tight.

"Are you okay?"

She pulls a hand out of the bag to wave me off. "I think I've got glitter on my vagina. It's *really* uncomfortable."

Dad turns, biting down on his knuckles to stop the laughter. I can't blame him. Her honesty and expressiveness are some of the things I like about her. It makes her unique.

After knowing her for as long as I have, and knowing her quirks, I still haven't figured out why she always has all these sex toys or objects. Yes, she explained why she has them, but she never explained why she always seems to have one in her bag.

She places down a glass jar of hot dog sausages, and Dad chuckles. I give him a warning glare but he shrugs, mouthing, "Hot dog sausages?"

"Aha, I've found them," she states, dangling a set of keys from her fingers. When she turns to the room, the colour of her cheeks matches the colour of her hair.

"Charlotte," I muse, stepping closer. "This is my dad, Silas, and my sister, Nora."

Her eyebrows shoot up before a blinding smile stretches over her face. She rushes over to Nora, pulling her in for a hug. "It's so good to meet you," she greets, pulling back. "My gosh, you're so pretty."

"Thank you," Nora replies, taken aback by the compliment.

Dad doesn't bother hiding his amusement when she turns to him. "And I see where Drew gets his handsome looks."

"Hey," I argue lightly, pulling her to my side.

"Why do you have hot dog sausages in your bag?" Nora asks, like that's the weirdest object Charlotte pulled out.

"And is that a muffin?" Dad asks, tiptoeing to get a better look at what's left in her bag.

Charlotte scrunches her nose up at the sausages. "I'm not actually sure. But I'll keep them in case I ever come across a stray cat or dog and they need feeding." She smiles at my dad. "It is."

"I never thought of keeping food on me," Nora murmurs.

Dad's horrified expression nearly has me bursting into laughter. "No. Think of the rats."

Charlotte nods sympathetically. "Happened to me when we went camping. I left bird seed bars in my bag and rats got inside the tent. Landon was not happy."

"I bet," I muse.

She suddenly stops putting her things back into her bag, taking in the room. "I have got the right day, haven't I? I mean, I've not interrupted family time or anything?"

I slide my hand down her back, causing her to shudder. "No; Dad and Nora just popped in to say hi before heading home."

"You don't have to go on my account," she stresses. "I can come back another day."

Nora laughs. "Your muscles hurt after each session, don't they?"

Charlotte pouts, her shoulders sagging. "Yes. I wasn't made for exercise."

Chuckling, I can't help but admire her honesty. "But you're doing so good."

Nora grunts. "You said that to me but then made me start extra lessons."

Charlotte tenses, slowly turning to face me. "You said that to me too."

"But yours is for another reason," I tell her.

Realisation dawns on her face as she slowly nods. "Oh yeah. I kind of really do need them."

"We will leave you in two in peace. I'm off to get this one home," he explains. "Even suspended, she still has to do all her homework."

"If you'd ever like some peace studying, you're more than welcome to come to Charlotte's Library on Main Street," Charlotte offers.

Nora beams. "I'd love that."

"It was lovely meeting you, Charlotte," Dad tells her before turning to me. "Son."

I give him a subtle nod. "Dad."

He takes one more look at Charlotte, before turning back to me. "I see it."

Charlotte, not understanding, starts wiping her face. "Do you see more glitter? I swear, it's going to take me weeks to get all of it out."

I chuckle, pulling her against me. She curls her hand into my T-shirt, beaming up at me. I love how comfortable she is around me. "I'll see you later, Dad."

After our goodbyes, I turn to Charlotte. "You ready to make your muscles hurt?" She straightens, placing her hands in a superhero pose. "What are you doing?"

"Preparing myself."

I lift her easily, throwing her over my shoulder. I smack her arse, causing laughter to spill out of her. "I'm not that bad."

"Say that to my muscles," she cries out.

"Stop being a baby," I lightly scold.

"No, for that, I'm not doing it," she argues. I place her down on her feet and she looks up at me, my stern expression burning into her. She sighs. "Oh, okay. I'm ready."

"Then let me lock up."

TWENTY-SIX

CHARLOTTE

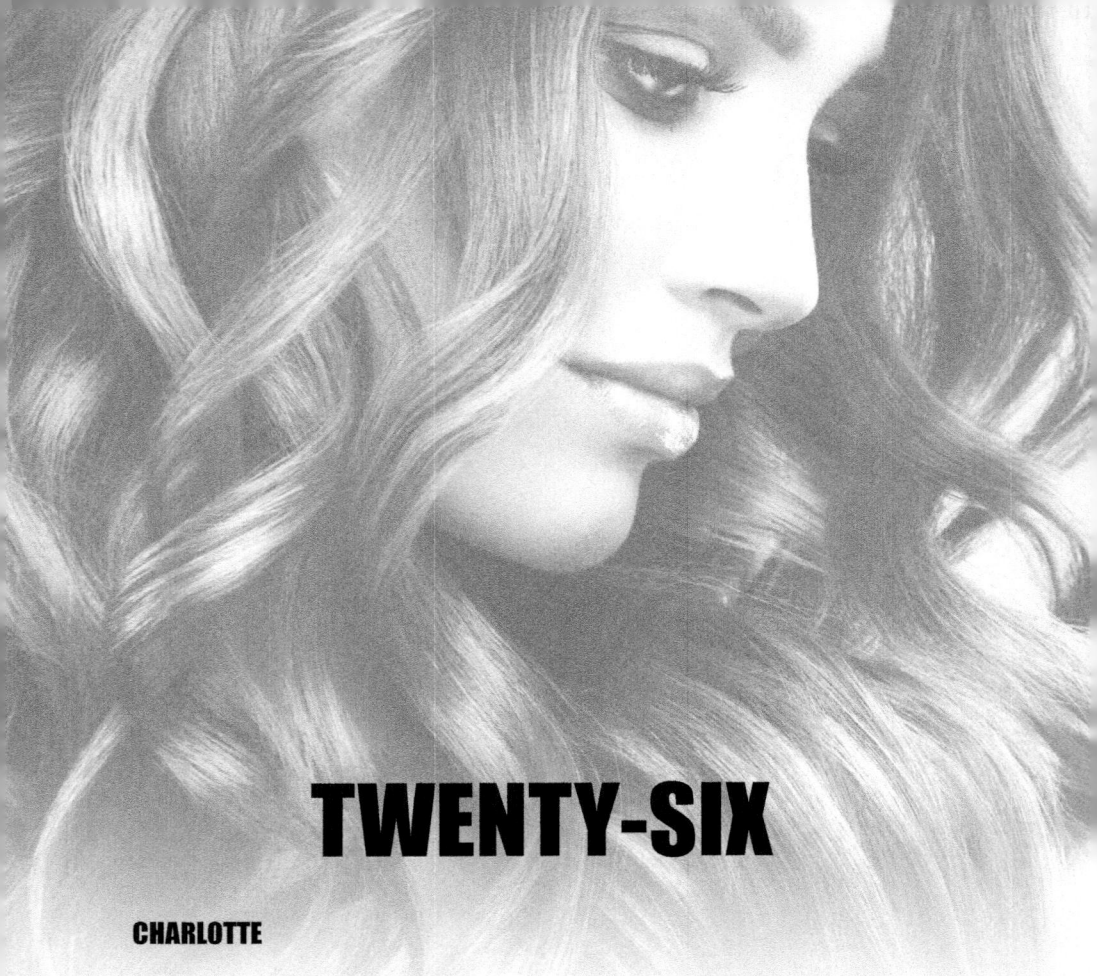

I blow out another breath as I fall to my knees on the mat. For the millionth time. "Come on, Charlotte. You can do this."

No, I can't.

Tears sting my eyes as I get to my feet. "I'm never going to be strong enough."

"It's not about being the strongest," he tells me, placing his hands on my shoulders. I shiver at the touch, just like I always do with him. "Do you remember the most sensitive areas?"

"Eyes, nose, groin, ankles, ears, throat, knees, and chest. Why?"

"Okay, so which of them could you use with me behind you?"

"Not your nose, throat or eyes because I can't reach them," I grumble. I'm sulking, I know it, but I really want to get this. Not just for me, but I want to make him proud.

He chuckles and spins me around until my back is to his chest. As soon as his arms wrap around me, I bend forward and groan when I make another mistake.

"No, stay there," he croaks out, his voice hoarse.

A shiver races down my spine, especially when his strong arms tighten around me.

"What do you want me to do?"

He doesn't say anything for a moment and the feel of him, hard and pressed against me, has me biting my lip to stop the moan threatening to slip free.

"I want you to grab my ankle really hard, and I want you to yank it up as hard as you can whilst rising. Then—"

Taking him off guard, I reach for his ankle and yank up, following the steps. I hear him hit the mat hard and I turn, dropping his leg to the floor.

I squeal, bouncing up and down. There is so much joy flowing through me, I can't keep the smile off my face. "I did it. I did it," I squeal. "Just call me Jack."

Drew groans, sitting up. "I guess I'm the giant in this scenario."

Seeing him rub the back of his neck, I instantly feel guilty. "I'm really sorry. How bad did it hurt?"

He chuckles, then shakes his head before focusing on me. "This is what was meant to happen. I just didn't have time to brace myself for the fall. You did good. Really good."

I beam, puffing my chest out. "Can we do it again?"

He jumps to his feet, and I turn, excitement pumping through me as he steps up behind me. The body heat coming off him seeps through to me and I close my eyes, anticipating the feel of his hands on me. He doesn't disappoint, wrapping them around my chest, only this time, he grips my wrists, pinning them to my chest. "Now what do you do?"

I push back, my arse pushing into his groin. He hisses, his body tensing. I do it again, trying to push him back whilst trying to free my arms, but he's too strong.

"Fuck," he moans.

I suck in my bottom lip as my stomach quivers. "I don't know what to do," I whisper, the tension between us different, electrified. I can't see him, but I can sense it.

His hand runs down my arm, moving across my stomach to my hip. He pushes my hips, grinding me back against him. "You do anything you can. You bite. You scream. You dig your nails in. Then do any of the moves I taught you. Or improvise with those moves. Then run. You run until you are in a safe place and don't stop until you are."

His voice is low, raspy, and I absorb the sound, feeling tingly all over. I lean my head back on his chest, the move causing my chest to push out.

"Charlotte," he warns, his fingers tightening on my hip.

I step away, turning to him. My cheeks are flaming. "Sorry."

When I look up, his eyes are burning with need. There's a deep want, and it freezes me. I can't move. Can't find the words.

I close my eyes, images of him taking me at the hotel running through my mind. I want that.

My lids blink open, instantly meeting his gaze. His grows more intense, like he has read my thoughts, watched those images, and before I can say anything, he's taking a long stride toward me. His hands palm my arse and I grab onto his shoulders as he lifts me up. I wrap my legs around him, and before my mind can start picking at things, or questioning anything, I lean down and cup his cheeks, pressing my lips to his.

His taste is better than I remembered. I grind my hips against him, kissing him harder. Then we are moving. I don't pull away to see where. I don't care. All that matters is him. His touch. His lips.

His calloused hand runs down my back as he bends, taking me with him. Pulling back, my breaths mingle with his.

"Charlotte," he moans, gripping my hips.

We're sitting on one of the benches, me straddling his thighs, and it feels so good. I lean down as I roll my hips along his hard dick. "This can be classed as cardio."

"Maybe we—"

I lean back, unzipping the zipper that holds my sports bra together. My tits fall free and his jaw clenches, his smouldering gaze burning into me as the material falls to the floor behind me.

I don't have alcohol running through my system.

I don't have that courage, but I find myself staring down at him, and although I feel vulnerable, and out there, I'm not afraid to show him what I want. Every insecurity I have, each bit of shyness I possess, it's gone with that one smouldering look. I trust him. Looking back, I don't think it was ever the alcohol that gave me the confidence, it was him.

"Touch me," I shakily push out, unable to look away. There's a stark need in my voice, one I haven't heard before.

He grabs the back of my neck, pulling me to him until our mouths meet. I kiss him back, my tongue sliding against his.

His hand slides up my side, running over my ribs until he reaches between us, cupping my breast and squeezing. I moan, arching my chest into him.

"Fuck," he growls.

I was already hot before he touched me. Now I feel alive in a way I have only ever felt once before.

And that was because of him too.

I spread my thighs further apart and grind down, the friction causing electric currents to pulse through my nerve endings.

"I've never done it in a gym before," I tell him, my voice husky.

He pulls back, his eyes darkening. "Well, we can't have that," he rasps.

I pout, slowly shaking my head. "No, we really can't."

He hoists me up by my waist before setting me down on my feet. Reaching for my leggings, he slides them down my legs. Fortunately, I'm barefoot, so all I have to do is step out of them. He looks up, his pupils dilating.

"You amaze me."

The touch of his lips on my skin is smooth, yet the texture of his stubble is rough, adding to my arousal.

He blinks up at me as he runs his tongue over my feverish skin, up to my belly button. I moan, reaching for his shoulders. He bends, running his tongue further down before running it through the seam of my sex.

"Oh God," I moan. "Do that again."

He does, this time flattening his tongue to press down hard on my clit. He sucks, licks and bites the inside of my thigh, driving me to the brink of insanity. All my emotions are clashing together, thrumming, beating, and with each touch, they spiral.

His fingers slide through my wetness, using it as a lubricant as he pushes one inside of me. My fingers dig into the skin on his shoulder as my knees threaten to buckle.

He keeps up with the assault, pumping his fingers in and out, and each time I come to the brink of wanting to climax, he pulls back, leaving me spinning out of control.

It feels so good.

Torturously good.

He slides his fingers out of my sex, rubbing my wetness back and forth until the tip of his finger probes my arsehole. I grow tense, looking down at him.

"Drew," I whisper, unsure. This is one thing I know I can definitely say I haven't done.

I'm not even sure if I want it to be done.

"You can say no," he tells me. "I'll *always* stop."

He pleads silently for me to trust him. He doesn't need to, I do. Something must have flashed in my gaze because the next time he runs his fingers through my sex, then moves further back to probe my arsehole, he adds pressure.

My head drops forward, my legs automatically spreading a bit wider. It's a weird sensation. Not painful, not pleasurable. But I can't deny I'm aroused.

I grip his T-shirt, and understanding what I want, he pulls back, letting me lift his top over his head. Immediately, I swoon over the sight of his tattoos and strong shoulders.

I reach out, my finger lightly running over his nipple ring. "Does it hurt?"

"No," he rasps, standing. I step back, his tall body towering over me. He tugs the tie loose on his joggers and pushes them down his legs before kicking them away. "I can't wait anymore."

I slide my hands up his chest, marvelling at the phoenix bird tattoo and others before reaching his shoulders. I press my body flush against his, leaning up on my tiptoes. "Then don't," I whisper.

He sits back down on the bench, reaching for my hips. "Straddle me," he orders.

I do as I'm told, climbing on top of him. I reach between us, grasping the girth of his cock, sliding my thumb over the tip. He growls, his fingers digging into my thighs.

"Please tell me you have a box of condoms in that suitcase you carry around."

I pull back, my lips twisting together. "Um, actually, I don't."

"So, you have handcuffs, lube, and a whip, but no condoms?"

"Um, I'm sorry?"

"Are you okay with me pulling out?"

Flashes of my dad and uncles' sex education lesson come back to me. I remember being traumatised, along with the other females in our family.

If he says he'll pull out, don't fucking listen.

"Yes," I whisper.

He lines himself up at my entrance before handing control over to me. I smile, sliding down his dick, inch by inch, taking in the wide girth. I feel stretched, feeling every ridge of his cock inside of me. It feels good. I moan, low, deep in my throat, my eyes closing as I savour every moment of him filling me. Not having a barrier between us… it heightens *everything*.

We should have done this before.

"Fuck," he grits out, dropping his head onto my shoulder. "So fucking tight."

I'm hoping that's a good thing.

Rising, I then drop back down, clenching around him. He cups my breast, lifting a little before sucking my nipple into his mouth; sucking, licking, biting. I run my fingers through the thickness of his hair, tugging hard as he toys with my nipple. Waves of pleasure shoot to my clit. It pulses, aches, desperately seeking climax.

"Oh God," I cry.

I grind harder, the sway of my hips causing him to go deeper each time. Tilting his head up, he captures my lips. It's wet, frenzied, leaving all thoughts to scramble together. I don't know which way is up or which way is down.

That carnal need is building up inside of me.

People were wrong about *sex* being sensual; intimate. I have experienced the opposite. It had been detached, cold, cruel. This… This is all me and Drew. What makes the act sensual is *us*. It's our connection; a powerful magnetism pulling us together. It feeds the fire that burns between us.

Everything we're feeling isn't because of the act, although it does help. It's each other.

"More," I plead, feeling brazen.

His eyes darken. "Stand," he orders.

I lift off him, whimpering when his cock slides out of my sex. His cock is wet with my arousal, and I lick my lips, turned on more than I ever have been.

"Hold onto the bar," he orders and I step forward, reaching for the bar on the treadmill.

A moan slips free when he grips the globes of my arse in his hands before ever so gently running his hands up the curve of my back. Pressing down on my shoulders, he pushes me forward and I go, stretching the muscles in my arms.

His hands stroke and caress as they run back down, the softness of his touch raising goose bumps on my skin. He only stops to once again squeeze the globes of my arse. It heightens the pleasure running through me.

"This arse has driven me crazy all night," he divulges as he presses against me. I moan at the feel of his cock sliding through my sex. "Do you know what you do to me?"

"No," I whisper, but I can only imagine it's something close to what he does to me.

"I'm about to show you."

His first thrust is cautious, gentle, and a moan of frustration bubbles out of me. His next thrust is harder, deeper, rocking me back and forth as he grips my hips punishingly. My tits swing from the force and I shudder in ecstasy.

Feeling the tips of his fingers in my hair, I tense, but then I feel my bobble sliding out, freeing my hair from the loose bun I had pulled it up in.

My core tightens the same time my knuckles bleed white around the bar. I want more. Need more.

Each rock of my body, the sound of our skin slapping together, is going to be my undoing. My knees threaten to buckle and sensing that, Drew's fingers tighten around my hip, whilst is other presses down on my lower back.

His grunts have my pleasure spiking. They're low, primal.

"Harder," I cry out, my chest rising and falling as I slam myself back to meet each thrust.

His other hand slides off the bottom of my back, gripping my hip punishingly. He uses it as leverage, pummelling in and out of me with force that knocks the breath out of me. With each thrust there's desperation and need, and I know he has been holding back.

I can feel it building.

The anticipation. The knowing of how good it's going to feel, yet the sadness of knowing it never lasts.

Our moans, whimpers and grunts mingle together. Each time I cry out, tightening around him, his cock pulses inside of me.

Each time he slams inside of me, the deeper he feels. It's ruthless, out of control, and I don't want it to stop. He fills me to the hilt, causing my clit to pulse.

My core is winding so tight, my skin clammy, and the tingling sensation is driving every nerve ending on fire.

A glutaral cry slips through my lips, my legs locking as my lower half spasms with my orgasm. The shock of my orgasm has my back bowing, and has a cry of pleasure wrenching from my throat.

For a few moments, all there is, is pure bliss. A moment where no sound or anything can penetrate.

I float back down to earth just as Drew's movements become unsteady. He thrusts once, twice, before he slides out, and the warmth of his cum spurts all over my arse and lower back. I moan, my pussy tingling in all the right places. I'm not sure if it's because if feel dirty, naughty, but the action makes me want him again. And again.

He leans over to the bench and grabs a towel to clean me up. Spent and lacking energy, I can do nothing but grip the bars tighter, too afraid that if I let go, my legs will give out on me. Exhaustion hits me as I try to catch my breath.

"Come here," he whispers, pulling me against his chest. He bends, kissing the crook of my neck before pulling back and turning me to face him. He locks his arms around me, and I look up, giggling with nervousness and happiness.

Amusement lights his eyes as he cups my cheek, and leans down, pressing a kiss overflowing with passion to my lips.

I sigh, pressing my body flush against his. He always manages to bring this side out of me. I have always been curious about sex. It had always intrigued me which is why romance is my favourite genre. The smuttier the better. But no one has evoked this feeling inside of me like he does. No one revs my engines like he does. And there has been no one in my entire life who gives me confidence the way he does. Not just with sex. Just being around him gives me a confidence boost. I never feel judged or mocked. He never gives me one of those 'pity' stares or the ones where someone's looked at me like I'm a freak. If anything, he finds my quirks endearing.

Yet, when the words form on my lips to ask what this is between us, I freeze.

"That was—"

"Go out with me tomorrow night," he rasps, tucking my hair behind my ear.

My eyes widen. "Do you mean like a date?"

His studies my face. "Do you think you are ready for that?"

My heart skips a beat, and I struggle to keep the smile off my face, so I don't. I beam, leaning up on my toes.

He arches an eyebrow, his arms tightening around me. "It's a charity event to raise money for The Shelter. I wasn't going to go this year, but I'd like it if you'd come with me. As a date. But not if you aren't ready."

I melt in his arms. "Of course, I'd love to go out with you," I tell him.

He bends down, meeting me halfway, his kiss bruising, punishing, yet filled with so much passion my toes curl.

I pull back, grinning like a fool.

I have a date.

A real one.

Things are starting to look up. I just hope it stays that way.

TWENTY-SEVEN

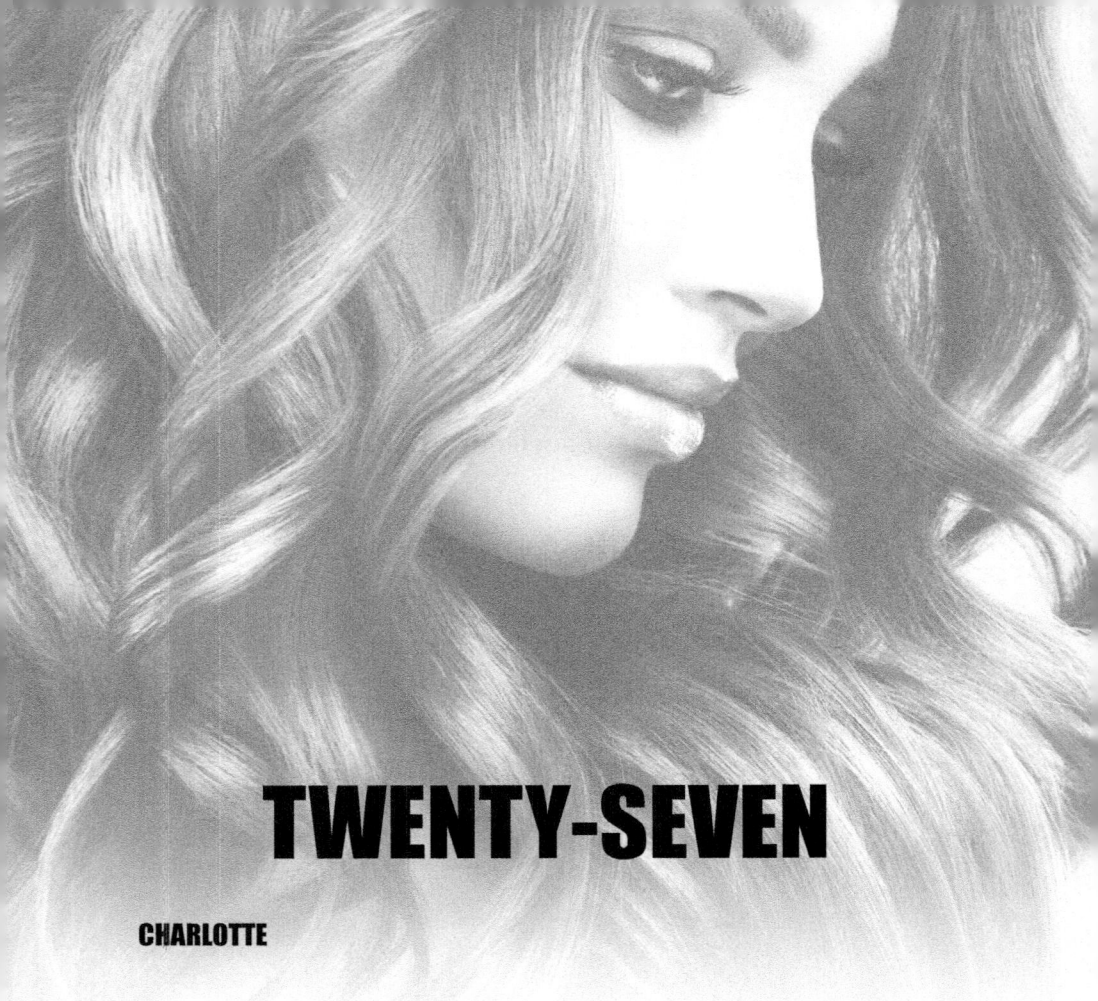

CHARLOTTE

My feet feel like they are filled with lead as we walk across the red carpet, bypassing the event photographer and the few news reporters who are outside, hoping to get a few shots of the headliner and the wealthy guests.

Drew had pre-warned me it could be a little overwhelming going in, but once inside, the atmosphere is different and the only photographer is the event's organised one.

He has been coming here ever since he was old enough to attend. His dad had also attended when he was younger. His friend was a fighter for the organisation and then his son when he retired. Silas isn't the only relative of Drew's who attends. Drew explained this is where his mum and dad met and had their one-night stand. He assured me Grace hasn't attended for a few years now, so I won't have to worry about bumping into her. I'm afraid if we do, I'll end up blurting out my sins over the hotel. That said, either Wesley or a representative for the family attend in their place.

My stomach is weighed down with nerves as we step inside the hotel. With its high-ceilings and marble floors, it seems much like the last hotel we were at, but there's a hint of richness here that the other place didn't have. I can't put my finger on it. Even as the staff direct and guide people, they have an air of money about them. There isn't a member of staff who has a stain on their shirt, one who forgot to wear the right shoes or even forgot to tidy their hair. Everything here is immaculate, including them.

I run my hand down my dress, self-conscious as a woman elegantly walks past, wearing a gold shimmer dress that falls in waves at her ankles. Jewels drip from her neck and ears. She screams money, wealth, but that isn't what is making me self-conscious. It's the sophistication, the way she holds herself as she walks. She seems sure, confident, and has a glow of air around her. Like she belongs.

I'll never have that.

The only time I've ever felt an ounce of that confidence is with Drew, but only sexually. Any other time I feel like a blithering idiot who speaks too much.

Drew, reaching for my hand, links our fingers together. He looks handsome in his white, crisp shirt, and black slack trousers. It's his wavy hair down, his leather jacket, and boots that add to his sex appeal. He has a body women want to reach out and touch. They wouldn't be able to help themselves. Even now, women of various ages are gawking and admiring his physique.

And who could blame them.

I also don't miss the looks some of them are throwing my way. I'm used to those looks. People give them to me all the time. This is why I prefer books, kids, and animals. They aren't judgemental or mean.

Pulling me against his chest, Drew then brushes my hair over my shoulder, causing a shudder to run down my spine. "Have I told you how gorgeous you look tonight?"

I melt against him, giving him a lopsided smile. "You have. Five times."

His pupils darken as he leans down, capturing my lips. "I guess it was worth mentioning more than once." He pulls back, putting space between us to look at my red suede dress. It's an off the shoulders, low cut, knee-length, and form-fitting dress. It clings to my body like a second skin. My boobs look pretty freaking good too. I have to remember to thank the girls tomorrow. It isn't me, but it is.

I kept my makeup light, not wanting to overdo it. My lipstick, however, is, and I love the blood red. My hair is in thick curls, two strands tied at the back with a silver daisy clip.

"So, what happens at these things?" I ask as we move forward in the line.

"Well, I come for the fights and to support a good cause. For the others, it's a hit and miss. Some are here to make and meet more connections, to show off, or for the good press. Then others are here solely for the cause and fights."

My stomach turns at the word fight. I can't deny I'm not the littlest bit interested. I am. But each time I really think about what we're walking into, I picture Landon in his hospital bed, bloody and bruised. I hear the sounds of the machines flatlining, the wails of my family crying out for their loved one.

"And people enjoy the fighting?"

His scrutiny has me shifting in my high heels. "It's not that kind of fighting. It's not watching someone walk down an alley to beat someone up." I tense, flinching at the reminder. That was what happened to Landon. "It's a sport; a combat sport people enjoy taking part in for various reasons."

I lean in so no one overhears and gets offended. "Do they not, like, get hurt?"

He chuckles, pulling me against his chest. "Babe, they are trained to block it out, to keep going."

I wind my arms around his neck. "I'm sorry. I'm being a baby."

He groans, dropping his head back. "I should have known. This is about Landon," he states, meeting my gaze. "Babe, if you want to go, we can go. We can go find a restaurant or club to check into."

I tuck his hair behind his ear. Even in heels I have to tiptoe to reach. "No, I want to stay…" I trail off, seeing Woods from Tease. A wide smile pulls at the corner of my lips. "Woods? What are you doing here?"

The two women in front of him turn at the sound of my voice.

Oh no.

"Shit!" Drew whispers.

"Drew?" Natalie calls out, excitement shining in her eyes. That dims the minute her eyes land on me.

Paying no attention to them, I turn back to Woods. He beams, pushing lightly past the queue to get to me. "Charlie, what are you doing here?"

I lightly shake my head, forgetting the two women strutting toward us. "Me? What are *you* doing here? I thought you worked for Tease?"

"Isn't that a strip club?" Eloise snidely remarks.

I beam, arching an eyebrow. "Yes, do you know it well?"

"God no."

Woods chuckles, poking me in the shoulder. "This one is a regular. Dave, the boss, threatened to ban her the first night she came, but look at that face. How could you ban that?"

I push his hand away, giggling. "He's just jealous I have moves."

His eyes widen in horror as he turns to Drew. "Be careful when she dances."

I press further into Drew. "I said I was sorry about that black eye."

"Why am I not surprised she dances?" Eloise bites out.

Drew tenses beside me. "Actually, she was there at first to research for a book she was writing," he tells her, before reaching a hand out to Woods. "I'm Drew."

"Keep an eye on this one tonight," Woods warns, but the smile doesn't slip from his lips. "I'm Woods, by the way."

"She stripped?" Natalie wryly gets out.

Drew gives her his attention briefly. "No."

I nod, agreeing with him. "I stayed 'cause I like it there."

"She really does," Woods comments before turning to me. "I need to get back to it. I'll catch up with you later."

I reach for his sleeve. "Wait, you didn't answer my question."

He gives the intruders a side glance before glancing at me, grinning. "I offer my services at the charity events. Dave knows and is always onboard with giving me time off."

"He's such sweet guy."

He chuckles. "I'll let him know you said that."

He leaves and I turn to Drew. "He's one of my favourite bouncers. He didn't get mad at me like the others."

"Why did they get mad?"

I shrug, glancing away. "I'm not sure. I mean, I don't think there's anything wrong with my dancing. I thought I did quite good. And no matter what Mathew said, I did not start that fight. Also, one didn't like it when he caught me feeling Nyla's boobs. I swear, you couldn't tell they were fake at all," I tell him, turning to Eloise, who is still trying to pull Drew's attention away from me. "Unlike yours. You should see if she'll tell you where she had them done."

Her lips clamp shut for a moment, her expression tightening. "You bitch."

I rear back at her outburst, my entire body shaking. "Excuse me?"

"As if you would say that," Natalie snaps. "Is this really who you want to be associated with?"

Drew snorts. "Even if she did say it to be a bitch, which she didn't, I'd still be standing right here. Eloise has done fuck all but make snide comments about her since they met."

"We came over here—"

He holds his hand up, stopping his sister. "To be nosey."

She huffs. "We'll speak to you later."

"You do that," he tells her, before taking my hand, pushing us inside the room where the event is being held.

I gape at the scene when we step through. Men and women are dressed to the nines, flouncing around with their jewels and drinks.

Large round tables surround the area around the balcony. It's loud in here, not just from the music playing in the background but the people talking. And not all of it is coming from up here.

Letting Drew's hand slip from mine, I make my way to the balcony bars, my breath hitching as I gaze at the scene below us. A large square ring sits in the middle of the floor below. Men and women surround the area, barking orders to the two fighters inside the ring.

I grimace at the sight of blood spurting from the guy's nose. The crowd below cheers, some standing while some remain sitting. The atmosphere is electrifying. The whole place is wired.

The two men in the ring step back from each other, both faces already swelling and bleeding. When the guy in the middle gives them an order and steps back, they go at it again, circling each other like predators.

A pair of arms wrap around me and I lean back into Drew's embrace. His hands press down on my stomach as he bends, pressing his cheek against mine.

"So, what do you think?"

I don't answer at first, too mesmerised by their movements. It isn't just their bodies, or hands, it's everything from their feet to the way they position their torso. It's an art form.

I glance into the crowd, watching the faces of those spectating, and they are just as mesmerised. Men look on with envy and frustration. Women ogle, salivating at the mouth, yet some are just as into this as the men. But it's the women trying to get closer to the fighters who hold my attention. There's an attraction there that I have seen with women and celebrity crushes.

"It's making me want to write a book about fighters," I murmur.

His fingers tighten on my stomach, pulling me closer against his chest. "Do your research as up and personal as you did with your last books?"

I nod absently, watching as one of the fighters are crowned the winner. A team rushes into the ring to attend to them both but it's one of the women who rushes straight up to the winner, jumping and wrapping her legs around his waist that I'm watching. "She seems happy for him."

"Maybe you could do one about a gym owner who teaches boxing?"

I grin, tilting my head to the side to look up at him. "That sounds like it could be interesting."

He nods, turning me in his arms. "And very hot. They could have sex on a weight bench."

I press my face into his chest. I still can't believe we did that; that I had been the one to initiate it. When I pull back, his smirk is downright dirty. "You're messing with me, aren't you?"

"A little, but I'd prefer it if you watched me rather than some other fighter."

I giggle at his pout. "If I ever do, you'll be the first person I come to."

"Drew, Natalie said you were here," Wesley announces. We turn, giving him our attention.

"Wesley, you look dashing," I tell him.

He grins, eyeing me up and down but not in a sleazy way. "And you look absolutely breath-taking, dear."

Drew reaches out, shaking his hand. "I didn't think you were coming."

There's a gleam in Wesley's eyes. "We've sponsored a new fighter. Tonight will be his first tournament."

"Which one is it?" Drew asks, pulling out his programme.

"It's Green. He's good. I've seen him practice."

Drew arches his eyebrow. "You've never taken this much of an interest."

Wesley steps closer, glancing around to make sure no one will overhear. "Between you and me; me and the guys from work have a little bet going tonight."

"Aw, will the winner be giving the funds to the charity?" I ask.

Drew presses his fist to his mouth as he covers up his cough. "Yes, Wesley, is that what will happen?"

"Oh, there's Dean. I must go say hello," he rushes out before stepping past us. He stops, turning back. "Oh, your sister is here tonight. She asked for the spare ticket."

"We've already seen her."

He nods. "Enjoy your night."

Drew chuckles. "You really got him there."

My brows scrunch together. "What do you mean?"

Bewildered, pulls me closer. "The money isn't going to Charity. They don't let them take bets here because they aren't licensed to."

My eyes widen, searching out Wesley, who is talking to an older fellow. "He wouldn't do that, would he?"

"Oh, he is, but his face when you called him out was priceless."

"I didn't know."

"That's what makes it funnier."

"What do you do at these things?" I don't want to bore him or make him wish he didn't bring me.

"First, I'll go find our table, then get you a drink. Then it's just a night of watching the fights and catching up with people. You'll also get to meet some of the fighters up here."

My eyes go round. "No way."

He pulls me to the other side of the room. "Don't sound too excited."

"Oh, there's your dad," I blurt out, staring at the table up ahead.

"You okay with him being here?"

I give him a side glance. "Of course I am. I wouldn't mind getting to know him."

I turn as we reach the table, pasting on my best smile. "Silas, it's good to see you again."

Pulling his attention from the lady he was in mid conversation with, he turns to see us. A grin spreads across his face. "Son, Charlotte," he greets, getting up. I give him a brief hug before stepping closer to Drew. Silas glances down at the clutch in my hand. "No bigger bag tonight?"

I wave my hand dismissively. "No. It didn't go with my outfit, and my other bag, Katnip chewed on the lid of an orgasm cream and it exploded everywhere."

He bursts out laughing, his eyes shining. The lady beside him winces. "Was it the Milo cream?"

I take a seat next to her as Drew converses with his dad, my eyes widening. "Yes. How did you know?"

"I'm Jackie, by the way," she greets. "And I had some. Expensive, but always does the trick."

"I didn't get a chance to use it. I get a lot of stuff via a friend to try out, but I never get to do the trying out part. The blueberry edible knickers were so good though."

A lady sitting across from us, clears her throat. "I prefer the strawberry ones."

"I'll have to try them," I tell her, giving her a smile of thanks.

Drew chokes as he takes a seat next to me. "Something you want to tell me?"

"Unless you want to try them?"

His dad laughs, slapping his son on the shoulder. "You picked a good one there, son."

I beam. "Thank you."

Drew runs his hand down my arm. "Would you like a drink?"

My hair brushes against my back as I turn to face him. "Maybe not wine."

He smirks, his pupils darkening. "You don't need wine tonight."

I lean forward, pressing my lips to his. "No, I really don't."

Because he is enough.

TWENTY-EIGHT

DREW

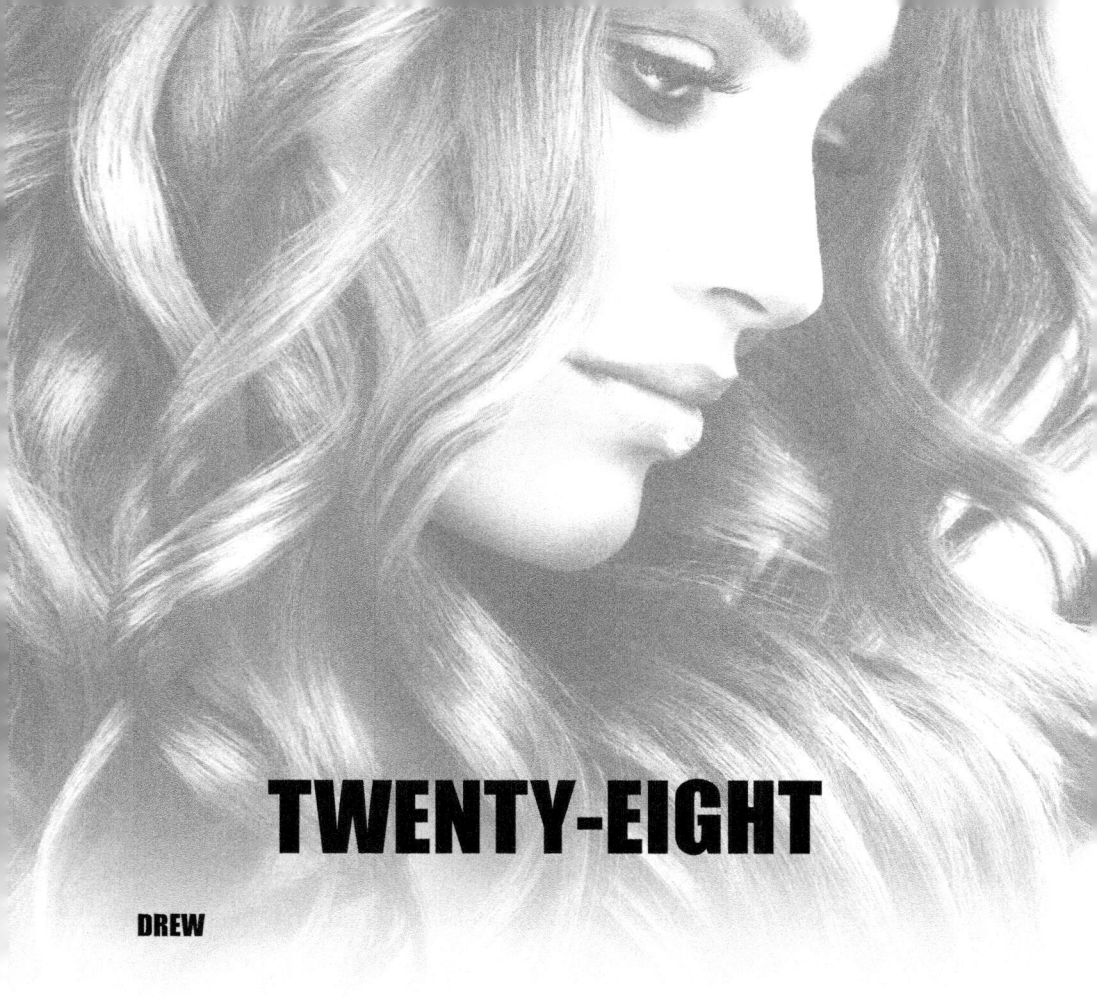

"**O**H MY GOD, CRUSH HIM!" Charlotte yells, holding her tiny fist in the air.

I wrap my arms around her waist, hoisting her up and away from the balcony. Who knew some so tiny could be so feisty and angry. Cheeks flushed, her eyes shining, she stares up at me. "Who does he think he is?"

My lips twitch. "Babe, it's their job."

Her attention pulls back to the fight, and Dad's friend, Gus, chuckles. "She isn't like your normal type."

I briefly check she hasn't nose-dived off the balcony before answering. "No. She's something else."

"She's special," Dad comments, placing a fresh tray of drinks down on the table.

Jackie nods. "Just don't let that girl tear her to pieces. She's been staring daggers at her all night."

I glance in the direction she looks, finding Eloise steaming at the ears as she glares over at us. I shrug. "Charlotte would break her without intentionally doing anything."

"What did Charlotte mean when she asked Eloise if she wanted a number?"

My shoulders shake as I run over what happened outside with the 'fake tits' comment. Dad splatters his drink everywhere. "She didn't."

"She hadn't even said it viciously."

Pride shines in his eyes. "She really is something."

Something hits me in the chest as I watch her half hanging over the balcony. "Yeah, she really is."

"Get him, Rampage. Take him down," Charlotte roars, and I dive to catch her before she falls over the edge.

I meet Woods' gaze over the balcony, shaking my head at his grin and the 'told you so' expression. "Fuck you," I mouth back.

"I want to fight. I want to take him out. He hit my Rampage," she cries.

Rampage is the headliner, the one the women all went hot for and someone I knew my sister and her circle of friends crowded whenever he was at an event.

It seems Charlotte isn't immune to his looks either and has been drooling over him since he came out half an hour ago to watch some of the other fights. "Babe, are you forgetting you came with a date?" I ask, earning chuckles from our group.

She turns to me, pouting. "But he's so pretty." Her attention gets pulled back to the fight when Axe, the other headliner, takes a cheap shot at Rampage. "Rampage, get your head out of your arse and finish him like a Chinese dinner." She pauses. "A vegetarian one because we love animals." She stops, turning to the group. "We love animals."

Dad, having just scoffed half a burger in his trap, gives her a thumbs up, nodding. "You tell him."

She nods, leaning over the balcony. "Rip him to shreds," she screams.

Rampage glances up, amusement written all over his face before he goes in for the next round.

"Babe, really? Stop drooling all over him."

She wraps her arms around my neck before sitting down on my lap. "This place is awesome. I feel so alive right now. I could totally take one of them on."

"And win," Dad adds, egging her on.

That look is one I'm becoming all too familiar with. "No, Charlotte."

Her gaze goes over my shoulder. "Harriet!"

She dives over me, nearly twisting her ankle to reach Harriet. "Charlotte," she squeals, reaching for Gabby next to her.

Gabby fist pumps the air. "Partayy," she yells.

Charlotte giggles. "Where are the rest of the girls? How come you are here?"

"We heard you were coming tonight so Woods hooked us up with standard tickets."

"Shouldn't you be downstairs?" Charlotte asks, frowning.

Harriet waves us off. "Like Woods could keep us from finding you. We just had to wait for the right time to sneak in."

"It wasn't hard," Gabby comments.

Charlotte reaches for their hands, pulling them closer to the table. "You have to meet everyone."

After introductions, people begin to shuffle around to make room for the girls to sit down next to Charlotte.

Charlotte takes a look down at the fight that is nearing the end. "You've got this, babe."

Harriet turns to me. "Did someone make her do a shot?"

I grimace. "Yeah, why?"

Gabby sighs. "Never give her a shot. She always gets boisterous and loud on shots."

Harriet slaps the table. "Horny on wine."

"Cranky on cider."

"What about Vodka?" Dad asks, grinning.

Both of the girl's shoulders drop. "You really don't want to know."

"She's happy," I comment, and both girls seem pleased with the answer. My eyes widen and I shoot across the chair to reach for her, pulling her back into her seat. "You're gonna fall."

"That lolly sucker tried to punch him even after that guy that keeps getting in the way called it."

"That's the ref," I remind her, my lips twitching. I pull her into my lap. "You having fun?"

"The best; you're the best," she tells me, leaning into me before her gaze narrows on the empty plate in front of Dad. "That's not an animal, is it? We discussed this and animals are our friends."

"The cow had it coming," he tells her, his lips twitching. "I'm saving the environment."

She shakes her head in disappointment. She doesn't really care that he's eating meat. I've seen her family eat. I think she just likes playing him up.

"Are you staying for dancing later?" Harriet asks.

Charlotte's eyes light up. "Dancing?"

My shoulders shake as I lean in, pressing a kiss to her neck. She shudders, cuddling closer. "If you don't get us kicked out before then."

She pumps the air. "Yes."

Polly, a wife of one of Dad's friends, leans forward. "Make sure you come to the next one. These things were starting to get boring but you have made this night enjoyable."

Charlotte's chest puffs out. "Thank yo— Oh my God, is that Rampage?" she yells.

I see him walking through the crowd toward us, now wearing a T-shirt and cleaned up from the fight. I stand at the same time Charlotte does. More to keep her from pouncing on him than anything.

"I'm your biggest fan," she yells. "You really knocked him out."

He grins, giving me a chin lift. "I heard."

"Holy fuck balls," Gabby sighs. "Why am I gay again?"

"You love vagina," Charlotte answers, sighing dreamily at Rampage.

His gaze moves past Charlotte to Harriet, who was staring dazedly up at him. "Good fight, man."

"Thanks, although my manager said you were paying more attention to your missus."

Laughter bubbles from my chest. "She got a little excited."

"You know him?" Charlotte asks.

"Who do you think trained him?"

Her eyes widen. "That is so hot."

Hiding his smile, Rampage takes a step forward. "Thank you for the cheering tonight."

"Was it a little much?"

"My opponent asked how much I paid you to cheer me on."

Charlotte chokes. "Dude, I can totally talk to him for you."

I pull her back when she goes to walk off. "Maybe not."

"Or not. I'm good with my mouth."

Eloise sidles up next to Rampage, Natalie next to her. "Fancy seeing you here," Eloise drawls, running her finger down his arm.

He rebuffs her touch, his gaze going to the woman behind us. From a quick glance, Harriet is trying her hardest not to look, but from the way her body is coiled tight, she has noticed him.

"I'm a fighter," he deadpans.

Natalie laughs before her gaze comes to me. "Drew, could I have a moment to talk to you somewhere privately please. It's important."

Natalie can be manipulative but something in her tone has me nodding. I glance down at Charlotte. "Can I trust you not to fall head-first over the balcony if I leave?"

She waves me off. "Of course not. Rampage can keep me company."

I roll my eyes, turning to him. He holds his hands up before I can speak. "Mate, her hair caught my attention but as soon as Neil said she was yours, I had to come up and see for myself."

"She has that effect on a lot of people."

"Believe it," he mutters, his gaze going back to Harriet.

"Yo, Charlotte, did you get to try the three-ninety-six, turbo, triple twist vibrator?" Gabby yells.

Charlotte's nose scrunches up. "It looked a little confusing with all the dials."

Harriet snorts. "She never tries them. She only picked it because it came with that fluffy feather whip and had glitter on the control."

I chuckle, leaning down to capture her lips. "Be back in a minute."

When Eloise goes to leave with us, I turn to Natalie. "I thought you wanted to talk privately?"

"I do. Eloise is family."

"So is my dad and extension, everyone in this family."

Charlotte leans on my arm. "Eloise, if you want, we can find that number?"

Dad chokes on his beer. Eloise's smile is brittle. "Rampage can keep me company, that is, if Drew doesn't get pissed at him again. He can be overprotective."

"He wasn't angry about you," Rampage answers before I can.

She waves him off. "You don't have to lie to protect her," she sweetly tells him.

I snort, pushing away from them. I jerk my chin at Natalie, and head to the back hallways. The music is drowned out the minute the door closes.

"If you are here to bad mouth Charlotte, you can forget it."

She places her hands on her hips, narrowing her gaze on me. "Do you think it's really wise to date her? She's a stripper, for god's sake. She's embarrassing, Andrew. She's done nothing but make a mockery of you tonight and you let her. How do you think Mum is going to react when she finds out?"

"Like I care what she says," I snap. "She's having a good time. No one but you has had a problem with it. She's not uptight. And for the last time, she's not a stripper."

"She goes to Tease."

"She was doing research for a book."

She stomps her foot. "People are going to think we are common."

"I am common," I growl, and she wisely clamps her lips shut. "You stand there trying to belittle Charlotte, and yet, she has worked her arse off to get where she is. She owns a library, and is a successful writer from what she has said."

"Eloise has been in your life since you were kids. You slept with her, Andrew. How can you just keep brushing that aside?"

"I'm going to stop you right there," I tell her, my voice low, menacing. "Eloise was a drunken one-night stand."

She takes a step forward. "Andrew. Give her a chance. Don't waste your life on someone like that girl out there. She's immature and beneath you."

"See you later," I gripe out, wishing she were more like Alison. It would be easy to like her then. She makes it so hard that there are times when I wish I didn't have to be in the same room as her. The only reason she gets away with half the crap she says and does is *because* she's my sister.

"Andrew, wait," Eloise calls out, coming in from the other door. I groan, running my fingers through my hair.

"You've been planning this all night, haven't you?" I declare, narrowing my gaze on Natalie.

"Just hear her out."

"No." I turn to leave, but her next words have my hand pausing halfway to the door.

"I was pregnant with your baby."

I slowly turn around, not saying anything. Running her hand down her black sparkly dress, she tries to appear nervous when I know she's anything but. Natalie gives her a warm smile, prompting Eloise to take another step forward. She flutters her lashes.

"I know I should have told you. I kept it from you and I can understand why you would be angry," she tells me, her voice shaking. "I tried on so many occasions, I swear, but you never gave me the chance. I'm hoping you'll give me one now."

"Andrew, please, hear her out," Natalie pleads. "She wants that back. She can give you that back."

Do they both think I'm stupid?

Nervously, Eloise glances away from Natalie. "She's right, Andrew. We can work this out. We are meant to be. Me falling pregnant proved that."

When I still don't say anything, Natalie blows out a heavy breath. "Andrew, I know she kept it from you, but can you blame her? You blow hot and cold."

"Are you done?" I ask her, not even sparing Eloise a glance.

Natalie gasps. "Andrew."

Eloise takes her arm. "It's fine. He needs time," she tells her before turning to me, her expression fake with anguish. "I know this is a lot to dump on you, but when you are ready, I'm here to talk. Okay?"

Does she think talking in a sweet voice will butter me up, will make me believe the crap coming out of her mouth?

And the tears.

I inwardly snort. "Mum is going to hear about this," Natalie threatens.

I stop myself from storming out, knowing Mum will believe the shit coming out of her mouth. I narrow my gaze on her. "You believe this?"

Natalie sniffs. "I was there for her."

"Really?"

"Andrew, this girl has you being an insensitive prick. How can you treat a long-time family friend like this, someone you shared something so special with?"

"Because the only thing I remember from our encounter was pulling off the used condom in the morning," I snap, and she pales, stepping back.

"We had sex more than once," she argues.

"No, we didn't," I tell her, my voice firm. "I might not remember much from that night, but I remember passing out blind drunk, which explains why I still had the condom fucking on."

"We had sex, Andrew. I was pregnant. I lost our baby at eight weeks."

I think back to that year. I had argued with Mum because I switched to fitness *and* business. She had been so mad and I went out and got shit faced. The same year, I had to stay with Dad because it had become too much at home. Eloise, I have no clue. She isn't on my radar now, and she certainly wasn't then.

"If you lost a baby, I'm sorry, but I wasn't the father. I don't appreciate you telling me I was either."

Her expression tightens. "You are only saying this because of her."

"Why are you so threatened by her?" I ask, my words biting. "Even with her out of the picture, you still wouldn't stand a chance, Eloise. I don't like you like that. At all."

"You'll see we belong together," she argues, tears gathering in her eyes. "Everyone wants us together. It's just you who won't see it."

I throw my hands up. "Because it's only my decision that matters. Just because someone says it should be 'so' doesn't mean it should be. I'm sorry you're upset, but I'm done here."

"Andrew," Natalie yells.

I stop with my hand frozen on the door handle and turn to her. "Don't, Natalie. I understand her being your friend, but you're my sister. You more than anyone should know when the bitch is lying and stand up for me. Instead, you enable her lies to continue, and in turn, could have tarnished my reputation."

She has the gall to look ashamed. As she should. "Andrew."

I leave, slamming the door closed behind me. I head back to the table, coming to a stop when I find it empty.

"What the fuck?" I whisper. I glance around and on the other side of the room, is Charlotte, leading a conga line with nearly every fucker in attendance behind her.

She waves from the other side of the club and I chuckle, my mood lightening. Dad breaks off, coming to stand beside me. "If I was—"

"Not even then," I warn him, knowing what he was going to say.

He chuckles. "You can't blame a guy for trying."

I watch her draw closer, her smile lighting up her entire face. "Best date ever."

No. She is the best date ever. She moves past, and I arch an eyebrow at Rampage, the bulky, muscled guy in line. He shrugs, grinning. "And here I was afraid of tonight being boring," he yells.

He moves past, and when I spot Howie, one of the event organisers who is in his eighties also in line with his wife, I chuckle. "Bring her again next time," he calls out.

Dad claps me on the shoulder. "They love her."

I turn, arching an eyebrow. "How could they not?"

He tilts his head side to side. "You got me there," he replies, his forehead creasing. "What did Natalie want? And don't think I missed that bitch following behind."

I sigh, running a hand through my hair, and quickly run over everything that was said. "I just don't get why she would take up for her like that."

"I do."

"What?"

"It's no lie Eloise gets around. She's a snake waiting to strike, but I've been hearing rumours."

"What rumours?"

"Her dad has threatened to cut her off if she doesn't hurry up and get married. He wants a male heir for his business and he's too old for any more kids."

I snort. "And she's picked me?"

"They've all picked you," he points out. "But like I said, she gets around, and it wouldn't surprise me if she wants you to give her a chance so she can get pregnant."

"To trap me," I surmise. "Natalie has always teased about her becoming a real sister eventually. Now I know why."

Dad shudders. "That woman is made of ice," he tells me, before laughing at the dance Charlotte has them all doing. "Unlike that one. She's all warmth."

"And she's mine," I warn him, grinning. I leave him laughing to go and get her. All these fuckers have had her for long enough.

TWENTY-NINE

CHARLOTTE

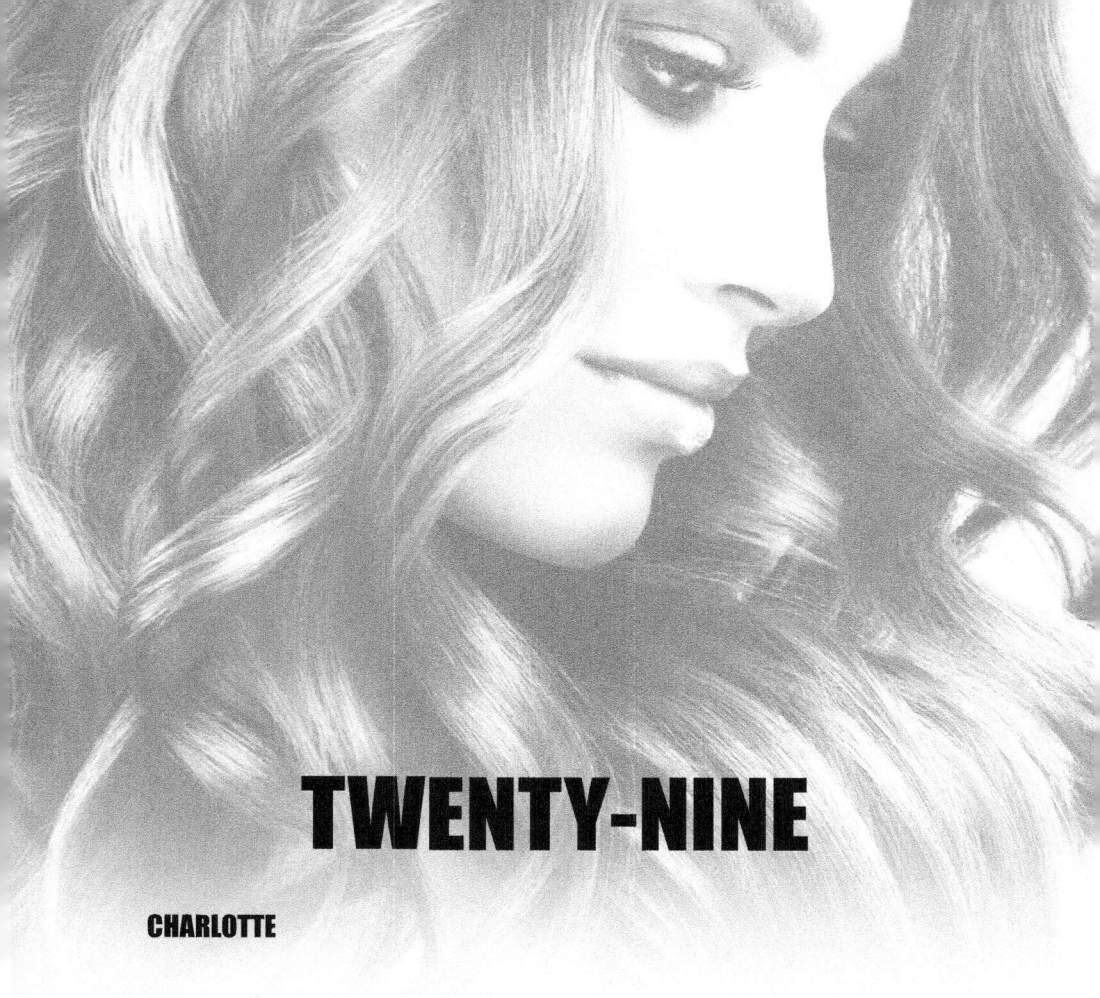

Tonight has been filled with so much laughter. My face aches from being unable to keep the smile off my face. And there's a fine shine of sweat beading on my chest and back from all the dancing I had done.

To top the night off, people are interested in my library. The fighter pauses, glancing up from his phone. "And this is on Main Street?"

"It is. We have various books on the subject, and if one of them isn't the right fit, I can order some in for you. It's not a problem."

"What are you doing now?" Drew asks, his arms snaking around my waist.

I lean back into him. "Trevor needs some coursework books. I have them. I was just telling him studying in this light isn't good for the brain."

Pressing his lips against my shoulder, I feel him smile. "Yeah, sorry for taking her time up, man," Trevor announces, yet his focus is still on his phone. "Thanks again, Charlotte."

Dev and his wife, Michelle, step forward. "And thank you for those tips. We'll get on it."

"You're welcome."

Once they leave, I turn, placing my hands on Drew's chest. His gaze flicks away from the couple who have just left us, to me. "What tips?"

I lean in. "They heard about the sex toys from someone at our table and asked what I'd recommend so I recommended this book at the library. It has some amazing tips on how to spice things up, and oddly enough, it's the same list I went by first to see if we had, in fact, done every position."

His lips twitch, but the normal happiness isn't there. Ever since he headed off with his sister earlier, he has been tense, not fully here with me, and I'm beginning to worry it's me. Sometimes I can get carried away and I've been told once or twice to grow up.

"And have we?" he asks.

"Well, if you include destination and then a certain area on my body, then no, we didn't do it all."

His pupils darken as he pulls me flush against his chest. "Maybe we should rectify those."

"Hmm, maybe," I tease.

He leans down, pressing his lips to mine. I press against him, clutching his jacket. When he pulls back, his pupils dilate. "Tease."

I shrug. "Are you having a good night? I feel bad it's our first official date and I've been wandering around."

He brushes my hair off my shoulder. "As long as you're having fun, I don't care. I'm glad you've enjoyed tonight."

I wrap a strand of his hair around my finger, fluttering my lashes up at him. "Are you sure? Because you don't seem okay? You seem off. Was it your sister?"

He lifts me up, spinning me around until he lands me on the stool. He steps between my legs. "I won't get into now, but I'll tell you later. I don't want it to ruin the night."

"I won't let it," I promise, seeing the hurt flickering in the depth of his eyes.

He sighs. "Eloise has made up some bullshit that isn't true about me. My sister is feeding off it," he explains. "I'll tell you the rest when we don't have prying ears."

I nod, understanding he wants privacy. "Okay."

He tilts my chin up. "I am going to tell you, but I'm not letting them ruin tonight. It's what they want."

Giving him a lopsided grin, I then pull him closer. "Have you enjoyed tonight?"

Pressing his lips to mine, I soak in the warmth. "I have. It's been one heck of a date."

"I didn't embarrass you?"

He gives me an annoyed look. "Not once."

My shoulders sag. "I was a little worried."

He smirks, shaking his head. "Babe, you know how to have fun, to let yourself be free. Don't ever apologise for that."

"Most people can't handle the weird."

"The weird is what draws people to you."

"Really?"

He pulls me against him. "But I'm the only one who matters. Remember that the next time Rampage walks past."

I giggle. "I think he has a thing for Harriet."

Drew scans the bottom floor of the event room we're in, stopping at something and groaning. Seeing his dad still trying to master the Gangnam Style dance, I begin to laugh.

"He's so wasted," Drew groans.

"Who is with Nora tonight?" I ask, laughter spilling out of me when he gets one of the older ladies to do it with him.

"She's okay on her own, but I know tonight she has a friend staying over with her. I will warn her about Dad though." He pauses to groan as his dad lands flat on his arse. "Yeah, I think it's time for him to get into a taxi."

"Ohhhh, I need to go for wee. I'll meet you in the lobby."

"I think most people are leaving now too," Drew confirms.

They are. The ones who don't want to continue listening to club music, head for the lobby to wine and chat. The rest of us are living it up in here dancing until our feet scream not to.

Leaning up on my toes, Drew grins, lifting me at the waist so I can kiss him. I love kissing him. And so many times tonight, he's found more reasons to do it. Not that I'm complaining.

Pulling back, a shudder rolls over me. A good one. A really good one. "Can we have sex tonight," I blurt out.

He leans down, capturing my lips once more. "Yes, because I've been dying to know what you are wearing under this dress."

I run my hand down my dress. "Not a lot if I'm honest. You'll be disappointed."

He laughs, pulling me close. "Never change who you are, Charlotte."

"I won't," I promise, then gently push him away. "Now go get your dad sorted. I want to have sex."

The guy walking past begins to choke on his glass. His gaze runs up and down my body before turning to Drew. "Lucky fucker."

I leave Drew to sort his dad and head for the toilets, yet when I spot Harriet and Gabby, I make a beeline for them.

"Toilet break?" Gabby asks, spotting me.

"Yes, then I'm going home because I really, really want to have sex with Drew."

She high-fives me before grabbing Harriet's hand. "I don't know why he keeps staring my way when he has all those girls hanging off his arm."

Gabby snorts. "Admit it, you want to ride his bone."

"I do not."

"You so do," I declare.

"You two are so unfair."

We reach the lobby, and seeing the toilet sign up ahead has my bladder weakening. I really do need to go. We rush inside, and I quickly take care of business before going to the sink to wash my hands.

Harriet looks at me through the mirror. "He's good with you. I like him."

"I like him too."

"Me three," Gabby sighs wistfully. "The way he picks her up just so she can reach his lips. Dudes. Sigh."

"He's only done that a few times," I remind her, shaking my head.

She shrugs. "Still hot."

"Come on, I need to meet him outside."

Eloise has other plans, blocking our path at the door. There's a dark smudge under her eyes, like she has been crying. If we had been friends I'd be hugging her right now. Because despite everything she has said to me, she seems like the kind of person who wasn't hugged enough as a child.

"Are you okay?" I ask.

She angrily wipes at her cheeks. "What do you care?"

"Dude, tone it down," Gabby presses.

Ignoring her, Eloise turns to me. "He's not going to love you. He won't even stay with you. This is just a short fling for him, another way to get back at his mum."

I fiddle with my clutch. I might not know for certain what the future holds or what Drew wants, but I can't believe her words. "No, it's not."

"Please tell me she's not an ex," Harriet bites out.

Gabby stands on my other side, crossing her arms over her chest. "I never get why they always make this scene."

"She's not his ex," I whisper from the side of my mouth. "They had a one-night stand."

Eloise laughs bitterly. "You think you are better than me? You aren't. We're meant to be together."

"If you were meant to be together, why aren't you?" I ask softly. Even being a bitch, I still can't find it in me to be mean back to her. She looks truly devastated.

"Because of you," she screeches. "This wedding was meant to be our chance to rekindle what we once had and you are taking it away from us. If you were any kind of descent human being, you would leave him alone and let him be happy."

"I'm not trapping him," I whisper.

"She's the best human we know," Gabby snaps, swaying slightly.

I beam, patting her arm. "Thank you."

"Yes, you are. You are putting a wedge between Andrew and Grace. And now even Natalie. How can you do such a thing? You are an embarrassment to him. I saw him tonight. He couldn't even look at you. No. But he looked at me," she tells me, pointing to her chest. "We're planning on having a family together."

"That's a lie," I tell her bluntly.

I might have been made a fool of in the past, may have been deceived and manipulated by those around me, but Drew wasn't one of them.

Her lips twist into a snarl. "No, it's not. And you know it. He hasn't brought you around us much and there's a reason for that. Hell, he didn't even sit at his table tonight, but his dad's, and it was because he didn't want to bring you into our world. He knows there isn't any point because you won't be staying. You don't belong."

"She was sat with his dad and friends," Harriet bites back.

Eloise arches her eyebrow. "Because that family have people coming and going all the time. It makes no difference to him."

I turn to Gabby, feeling my eyes well up with tears. Not because I believe her but because I understand what Drew meant when he said his family had high expectations and it suffocated him. "I don't believe her."

"Hey, don't get upset," Gabby soothes.

Eloise, smug as all hell, and no longer slouching, straightens. "Believe it. He wants me."

"I'm not getting upset. I'm getting angry," I growl.

"Oh fuck," Harriet whispers, stepping away.

I place my hands on my hips, staring Eloise down. "Why do you want him?" Her lips move, but no words come out. "Answer me."

"Because we are meant to be together."

"Why though?"

"Because our families—"

"Because your families said so. Not Drew. *Them*. He is a person most capable of making his own choices in life and you stand here trying to take that away from him. I might not have known him long, but I do know he never does something he doesn't want to do. If I was embarrassing him, he would have taken me home. If he didn't want to bring me here, he wouldn't have even mentioned it. And as for the table situation, Drew already explained to me he has two chairs here at the event. It gives him a choice of who he wants to sit next to, but he's always sat with his father since he's more comfortable there." I exhale slowly. "As for your predicament, it's a fantasy. I can relate. I've lived in books for years. What your excuse is, I don't know. If he wanted you though, he wouldn't deny it. He's not a man who hides from what he wants."

"Which I guess means he wants you, since he's always going after you," Harriet surmises.

Face red, coiled tight with veins bulging at her neck and temple, Eloise comes at me. "You bitch."

My body freezes for a moment, my intake of breath getting trapped in my lungs. I can't be hurt again. Not ever.

Crying out, I push her back before she can hit me, knocking her into a woman stepping through the toilet doors.

Gathering her bearings, the woman straightens, going right for Eloise.

"Oh shit," Gabby whispers as another woman is knocked over, getting pulled into the fight.

I watch in horror as two men come rushing over. "Get off my wife," he roars, trying to pull the blonde off who I assume is his wife.

"Don't touch my woman," the other guy bites out, his fist flying out and landing on the guy's nose.

I whimper. "Oh God."

"He's mine, bitch. Mine!" Eloise roars, extensions hanging off her head.

Attentively, I step over an out cold woman, making my way around the ever-growing fight. I get out of the fray when Woods storms over, pausing when he sees me. "Why am I not surprised you're involved."

I get shoved in the back and he catches me, pulling me out of harm's way. "Go!"

"I'm coming for you," Eloise roars, before another woman jumps on her back, stopping her from coming at me.

"Oh fuck!" Gabby whispers. "That had to have hurt."

"Charlotte!" Drew roars, knocking a guy out of the way as he gets to me.

"Girls, I'll speak to you tomorrow."

"Go!" they order. "We're going back for one more drink."

Drew grabs my hand, pulling me back. I watch the girls for one more moment, making sure they get back into the event okay.

"Come on," Drew orders, pulling me toward the exit. "The police will be called."

I begin to run as fast as I can in my heels. "Come on, before they arrest me."

"Arrest you? You've done nothing wrong," he calls out.

I push open the door, paling when I spot police cars coming down the road. "I pushed Eloise when she came at me. It had a domino effect because before I knew it, they were all fighting."

"Eloise—"

"Let's go," I order, pulling him in the opposite direction the police are pulling in from.

He tugs on my arm when we come to a side road, and drags me down there, pushing me against the wall. "Did she hurt you?"

Panting heavily, I glance up at him. "No."

"What happened?"

I quickly run over everything she said in the toilets. "I didn't believe her," I finish.

"You have that much faith in me?"

I run my hands up his chest, stopping at his shoulders. "I've been fooled a lot during my life, but with you, I can't explain it. I trusted your actions and words more than I did hers. Does that make me a bad feminist?"

"No, it makes you intuitive," he admits. "What she said, none of it was true. Earlier, she ambushed me, stating the night we spent together resulted in a pregnancy that she miscarried."

"Drew," I whisper.

He shakes his head, quickly explaining everything that happened when his sister pulled him away earlier. The more he tells me, the closer I press against him, wanting to comfort him.

"Why would she say those things?" I ask, then a thought occurs to me. "Your sister wasn't with her earlier. And Eloise looked pretty upset."

"Hopefully she saw through the lies." He shrugs. "I'm pissed she'd think so little of me."

"I'm sorry you had to listen to that."

"What's worse is, Eloise knows the pressure my mother will rain down on me if she tells her. And what's worse, my mum will probably know it's a lie and go along with it anyway."

My heart constricts. "What will you do?"

"Fuck all. Because it's all bullshit and even if it wasn't, it still wouldn't be a reason to force myself into a marriage with her."

I relax against him. "She thought she could guilt trip you," I guess.

"Yeah, but it's not going to work. I'm not sure why they've deluded themselves into thinking otherwise."

"The things she said... I don't want to come between you and your family."

His gaze softens. "You wouldn't be the one getting between us. It's them getting between us."

My pulse picks up. "There's an us?"

His pupils darken. "Fuck yes."

"And I didn't embarrass you?"

Cupping my cheek, he brings his head down, resting it against mine. "Never."

"Good," I whisper, feeling good all over. Even my vagina is feeling extremely happy right now.

He pulls back a little, his expression bewildered. "You really stuck up for me?"

"Of course. I always stand up for what I believe in."

"You started a full-on brawl," he teases.

I press closer, needing his touch. "Because I was taught to never do things halfway."

He leans down, groaning into my neck. "I want to pull up your dress and fuck you right here, but you deserve a bed."

I giggle, running my fingers through his hair. "Then take me home."

THIRTY

DREW

Stepping into the bedroom, my gaze goes right to the bed where Charlotte is sleeping. Her bright red, thick hair fans out across the pillows. One leg is hitched up, wrapped over the blanket, along with her arm. She was in the same position when I woke up earlier, only her arm and leg were draped over me.

A light snore passes through her thick, luscious lips, causing me to chuckle. Her makeup from the night before is smudged, her lipstick smeared, and mascara has run under her eyes.

And yet, she is still the most beautiful girl I have ever met.

And if my bladder hadn't been screaming at me to use the loo, I'd still be cuddled up to her, which is how I would have preferred our night to go.

It hadn't. When I checked my phone for the time, I couldn't ignore the millions of missed calls and messages filtering through.

I called my dad and Nora first, and once I got off the phone with them, other guests who attended last night's charity fight called, checking in on Charlotte. Even Rampage, someone who had met her briefly, called after hearing someone tried to attack her and then wanted to know if it was true that she and her friends had caused a riot in the hotel. I still can't believe it happened. I'm angry Eloise went after her, and hearing other people bringing it up, each time the story changing from bad to worse, I want to go give Eloise a piece of my mind. But I have a sinking feeling it's the attention she wants. She wants me to go to her.

Everyone else thought it was hilarious someone so sweet and small could cause such chaos.

Then Mum called, accusing Charlotte of attacking Eloise, and told me the invite to the wedding was revoked for Charlotte. Luckily, I had already spoken to Alison and she was livid on Charlotte's behalf. She hated that Natalie and Eloise did what they did, more so once I ran through everything they accused me of. Her screech of anger is still echoing through my ears and I have no doubt Natalie is going to hear it from her twin at some point today.

Fortunately, I didn't have to listen to Mum continue to go on about how common and unladylike Charlotte is since my battery died.

Charlotte didn't once let what they did taint our night, and when we got back, she proceeded to show me just how much she had enjoyed our first date. My redhead is an enigma. She wants romance, sweet kisses and hugs, but she also wants it dirty and rough. She's the definition of 'lady in the streets, freak in the sheets.' And it blows my mind every time she suggests we try something new or is willing to switch it up. She's open to experimenting as long as it feels good.

And fuck does it feel good.

Her confidence is astounding after everything she has been through. Her pure heart is what has pulled her through. She thinks it's because of her family and the self-defence lessons we've been working on. But it isn't. It's her heart. She has managed to do what many victims aren't able to: separate a violation to a sexual experience. Even under her sweetness, her rose-coloured blushes, my girl is highly sexual. No one has the right to take that away from her. No one.

Setting the tray on the other side of the bed, I then take a seat next to Charlotte, taking in her room. It's a girly room, yet modern. There are a lot of crazy knick-knacks too, but they suit Charlotte's personality. I also notice there's a lot more pink frilly stuff and glitter than there was the last time I was here. This seems more her. The only thing that worries me is the fact she has butt balls that light up and is using them as decoration. When I asked her about it last night, she said it's a night light her friend from Tease gave her.

Katnip sits on her dressing table, her judgy eyes focused on Charlotte sleeping. It's creepy to the say the least, especially when she suddenly does a head tilt, like she's contemplating how or when would be the best time to strike. I can see why Landon and his family are worried for Charlotte's safety. That cat has fucking issues. If I hadn't seen how cuddly and loving the cat could be, even I would think it was soulless.

Pulling my attention away from the bipolar cat, I lightly tap Charlotte on her shoulder.

"Charlotte, wake up," I whisper, before running my finger down her arm.

"My kung fu is strong," she grumbles, shoving her face into the pillow where the snoring continues.

I chuckle, and lean over to brush away the hair that has fallen over her face. "Charlotte," I call out.

She slaps her lips together, turning away from my touch. "One more minute and I'll defeat him."

"Charlotte, babe," I call out, shaking her once more.

"My vagina doesn't want another round," she mutters, moving away from my touch.

Laughter spills out of me and I take a minute to gather myself before shaking her a little harder. "Charlotte, babe, wake up."

She knifes up in bed, glancing around the room before turning to me. I chuckle at the hair knotted in a ball at the side of her head. "Drew?"

"Good morning," I greet.

She yawns, stretching her arms into the air. "What time is it?"

"Just after ten."

Her gaze softens on the eggs I made. "Is that for me?"

"It is," I reply, pushing it closer to her. "What are you doing for the rest of the day?"

"I need to go into work at some point," she admits, before biting into a piece of toast.

"Spend the rest of the weekend with me."

She finishes chewing her toast. "You want to spend the weekend with me? Here?"

"Yes," I tell her, and her shoulders slump, a lost look in her eyes. "But I want to take you out on my bike first."

The light appears back into her eyes, making me relax. I'll have to remember to question her about it later. "You want to take me out? Like, out, out? In public out?"

"Yes," I chuckle. "And after, I thought we could bring my projector around. The white screen will hang off your tree and we could watch a movie outside. If you want."

Suddenly, she slaps her face. "I don't want to wake up."

Laughter spills out of me, and I grip her wrist, stopping her from slapping her face again. "Stop. You're awake."

Her eyes bug out. "Really? This isn't some dream?"

I lean over, pressing my lips to hers. "Would that happen in a dream?"

Her pupils darken. "You do a lot more in my dreams."

I rest my forehead against hers. She kills me. I groan low in my throat. "Charlotte."

"You really want to spend time with me?"

Tilting her chin up, I lean in closer, meeting her gaze. Her insecurity is killing me. "One day you'll realise your importance to people."

She grips the bedsheet puddled in her lap. "I'd love to spend the day with you, Drew."

Pressing another kiss on her lips, I then get up, straightening out my creased shirt. "I've got to go home, get showered and changed, and then go check on the gym. I missed calls from Landon, but my battery went before I had a chance to talk to him. I'll be back to pick you up around twelve? Is that okay?"

"More than okay," she whispers.

Kissing her one last time, I then turn to leave. "See you soon."

I close the bedroom door to, and laugh when I hear her muffled squeal of joy. She really is a breath of fresh air.

"Katnip, no..." she cries out.

A chuckle slips free as I let myself out.

PULLING UP OUTSIDE the gym, I gape at the destruction that awaits me. All the front windows are smashed, including the entrance door. The area has had a few broken windows and a couple of incidents involving graffiti, but never something this severe. Taking a look at the other buildings, none of them have been touched.

There are police questioning staff and Landon is amongst them, running his fingers through his hair with a haggard expression.

I get out, slamming the door to Dad's truck that he let me borrow. It's easier to cart my bike and the stuff we will need for tonight in there than doing a dozen trips back and forth. Now I'm wishing I had gone straight to Charlotte's. I don't want this ruining our day together. She had been too excited about me taking her out for me to let her down now. Whatever happened here isn't going to change my plans.

Landon turns at the sound of my door slamming shut, and his shoulders sag when he spots me. "Where the fuck have you been?"

"What's going on?" I ask, gritting my teeth as my boots crunch over the broken glass. "Who the fuck has done this?"

"Calm down," he tells me.

I give him a hard look, not wanting to be fucked around right now. "Tell me!"

He shoulders drop. "As you can see, someone has smashed the windows; they've also vandalised your office. It's a mess in there," he explains. "I've been trying to get a hold of you all morning and left messages for you to get here."

I step past him and through the broken doorway, following the scrape someone had run along the floor, the reception desk, and then back to the floor leading to our office. For it to cause that kind of damage, it would have needed a steel bar.

I'm taken aback when I step into the gym area. All the equipment has been left untouched. There isn't a single thing touched or damaged in here. "What the fuck?" I grit out, stopping to let Landon answer.

"I don't know either."

"This was personal," I guess.

He avoids looking me in the eye. "There's more you need to see in the office."

What isn't he telling me?

Stepping inside, I suck in a breath at the mess that is contained to one side of the room. "It's only my side that's been trashed," I point out.

"Yeah. And you received those," Landon tells me, pointing to a vase of white tulips on the broken desk.

The hairs on the nape of my neck stand on end, and ignoring the newcomer, I move toward the vase.

"Sir, we have forensics coming."

I narrow my gaze on him, and he clamps his lips shut. I take off the lavender coloured note wedged into the petals and vase. "Has someone read this?"

Landon shakes his head. "No. I have been waiting for you. My family know about this. We think it's someone trying to warn me off and they got the wrong side of the room."

I pull out the card, not answering him.

She taints them all.

She paints them red.

Give her a chance, and she'll stain you next.
Leave while you can.
This is my gift.
I won't give up until she's at rest.

"This isn't about you," I rumble.

Landon takes a step, his brows reaching his hairline as he scans over the note. "What the fuck?"

"This is because I'm spending time with Charlotte."

He narrows his gaze. "You spent, what, a handful of times with her? This has to be because I've been looking for him."

"I took her on a date last night," I admit, giving zero fucks for his reaction. He grits his teeth and looks away. "I think someone doesn't like that."

"Then it's Scott doing this. It's the only explanation."

"Not the only one," I murmur. "Did you speak to any of the women on the list?"

"Not yet. Me and Aunt Kayla are going up to see one next week. She's away with her husband at the minute," he explains. "The rest don't feel comfortable talking to us. Kayla said to give them time."

"Let me know how it goes." I turn to the officer. "How long before we can reopen?"

"We should be finished up here in a few hours."

I give him a nod before turning to Landon, handing him the note. "Find the person in charge of her case. Give this to them, no one else. They'll want to know."

"What are you going to do?" he asks, as I pick my phonebook out of the pile of papers scattered all over the floor.

Handing him the phonebook, I grin. "I'm going on a date with Charlotte. No fucker is going to push me away from her." I narrow my gaze on him. "Not even you or yours."

He curses, stepping forward before stopping himself from doing something stupid. "You always were a stubborn motherfucker."

My grin spreads. "Get used to it because I'm not going anywhere."

"What does Charlotte have to say about that?"

I shrug. "You'll have to ask her; but just so you know, I'll take it personally if you warn her away from me. Now I've gotten to know her, I won't let you or anyone else fuck it up."

"And what are you going to do if we do?" he argues, a sharp bite to his tone.

Stopping at the door, I turn to him, letting him see how serious I am. "*Fight for her.*"

I leave, and hear him stomping after me. "Wait; where the fuck are you going?"

Sighing, I turn to him. "I've got somewhere important to be," I remind him, then point to the book I gave him. "You can call someone to fix the windows and door. Charge it to the business account."

"And what about all the members and staff?"

I shrug. "Send them home."

He watches me closely, eyes narrowed. "You don't seem very effected by this."

"I'm a calm person."

"Yes, but you protect what's yours. I've seen you jump to defend this place when we've had trouble."

My gaze bores into his. "This isn't what needs protecting. Charlotte is."

With that, I turn and leave, trusting Landon to sort this mess out. Am I pissed someone has done this? Yes. But it's all replaceable and easily fixed. If the person had directed their anger to the entire gym, we might not have been able to reopen for a while. We're also lucky no one took advantage of the break in to actually steal equipment.

The gym has been my life for so long. I sacrificed everything to make sure it took off and made profit within the first two years of opening. The expansions made to the place had come from those profits and over time it had increased. When Landon became partner, it was to give me time for other aspects of my life. However, I found once I had all the free time, I didn't have anyone to really spend it with. I could go out with my mates to the pub and have a drink, but I had no one to go places with. And it sucked. I had contemplated getting a dog until I babysat Rex, Landon's dog. The animal had separation anxiety whenever he parted with Landon.

My phone dings with a message alert as I open the truck door. I lean over the console, taking it off charge. I have missed calls from Mum, Nora and Charlotte. I click on her message first.

Charlotte: Mum has just called me. Is it true? Has someone smashed your windows because of me? Drew, I'm so sorry. I'll pay for the damage; everything. I'm just so sorry. Please, please, call me back. Please. I'll do anything to make this right.

Drew: Please don't get worked up over this. None of it is your fault or your responsibility. I'm on my way. I'll speak to you when I get there.

Charlotte: You don't hate me?

Charlotte: Don't read that if you're driving.

Charlotte: Sugar, or that.

Charlotte: I'm going to curl up in a ball and cry.

My shoulders shake with silent laughter as I slide into the truck. I quickly type out a reply.

Drew: Be there soon, gorgeous. And make sure you have on thick jeans.

I pocket my phone and turn on the engine whilst glancing around at the crowd of people who have gathered to see what is going on. One of them could be the fucker messing with Charlotte, hoping she'll turn up at some point to see if we're okay. This is, after all, her cousin and best friend's gym, and mine, the guy she is seeing.

I think back to the note that was left as I pull out of the space. It sounded like an ex-lover who wanted her to himself. But there is a slither of doubt that I can't push away that makes me think there is something more to these notes. Stalkers have obsessions. This person isn't obsessed with Charlotte in way they deem her as a belonging or theirs. It's an evil rooted so deep it's going *after* Charlotte.

And I'm going to stop them.

THIRTY-ONE

DREW

There's nothing more freeing than being on a motorcycle. Just like being in a car, the places you can go are endless, but with a bike, it's something else entirely. It's thrilling, enticing. There is nothing but you, the rumble of the bike beneath you, and the wind whipping around you.

Today, however, it isn't just me left to my thoughts. Today I have Charlotte on the back of my bike, her fingers clenching into my jacket. The excitement, the exhilaration of the ride… I can feel it vibrating off her and into me. She had been so tense when we rode off, but the minute we got out of the town and onto the empty roads or motorways, she relaxed. At one point, I watched as she leaned her head back a little, soaking in the feeling you only get on a bike.

I knew she'd like it, if not love it. For someone with deep roots in her life, she's still a free spirit at heart.

I clutch the throttle, then twist, accelerating up the hill faster and taking the bend with practiced ease. The countryside flies past us, the scent of country air, hay, and horse manure hitting us in the face as we speed through.

Easing on the throttle, I slow down through the village, passing children who are playing in the small park. They all stop at the sound of the bike rumbling through the street, the boys racing over to the gated fence to get a closer look.

Charlotte waves quickly before grabbing for my jacket once again. I grin, speeding up the bike once we hit the main road more, and moments later, take a right turn, riding higher and higher through the windy roads.

We're close to my favourite spot; a place a lot of locals and tourists come to visit. The cliff top is known for its beautiful view, and people spend the day travelling to see it. The food trucks come into view and I slow the bike down before coming to a stop in the first available spot.

As always after a long drive, my legs buzz from vibrations and my heart races from adrenaline. I rip my helmet off, throwing it over the handlebars before sliding off the bike.

Charlotte's a sight to be seen. Thanks to Nora, I had a jacket, boots, gloves and a helmet to fit her. In her dark jeans and leather jacket, she reminds me of a model on a cover of my motorcycle magazine.

Whipping the helmet off, Charlotte grins up at me, her entire face flushed and filled with life. Happiness doesn't just shine from her, it radiates from her.

"You like?"

She sighs, settling back to tilt her head up into air, soaking it in. When her gaze locks on mine, there's a fire there. "Drew, that has to be the best experiences of my life. I've bungee-jumped, zip-lined and swam with sharks. But none of those even compared to what I felt sat behind you on this bike."

I help her swing her leg over the bike and step between her thighs. Her thick, red hair had fallen free when she took the helmet off, so I tuck it behind her shoulders. "You're beautiful."

She melts against me. "You are too."

Landon's words earlier are an echo in my mind. I don't want them to get to me or play a part between Charlotte or I, but I know her well enough to know she'll never broach the subject. "Charlotte, there's something I want to talk to you about."

"About the vandalism?"

I avoided talking about the gym, wanting her to enjoy the day. I know I'll have to talk about it. I'm just hoping we have more time before conversation turns sour. "This is about us."

The light in her eyes dims and she folds her arms in front of her, ducking her head. It's like I have sucked all of the joy out of her. "About us?"

I tilt her chin up with my finger. "Don't do that."

"Do what?" she whispers.

"Think the worst. You never give yourself enough credit or worth."

"I don't mean to."

I wrap my arms around her, pulling her flush against me. "I know."

She gulps, still looking vulnerable with her green doe eyes blinking up at me. "What did you want to talk about?"

I rub the back of my neck, finding this harder to bring up than I thought it would be. "We've, um, we've been spending a lot of time together."

Her brows dip. "Do you want some space?"

"What? No. I want to spend *more* time with you."

She beams. "I'd really like that."

"But not as friends."

She shakes her head, her baffled expression amusing me. "Not as friends?"

I step closer, cupping her jaw. "I want to be more than friends."

"More than friends with me?" she breathes.

"Yes," I whisper, bringing my lips down.

"Why?" she blurts out, and I pull back, confused by her question.

"Why, what?"

"Why would you want to be more than friends? What do you want to be?"

I sigh, putting an inch between us. I'm not willing to give her more. "Because I want to be more than friends. I want us to be together."

"We are together."

My lips twitch. "As your boyfriend." Something lurks in the depth of her eyes and I feel like I've lost her for a moment. I gently shake her, ducking my head to meet her gaze. "Where did you go?"

Blinking, she regains focus. "This isn't a trick?" she whispers.

The heartbreak in her voice has me picking her up by the waist. She wraps her arms and legs around me as I walk over to the bench not far from the bike. I take a seat, keeping her on my lap. "Charlotte, this is no trick. I'm not *him*. I won't hurt you. I'm not saying I won't fuck up or get on your nerves, but you never have to be scared of me."

"I'm not scared of you," she whispers brokenly.

"Then what are you scared of?"

She gazes over my shoulder, seeming lost in thought. When she turns back, her eyes are glistening with tears. "I'm scared this isn't real. I like you. *Really* like you. But what if it's all a dream? What if I'm being blind to what's really happening again?" She exhales. "I want children, Drew. I want a husband."

"This is real." I grab her hand, placing it on my chest. "Feel that. It's real. And Charlotte, I've never once said I didn't want those things. But we are new. We have all the time in the world for those things."

Landon had already mentioned what she wanted, so I have been prepared for this to come out. It isn't that I'm telling her what she wants to hear. I'm telling her the truth. I don't know what tomorrow will bring. No one can. But I'm willing to try. And if we end up married and having kids, I won't balk at the idea. Charlotte is someone I can see a relationship lasting with; a relationship that grows and doesn't dwindle or become stuck in a rut.

She hiccups. "But what if I don't?"

"What do you mean?"

She presses down, getting comfy. "Have time. My mum, not many know this, but she struggled to get pregnant. She had a condition that caused her egg count to be low. Her mum wasn't the best mum— she didn't deserve kids— but she struggled to get pregnant which is why my mum was an only child."

Realisation dawns. "You're worried you'll be the same."

She nods, wiping under her nose. "I am. It's not hereditary, but that fear is there. The older Mum got, the more she struggled. After the third attempt of IVF, she fell pregnant with Jacob. If she had left it longer, the worse her condition would have gotten. At my age, she was already married. She had a plan. But I'm not married, Drew. I don't have that head start like she did."

"Have you ever gone to see a doctor?"

"No. I've been too scared."

"I'm all in, Charlotte. I swear. But I can't promise tomorrow. No one can. I'm not going into this thinking it's temporary," I admit, keeping her attention on me. "But you also can't live your life rushing. It's meant to be lived." I'm hoping my next words don't offend her. "You also shouldn't be with someone because you think it will happen, Charlotte. You'll end up with the wrong person."

She flinches, ducking her head. "I know. I think it's why I pushed and pushed myself to give Scott my all. I thought I wasn't trying hard enough."

"With me, just be you. I like *you*."

"I'm nutty, crazy; I like glitter, I wear fluffy kitten jumpers, and I can't bake. Well, I did bake something good the other day, but it seems it was a fluke."

"And?"

She startles. "It doesn't bother you?"

"Charlotte, you have many contributions to who you are and your personality. Not one of them bother me. The nutty, the crazy, and all those other things you listed, just add to who you are. And I happen to really like who you are."

"And you want us to be together? Like a real couple?"

"If you are ready for that," I agree.

She bites her bottom lip. "I do. I want you. I always want you." She groans. "I'm not saying this right."

"I think you're saying this perfectly," I muse, wagging my eyebrows.

She pushes my shoulder lightly. "Not what I meant," she tells me, unable to keep the smile off her face. She loses it just as fast. "I'm scared."

"You were scared to get on the bike."

She shivers as the wind picks up, blowing her hair around her face. "I know."

I run my hands up her thighs. "And what did you feel once you got used to it, once you trusted me to keep you safe?"

"I loved it."

"So trust me now to take care of you with this and not hurt you."

I watch as her resolve breaks. "I do really like you. And you're so pretty to look at."

My lips twitch. "Thank you."

"Boy, Drew, is that you?"

We jump at the sound of the loud, booming voice. Turning to my uncle, I grin. "Uncle Malcom," I greet.

Charlotte squeaks, sliding off my lap to stand. I follow, taking her hand. "Uncle?" she whispers.

I pull her toward the food truck that is sheltered from the elements in an alcove. My uncle leans out of the front window, a big grin on his face. He holds so much resemblance to my dad that you would never guess they have different mothers. The only difference between the two are my dad is always covered in oil and my uncle is covered in food grease or fat.

"Malcom, this is my girlfriend, Charlotte. Charlotte, this is my uncle, Malcom."

Charlotte's fingers clench around mine and I tilt my head, finding her staring up at me with so much wonder and awe.

Malcom wipes his hand down his blue and white apron, and holds his hand out to her. "I've heard a lot about you from my brother. Said you were the best doll he's ever partied with."

I groan. "Dad would say that. She didn't wake up in his bed nagging at him."

Charlotte pulls her hand back. "It's so good to meet you."

He flashes his teeth at Charlotte. "No starting a brawl up here, doll. It's a long way down if one gets going."

Charlotte's breath hitches. "It was a misunderstanding. I swear. One minute she was there in my face, the next…" Her eyes glaze over. "It really was a misunderstanding. And everyone else, um, just got caught up in it?"

"I bet," he tells her, before leaning back. "What are you guys having? I can have Bruce whip you up something good."

"Charlotte's a vegetarian," I tell him, knowing he'll love the fact.

"I'm sorry. If I ate it, I would totally order something. I swear," she rushes out, most likely not wanting to offend him.

"Me too, sweetheart," Malcom grins. "This is the veg truck. The one next door is meat."

Her eyes widen as she scans the area where people are sat eating. "But they are all queuing here."

"Best burgers about, that's why."

She smiles. "Then I'd love a burger, please."

"Be five, ten minutes. I've just got to get these orders done first."

I wave him off. "Take your time. Just yell when you are ready."

"Take these first," he demands lightly, handing over two steaming cups. "It's hot chocolate. It's nippy up here."

Charlotte laughs as she takes the mug. "It is a little windy."

Taking her hand, I walk us over to the north side of the cliff, not far from the food trucks. The fresh air, the scents of food cooking... it's heaven.

Charlotte staggers to a stop as she takes in the view. "Wow."

I step up behind her, wrapping an arm around her and pulling her against my chest. "I know."

"This is beautiful, Drew," she breathes out. She pulls out her phone with one hand, snapping a picture of the view. For miles, all you can see is greens and browns. It's breath-taking.

"Here," I comment, reaching for her hot chocolate. I place them down on the rock then grab her phone and turn us until the view is behind us.

"You want a photo?"

I glance down at her, wondering if there will be a time when she stops second guessing stuff. "Yeah. You can send it to me after."

She leans in as I bend down, smiling wide as I snap a picture of us together. Her laughter is carefree as she takes a look at the photo. "We aren't getting the view in."

"Would you like us to take a picture?" a young woman asks, her man standing beside her.

Charlotte reaches for the phone. "Would you mind?"

"No, of course not," she replies, taking the phone.

Charlotte rushes back to my side, her smile so blinding it's powerful. It knocks me off my axis and for a moment, I can do nothing but stare. The unexpected warmth twists in my gut.

I have been with beautiful girls before. I have even been with a nerdy girl and one chick who wore a lot of pink. Each irritated or bored me. Charlotte, however, is a combination, but there is something about her that can't be explained or rationalised. It's a part of her soul that she wears for the world to see. It makes her different and stand out from others.

"Are you ready?"

Charlotte straightens, turning to the camera, her smile still intact. I slowly do the same, but this time, I gulp, swallowing past the lump low in my throat as the realisation hits me.

I think I might be falling for Charlotte.

THIRTY-TWO

CHARLOTTE

Just as planned, Drew finished our day together by setting up his projector outside in the garden under the stars. The white backdrop is pinned to the tree and pegged to the floor. If it weren't, the light wind would have it wrapped around the branch right now.

We laid out a tarp on the ground before putting my portable sofa bed on it. It was only a thin, cushioned mattress and has mostly been used for visitors to sit on when there haven't been enough seats. Tonight is the first time the actual bed part is being used. And I like that it will now hold a special remembrance to me.

The night air is chilly, but thankfully we have blankets and pillows to keep us warm, and thanks to Lily, we have a heat burner. The scene is every woman's dream. He even hung some fairy lights I had left from Christmas and wrapped them around the patio area. It fit the mood after the perfect day we spent together.

I've read a lot of romance novels, had melted at the most romantic scenes, but none of them hold a candle to tonight. This isn't romantic fiction, a made-up story to make women swoon. It's real, and my heart aches from how full it is.

The stars are bright, twinkling down at us lying below them. This is what I have been looking for this entire time.

It isn't just about the relationship, or the sex; it's also companionship. It's a connection that burns so bright it's almost blinding. A friendship that's built from attraction.

I can't deny the pull between us anymore. I went into this not knowing where it would end or if it would happen again. Now I find I don't want it to end. And slowly, he hasn't just become a friend, he's become someone I don't want to spend a day without talking to. He's the person I first think of when I have news. It's no longer a member of my family, but him. I wasn't even aware of that fact until today.

However, I think I may have scared him because of the movie. He's still staring at me and the next movie has already begun to play.

Using the sleeve of my jumper, I wipe away the tears that have fallen free. My heart is shredded into pieces. Some films know how to break their viewers.

"I can feel you judging me," I tell him, trying not to sound snotty.

"I'm totally judging you," he confirms, a grin splitting across his face.

I gently drop down over his chest, resting my chin on my hands. "Stop. It was sad."

"Charlotte, he was a serial killer who killed nine main victims. That isn't including the ones he killed along the way to get to them."

The lump in my throat aches. "He was just misunderstood." I sniffle. "They tortured him unnecessarily."

He chuckles, and wraps his arms around me before turning us, him looming over me. He brushes my hair out of my face. "You are seriously too empathetic toward others. He killed three innocent children."

I lightly shove his shoulder. "They could have just tied him up and called the police."

A noise from Lily's garden has Drew lifting his head to check it out. "It was Jaxon again."

I run my finger over the crease between his eyebrows. "He's just checking on me. They are worried."

"I'm insulted they think I can't take care of you."

"I told you they were protective of me. I think Jaxon is doing it more for his sister. She's been pretty upset about Landon watching my place."

"They'll be fine. She brought him lunch the other day and they seemed to be in a better place. Landon was just kicking himself for not being there for you."

I hesitate for a moment, but I have let him change the subject all day. "Speaking of Landon, will you please tell me what happened at the gym now? He wouldn't tell me when I spoke to him earlier. He told me not to worry."

He sighs and rolls onto the mat beside me. Tucking my hands under my cheek, I give him all my attention. This has played on my mind off and on. Drew has been able to distract me all day.

"It's nothing major. Someone smashed the windows and broke the door. There was no permanent damage."

I place my hand over his chest, feeling it pulse under my touch. "Drew, there is more to it than that."

"Charlotte, you just got upset over a bunch of teens who killed a serial killer. I'm not telling you the rest for you to take on that guilt."

My stomach bottoms out and dread hits me. If he isn't telling me, it has to be bad. "Please, tell me. I'll imagine the worst if you don't."

For a moment, I think he's not going to tell me, but then he groans, closing his eyes briefly. "The damage was to all the front windows and door. The entire front wall of glass was shattered. They took an iron bar or something and scraped it along the floor, the side of the reception desk and then to my office. The office was trashed too."

He isn't telling me the entire truth. "What aren't you telling me?"

"It's not important."

Tears gather in my eyes. "Yes, it is. Mum said over the phone they think it's the same person who sent me flowers, but she wouldn't tell me why they came to that conclusion. And I know you know why," I tell him, my voice breaking. "I'm so sorry, Drew. So sorry."

"It's not your fault," he assures me, letting out a weary sigh. "It was only my side of the office that was trashed. Landon's went untouched."

My breath hitches. "Why?"

"There were flowers left for me. That's why they know it's from the same person going after you. Landon thought they had done the damage and left the flowers for him. He assumed they had just gotten whose side of the office it was, wrong."

"But it wasn't?" I whisper.

He shakes his head before reaching out to run a hand down my arm. "The note was basically threatening me to stay away from you, or at least, that's how I read it."

I sit up, my eyes widening. "Drew, you need to go. I don't want you being targeted because of me." He laughs and my chest hurts. "Stop. I'm deadly serious, Drew. Someone threatened you away from me. You need to listen until we find out who it is."

He sobers, and a shiver races down my spine at the lethal intent in his eyes. "No fucker is going to push me away from you, especially not some creep who is out to hurt you."

"This is serious, Drew. I'm not going to let you get hurt. I can get Landon or Jaxon to watch out for you. You'll be protected."

He drops down onto his back, laughter booming out of him. I slap his rock hard chest.

"Charlotte, hear me when I say this, I can take care of myself. You don't need to worry about me," he declares fiercely.

"Why would you still want to be around me when someone has done that to your business *because* of me? I know how much it means to you."

He pulls me against his chest and I go willingly, loving the feel of his hard abs under my fingertips. "If you haven't already guessed, I really like you."

My heart stutters at hearing those words. "I really like you too."

He smirks. "I know."

I pout. "Be serious."

"I am. I've never let anyone come between me and what I want. Not my mum when I wanted to change courses. Not when I opened the gym. Not when I wanted to visit my dad. And the same goes for you. I won't let anyone come between us. Not Landon, not your family, and not this person sending this crap to you."

More tears gather in my eyes. I'd claim I wasn't always this much of a crier but it would be a lie. I cry when I'm happy. I cry when I'm sad. But right now, I'm so overwhelmed, I can't hold them back. Even with the threat shadowing me, I'm the happiest I have ever been. His words aren't a declaration of love, but they feel as close as.

"You really do like me."

He rolls us again, hovering over me. He's careful not to crush me, leaning up on his elbows. "I've been telling you that from the start, just not with words."

I run my fingers through his thick, curly hair. "Yes, but I didn't believe it until now."

"Then I'm not doing it right," he whispers against my lips. My thighs clench around him at the sound of his husky voice.

His lips are cool against mine and I relax back onto the makeshift bed, running my fingers through his hair as the kiss deepens.

Butterflies flutter in my stomach. "Drew," I moan.

Wild tremors rake through my body, a surge of warmth that always has me feeling a sense of free falling. With just a kiss he can send me speechless and mute my inner conscious. And it's led back to freefalling. Constantly feeling that flutter in your stomach like you are on a rollercoaster. It sends me into a tailspin each and every time.

Each flick of his tongue, each moment of feeling him thrust against me, is one more minute of him driving me insane.

I'm not sure how much time passes, but a lick of heat covers my flesh from wanting him so much. Our hands continue to run over each other, the touches innocent, yet intimate, and our legs become tangled together.

A broken moan slips past my lips. "Drew." He is torturing me.

He glances up, his gaze flicking to Lily's back garden. "I think they've gone to bed."

"Probably," I murmur, pulling him back toward me. I don't want him to stop kissing me.

Ever.

He grins, his fingers sliding under my leggings. I tense, tilting my head up to meet his gaze. There's a moment of pause, a moment where I'm not sure I'll be able to do it, especially out in the open. But there's something in his soft expression that doesn't have me recoiling at the silent offer, but instead, arching into his touch.

There's a dark hunger staring back at me as he leans back, lifting the blanket we had brought out and pulling it over us, blanketing us both.

His hand pushes further into my leggings and under my knickers. The minute his skilled fingers slide through my sex, my eyes close and a wave of pleasure uncoils in my abdomen. I have been wanting this all day. Wanting him.

My sex clenches around him as he inserts one, then two fingers inside of me. "Drew."

He inclines his head, running his nose along my jaw before nipping my earlobe. "You feel so fucking good around my fingers."

"Oh God."

I arch into his touch, groaning as he presses the heel of his hand against my clit. The confinements of the leggings and knickers have the pressure increasing. The material of my knickers are damp and it only adds to my arousal.

"Ride my hand," he demands.

I reach up, running my fingers around to the nape of his neck, using it as leverage to rock against his hand. He leans down, his lips brushing mine, yet neither of us move in for a kiss. He doesn't look away, his gaze locked on mine as he pumps his fingers in and out of me. My sex clenches each time, the pressure building and building. The heat coming from both of us, the naughtiness of being outside, is becoming too much.

I want to prolong this moment as much as I can, yet I know I won't be able to, not when he makes me feel so much.

"Come for me," he demands, his tone rough.

My neck arches, and my toes curl into the thin mattress beneath me as my orgasm tears through me.

Before I can come down, I feel him lean down, rolling my leggings off, taking my knickers with them. I hear him fiddle with his own shorts before he looms over me, ripping his shirt off with one hand. The move itself is beyond sexy, but then my eyes catch sight of the tattoos and nipple piercings, and I'm certain I just had a mini orgasm.

"Top off?" he asks.

I melt at him asking, and lift up, taking the jumper and T-shirt off, leaving my bra on. His pupils darken as he runs a finger over the soft globes before palming my tits, his fingers digging in.

"So fucking hot."

I could say the same thing about him.

He hovers over me, one hand between us as he lines his cock up before slowly thrusting inside me to the hilt.

He groans, shoving his face into my neck. "You'll need to be quiet," he rasps. "We don't want Jaxon coming out and spotting us."

My sex clenches around him, causing him to growl low in his throat. I grip his sides, holding onto him as he thrusts back in, sliding my body up the mattress. My thighs are still aching from the bike ride, but right now, it feels like the good kind of ache, the ache you know you'll remember for the right reasons.

My neck tilts a little, giving him access as he peppers kisses along my jaw and down my neck, to my collarbone.

"Faster," I plead, punctuating the word by digging my fingers into his shoulders. I need more friction, more of him. He touches me like an instrument, one he knows how to play, and my body sings to the tune. I'm high on lust, need. I want more, so much more, but then I think when it comes to Drew, I'll always want more.

He pulls back a little, resting up on his forearms. "No."

"Please," I beg, thrusting up, but he presses down, using his weight to stop me from seeking more.

It's torturous. Each time he hits the spot, it's deliriously slow, yet it feels just as powerful.

He brushes my hair away from my face, keeping his hand cupped at my jaw. "What are you doing to me?"

I know from the last time this is a hypothetical question. "Probably not the same as what you're doing to me. Please, Drew, go faster."

He smirks, and it's devilish and naughty. "No. I have you exactly where I want you. Trust me to give you what you need. You'll feel it soon," he rasps.

"I feel it now," I whisper, unable to look away.

His lips are hard, punishing, and yet, his pace stays the same. Never once slowing, or speeding up. Pleasure floods my entire body. Each breath I take, each move I make, I feel it.

He was right.

I can feel everything.

It's raw, real, and as we gaze into each other's eyes, it feels like a part of my soul has left to join his. I'm bursting with emotions and each time he slams inside of me, it only creates more.

As corny as it sounds, it doesn't feel like it's only our bodies connecting. I'm not spiritual, but if I were, then this would be a defining moment for me. Because I have never felt more alive than I do in this moment.

I press my knees to his side, the move causing me to take more of him. He fuels the fire between us, licking and nipping at my neck.

The pressure I have become accustomed to is building once again, sending me into a frenzy.

My body jerks as each thrust gets rougher and rougher, and the moment he nips at my jaw, I explode, crying out my orgasm as a blinding light bursts behind my eyes. My legs begin to shake. The ripple of pleasure runs down to the tips of my toes. My pulse is racing so hard, I feel like my heart is going to explode. For that one single moment, it feels like euphoria.

"Fuck," he growls, his fingers pulling at my hair a little.

He rocks above me, the lines and muscles in his face straining, like the torturous pace is killing him as much as it had me.

His body coils, and a breathily groan slips through his lips. His ripped body pulses with his orgasm and tingles spread through me.

My entire body goes limp and the pressure of his weight increases above me.

That was intense, powerful, and my sex still tingles, sensitive from the orgasm that shot through me.

He can bend me to his will sexually. I'll give him anything he asks for. But as I replay everything that happened, add in where we are and the day we shared together, I know I'll never get another moment like this one again.

I'm not saying the next time will be bad. It will be a new kind of special. But I know deep in my heart, there is no repeating the moment we just shared, or the intensity.

Lowering his head, he rests his forehead against mine, panting heavily. I run my fingers over the hard groove of his muscles, finding his skin coated in a sheen of sweat. I rest my palm against the heavy beat of his heart, my own tightening.

I feel like I can't breathe and it has nothing to do with his weight.

He puts a little bit of space between us, and brushes my hair out of my face, his gaze and touch gentle. I suck in a breath, wondering how someone so large, so powerful, can be so gentle. He makes me feel like I'm a delicate artefact.

"Charlotte," he murmurs, his voice raspy.

I shake my head, and swallow past the lump in my throat. Something definitely passed between us. Something monumental, and everlasting.

But I'm too scared to grasp it right now, too overwhelmed to figure out what it means.

Instead of telling him that, I reach for him instead.

"Hold me."

THIRTY-THREE

CHARLOTTE

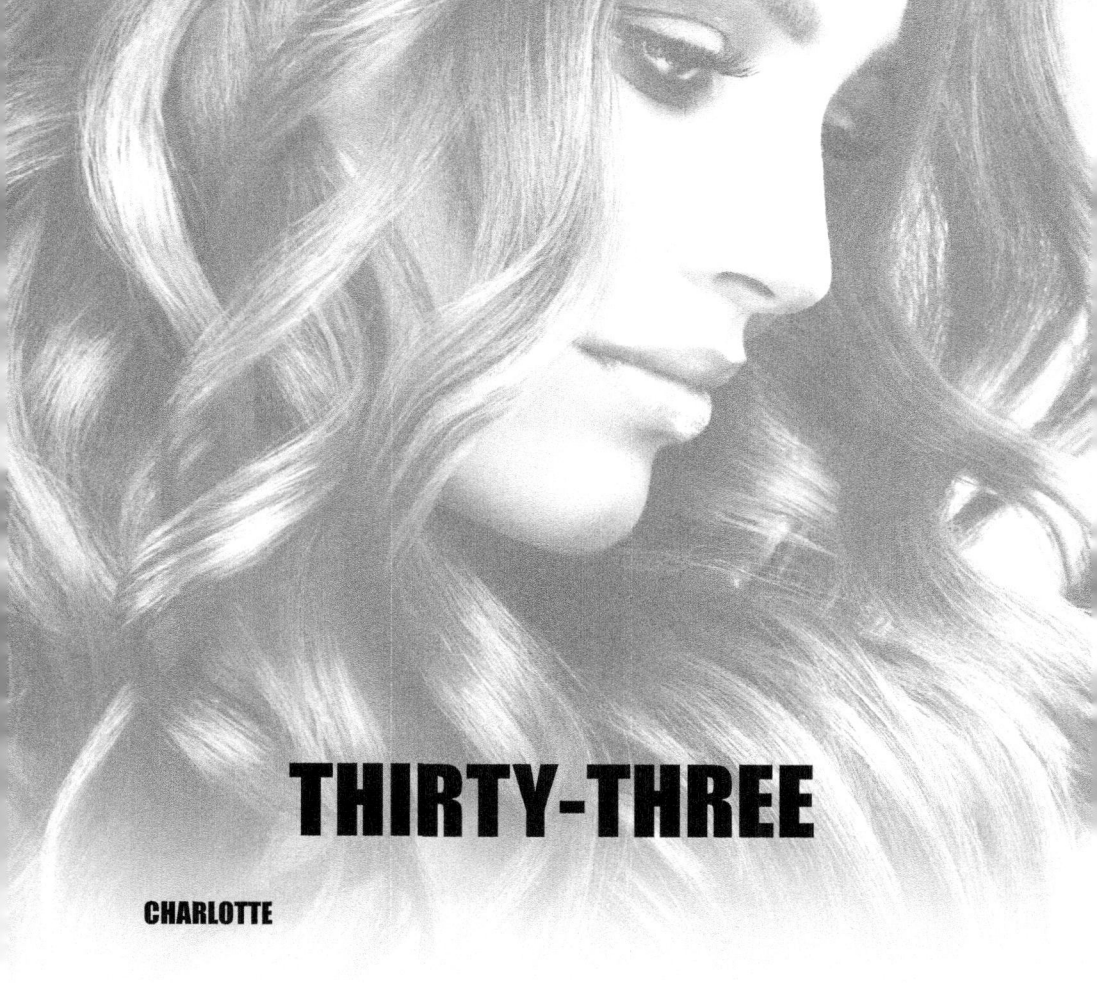

A SMILE LIGHTS UP MY FACE AS Drew steps up behind me, wrapping his arms around my waist. He leans down, pressing a kiss to the side of my face. "Morning, beautiful."

I tilt my head and glance up at him. "Did you sleep okay?"

His pupils darken. "I slept really good."

I blush, ducking my head. Yesterday we hadn't moved out of bed for anything other than to open the door for the takeout or go to the toilet. I'm sore in places I never thought I could be. I think I may need to stretch before and after at this point.

Do people stretch before sex?

I'll have to look it up later and double check I'm not doing it wrong.

"I made cookies." He grimaces, staring down at the fresh tray I pulled out. "You don't want one?"

"Um, I, of course," he tells me, grabbing one. I watch as he takes a bite, smiling when he groans. It isn't out of disgust or pain. It's one of pleasure. His eyes widen, and moments later the cookie is gone and he's taking another. "These are seriously good."

"I'd really love to know what I did right today to get them to taste so good," I muse.

"You know your other baked goods are a health hazard yet you still give them to people?" He doesn't seem pissed, only amused.

I shrug. "My cakes I can't exactly try. It wouldn't be hygienic to hand someone a cake with a slice missing."

"And the famous muffins I've heard so much about?"

I'm still mad Landon told him my muffins were a self-defence weapon. They weren't that bad.

"It's chocolate; that always smells good to me."

He chuckles, leaning down to press a kiss to my lips. "I really hate that we have to go into work today. I want to stay and eat cookies."

I grab the container I filled earlier. "I made you some to take to work."

He takes the container, eyeing it warily. "How do you know these ones aren't toxic?"

I giggle, shaking my head. "Because I tried one."

I love how he doesn't try to fake they're good. My family tends to force themselves to eat it or lie about not being hungry. And we all know a Carter is always hungry. But it's fun to mess with them.

"What time do you have to be in?"

"An hour ago. But I messaged Rita yesterday to call in a temp to cover Marlene for a while."

"The chick that was poisoned?"

I bite my lip. "She won't answer the phone to me but her sister or friend did, and she passed on a message."

"What did she say?" he asks, taking a swig of his coffee.

"She doesn't know if she will be coming back to work. She still has another week of paid leave so I'm hoping she will let me know by then."

"Doesn't she screw up a lot? Or is that Rita? I remember Landon moaning about someone who worked there."

"That's Marlene," I admit. "What time do you need to be in?"

He grins. "An hour ago, but I messaged Landon to open up so we could have a lie in. But you weren't there when I woke up."

I press my body flush against his. "I'm sorry. I wanted to make you some eggs but then I panicked in case you drank a protein shake instead."

He glances around the kitchen. "Where are the eggs?"

I duck my head. "In the bin. I kind of burnt them."

He chuckles, wrapping his arms around me. "I'll make you breakfast next time."

"You want to stay again?" I ask, surprised.

"Why did you say it like that?"

I shrug. "Because most men would be put off by the pink and glitter in my room. You aren't exactly the type who seems to be okay with those things."

"They're you. I like you. And no offence, sweetheart, but a bed is a bed. I couldn't care less what's on the cover."

Warmth fills my chest and I lean up, pressing my lips to his. "You are amazing."

Before he can answer, my phone blares with a call and I grab it from the counter. My brows pull together at the unknown number. It's the same area code but no one I'm familiar with.

Drew tenses. "Who is it?"

"I don't know," I whisper before answering the call. "Hello?"

"Miss Carter, it's PC Megan Brown."

I straighten, my hands shaking. Megan is the officer who interviewed me at the hospital the night Scott hurt me. She had been the one to recommend counselling and gave me details on victim support, one I didn't take her up on.

"Hi," I whisper.

Is this it? Is this the moment she will tell me she found him?

"I have an update about the case. Are you free to talk?"

"I am," I tell her, letting Drew pull me against his chest. He runs his hand down my arm, soothing me.

"Amber Cooper woke up yesterday and had her sister bring in the photo of who she believes to be Scott Taylor. We would like you to come in and see if you can identify the man in the picture. Are you free this morning?"

"Um, I am," I croak out. "Is Amber okay?"

"From what her sister said, she still has a way to go regarding recovery. We will be interviewing her in the next week or so if this turns out to be the man we are looking for."

I hadn't heard from April for a few days, but I'm happy her sister is awake and doing okay.

"I just need to finish getting dressed, then I can drop by?"

"That's perfect. Just ask for me when you hit reception. They'll call for me."

"Okay, thank you."

I end the call and turn in Drew's arms. "Amber woke up and told April where to find the picture."

"This is good news, right?"

"What if it's not the same person? What if I'm getting my hopes up? Before, I just wanted to forget everything that happened. But now…"

"But now?"

"Now I have something to compare it to. What he did was wrong. It wasn't me. *I* didn't do anything wrong. It wasn't because I was weird or a freak. It wasn't because of me."

For so long, I have blamed myself for that entire night. Not anymore. And if it is Scott messing with me and my loved ones, I want to make sure they get him.

He cups the back of my neck, pulling me against his chest. "It was never your fault."

"I know that now," I breathe into his shirt, trying to hold back the tears, but it's useless.

"And you aren't weird or a freak. Never say that again," he orders, his voice rough.

I pull back, swiping the tear that rolls down my cheek. "I need to get ready and go. And call Mum to come and get me. After the crash, I don't want to…" I pause, fighting back the memories. "I can't drive my car. Not yet."

"I'm taking you. If you want to call your mum to come, we can pick her up on the way, but I'm not leaving you."

I hiccup. "You aren't leaving me?"

His expression softens. "No, babe, I'm not."

Tears burst free and I rush at him, wrapping my arms around his waist. "I didn't want to be needy or clingy but I really want you with me."

"I'd be there even if you didn't," he assures me. "You shouldn't be alone."

"I think I more than really, really like you," I blubber.

PRESSING MY FACE into Drew's jacket, I inhale sharply. His muscles tense beneath me as he wraps an arm over my shoulder. Mum is just as tense, her fingers tightening around mine.

It's Scott— if that is even his name.

The beautiful redhead next to him is Amber and she looks happy and so in love in the picture. Scott's smile is charming, giving her the same wonder-filled expression he used to give me, like he can't believe he met the woman he wants to spend the rest of his life with. It had all been a lie, like an actor playing a part. He played the game and he played it well.

For what feels like months, I have been praying this had been a misunderstanding and he hadn't hurt anyone else. But he had, and the same foolishness I felt each time I thought of him, increases tenfold.

When PC Brown slid the photo toward me, I saw the very thing I had been blind to the entire time we were together. It was beyond the charm and sweet words. He had hidden it so well and if I didn't know now to look for it, I would never have seen it. There was a narcissistic man consumed with darkness. A sadist who picked his prey by their kindness and vulnerability.

Seeing him, even if it had only been a photo, had brought back all the memories that have haunted me since that night. I saw the tightness in his eyes, the clenching of his jaw. Everything assaulted me from the feel of his hands on me to how rough he had been inside of me.

I whimper, closing my eyes as I try to breathe through it all.

"Do you have any idea who he is now?" Mum asks.

I turn to face PC Brown, wanting to know the answer myself. I can't move out of Drew's arms though, needing his comfort. This has been harder than I realised.

PC Brown sits forward and from her blank expression and the flicker of her gaze, I know it isn't going to be good news. "I'm afraid not."

"How are you going to find out? Surely there has to be someone who knows him."

"That's the next thing I'd like to discuss," she explains, turning to me. "We want to do a press release. We will post this picture and ask for anyone who recognises him or thinks they do, to call in."

"Will I be mentioned?"

"No. It will remain anonymous and be read as, 'in regard to an assault charge' or something along those lines. This is our last shot at finding him."

I chew on my thumbnail. "And the notes and flowers; do you think they are from him too?"

"I'm not sure until we bring him," she admits. "I'll be straight with you; I didn't think we would get this far in the case. I've been searching every avenue and coming up with nothing."

That isn't exactly true. Landon had mentioned Drew's dad, Silas, finding a little information. We just aren't sure if it was useful yet.

"Do you need us for anything else, because I'd like to get Charlotte home," Drew announces.

PC Brown shuffles her papers into a pile. "No. That is all for today. The press release should be going out sometime this week or maybe next. But I'll let you know."

We stand, and say our goodbyes. Once outside, the fresh air feels cool on my face. I soak it in before turning to Mum. "Thank you for coming with me."

"I'll always be with you. I need to call your father. He should be finished with his case soon and will want to know what happened," she tells me, then stops, taking me into her arms. "You were really brave in there."

"Thank you," I reply. "Go call Dad before he searches for us."

"True." She steps to the side to make the call.

Drew pulls me against his chest, his strong, large arms wrapping around me. "How are you feeling?"

"I'm not going to lie, it feels weird seeing him again, even if it was on a picture. I have this tightness in my stomach and for a moment back there, I thought I was going to be sick."

"It's from seeing his face again," he mutters.

"What was I thinking?" I murmur. "I should have seen it. It's all I see now. Looking at that picture, I felt revolted. With him, with myself."

"Stop," he demands, running his fingers through my hair. "You aren't going to blame yourself. You can't change what happened. No one can. But we can change the outcome by finding this fucker. He needs to pay for what he has done."

"You aren't just a pretty face," I muse.

He arches his thick brow. "What's that supposed to mean?"

"It means you are quite intuitive."

"You mean I'm right," he adds, giving me a pointed look.

I roll my eyes. "Yes. That."

"Are you ready to go home, sweetie? Your father said he will meet us there."

I glance at Drew and chew on my lip. "I need to go to work. I can't go home. I'll stew on this all day."

"You sure?" Drew asks.

"Honey."

I turn to Mum. "I want to go to work. If Dad still wants to see me, then we can meet him there, but I can't keep putting my life on hold."

Her gaze softens. "All right, sweetie. We can arrange that."

Drew pulls open my door, letting me inside. It won't take us long to get back to the library. The police station isn't that far away.

As I sink into the leather seat, my mind still whirls on the picture. I'm hoping with it, we finally found him because I have so many questions. Why had he lied? Why did he hurt me? Why did he give me a fake name?

Mainly, I want to know *who* he is or if anything he said to me was real. I'm not even sure why it matters, but it does. They are questions which have been running around my head from the very beginning, since I found out he lied about who he was.

PC Brown had been the officer to give me the bad news. My mum had sat beside me, my dad on the other, and something inside of me broke that day. It tore me in half. I gave and I gave to everyone I came into contact with. I gave them all of me; including my love and trust. There was no in between. And that had all been torn away from me. I didn't do it for recognition or praise. I did it because it's who I wanted to be. I always strived to be a better person.

But that day, all I could ask myself was: what was the point? What was the point of being this person if it gave power to people like Scott who want to tear me down.

For weeks after I couldn't even look in the mirror. I would see myself and feel so much self-loathing, it choked me. It was so deep rooted I hid it well. I felt dirty, cheap. I faked each day until one day, it hit me.

I wasn't this person.

But that didn't mean I wasn't desperate for answers. It was like my subconscious needed them to heal.

Drew parks outside the library and grips my hand. "Are you sure you want to go in?"

Shaking the thoughts from my mind, I give him a nod. "I do. I have so much running through my head I need something to pull my focus away from it."

"It might not seem like a lot right now but the police having his picture is a huge step. They'll find him. There's no rock he can hide under."

He always knows what to say to me.

I also like how he doesn't declare he'll find him and kill him. It's what the men in my family have threatened to do over and over. It's a needy behaviour on my part, but I like that he's more concerned with me than looking for him. I love Landon. He is a huge part of my life, but I see him less and less than I did before the attack. He has been spending all his free time following leads to find Scott.

"Fingers crossed."

I push the door open and slide out. Mum does the same, her brows bunched together as she gazes down at the phone.

"Mum? You okay?"

She pastes on a smile. "Yeah, I'm just going to call Lake. She was going to pop over but somehow, the time between us leaving the police station, to now, Max has come out of work and locked her in the house."

My eyes widen. "Locked her in?"

She reads the message and bursts out laughing. "Max said she kept making eyes at Drew so she wasn't allowed near him." Drew chuckles, not taking it offensively. "I'm just going to call her. I'll be inside in a second."

"All right, Mum."

Drew takes my hand, leading me up to the library. "Your family are nuts."

"But they are happy. That's the main thing."

"Why the fuck didn't you tell me you were going to the police station?" Hayden yells, storming inside the library like I stole her last meal.

"Well, some people are happy," I mumble, letting go of his hand. "Hayden, we literally went to the police station after she called. We didn't have time."

"You had time to pick your mum up."

"She's my mum," I remind her.

Hayden's boyfriend, Clayton, steps forward, pulling Hayden in front of him. "What she means to say is, she hopes you're okay and it went okay at the station."

Hayden narrows her gaze on him. "No, I fucking didn't."

I giggle, sobering when her glare turns my way. "I really am sorry."

She huffs. "I know," she replies. "How are you doing? Did it go okay?"

Clayton groans as I struggle not to laugh. "I'm okay. It was hard to see the photo but I'll be fine."

"Did they say—"

Seeing there are people in the library, people I speak to on a regular basis, I interrupt. "How about we not talk about that here."

"Oh, alright," she groans.

THIRTY-FOUR

DREW

Leading Charlotte over to the large table and chairs bundled together, we take a seat, Hayden and her fella following.

I quickly pull out my phone, checking my messages to make sure Landon got the gym covered whilst we were out.

He had.

Which means it won't be long until he arrives.

"What was you doing with her?" Hayden asks, and I look up to see she is directing the question at me.

"Um," Charlotte hums, her cheeks blossoming red.

My lips twitch a little at her discomfort. I reach for her hand under the table and Hayden's gaze narrows in the direction. "I stayed the night with Charlotte."

Hayden glares my way and I swear, my balls shrivel. I have met a lot of empowering, strong women, but never someone who is scary like Hayden. She doesn't threaten, she just does it. And what scares me the most is her being a Carter with the skills of knowing where to hurt a guy and giving zero fucks about it. Her fella is a brave guy sleeping next to her every night. I have seen her fight with her brothers and it wasn't pretty.

"And when did this little development happen?" she asks, and with the way she's looking at me, I'm willing to bet she's picturing a hundred ways she can hurt me.

Unblinking, I keep my focus on her. "I'm not sure it's your concern."

Charlotte tenses, her focus on Hayden. I gently run the pad of my thumb across the top of her hand. I want to reassure her that I'm not angry. She already has a lot to process and doesn't need to deal with me and her family bickering.

Hayden sits back, smirking. "I do like you, Drew."

I snort. The girl doesn't like anyone other than family and sometimes even then I find it debatable. Before I can reply, the door of the library slams against the wall, the sound echoing throughout the library.

I tense, ready to move to protect Charlotte, but I needn't worry.

"Oh no," Charlotte whispers, suddenly tensing.

Landon trips inside, nearly falling into a display table. Liam, his brother, is right behind him, his expression livid.

Landon spins around, glaring holes into his brother. "I didn't fucking steal your lunch."

"Yes, you did," Liam yells. "I know it was you. It was there one minute and gone the next." He points to Landon's stomach. "In your fucking stomach."

"You're being ridiculous. Paisley feeds me."

Liam snorts. "Don't patronise me. Like that will stop you from eating other people's food."

"Oh no."

I turn to Charlotte, finding her pale and not staring at the brothers' arrival but up at the top floor of the library. I tilt my head up, my eyes widening when I spot her uncle sitting on the banister, his back resting against the pillar behind him. One leg is bent and resting on the banister and the other is dangling on the other side. In one hand he has some kind of water gun device—although I have never seen one like it before. In the other he has a sandwich. However, on the carpet near his feet, there are other food wrappers like he has been staked out up there for a while, which I highly doubt since I would have sensed him.

Maybe.

"Accuse me again, I dare you," Landon warns, stepping up to his brother.

Hayden, not looking up from the pasta she suddenly has in front of her, speaks up. "Dad ate it."

Maybe *I shouldn't* play mind games with her.

Because I haven't seen her turn around once since she sat down and her dad was definitely not there when we all arrived.

"We've not even seen Dad today," Liam tells her, forgetting his beef with Landon for a moment.

"No, you didn't," Max announces, and both Landon and Liam tense, slowly turning to face their dad. "You two disappoint me."

Hayden snorts. "Like that's new."

"Shut up, Hayden" Liam snaps.

She grins, glancing at her brother. "Still hurt I'm the favourite?"

"Whatever helps you sleep at night," he retorts.

"Why are you sitting up there?" Landon asks. "Like a creeper."

"Is that my fucking lunch?" Liam cries. "*Dad*, I've been looking forward to that all day."

"Then you shouldn't have waited," Max scoffs. "Did I teach you nothing?"

"Why do you have a gun with you?" Clayton asks.

"Because I heard Charlotte had to go to the police station and I wasn't sure if it involved the giant."

"Really?" I mutter, rolling my eyes. The giant comment is becoming old now.

"Got a good advantage on you now, haven't I, boy?"

I roll my eyes, not worried in the slightest. "Not really."

"Max Carter, get your fucking arse down from there right now," Lake snaps, stepping inside, her hair a mess.

Max gulps, jumping down from the banister. "The light of my life, the apple of my eye, what do we owe this pleasure?"

"Don't, Max. Really, just don't," she warns him. "I had to climb out of the bedroom fucking window."

"I'm not sure I like your tone," he snidely replies.

She huffs out a breath before turning to her son. "Don't worry about your food. I've called your uncle Malik to bring takeout, so there is plenty for you. He is on his way."

"And your uncle brought drinks," Kayla announces, stepping through the door with Myles.

Myles walks over, bending down to kiss the top of his daughter's head. Her eyes close and a small smile appears on her face when she tilts her head to look up at him. "You doing okay, baby girl?"

"I'm doing okay, Dad. Thank you for coming."

"Always." He turns to me, and doesn't say anything for a moment. "Thank you for being there for her."

I give him a nod. "It's not a problem."

He takes a seat further down and the movement makes me lose focus of the rest of the room. More Carter's are piling inside and I take my eyes off the ball for one second.

One second.

Because if anyone is a threat to me in this room it's Charlotte's dad. She loves her parents and their say means a lot to her. If they truly dislike me, there is no way Charlotte will carry on seeing me.

My chest hunches over as a sharp ball of pain smacks me in the shoulder. The impact has my entire body tensing and my teeth clenching together. I can't show them it fucking hurt.

I slowly turn to face the culprit and come to a stand, the chair scraping along the floor. My gaze never once wavering from the man in question. Max's eyes widen and he wisely steps back, his hands held up. "It's the trigger mechanism. I swear."

Myles chokes out a laugh. "You are such a fucking liar."

I keep my gaze on him but lean forward, grabbing a napkin Hayden has in front of her to wipe off the gooey mess on my shoulder. "This was my favourite T-shirt."

Max wipes a hand down his face. "I'll clean it. Just sit the fuck down. There's no need to get testy."

I take a seat. I didn't realise how tense it had gotten until I take in the room. They all visibly relax, glancing away from the spectacle.

Charlotte, however, doesn't. She reaches into her bag, pulling out a zip lock bag that has the last one of her cookies. She shoves half into her mouth, whimpering. "It's too much," she cries.

I chuckle at her expression. She's going to give herself indigestion with the way she's going at the cookie.

Hayden reaches over, snatching it from her hand and taking a huge bite. Her eyes go round, and her brows shoot up to her hairline. "Fucking hell. These are really good. Where did you buy these from?"

"I made them," Charlotte replies absently, staring longingly at the cookie.

I slide Charlotte back from the table. Landon, Liam, Myles, Max and another guy who I'm sure is another cousin, dive for the cookie Hayden has in her hand, but without a care in the world, Hayden pops the last bit in her mouth, chewing with a smile on her face.

Dejected, the others pull back and then turn to Charlotte. "Do you have more?"

In the middle of searching through her bag for most likely another treat, Charlotte pops her head up. "I only had that one left. The rest I gave to Drew to take to work."

All eyes land on me, and I swear, if looks could kill, they'd have sent me six-feet under. "Don't look at me. They're all gone."

Charlotte's head swings my way. "You threw them away?"

"Babe, I ate them whilst waiting for you to get ready."

Her lopsided smile melts my heart. "You thought they were that good?"

I lean down, not caring her family are there, and capture her lips. "They were the best," I tell her, then lean down to her ear. "But you taste better."

Her face is beet red when I pull back. Max, who is visibly struggling not to say something, drops down into the closest chair. "I can't fucking believe this. *Every time*. If I didn't see how much Hayden had enjoyed it, I would never believe it."

"Believe it. They were so fucking good too. Hit the spot right on."

His fists clench but a look from Lake has him placing them under his thighs. I grin.

The sharp angles of his jaw clench. "Give me another reason to come at you. I dare you."

"Max," Lake hisses.

I shake my head. It's adorable he thinks he can take me. "It's okay."

"No, it's not," Charlotte whispers. "Max, please, be nice to Drew."

"Charlotte," he starts, but something Lake does has him hissing out in agony.

Charlotte tilts her head up and leans into me. "I'm sorry. I'll make you some more later."

Pulling her into my arms, I give her uncle a triumph smirk. "Thanks, babe."

"Dead," Max mouths. "So dead."

Once again, the library door slams open and Madison and Faith step through with Beau, Faith's fiancé. I've met them a few times, hoping they could find me a trained dog. She found a few but none that I connected with.

Which reminds me, before I left, there was something else I wanted to talk to her about.

"What happened? Did they find him?" Madison asks, before taking in the rest. "Dad will be here soon. He's picking up food but he can't stay long before he has to get back to work."

Charlotte quickly runs down everything we learned today. None of them look hopeful. Landon looks like he's about to burn the world down.

"Did you get a copy of the picture?" he asks.

"No," she replies. "But it will be in the paper soon. You'll see it then."

Feeling her anxiety, I pull her against me. "Remember, no one but your friends and family will know what it's about."

"I know. It's just scary it got to this point. I know I'm not, but there are times when I wonder if I'm blowing things out of proportion."

"No, sweetie, you aren't," Kayla assures her.

"Listen to your mum," Myles gently warns. "She's right."

Kayla stares at her husband with doe eyes. "Are you only just getting that?"

His expression gentles and a small smile kicks at the corner of his lips. "I've always known that."

"One, get a room, and two," Hayden states, turning to Charlotte, "the fucker deserves everything he has coming to him. He'll wish the police got a hold of him before I do."

"Hayden," Charlotte whispers.

Hayden sits back, holding her hands up. "Okay, I'll drop it."

"Do you think Liam could hack the police records again?" Max asks, looking lost in thought.

Myles taps his chin. "He was saying he needed to keep a low profile after something he did for the Hayes."

Landon leans forward. "That's true."

Lake places a bottle of water down in front of us. "As long as he's caught, I don't care how it's done. But for right now, let's eat."

Max's head snaps up, sniffing the air. "Food."

"You aren't getting any," Liam snaps.

Max eyes his son like he just said the most ridiculous thing. "And why would you think that?"

"Because you ate my food. You don't get any more."

"Puh-lease. Like that was enough to touch the sides."

"Stop arguing," Lake warns, giving both her husband and son a warning look.

My phone begins to ring, and I pull it out of my pocket, seeing 'Dad' on the screen. I tap Charlotte on the arm. "I'll be back in a minute."

"Okay," she whispers.

I give Malik a chin lift as I pass him, moving through the stacks of shelves. I call Dad back, having missed the call.

"Son, where are you?" he greets.

I become alert, my body tense. "I'm at Charlotte's library. What's happened?"

"You tell me. I've just had Nora show me some tak—"

"Tik Tok," Nora yells.

"That. And it's your gym in the video with the windows put through. And by your fucking silence, I guess you already know. What I want to know is why the fuck didn't you call me?"

"Fuck!" I run my fingers through my hair and move further into the library. I come to a stop at seeing a woman standing at the end, her gaze running over a shelf of books. Our gazes lock and she jerks, before going back to her business. "Hold on a second," I tell Dad, moving away from the woman and down another aisle.

"What's happened, son?"

Happy I'm away from prying ears, I explain. "It's the same person sending Charlotte that stuff."

"The one we think is her ex playing mind games with her?"

"Yeah. We went to the police station this morning. That woman in the coma woke up and got her sister to hand in the photo. Charlotte confirmed it's the same guy."

"Fuck, is she okay?"

"What's going on?" Nora asks.

I wait for Dad to relay what had happened. "I didn't find out about the gym windows until I left yours the other day. And it slipped my mind about calling you."

"Wait, it didn't happen today? Why the fuck are we only hearing about it now?"

"I spent the weekend with Charlotte. Landon dealt with it and it's all fixed now."

"You didn't answer about Charlotte. She okay?"

"She seems okay, but it's Charlotte. She's always happy. I'm going to keep an eye on her though."

"Good. Send her my love," he tells me. "And next time something happens, fucking call me."

"I will, but until we find out who is doing this, it won't stop. And if they are upping their game by targeting me, they are getting jealous, angry."

"I bet. But soon they'll realise they fucked with the wrong person. I've still got my mate looking into it. If they have a picture of him it won't be long now. It might take time but we'll find out who this guy is. And if it's not him doing this shit, then my guess is it's someone who is connected to him."

"My thoughts exactly," I agree. "Charlotte's done fuck all to deserve this. She's innocent. And when I get my hands on the person doing it, I'll make sure they understand that."

There's a shuffle over the phone before I hear Nora. "Tell Charlotte I'll come visit her library soon."

I chuckle. "I will. But I will warn you, if she introduces you to a Hayden, run."

"Why? She a bitch or something because I'll totally put her in her place."

Laughing. "No, but she's just like you and the two of you together might end up with a trip to the police station."

"This family sounds so cool," she gushes.

"I'll speak to you both soon," I tell them once I spot Faith coming toward me.

"Talk soon, son."

"Love you, brother."

"Love you too. Speak later," I tell them, and then end the call. I face Faith. "Everything okay?"

"Yes, Charlotte didn't know what you'd want to eat so I said I'd come look for you. She needs to eat something healthy. When she stresses, she eats junk food."

"She'll get through it," I assure her, seeing how concerned she seems to be.

"Please don't hurt her. I don't want to be another Carter who threatens you. It's not my intention to. I want her to be happy and if that's with you, then I'm team you. But please, from one human being to another, don't hurt her.

She might brush a lot off but one day, that will all come to an end and she'll explode."

"I'm not going to hurt her. I can't promise you what will happen in the future. But if that time ever comes, I can promise to do it amicably."

"That's all we can ask for," she murmurs, before her shoulders drop and a sigh escapes. "I guess we should get back."

"Actually, there's something I've been meaning to ask you."

She pauses, curiosity marring her expression. "Oh yeah?"

I run through what I want and why, and her face lights up, a wide smile spreading over her face. "I can do that."

"Thank you."

"Now, can we eat because I'll be surprised if there's anything left."

I chuckle. "Let's go eat."

THIRTY-FIVE

CHARLOTTE

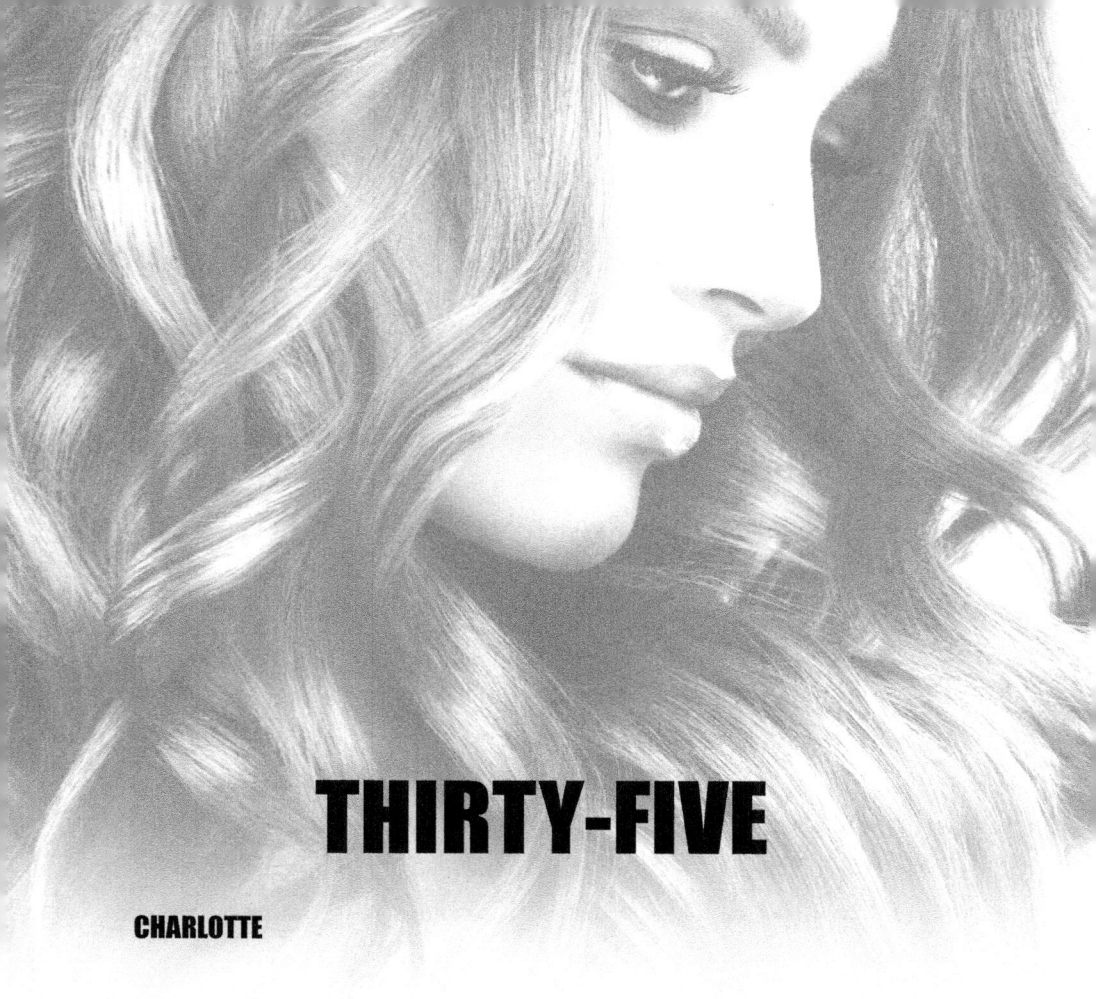

A SOFT BREEZE PICKS UP MY HAIR, stirring the strands around my cheeks. I had come outside, needing a little calm with my cup of tea. Last night was spent tossing and turning, images of Scott invading my dreams.

My mind wouldn't block it out, wouldn't let me rest, and it's making me scattered minded. Yesterday, after everyone left the library, I couldn't find my keys. I had hoped they were here at home but after searching all this morning, I'm giving up hope that I'll find them.

Two arms wrap around me from behind and I smile, breathing in Drew's intoxicating scent. "Morning."

"Have you been up long?"

I glance at the watch on my wrist, grimacing. "I've been up a while."

"Why didn't you wake me?" he asks, pressing his lips to the corner of my mouth.

Sighing, I lean into the gentle touch. I didn't want to leave him in bed this morning but I also didn't want my fears keeping him up.

You didn't want to scare him away.

I clench my eyes shut at the wave of pain shooting through my chest. My inner conscious is right. I don't want to scare him away. I know it's my insecurities talking, but I can't help it. Sometimes, I fear he'll take one look at me and wonder what he's doing with me. My personality isn't for everyone but add in the issues I'm having and I'm a disaster.

Will he stick through it with me or leave?

"I'm sorry. I wanted to get an early start and try to find my keys. Mum's spare set don't have the keys to the safe and back room," I explain.

He snatches the mug off me, taking a sip before passing it back. "If you can't find them by the end of the day I'll have a friend of the family come and change the locks for you."

I relax back into him. "I'm so lucky to have you."

He slowly turns me in his arms. With his head bent, he meets my gaze. "Charlotte, if anyone in this scenario is lucky, it's me."

Leaning up on my toes, I press a kiss to his lips, humming in my throat when I taste the peppermint on his tongue.

His phone rings, pulling me out of my thoughts. Taking his phone out of his pocket, his expression becomes wary. He answers, lifting it up to his ear. "Hello? How come? Can't you book somewhere else?" He pauses, listening to whoever is on the other end. "I'm sorry, Alison."

"Is everything okay?" I whisper, unable to stop myself from interrupting.

"The girls hen party plans for this weekend have fallen through and Joseph now has to go away for work. He can't get it off or change plans with the wedding so close."

An idea comes to mind. "Can I speak to her?"

Surprised, Drew nods. "I'm handing you to Charlotte."

I take the phone and give Drew my back, already feeling my cheeks heat. "Hey, Alison."

"Hey, Charlotte. You okay?"

"I'm good, thank you," I reply before taking a breath. "I know this probably isn't your scene but there's a strip club called Tease."

"I know the place," she replies.

"Well, I've been out there a few times," I announce, leaving out the part that I went there every Friday. "It's a really good night out and you don't need to book. I could even tell my friends you are going and they'll make sure you have a good night."

"You are friends with strippers?"

I beam, standing straighter. "I am and they are awesome. You'll love them. Just don't go near Trixie. She only wants the tips and then cheats you with the time of a lap dance."

Drew coughs, and rushes into the kitchen.

I guess the cough is back.

"Um, I, well, that's something to think about."

"Think about it. And you never know, you are hot and Dave might not shout at you if you want to try out a pole."

She bursts out laughing. "I'm not one to strip."

"I didn't strip either," I tell her, pouting. I had courage, but it never stretched that far.

"You know what, I think I might. Can you let them know I'll be in this weekend and it will be for a table of twelve?"

I squeal. "I'll tell them. You'll love it, I promise."

"You should join us."

"I'd love to but I have some work to catch up on," I lie. I don't want to go back there in fear of Scott turning up. Which right now, doesn't sound like a bad thing. I want him caught. He has hurt too many people and needs to face the consequence of his actions.

"Oh no. Maybe another time."

I perk up. "Definitely."

"Tell Drew I'll speak to him in the week and that I'm okay with him not staying overnight after the rehearsal dinner."

"I will."

We say our goodbyes and I step back inside, finding Drew holding Katnip, who is purring against his hair. He spots me and puts her down on the floor. His lips twitch as he takes my phone. "Is she going to the strip club?"

"Yes."

His brows pinch together. "You okay?"

I hand him his phone. "She said to tell you she's okay with you not staying overnight after the rehearsal dinner," I relay to him. "How come you changed plans? If this is because of me, and the fight at the charity event, please, don't. I don't want to cause drama between you and your family. I can stay at home; it's not a problem."

He pulls me against his chest. My hands go flat over his hard pecs and I bend my neck right back to look up at him.

"This isn't about that. Mum is on a rampage over Eloise. I'm not sure what's gotten into her but she's taken her side and I'm done with it. She might not ruin the rehearsal dinner or the actual wedding by causing a scene but I know my mother. Nothing will stop her after the events are over, and I'm done listening to it."

My chest tightens. "I'm so sorry, Drew. Have you explained your side of the story?"

He shrugs. "I don't need to. Apparently, they already filled her in on my part and they picked it apart, saying I'm lying and in denial."

"Oh no," I whisper, hurt on his behalf.

"So yeah, that's why I don't want to stay over. Although it wouldn't ruin the actual event, it would ruin Alison's day and I don't want that. We still have three weeks left until then so hopefully things change."

Noticing for the first time that he's dressed, I ask, "Are you going into work?"

"I am. What about you?"

"Me too. I have tons of stuff to catch up on and I have a birthday party coming in later."

"A birthday party at a library?"

I chuckle, having seen this reaction before. "Yes. I have the space. It's cheap. And the kids love having Disney characters dressed up coming to see them."

"You dress up, don't you?" he guesses.

I grin. "All the time, but not today. Today I'm short staffed and have hired other people to come in. The kids love it."

"Have you had breakfast?"

I nod. "I had some marshmallows earlier."

He swivels his head to the side at the empty bag of chocolate covered marshmallows. "You ate the whole bag, didn't you?"

I pout. "I really did."

A smile teases his lips. "And you have no regrets."

"None whatsoever," I reply truthfully, grinning. "Are we still doing self-defence this week?"

"Of course," he answers. "Grab your stuff and I'll walk you to work before I leave."

"Ah, ever the gentlemen."

He slaps my arse, causing me to giggle. "You bet your arse. Now get moving before Landon tears me a new arsehole for making him open on his own again."

"Let me grab my bag and shoes," I tell him, moving down the hallway to grab them. I pull open my shoe rack, grabbing my pumps. Katnip takes the opportunity to jump out from her hidey spot on the shelf above and I squeal. I only have a second to react before she can latch onto my face. I grab her, clutching her to my chest, and relax when her claws dig into my chest. It's always better than my face.

Drew comes racing out of the kitchen, takes one look at Katnip, and sighs.

"What? It's a work in progress."

He chuckles, taking her from me. He holds her up until their gazes meet. "You, cat, need to be nicer to your mother," he scolds.

I finish sliding on my shoes before grabbing my bag. "You ready?"

He reaches for his keys off the side and nods. "Let's go."

We head out and I lock up behind us. I fiddle with the strap of my bag. "So um, are you, um, coming over later?"

He wraps his arm around me and pulls me against his chest. "I'll come over after I've finished work and take you out for dinner."

The tightness in my chest eases. "I'd love that."

I unlock the door to the library and stop, turning to him. "Thank you for staying with me last night."

His eyes heat. "Oh, it was my pleasure."

He wraps his arms around my waist, and lifts my feet off the ground. I smile, leaning up to press my lips against his. He kisses me back, his lips soft, moving slow and gentle, and after one last flick of his tongue, he reluctantly pulls away, sliding me down his body until my feet meet the ground.

"I'm going to miss you," I blurt out, inwardly groaning at my running mouth.

"I'll miss you too. If I do get a chance, I'll bring some lunch for you. Keep you company. I'll message you."

"I'd love that."

He presses another kiss to my lips before putting space between us. I like that. That he needs to, to stop himself from touching me.

"Later," he drawls.

"Bye."

With a dopey smile on my face, I push through the library door, locking the main one onto the latch to keep it open before pushing through the second doors. These are the ones we couldn't lock last night due to the keys going missing.

I hit the alarm code and step inside, flicking on the lights.

Nothing.

I do it again, my brows pulling together. Again, the lights don't even give off as much as a buzz.

Which is strange since I have them looked at for insurance purposes every year.

A strong feeling of impending doom hits me square in the chest. I stagger backwards, my heart racing as a sliver of fear races down my spine.

Scanning the library, I try to find the source of my fear. I can't pinpoint what is out of place.

The hairs stand on end on the back of my neck and arms. I'm not sure how I know, but I have this sinking feeling I'm not alone in the library.

"Hello?" I call out, groaning as I slap my forehead. "Yes, because a mass murderer is going to pop out and say hi."

Still, there is no sound, no movement, which feels even worse than if there had been. It's eerily quiet.

The library doesn't feel right. It isn't because the light isn't as bright without the main lights on. It isn't the smell, which for some reason smells earthy and of mould.

I can't place it. I take another step back but then, as the clouds clear outside, a stream of light shines through the window, landing on the cause of my anxiety.

I scream.

I scream so loud my throat hurts.

I will my feet to take me outside, but I can't move. I struggle to catch my breath each time I scream, the sound scratching at my windpipe and leaving it raw.

Scott.

Pale, motionless, and eyes still open and blank, he's propped up against the bookshelf, facing the doorway. Ghostly, with shrunken cheeks. I shriek even louder.

Dried blood coats the side of his face and hair and even though the wound has long healed, the side of his skull looks crushed in.

"Fucking hell," Drew hisses, picking me up and taking me outside. I'm still screaming, clinging to his hoodie, the sound shrill, piercing. Only this time, my eyes have the will to shut.

But I still see him behind my lids.

Drew sits us down and begins to rock.

"Police please. We found a dead body," Drew announces, his body tense. I don't hear the rest; I can't, but I can feel the rumble of his chest.

It stops and suddenly, the back of his hand cups the back of my head. I flinch, my screams turning to whimpers. "Charlotte," he whispers.

I can't.

That was Scott.

He's dead.

And that imploding doom I sensed earlier, intensifies. If it wasn't him sending me those flowers, then who was?

And are they the reason Scott has been murdered?

"Charlotte," Drew whispers, pressing a kiss to the side of my face.

My body bucks as sobs tear through my chest. "I watch crime shows. I love horrors."

Drew tenses. "Um—"

I lift up, getting his face. "They were my favourite," I screech, my pulse racing. "But t-that was different. It, i-it wasn't on the screen. It was real life. And they lied." My breath hitches. "He… He…" I struggle to catch my breath and my eyes begin to bulge.

"Charlotte, breathe," Drew orders, his face paling.

My eyes roll, and the last thing I remember is the world around me falling away.

THIRTY-SIX

DREW

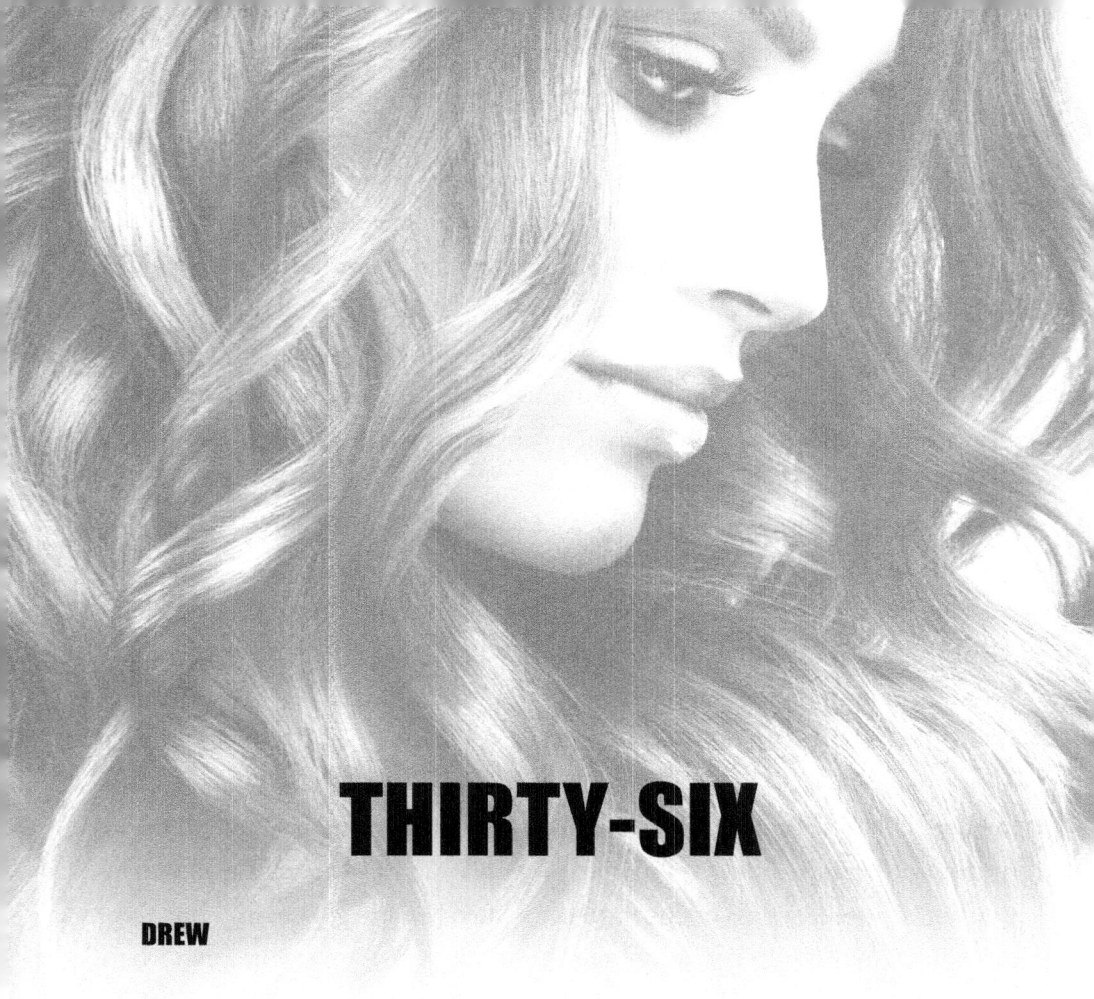

Charlotte stays cuddled into my arms as we walk through the house. It has been a long twenty-eight hours since she walked into the library and found her ex's gruesome corpse.

After being released late last night from the hospital after she went into shock, we brought her home. None of her family argued when I told them I was staying. Her parents didn't leave either, camping out downstairs, and her brother took the spare bedroom. Landon would have stayed too if there had been room. At one point it seemed like he was ready to camp outside her bedroom door.

When the police knocked this morning, wanting to bring Charlotte in for questioning, all of them rallied to support her. Only, the police wouldn't let us in the room whilst they questioned her. It caused a bit of stir and whatever they said to her, had made her curl into herself. She hasn't spoken a word since she came into the waiting room and the officer who was dealing with her case explained they will have to speak to her again at some point.

With Landon and I putting one of our team in charge at the gym, neither of us have to be back in work for a few days. Which is a good thing since I don't think it's wise to leave Charlotte alone right now. She has endured a lot since I met her, yet she has pulled through, her strength shining for us all to see. However, the light she carries, the care and love she shares with others… it dimmed yesterday at seeing the corpse.

I still have moments where it's all I can see. The dirt caking his clothes that looked like someone had rushed to put on him. None of the buttons had matched and his trousers had been undone. His injuries were out of anger. Someone had kept hitting him long after his death, and I don't need an autopsy to confirm that.

What kept me up most of the night was Charlotte's screams. I had been in the car, rolling down my windows when I heard it. Filled with torture, and anguish, I had slammed my breaks on, not even bothering to shut it off before racing up the steps. I didn't even think twice after I saw the body, the reason for the soul shattering cries coming from her. I lifted her and got out of there. Over an hour it took me to get away from the scene to head to the hospital where they had taken her. An hour of not knowing if she was okay or how she was doing. An hour of her thinking I had abandoned her. I needn't have worried. By the time I arrived, she still hadn't woken up.

She seemed better this morning, but that cloud still hung over her and everyone could sense it. And then the police turned up.

Helping her to the sofa, I take a seat next to her. She curls into me, her head resting on my shoulder.

Kayla sits on the coffee table in front of her, reaching out to brush her red locks off her face. "Honey, do you want to talk about it?"

"I think they think I killed him," she whispers, sounding so broken.

I tense, sitting up, and lift her upright. "What the fuck? Why on earth would they think you had anything to do with it? He's the one who hurt you."

Kayla pales, her grip on Charlotte's hands tightening. "We will sort this, honey."

"Why did they think you did this?" Myles asks, placing a hand on his wife's shoulder.

"My statement to the police that night," she whispers.

Landon sits down next to Kayla, his forearms resting over his thighs. "Charlotte, I need you calm for a moment. You need to tell us exactly what was said so we can help you."

"In my statement, I told them I hit him over the head. It was with my *Kama Sutra* book. I swear." She hiccups and I wrap my arm around her. "I didn't use anything else. It was that book. But they kept saying maybe I mistook what I held and it was a crow bar or something. Mum, I didn't. I swear."

"Hey, honey, I believe you," she soothes, rubbing her thumbs over the top of her daughter's hand.

"Then they said there was excessive damage to his groin area. I kicked him once and squeezed his balls. It was to get away, but he got up. I swear, he got up."

Landon's stoned-faced expression has me tensing. I'm guessing this is the first he's heard of the inner details of that night. And knowing she had to go to these lengths to fight him off, it's just now hitting him.

Just like it is me.

She came to me that night and unbeknownst to me, I'd get to know her, care for her and maybe even more than that. I hurt for her that night. Now, it cuts deep, wishing I had done more after I dropped her off. Maybe if I had known where she lived that night, I could have gone back to see if he was there, to teach him a lesson. All this continued pain could have been avoided.

"You did what you needed to, to get away."

"I also told them I scratched him and that I drew blood. He had those markings on his face. They have no evidence, but they said once the reports come back, they'll need me to go in for questioning again."

"But that Megan officer said they didn't arrest you," Kayla murmurs.

Charlotte wipes her eyes. "Because there isn't enough evidence. I didn't kill him. I swear."

"We know," Landon assures her.

Hayden snorts. "Someone fucking did. I don't get why people are getting testy about it. The world is a better place."

"He had children."

"Who he may have hurt," Hayden argues.

Charlotte's lips quiver. "I won't make it in prison. Do they let animals stay with you? Can you read romance books or do they only give you stuff like dictionaries? What if I have to eat meat because it's all they have? What if someone makes me her bitch?" she cries.

I pull her tighter at her outburst. "Nothing is going to happen to you."

She glances up at me. "I'm going to prison and you won't see me again."

"You aren't going to prison."

Her gaze down, she shakes her head. "Yes, I am."

I rub my hand down her back. "What makes you think that you are? You didn't do it. They'll need evidence, Charlotte, and there is none."

Her gaze goes to her family in the room, her lip quivering. "I'd go to prison for you. Whichever one of you did it, I will. I swear. But promise me you'll look after Katnip."

"Why are you looking at me?" Hayden argues defensively. "I don't even know what the dude looks like."

"You didn't kill him?"

Hayden snorts. "No, and if I did, I wouldn't drop him off at your library like a goddamn present. I'd make sure no fucker found him again."

"Good to know," Jaxon murmurs, pulling his wife away from the lunatic.

Her smile is snide. "Don't worry, you and yours are safe," she tells him, before tapping her lip. "Unless Reid pisses me off again."

"If you didn't, then who did?" Charlotte murmurs, fiddling with the pillow she pulled off the back of the sofa.

Hayden shrugs. "I thought Landon had done it, but again, he wouldn't be stupid or cruel enough to take him to the library."

Her brother snorts. "I thought Uncle Myles had done it."

Myles shrugs. "I thought Max, since he went missing a lot for days after."

Max gasps, placing a hand over his heart. "As much as I'd love to take the credit, I was stopping this one," he jerks his thumb at Maverick, "from tearing the entire town down looking for him. I didn't want the police to catch onto us looking for him. It would make us number one suspects."

"You kind of are," Jaxon murmurs.

"And who asked for your opinion?" Max retorts.

"I'm just saying, you are all here talking about murder like you are trying to solve who ate the last fucking cookie."

"Max did," everyone answers.

Jaxon rolls his eyes. "I'm just saying. Try to at least care that one of your own are accusing you."

Landon takes a glance around the room. "Anyone else care that the first person she thought did it was Hayden."

"My money would have been on Hayden," Madison pipes up.

"I thought it was Dad," her brother replies.

"I thought it was you," Hope tells him.

Everyone else gives their two pennies worth until they stare at Lily. Jaxon narrows his eyes. "Don't tell me you thought it could be one of them too."

She shrugs, grimacing. "I thought it was the giant. He was the only one here not accounted for that night."

All eyes turn to me, some hopeful, some resentful. "I didn't fucking kill him, although I wouldn't have lost sleep over it."

"And I thought me and my family were nuts," Jaxon mutters.

"I knew I liked you," Max announces, grinning.

"You've just ordered chains to use on him if he steps out of line," Maverick declares.

"That's for the new dog I'm getting," he fires back.

Lake's expression lights up. "We're getting a dog?"

He winces. "No. It died in transit and I can't go through that kind of loss again."

"Puh-lease," Hayden remarks. "What about the razor you bought?"

He narrows his gaze on his daughter, his posture tight and on the defence. "I want to cut my hair. Is that a crime?"

"You pay the barbers to do your hair," Lake replies warily.

He rolls his eyes, letting out a nervous chuckle. "God, you guys are so argumentative today. We aren't here for me. We are here for Charlotte. She's going to prison, for fuck's sake."

Charlotte's turns into a blubbering mess. "I don't want to leave and go to prison."

Kayla glares at Max before moving to take a seat next to her daughter, comforting her. "You aren't going anywhere. We will get this sorted, honey, I swear it."

"What did they say about the flowers and notes?" Madison asks.

Wiping her nose on the sleeve of the hoodie I gave her the first night I met her, she answers, her voice shaky. "They think I've been sending them to myself."

"And my gym?" I grit out. Do they think she faked that too?

"They think I got you to do it."

"Fucking arseholes," Hayden bites out. "They're going to be so fixated on pinning this on Charlotte, they are going to miss who really did it."

"She lost her keys to the library. They have to take that into account."

"They think I planned that or made it up," Charlotte explains.

"I was with you all night. They've not asked me where you were," I tell her. That has to account for something.

"They might want you in for questioning, I don't know. Officer Brown seemed to believe me, but that other guy was saying it was a lover's quarrel that had turned bad. They think I was mad that he had a wife, that I got angry when he wouldn't leave her, so I killed him. Then made up the false allegations so that when they found his body, I had an excuse."

"This is bullshit. The only reason they know he has a wife is because of the message you told them you read," Myles snaps. "They still don't know if his name is Scott."

"It's all in the papers now," Hayden adds. "The press latched onto the story quickly so the police have made a vague statement."

"But the police haven't released any details. They want to get as much evidence as they can before releasing the picture to the world," Kayla adds.

"They need to inform the wife before they release the picture. They are hoping they can find his identity before then or that someone comes forward to report him missing," Maverick explains.

"How do you know that?" I ask.

He glances at me, his expression void. "Because Beau, my daughter's fiancé, has kept us in the loop. He just messaged me."

"What do I do until then?" Charlotte whispers. "What if they never find out his true identity or who killed him?"

Maverick gives her a warm smile. "Go about your day and life, honey. The library is still closed for another week. Maddox has got people working to fix the electrics that were broken, and someone is coming in to change all the locks."

"This is such a mess," she murmurs.

"Speaking of press," Max begins, turning to Hayden. "How pissed off is pretty boy?"

"He's not a pretty boy," she retorts. She sniffs haughtily. "And he's fine."

Max chuckles. "You gave a vivid description of what you thought about the dead body they found in a local library. They quoted you word for word."

She shrugs, glancing at her nails. "I don't regret it."

"And mentioned your station," Landon adds, his lips twitching.

"He's not bothered. Some of the board members are, but they'll get over it. They always do. It's not the first time I've said something they don't like."

"You won't get into trouble?"

Hayden glances over Charlotte's head. "Never."

Charlotte relaxes, not sensing the lie. "I'm so glad."

Hayden had said the corpse could keep rotting and he deserved to die painfully. There was speculation of what he had done but because the police weren't going into detail, they didn't have the answers to report. But someone would soon find out.

There's a knock at the door before we hear it open. Faith steps through, her complexion pale as she's unsteady on her feet.

I hiss out a breath, seeing the pot in her hand.

"Blue Forget-Me-Nots," Madison whispers, standing from her place on the floor.

"What do they mean?" Charlotte whispers, on the edge of the sofa.

"They represent death. The name says it all. It's a reminder to not forget those who have passed. They are an emblem of remembrance. Whoever sent these, did so with the meaning, 'he will live on in your memories.' This is connected to Scott. These flowers are a slap in the face, wanting you to suffer further."

"Get them out of here," I bite out.

"There's a note," Faith shakily gets out as she hands her father the pot.

Max pulls off the note, opening the envelope before reading,

"His death is the price paid for love.

His grief does not speak.

But yours I'll seek.

And you, my dearest Charlotte, shall perish for your sins."

Charlotte covers her mouth with her hand, her breath hitching. "This isn't over," she whispers.

Mouth tight, Myles grabs the pot, smashing it against the wall. Kayla stands at his side, placing a hand on his chest as he heaves out a breath. "This isn't over."

"Myles," she whispers, her voice pained.

"No one hurts our daughter. No one. And if the police don't find them first, whoever it is will be sleeping next to that prick in the morgue."

I tilt Charlotte's head up to meet my gaze. "I'm going to go home—"

She grips my arm. "No, stay," she cries.

"Charl—"

She grimaces. "I understand. I mean, I can't make you stay. I wouldn't even if I could. I'm sorry. So sorry."

I press my lips to hers, taking her off guard. I pull back, resting my forehead against hers. "I'm not going anywhere, but I need some more clothes. I'll be staying here with you."

"We can stay with her," Landon tells me, a warning lacing his tone.

"You're more than welcome to if that's what she wants," I tell him. "But it still doesn't change the fact I'm not going anywhere."

"Thank you," Charlotte breathes, her fingers unclenching from my hoodie.

I kiss her head and get up, glaring down at Landon. "Don't leave her till I'm back."

Max snorts. "Look at you giving off orders. Thinks he's all—" I give him my best 'don't fuck with me' look and he holds his hands up, stepping out of my way. "Carry on. We'll keep her company until you're back."

"Thanks."

I step out of the room, hearing him mutter, "I could fucking take him."

I shake my head. Sooner or later, they'll get it: I'm not as easily scared off as what others may have been.

I'm here to stay.

THIRTY-SEVEN

DREW

CHARLOTTE AND I END UP BACK outside to watch a movie under the stars. The weather has stayed dry and the night air isn't as cold as it was the last time.

The past week has been draining on her and it's starting to show. It's beginning to be a bit of a worry, especially during the times she gets lost in her own head. Nothing or no one can pull her out of those times. So earlier, when she was busy trying to get Katnip out from under her bed, I told the others to leave and give her, and us, some space.

They mean well, all of them do, but it isn't helping her get back to her norm. They are worried about her, rightly so, and yet, it's that worry that doesn't let her forget she found her ex's—the same guy who assaulted her not that long ago—dead corpse.

Another reason I asked them to leave was selfish on my part. I have a surprise coming tonight and want some alone time with her. And not the kind that's whispered words in her room so her family can't overhear. I find she opens up more when she isn't trying to protect those around her, and when she isn't trying to mask the hurt in her words to save other people's feelings.

And she is hurt.

At first, I thought it might be because she still harbours feelings for him, and although she's never said it directly, I know that isn't why.

Outside, under the stars and the light glow of the lights and the white screen, she is the most relaxed I have seen her this week.

"How are you doing?" I ask, breaking the silence that fell between us once the movie started. Now it has ended, and for a moment, we were enjoying the solace of the peace and quiet. This week has been hectic with people coming and going. It reminded me again of the vast difference between our families. Well, my mother's and hers. My dad's side is almost similar.

What surprised me the most was not one member, save for her uncle, gave a shit about me inserting myself into her life. None of them worried, even if they didn't like us being together. I think given the circumstances, given my record with those around me, they knew deep down I would never hurt her or *any* woman. Or at least, I hope that's what it is. They are Carter's after all and could just be biding their time. There are times I see them staring at Jaxon and it looks like they are secretly planning where to hide his body. Every so often, I'll be on the receiving end of the same look.

"I'm good," she whispers, snuggling into my warmth. "Thank you."

"No need to thank me. I enjoyed doing this the last time," I tell her, giving her a pointed look.

A faint pink blush rises in her cheek. "Me too," she whispers. "But that wasn't what I was thanking you for."

My brows draw together. "What were you thanking me for?" I pull her lush body against mine and she cocks her leg over mine, snuggling closer.

"For realising I needed some space to think, and making it happen."

"Your family mean well," I remind her.

She traces patterns on my chest with the tip of her finger. "I know. I don't know what I'd do without them, but this week, the voices inside my head have been going a mile a minute. Add in all their thoughts and feelings and it's been deafening," she explains before lifting her head up. "I'm not crazy. I swear. It's my own thoughts I hear and because they overlap, all screaming at me to figure out, to compartmentalise, it's driving me mad."

I duck my head down and reach over, tucking a strand of her hair behind her ear. "I don't think you're crazy."

She snorts lightly. "I think I'm crazy."

"You've had a lot going on."

"I'm surprised you've not run for the hills. My family is crazy, but this is something else. It's a lot to deal with. And then there's what happened at the gym."

I bite my lip to stop the laughter from bursting free, but it's too late. She smacks my chest.

"Babe, they deserved it."

"But Harriet—"

"Was giving them what they deserved."

She sighs, dropping her chin onto my chest. "If you say so."

I do.

The girls had started rehearsing this week at the gym since they had some free time come up. Some of the members of the gym had made some lude comments and tried getting into the room they were practicing in. The girls took it upon themselves to get payback, not wanting to deal with that every time they wanted to go and practice. I'm not sure what actually happened, but the girls went out to use some of the equipment. Two clients were rushed to A&E for dropping the barbell on their chest. Three went flat on their face on the treadmill and the staff said the sight wasn't pretty after. I wish I had been there to see it. They all found it hilarious, especially when the girls started taunting them for their lack of willpower and strength.

Charlotte seems lost in thought once more and once again, I notice tears gather in her eyes. "What are you thinking about?"

"Nothing," she whispers.

I nudge her. "Talk to me."

"I don't think I can talk to anyone about this."

I pull her up my body. "I'll never judge you. Ever," I assure her. "This is about Scott, isn't it?"

She nods, glancing away. "I'm sad."

I gulp, my worst fear coming to life. Maybe I read her wrong. Maybe she does mourn his loss. And it isn't until this very moment that I realise what she has become to me. I know my feelings run strong. I would never have risked my friendship with Landon had they not. She drew me in like a magnet, and even if I had tried to pull away, to take a step back, it wouldn't have mattered. I would have always ended up here. With her.

Free-falling into something that's beyond something I have shared with any other girl or girlfriend.

I gulp. "About Scott?"

So many emotions cross her face. Confusion, pain, hurt, grief. "He had children," she whispers.

I try not to tense my body, but it's hard. This is the first time I have heard of him having kids. Or at least, I think it is. I know she didn't know about them before without having to ask; she is too kind-hearted and loving. She'd never have started something with him had she known. I know that with all my heart. She isn't built that way.

"Children?"

"The night he… that night I found out he was married, the night he hurt me, I read part of a message on his phone. Someone called Sophia had messaged him asking if he would be back to put the kids to bed. He had kids, Drew. Innocent children. They are going to be devastated when they learn of his death. I can't imagine what they will go through. It's tearing me apart inside."

She begins to sob and I clutch her under her armpits and lift us both up, sliding her into my lap. "You have the biggest heart."

"They will grow up without a father. I can only imagine how that will feel for them. Just the thought of my dad never being here, it rips me open inside.

I don't know how old his children are, but they must be young. This is going to change their entire life. And I… And I…"

"Charlotte, this isn't your fault. I get you feel for them. I do too. No kid should go through that kind of loss. But we can't change the outcome. None of us. They are going to feel it either way."

"I know it's not my fault he's dead. I wasn't the cause or maybe even the reason. But I keep running over it in my head. What if the person who killed him is the same person as my stalker? That would mean I am part of the reason. Maybe they knew he hurt me that night and killed him for it. Maybe he—"

I press my lips to hers, silencing her. Her breathing is ragged, harsh, and as I run my fingers down the curve of her spine, she begins to calm. "One, we don't know *who* killed him. If it even is the same person. Two, he had enemies. Any one of them could have found him and killed him for revenge. Don't feel guilty for his death."

"I don't. I feel… something. But it's not guilt. I'm sad for his family. For his wife. I didn't want him to die, even…. even during and after that night. But I'm not sad that he's dead." She sniffles, glancing over my shoulder. "That is what I feel guilty about. I'm a bad person for thinking like that."

"No, it makes you one of the best," I admit, and it pulls her attention back to me. Her brows pinch together. "I couldn't give a fuck that he's dead. For me, his death or not, he would have been punished and paid for his crime. Whether that was this month or in ten years. It would have caught up to him—and it seems like it has. Your family wish it was them who killed them. Even that cranky lady who lives next to Lily was ranting the other day when I went out to get milk about how she wished it had been her to do it."

"I want my life to be boringly normal again."

My lips twitch. She's hot when she pouts. "I hope that includes me."

"Always," she whispers.

A thought occurs to me, one I assume occurred to the police *before* they took Charlotte in for questioning. "If he has a wife, and children, he has to be known by other parents, neighbours. He would have been reported missing.

Why hasn't his wife reported him missing?" I put out there. "And you said he worked. Why haven't they?"

"Maybe they have," she admits. "Maybe they reported the real Scott missing."

"Maybe," I reply, but it's doubtful. "The first thing the police would have done was run through missing persons fitting his description."

"Let's talk about something else. Tell me what you'd be doing if you were at home."

I glance down at her, knowing this is the moment I let her in on how boring my life was until I met her. "If I was finished up at the gym, I would most likely be doing books for the gym or be asleep."

I can see her calculating the time. It's still early, too early for a grown-arse man to be going to sleep. "You wouldn't be out with friends?"

I shake my head. "Not really. We'd meet up once in a while but the gym takes a lot out of me. Some nights I don't finish until late. And then I'm around people all day, every day and sometimes, I just want to go home and chill."

"I get that. I love people. I love socialising. But I also love coming home and relaxing with a cup of tea."

I chuckle. "From the stories your family have shared this week, I'm inclined to doubt that."

Her cheeks blossom. "They were exaggerated."

"They said you once wanted to go to the beach so badly when you were younger that you took a train and ended up near a village in the middle of nowhere."

"I was being productive and not pestering my parents. Plus, Madison and Maddox came with me."

"And the time they told me about you hoarding animals in your bedroom?"

She bites her lip for a moment. "They were injured."

"See, always a social butterfly."

"And that doesn't bother you?" she asks, unsure.

"No. Not at all."

"It won't get too much when my family are always here?"

"No, because you'll be here."

Her expression softens. "My family mean everything to me. I love spending time with them. Sometimes I think it annoys them."

"Charlotte, I doubt anyone who loves you could be annoyed with you. They love you."

"I know. It's because they're always too busy being annoyed with Uncle Max to be bothered."

Chuckling, I reply. "Now that I'm more inclined to believe."

"They're the best family I could wish for."

I clear my throat as something else flitters through my thoughts. "Why didn't you become a vet? You love animals a lot. I've seen you feeding the birds, and even the other night you took food out for the hedgehog."

She lowers her lashes for a moment. "Because I could never stomach the thought of having to put them down. I couldn't be the person who took someone's family member from them," she explains softly. "I do volunteer to help Faith sometimes. I like spending time with the animals. I get to walk them, spend time with them."

I shake my head, pressing her flush against my chest. I grip her arse, and her lashes lower, her gaze on my lips. I grin at the intake of breath. "You are miraculous, Charlotte Carter."

She leans down, her plump, full lips a breath away from mine, when my phone dings with an alert.

I reluctantly pull back. This is the message I have been waiting for. Moments later, car tyres crunch along the road outside the front.

"You expecting someone?" she asks, watching me read the message on her phone.

"Yes, and I need you to wait here for one moment. Okay?" I place her down on the makeshift bed beside me, and lean down, pressing a quick kiss on her lips.

Facial expression filled with bewilderment, she nods. "Okay, but, um, should I be worried? Your smile is kind of freaking me out."

I chuckle as I get up, dusting off my knees. "Trust me, you're going to love this."

I leave her and head to the backdoor. "Bring some cookies back," she yells.

I'm bringing her more than cookies. I'm bringing her something that will make her forget she ever wanted them.

Heading through the house, I stop at the front door, scratching Katnip behind the ear where she's perched on the shelf beside her door.

Pulling it open, Faith and her fiancé, Beau, walk around the front of the car, the basket in hand.

"Did you receive the money I sent?"

"Yes, but like I said to you on the phone, the seller was asking for far too much."

I shrug, taking the basket from her. "I don't care."

"We've put together some food that will last a couple of days," Beau announces. "Where do you want them?"

I nod in thanks. "Will you pop them inside the door for me, please."

"I gave him a general check-up and gave him his injections," she announces before her vet mask vanishes and she grins. "Does she know about him yet?"

I smile back. "No. I'm about to surprise her now."

"I'm sure we will hear about it later or tomorrow," she tells me as Beau goes to her side, pulling her against his chest. "Just make sure she keeps him inside. He seems very docile and loving."

My smile spreads into a grin. "In other words, don't let Katnip near him."

Her shoulders sag. "Just don't let her bully him. That cat can be vicious."

"They'll be fine."

We say our goodbyes and I head back inside, stopping just before the kitchen doorway. I hold the cage up, finding bright blue eyes shining back at me. The ragdoll—the same cat Charlotte had dozens of things with their picture on—is pure white bar the tail and face. From this light, it looks like a speck of dust.

She is going to fall in love on sight.

I head outside and Charlotte pulls her attention away from the second movie playing, her eyes wide and on me. "Is that… is that an animal?"

"This," I begin, holding the cage up. "Is a present from me to you. He's yours."

"He?" she whispers, sitting up straighter. As I near, a gasp passes through her lips. "Is that a ragdoll?"

I grin, bending down and sitting next to her, setting the cage in front of us. Blue eyes sparkle as he presses up against the cage doors.

"Oh my God," she cries, her hands shaking as she reaches out. "He's beautiful."

"You need to give him a name."

"I- I don't know what to say." She trembles. "He's so cute."

She pulls him out, and I notice tears streaming down her cheeks as she clutches him to her chest. He immediately begins to purr, rubbing his nose against her chest.

"Hey, I didn't mean to upset you. I—"

Her expression stops me from going any further. A sob hitches in her throat. "He loves me. He really loves me."

"Babe," I mutter, amused.

"Drew, I- I don't know what to say. He's- he's perfect."

"So are you."

"This is the best present I could ever want," she cries. "He's so soft."

I run my fingers over his soft fur. "He's cute."

More tears.

She lifts him up, glancing into his doe eyes. "I'm going to love you so much." A little reptile meow escapes him and her entire body melts. She turns to me. "I love you. I love you so much."

"Me or the cat?" I whisper hoarsely. It feels like a truck has slammed into my chest.

She loves me.

"You. Him. But you too," she chokes out. "I'm sorry."

I grip her chin, tilting her head until she's facing me. "Never be sorry. I've not been in love. I wasn't sure if this is what it is. I am now. I can't imagine love feeling like anything else."

"You can't?" she whispers, her lashes fluttering.

"No. Because you are all I ever think about. You make me strive to be a better person. I hadn't realised I was lonely until I met you. You brighten up my days. I love being with you, I love being around you. I love you," I admit, pressing my lips to hers. "But don't say it back. Don't say it after receiving a cat. Say it to me when the dust settles with the stuff going on around you, when the exhilaration of this little guy isn't fresh. Say it to me then. Okay?"

She nods, tucking the cat closer to her chest. "I will. I promise, I will." Her voice is low, calm, and after pressing another kiss to her lips, her attention goes back to the cat.

I watch the joy and happiness light up her face, all of it a kaleidoscope of emotions as she plays with the cat. Content on just watching her, I sit back, hearing 'I love you' coming from her mouth inside of my head.

Is it love?

Who knows. She could have said it in the moment. I knew what I felt was more than lust or attraction a while ago. Saying I love you out loud is easy. *We* feel easy even if everything around us hasn't been. I'm not sappy, I'm not a romantic, but for her, she makes me want to be. She makes me want to spoil her, to see the world through her eyes.

She turns to me, her bright red hair blowing in the wind as she aims her blinding smile my way. I return her smile as I cross my arms behind my head and lean back.

Yeah, she is easy to love.

THIRTY-EIGHT

CHARLOTTE

My attention pulls away from the extravagant homes Drew drives past. Do families live there? Couples? Or is it a rich woman or man living alone? I think of all the homeless people, all the people struggling to fit their families into their homes, who would jump at the chance to live in one. I don't begrudge the rich for the things they have, I'm just upset life has to be this way. It makes me grateful and lucky to have everything I have in life, and it isn't just my home or my library, but the people in my life who enrich it.

"We are nearly there," Drew announces.

"Okay," I reply quietly, nervous.

I'm not nervous about seeing his family again, although they are part of the reason. I'm worried because of the outfit I bought. The dress doesn't match the cardigan I was forced to wear.

I can already feel their stares, their judgement, and although I can handle it, I don't want Drew to have to listen to it. It isn't fair on him, especially when there's already a rift between them.

I pull the white cotton cardigan tighter around my chest, hoping like hell they don't make me remove it.

Drew pulls up a wide, thick driveaway and the house that comes into view has my stomach turning.

White rendered walls gleam outside, making the blood-red door stand out. There's a climbing rose bush that arches over the left side of the house, over a window.

I fiddle with my cardigan again and after putting the car into park, Drew turns to me, placing his hand over mine. "You don't need to wear the cardigan," he tells me, his lips twitching.

I narrow my gaze on him. "It's not funny."

"It's a little funny."

He's right. It is a little funny. For nearly a year I have tried my hardest to build a bond between Katnip and I. But I think my cat has some sort of mental issue. Because from the minute we introduced her to Snowball, my cat has changed. Every time he comes to me for fuss—which he does often—she will get so jealous and claw at me until I set him aside. Only then will she curl into my lap and begin to purr. If I pick her up when Snowball isn't around, she claws at me like my life means nothing to her, like the hand that feeds her means nothing.

I can't make heads nor tails of it.

Today, Snowball had been staring at the wall—he does this often too. I bent down to pick him up and Katnip came out of nowhere, clawing me anywhere she could get a grip. One thing led to another, and before I knew it, I was climbing the tree, trying to get the sulking cat down. I ended up once again hanging upside down, Drew once again saving me from hanging there until a family member passed by and found me.

It's a work in progress.

But at least she has stopped hating me.

It just doesn't help that I now have scratch marks all over my chest and down my arms. I look like I went toe to toe with Freddie Krueger.

"I look a mess."

"You look beautiful," he declares.

I sigh, unclipping my belt. We're going to be late if we stay out here hiding and I don't want his family having something else to pick about.

He slides out of the car and I follow, meeting him around the front to take his hand. "Do you think they'll be okay?"

He chuckles, stopping to pull me in his arms. "They're cats. They love solitude."

I pull my phone out, sending a message to Lily. "Just to be sure…"

Charlotte: If you have time, and if you don't mind, will you go and check on Katnip and Snowball for me please.

Charlotte: It's okay if you don't want to.

"Who are you messaging?" Drew asks, not in annoyance, but in amusement.

"Lily. She's the closest. It will probably be Jaxon that goes." I bite my lip. "But I don't think he'll actually check on them."

My phone dings with a message.

Lily: Will you be mad if I told you I'm already here? They're both playing with the new toys I bought them.

I chuckle and show the message to Drew. Lily has popped over a lot to see the new kitten, and has threatened to take him a few times.

Charlotte: It's fine. And thank you.

I drop my phone back into my bag and beam up at Drew. "I can relax now."

He chuckles. "I'm glad. It's nice to see you smiling again."

I know what he's talking about and I don't want to think about it. Not tonight. And yet, I can't help but think back on the conversation I had with Officer Brown the other day.

"We have his identity."

My heart races at hearing the words I never thought I'd hear. "You do?"

"Scott Parish."

Scott Parish. Just hearing his name in my mind feels foreign, and a sliver of ice runs down my spine.

"Did you... Did you find out who killed him?"

"We are still looking into his case, and we aren't at liberty to discuss this with you just yet."

"I understand," I whisper, grateful she even called me since I'm the number one suspect. A thought occurs to me. "Did you... did you contact his wife?"

"We have spoken to Sophia Parish. She wasn't aware of her husband's affairs."

I close my eyes, my heart aching when I imagine what she is going through right now. She doesn't deserve this. In one day, she has learned her husband, the father to her kids, not only cheated, but was murdered. "Did she say why she never reported him missing?"

"As far as Mrs Parish was aware, he was working away in Scotland and was due back in two weeks."

"She didn't get suspicious when he didn't call?"

She sighs and I hear the background noise disappear before she replies. "She received messages from his number. When she asked why he wasn't answering, his reply was his signal was spotty or he was in meetings. We know this isn't true and we are trying to track where the messages came from through the GPS."

"So you'll be able to find out where the messages came from?"

"Hopefully," she explains.

"Would she..." I close my eyes. "I'd like to speak to her, to explain and apologise. I'd never have gotten involved had I known he was married."

"She's a grieving widow. She's asked us and the press to respect her privacy. She wants time to tell her children that their father isn't going back."

I glance up, finding a few people in the library listening into my conversation. I roll my desk chair back and turn, lowering my voice. "Okay."

"I'll call you with any other updates."

"Thank you."

Drew brings me back to the present. "I'm sorry. I've brought up bad shit for you."

I shake away those memories and step forward, wrapping my arms around his waist. "Don't be. It just hasn't sunk in yet."

"Give it time. It's only been a few days."

"I know," I whisper.

We turn back to the house and the red door opens. Stood in the doorway, intimidating and unapproachable, is his mother.

She storms down the steps, Wesley following her with a tight expression. "Grace, please, not tonight."

She ignores her husband, her daggers and thorns aimed at Drew and me. "What on earth has possessed you to bring that girl here?"

"Good evening to you too, Mum."

"Answer me," she snaps, her voice just lower than a screech.

I step closer to Drew, curling my arm into his. I don't know what is going on. Why she is acting this way. "Mrs Wyatt, I—"

She holds her hand up to my face. "Do not speak to me."

"Mum," Drew scolds, his voice tight, and his expression pinched. "Do not ever speak to her like that again."

"You brought her to your sister's rehearsal dinner after everything she did."

"She hasn't done anything."

"She attacked poor Eloise!"

"I didn't hurt Eloise," I explain, recoiling at the lethal look she throws my way. "I pushed her. That's all. And that's only because she came at me. It was an immediate reflex."

"You are trash, and my son can do a lot better than the likes of you."

I stiffen. "You mean Eloise?"

"Yes, Eloise. She is respected amongst all, and has manners. You—"

"And what about your son? What about what he wants?"

Her expression is livid as she turns to Drew. "Do you care that you're embarrassing our family name?"

"I'm not the one embarrassed, Mum."

She continues like he hadn't answered. "And don't think we didn't hear about what happened at that place you work. We had a friend look into it and they reported back that it has something to do with this case."

"Grace," Wesley murmurs, trying to pull her away. She pushes him away.

"And if that wasn't the worst of her transgressions; there was a body found in that place she works at. How could you do this to us, Drew? How?"

His silence has the hair on the back of my neck standing on end. "Maybe we—"

"I'm here for Alison, and Alison only," he tells her, his voice harsh, the bite in it sharp and unforgiving. "But before we walk through that door you need to realise that I won't be coming back, not until you apologise."

"All this because of this, *this girl.*"

"Please, stop this. Don't. You are family," I plead.

Drew takes my hand, running his thumb over the top. I look up, but his attention isn't on me. It's still on his mum. "One, Eloise is a manipulative bitch." His mother gasps. "Her father is threatening to cut her off if she doesn't get her act together and marry. She thinks marrying me will get her back in her father's good graces. And you want me with her because of your reputation, Mother. You don't care what I want or about the lies she has spread about me. You are too self-centred to care."

"Don't you dare—"

"And if you knew about the gym, why didn't you call me? Dad called me the minute he found out and wanted to come and check up on me."

She rears back, her hands shaking. "Because that place is an embarrassment. You could have been anything you wanted and thrived at it, but you chose to do *that*. The damage has done you a favour. You still have time to go back to school. Be something—"

He groans. "I'm not going to close the gym and I'm not going back to school because you aren't happy. I'm doing a job I love; one I'm damn successful at. My gym makes a high percentage of profits each year but that doesn't matter to you. It doesn't matter that it thrives. *None* of it matters. Because it will never be good enough for you."

I squeeze his arms as tears gather in my eyes. His sisters, Alison's fiancé, and Eloise pile out of the door to watch the argument unfold.

"Drew."

The hurt in his voice has my stomach bottoming out. "And if you held any kind of remorse, if you had even a tad of decency, then you'd apologise to Charlotte. Not only for how you've treated her from the moment you met her, but because you've just brought something up that was traumatic for her. You didn't ask who was found or why they were dumped in her library. And I'd like to say that if you did know, you wouldn't have mentioned it, but you would have."

"Drew," I whisper, my fingers digging into his arms.

I don't want this. I don't want to be the person who comes between family. I don't want Drew hurting, and the anguish I heard in his voice… it has my knees locking together.

"I was there," he grits out, still glaring at her as he slams his fist against his chest. "I heard her screaming so loud the windows shook. I saw him. I saw what was done to him. And you threw it out there like it meant *nothing*."

My eyelids pinch shut at the reminder. *All this time.* I have been selfish once again, not realising how badly this affected him, how deeply it had traumatised him, like it had me. I hadn't asked him. All these weeks and I hadn't asked him if he was okay. It makes my gut clench.

I should have asked.

I whimper, trying again once more to pull him back. "Drew."

"Son," Grace whispers, pain shining for a moment before she masks it. But I saw it.

She loves her son.

"No, Mum. I'm done. I've taken your criticism for years and I did it because I love you. But I'm not going to have you do the same thing to her. I won't let you or anyone run her away."

Eloise steps forward, tears running down her cheeks. "Can't you see what she's doing? She's trying to put a wedge between you and your family."

He doesn't even spare her a glance. "This has nothing to do with you."

"Eloise is right. This is because of her. She's gaslighting you. She's pushing away those who have your best interests, who love you."

"Do you have my best interests?"

Grace has the audacity to look taken aback, like moments ago she didn't show signs of remorse. If I hadn't witnessed it myself, I wouldn't have believed it. "Of course, I do."

He snorts. "No, you really don't. Otherwise *she* wouldn't be here."

Wesley steps forward. "Maybe we should all calm down and take a minute."

"No, Dad, let him speak," Natalie drawls.

Eloise wipes her tears away. "This is my fault. If I hadn't told you about the baby…" She gulps, glancing away like it's too hard to face him. This girl doesn't realise I have grown up a Carter and can spot a bull-shitter a mile away. When she continues, her voice is raspy, filled with a fake emotion so good, the others move a little toward her, all except Alison. "If I hadn't told your family about the baby, this rift wouldn't be here."

"Honey, no, it's not your fault," Grace coos, stepping closer to comfort her.

My spine straightens at the sign of affection she willingly displays for this woman and yet her son, pours his heart out, and she stands there, frozen, like an ice queen upon her throne. She has no right. None at all. "You are a very mean lady."

Her attention snaps to me. "Excuse me?"

"You're mean."

Eloise scoffs, her nose tipping up. "Are you going to run back and tell your mummy?"

I don't glance away from Grace. "Your son is hurting. He's upset. And you are comforting the girl making up lies about him."

"Charlotte," Drew soothes, reaching for me, but I side-step him.

"No, they need to hear this," I order.

His lips twitch. "Okay."

I point at Grace. "You have a son who runs a successful business. So successful he has fighters lining up to use his gym, to train with him and my cousin. But even if he wasn't successful, you have a son who respects women. Who helps a half-dressed, beaten woman late at night," I choke out, tears falling down my cheeks. "You have a son who may look a little rough on the outside, but is the kindest, most loving man on the inside. Someone who teaches self-defence classes for free to help survivors of violence." I give them a moment to digest my words, but I know, from the cold look she is giving me, it isn't enough. They need it all. If she can't accept her son after this, she doesn't deserve him. "He saved me. Not just the night I staggered into his gym, but after. He helped me when I refused to admit I even needed help. That's the man who stands before you. Why you continue to belittle him, belittle his achievements like they mean nothing, I'll never understand." Drew's hand runs down my arm and I shiver, even as I press into the touch. With another deep breath, I continue, this time addressing Eloise. "I understand why you want him. He is everything a woman could wish for. But he's not yours. He's never been yours. And telling people otherwise, you're only embarrassing yourself."

"You ginger bitch," she sneers.

I run my fingers over my red curls. My brows pull together. "I prefer the term redhead."

Eloise heaves out a breath. "Are you really going to let her do this? Her verbal diarrhoea is not needed here. If not for me, then take a look at your family, look at what it's doing to them. You don't want that."

"You helped her?" Alison asks, her voice barely a whisper as she clings to her fiancé.

"Yes," he replies, tensing.

Alison's gaze snaps to mine. "You were hurt?"

"So much so that when the doctors were examining me, I wanted to die. I had my mum, who I love so, so much on one side, and my dad, who is my hero, on the other, and yet I wanted to die. The meds numbed the pain internally and the injuries covering me, but they did nothing to numb my heart," I choke out as Drew's embrace surrounds me. My gaze never once leaves her, even though I can feel the stares from the others on me. "And then I clung to the hoodie I had on. It still had his scent on it and I was suddenly transported back to the gym where I finally felt safe. I remembered the soft words he gave me, the gentleness in his touch and the kindness in his heart. I remembered how he got me home. He made me feel safe." I stop, the ball expanding in my throat as I turn to his mum. "That is the son you raised. It doesn't matter if he's a doctor, gym owner or a litter picker, because he's a good man."

Drew kisses the top of my head as he runs his hand down my arm. "We are going to go," he announces. "We'll be here tomorrow, but for tonight, it's best if we leave, but say now if you don't want us coming."

It takes a moment for Alison to snap out of her haze. "No one is going to start anything tomorrow. Are they, Mum?" Her tone holds no argument.

Grace, who still doesn't look happy, nods. "No," she croaks, staring at her son like it's the first time she has seen him.

"You can't be buying this," Eloise pipes up.

"Shut up!" I yell, startling everyone. "Stop making it worse for them. Let them heal. Leave him be, for heaven's sake."

"But—"

"But nothing," I snap, my hands and knees shaking.

"Maybe it's best if *you* leave," Natalie declares.

The hurt on Eloise's expression may have made me feel sorry for her had it not been for the ugly snarl she sends her back. "We were going to have a baby."

"There was no baby," Natalie snaps.

"What?" Grace asks, looking between the two.

Natalie doesn't say anything for a moment until she turns to her brother. "I'm sorry. I'm sorry for being a bitch to you, and I'm sorry I cornered you at the fight."

He nods, and suddenly, Eloise pales. "Natalie."

Natalie shoots her a glare. "Don't," she warns, then turns to her brother. "I figured it out that night. She's had a coil since she was sixteen. She must have it changed every five years and I ran through it in my head. She had it changed the year before, right before my birthday because I went with her."

"Natalie," Eloise hisses.

"I left that night because I wanted no part in it but then she came the next day and said Charlotte attacked her, and I believed her. I believed her because she's always been there for me," she explains, before turning to me. "I'm sorry. I'm sorry for what you went through, that we treated you like that. We're sorry."

I nod, and my fingers tighten around Drew's.

Eloise screeches so loud, and stomps her foot, that I have to take a step back. "She's gay!" she yells, pointing to Natalie.

Grace falls back into Wesley. "You are a gay?"

Natalie snorts. "It's not a thing, Mum. Get over it."

"Get over it?"

I swear my ears bleed from the sheer volume of Grace screaming. Natalie waves to us before heading back into the house, his mum and Wesley following her.

Eloise takes one last look at us before stomping away, going to toward a car.

Alison and her fiancé step forward. "So *that* happened."

Drew chuckles. "We really are sorry your party was disturbed."

She waves us off. "They've probably not even noticed we've left," she admits. "You don't have to go. The bitch has gone."

"We do," he states. "If you don't want us to be there tomorrow, please, just let me know. I won't be offended."

Her nose scrunches up. "I will be. I'll speak to Mum later but after that little speech, I can't see her being a problem. She's just too stubborn to admit when she's wrong."

I paste on a smile. "I'm sorry for yelling and for ruining your night."

Alison tilts her head, scanning me over like she's analysing me. "Have you ever heard Ava Max's, *Sweet but Psycho*?"

My nose twitches. "Um, yes, why?"

"The song reminds me of you. I'm not sure if it's the red hair, but you have a fire inside you."

"Isn't that about a girl who poisons her cheating ex?"

Alison laughs. "Not literally about you. Just parts. Although I could see you reacting that way if Drew cheated."

I can't smother my laughter. "I wouldn't need to. My family would get there first."

Drew gulps. "On that note, we are going to go and let you get back to your family."

Alison walks over and pulls me into her arms. "I'm glad you're okay."

The back of my nose burns. "Thank you."

She pulls back, gives me a reassuring smile, before hugging her brother. "Love you."

"Love you too," he tells her before she leaves, her husband pulling her into his arms.

We head back to the car and I stop at the door, grimacing. "I'm sorry."

He presses my back to the door, brushing my hair over my shoulders. "Don't ever apologise because of them. This has been a long time coming."

I grip his waist. "Still, that was a lot."

"I'll get over it," he tells me, before leaning down, pressing his forehead against mine. "What I won't ever unhear is that you wanted to die."

I tense, my blood freezing. "I couldn't stop the thoughts."

"Promise me," he croaks out before clearing his throat. "Promise me if you ever feel like that again you'll come to me."

I smile, running my fingers through his hair. "You'll never have to worry about those thoughts again."

"Yeah?"

"Yes, because the morning after, I realised I had a lot to live for, even if I didn't know what that was."

"Good," he breathes out.

I hike my leg up, running it up his leg. "Now we have the night free, what should we do."

His eyes darken as he runs a hand up my thigh, stopping to cup my arse. "We have most nights free."

I pout. "But we're all dressed up." His muscles tense as I run my finger down his hard abs. "It would be a shame for that to go to waste."

His fingers tense on my arse as he leans down, his lips a breath away from mine. "What I have planned doesn't involve clothes."

I grin, glad the disaster of tonight has been somewhat washed away. "Oh yeah?"

"Yes," he replies, his voice like silk, rich and dark. "Get in the car."

I drop my leg and turn to pull open the door, and before I can get in, Drew pulls me back, running his hands over my stomach. "Thank you."

"For what," I whisper. His breath against the sensitive area under my ear has the tiny hairs standing on edge.

"For what you said, for how you see me. *Thank you*."

"You never have to thank me for telling the truth."

He runs his nose along my neck, a small groan passing through his lips. "No, but I will."

He helps me into the car, and before he can shut the door, I see the appreciation on his face. It's deep, strong, and it makes the back of my throat burn. My words hadn't just meant something to him, they had meant everything to him.

And I realise, I'm not the only one who has insecurities. He has them too.

People see my size and find me intimidating.

Women are sometimes scared of me.

I remember him saying those words; how he hated that he couldn't get them to see him differently. I close my eyes, stopping the tears from flowing. For as long as we are together, whether that is for a day or forever, I promise to make sure he knows how special he is.

Because he isn't just my hero, my saviour.

I swallow deeply as it hits me.

He's the man I was searching for.

He's the one.

The love of my life.

My forever.

My dream.

THIRTY-NINE

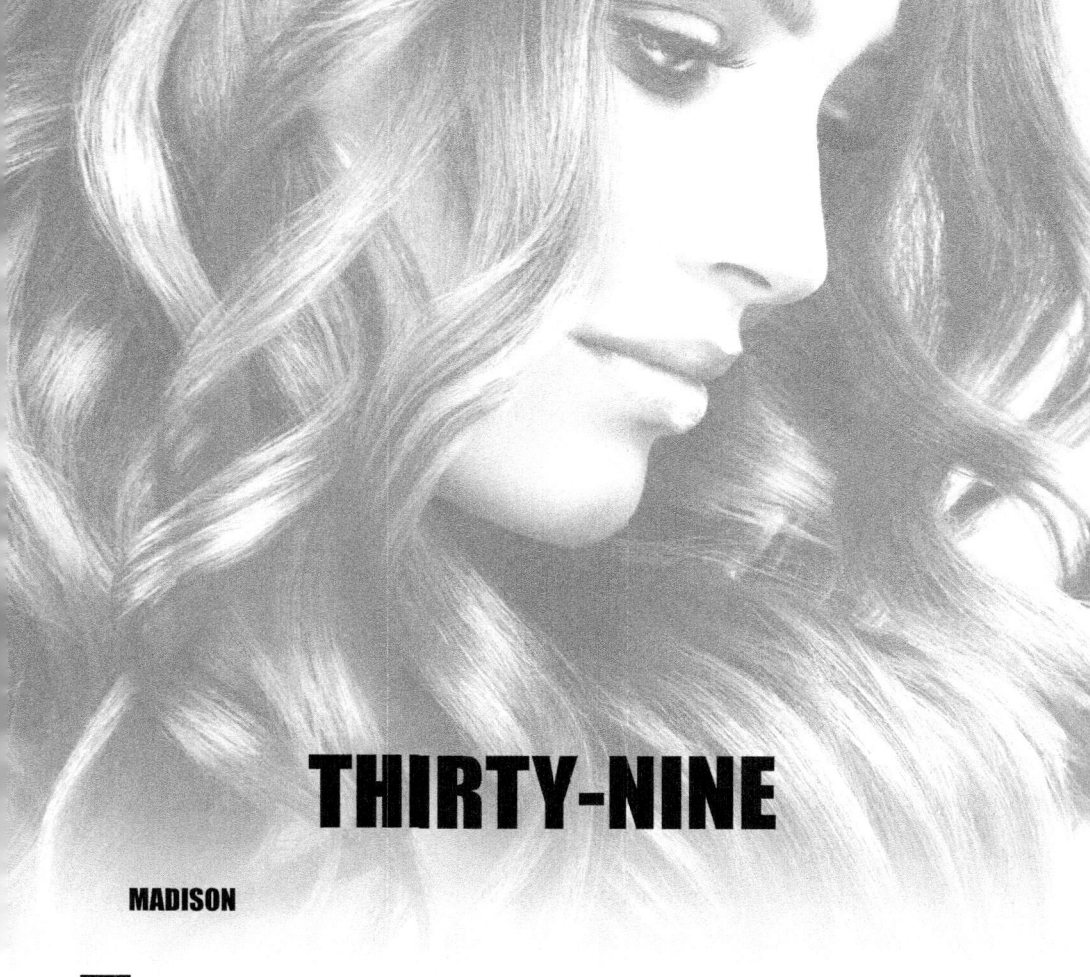

MADISON

LIFE.

It isn't just the babies birthed or the essence we breathe. It's all around us. Life is in the air, in the trees, in the weeds that grow in your garden. It's in your home, in your work, and in those around you.

For as long as I can remember, the earth has fascinated me. How a flower blossoms from a meagre seed, how fruit and vegetables grow from the ground or from a tree.

All of it.

And with each plant, each flower or piece of food, I became more fascinated, wanting to learn everything I could about them. Flowers come first. My aunt Teagan had taken me to the flower shop when I was little and seeing all those vibrant colours come to life, made into bouquets or arrangements, I had to know more. From there, I studied every one of those flowers. Some I remembered, some I didn't. Either way, they all held meanings or sentiments.

When Charlotte first admitted about the flowers she had been receiving, my attention to detail screamed at me to find out what they meant and where they had come from. It has been an obsession of mine since that day, and it's killing me that I can't find out where these plants have been coming from.

Hayden turns down the radio that has been playing some crazy rap song. "Are you going to sulk all the way home or are we going to hash this out?"

"Stop making it sound like you have hours left of the drive. We are going to be back within the next thirty minutes. If these arseholes learned how to drive, we'd have been back way before now." I honk the horn when another dickhead cuts in front of me, forcing me to put my foot on the break sharply.

Hayden grabs the dashboard, breathing heavily. "I love my life and I don't want to die."

"I'm not the one driving like a race car wanker."

Throwing herself back into the chair, my feisty cousin lets out a breath. "I'm sure we'll find someone willing to speak to us."

She's on about the flowers again. I'm still searching for the person who purchased them, to no avail.

"It's pointless. No one is going to tell us. Maybe they'll tell the police. I don't know. It's the only lead we have on who is doing this."

"Landon has gone with Aunt Kayla to visit that last girl."

"The one who kept putting it off?" I reply.

"Yeah. Apparently, she saw the news with his picture and recognised him. She wants to help Charlotte."

"Help her how? They can't stop the police looking at her as a suspect; not now they know who he is. We wanted their help searching for him, or at least to find out his real name. None of us knew he was fucking dead while we were searching for him."

She glances down at her phone. "He said it's the same story as the others and she wasn't much help with any clues as to who it is. None of them received any flowers after."

"Didn't he say weird shit happened to them after?"

She nods as I maneuverer the car into the next lane. "Yes. One lost her job.

One of them were disowned by their family after a picture of her stripping was revealed. And I'm sure the last girl said she was broken into the week he left her." I watch as she grips her knees, her breath shuddering. "He did the same thing to each girl. Charming, sweet, and attentive but the minute he got them in that bed, inside them, he turned into a brutal prick. He didn't stick around after, leaving them lying there, broken and hurt as he hurled abuse at them, saying they were dirty and unclean."

"Charlotte said he didn't do that. He tried to—"

"Control her," Hayden interrupts. "With Charlotte, he had a hold on her that I think he didn't get with the others. I could be wrong but that's my thought on it. He hurt her, I'm not disputing that, but it wasn't the same as the others."

I clench my fingers around the steering wheel. I can't imagine what she went through, how she felt. "I know."

Both of us cease speaking and I know, like me, she is thinking about Charlotte. Our kind, sweet Charlotte. She is the person who mediates conflict if one of us falls out. She is also the person who has unintentionally caused arguments. Every time one of us pushed her treats on another, we fought about it. And she's the type of person who thought we were fighting over which one of us got to eat it.

She hums tunes when things get tense. Heck, she feeds stray animals and some of them aren't even friendly, yet she'll smile and coo at them like they are a cute kitten.

Even with all her kindness, she holds a fieriness inside her, one that only comes out when she is pushed.

That's our Charlotte.

Knowing a monster had her in his grip has us all feeling guilty. We should have done more, should have seen it coming. The males in our life might be overprotective, and we had warned them off, telling them they had been ridiculous. Yes, they went over the top with it at times. What they did to Jaxon, and in turn Lily, had been horrific and none of us wanted to go through that each time we found a partner. But had we been too hard on them? Had they been right to worry? Seeing what Charlotte has gone through… I'm not sure I want to take a chance. The only reason I'm conflicted is because of how happy she is at the moment. She has always been happy but for those months with Scott, she wasn't herself. She lost weight and questioned everything, even the clothing she wore. Drew brought her out of her shell once again and the bounce in her step, the twinkle in her eyes, it's stronger and brighter than it ever has been.

The silence of the car is broken by the ringing of Hayden's phone. At a quick glance, she's confused as to who is on the phone. "This is a call extension from work. Why would they be trying to put a caller through to me when I'm not due in today?" she explains before answering, putting the phone on loudspeaker. "Hi, Chrissy. Everything okay?"

"We have someone on the other line wanting to speak to you. She said it's important and about the library."

I pull over into a vacant space on a side street and stare at the phone.

"How does she know I'm a relative or that I work at the station?"

"She saw your picture in the paper and they mentioned the radio station."

"Put her through," Hayden orders gently.

We both share a look as the voice on the other line comes through. "Hello?"

"This is Hayden. Can I ask who I am speaking with?"

"My name is Milly. I'm calling about the library you spoke about in the paper. About the dead body they found."

"What do you know of it?" she asks, her voice gentle.

A forced laugh echoes down the phone. "I know enough to know that what happened to that girl isn't speculation, that she isn't the reason for his death."

"Do you know who is?"

"His wife."

My brows pinch together and Hayden and I share another look. As far as we have been informed, his wife didn't even know about his affairs or that he wasn't at work. According to the officer Charlotte spoke to, his wife is grieving and wants privacy.

"His wife doesn't—"

"She's unstable. Do not believe a word she says. If he's dead, he pushed that crazy bitch too far."

Hayden lowers her voice, her hands trembling around the phone. "How do you know all of this?"

"Because the two are a match made in heaven. He hurt my sister. Jade was nineteen, had her whole life ahead of her, and he destroyed her."

"Had?"

"She killed herself. She couldn't cope with what he had done, what his wife had done."

"What happened?" Hayden asks, as I struggle to stop myself from firing questions at her.

"Jade met Scott Parish whilst studying at school. He was five years older. They hit it off and as months passed, she seemed more and more withdrawn. I went up one day to visit and I found her; her sheets bloody, her body covered in bruises and cuts. I stayed with her until she recovered. She wouldn't go to the police or seek medical attention. He had her so brainwashed that she blamed herself. Her friends told me they saw it coming but nothing they said to her registered. She would ignore their opinion and advice and they had to watch as he belittled and made her the shell of the person she once was."

"I'm sorry," Hayden whispers. "So sorry he put her through that."

"It's not him who did the worst. It was the wife, Sophia. She showed up during Jade's class, screaming at her for being a homewrecker. He had been trying to contact Jade for weeks but I kept her from the phone, deleted the messages, and the calls. And his wife must have seen them. I don't know. The school asked her to leave for the day. She was embarrassed, upset since that was the first time she had found out about the wife.

"Her depression got worse after that. She was being bullied by people spreading the rumours going around from that incident in class. Sophia didn't give up terrorising her. She called once to tell me someone put tomato sauce in her bed, and left threatening notes. Men would try to rape her then claim it's the service she charged for. She'd leave class, and Sophia would be there, watching, taunting. It didn't matter that Jade had told her she hadn't spoken to or seen him since that night they slept together, this woman didn't believe her.

"I went back up one week, hearing the anguish and depression in her voice.

She was so skinny and frail. I'll never forget that image. I wanted to talk her into coming back home with me. His wife turned up at the house that first night, banging down the door screaming, and I answered. I threatened her; I told her that if she ever came back, I'd go to the police. I went home a week later; my job wouldn't let me have any more paid time off. I shouldn't have left."

"What happened after you left?"

"Sophia beat the ever-loving crap out of her. Her friends called me and said they were going to take her to the hospital so I got in the car and headed down. I got a call halfway saying my sister had slit her wrists."

My hands shake, tears streaming down my cheeks as I listen. "I'm so sorry. So very sorry for your loss."

"Thank you," she chokes out. "I know that isn't the worst she had done to her. I knew she was keeping things from me and from her friends. But the two of them destroyed her. He deserves to be dead, but she deserves to rot."

"We've not even been allowed to know who she is. Someone was sending my cousin, Charlotte, flowers the night he hurt her. They've continued to send them since, all with threatening poems. But the police seem to believe her story. We don't even know where she lives or who she is."

"I have a picture."

Hayden gulps, and her fingers tighten around the phone. "You have a picture?"

"I can send it to you. I gave it to the police years ago but the image is a little blurry and they never found her. I only knew her first name but when I saw his image in the paper, I knew it was the same couple. I had only met him once and it was over a phone call, but I'll never forget it."

Hayden rattles off her number. "I swear, we will make sure she gets what's coming to her," Hayden promises. "Leave your number with my assistant. I'd like to keep in touch if that's okay with you."

"Thank you," she croaks out.

"What for?"

"For believing me. I might not be able to see your face, but I can hear in your voice you want justice for them both."

"I want justice for them all," Hayden declares.

Milly's breath hitches. "All?"

"There have been loads more, but I swear to you, it will never happen again. I really do need to go, but I will call and explain the rest when I get time. I just think the police officer and my cousin need to hear this."

"I understand. Thank you for taking my call and listening to me. And I really hope your cousin sorts everything out."

"Me too."

They say their goodbyes and moments later, her phone dings with a message. I watch as her eyes widen. "So that's Sophia."

I lean over the parking break, and my heart begins to race as I snatch the phone out of her hand. "Oh my God," I breath.

"What?"

"I know that woman."

"You do?"

"Yes. Although her hair is a different colour to that blonde."

"Who is it? What do you mean?"

I turn to her, my pulse beating rapidly as I think of what this means. What it means for Charlotte.

"It means we need to get to Charlotte. It means she's in danger. She knows this person too."

Hayden takes the phone back, her lids squinting at the picture. Her eyes widen as she slowly turns to me. "Fuck."

My thoughts exactly.

FORTY

CHARLOTTE

I TWIRL AROUND THE KITCHEN, humming along to Katy Perry's, *Roar*. Life is so good. The smell of brownies fills the air; *love* fills the air.

I still haven't made up my mind on when to tell him. He told to me to wait until everything has calmed down, and that the stress of the case isn't hanging over our heads. However, last night, after hours in bed together, I wanted to tell him then. I wanted to scream it from the rooftops.

I pick Katnip up from the counter, moving her away from the food before she gets a chance to steal it. "Not for you, kitty."

Meow.

She swats at me, trying to play with a strand of my hair, but I tusk, placing her down on the floor. "Nope. You aren't chewing on my hair either."

I have spent hours curling my hair into stronger curls than the thick, bouncy, loose ones they normally are. I tied most of it back from my face in braids, putting those pieces into a bun at the back of my head, leaving the rest to flow down my back. My makeup is already done too. All I have to do is put on some lipstick, throw on my dress, and spray on some perfume. And I am good to go.

We still have two hours until we need to leave for the wedding, three until it starts, but I was so excited, so full with life, that I couldn't keep still and wait around. I didn't need to go into work like Drew did. And I didn't want to lose track of time by baking first. So I compromised and did my hair and makeup before I began baking. All I'll have to do once it's time, is slide on my dress.

My phone rings from the kitchen counter and I twirl, still singing along to the lyrics. Seeing Nora's name on the screen, pleasant surprise fills me.

"Nora, how are you?"

"Charlotte," she breathes out dramatically. "I'm at the library looking for a couple of books I need. I'm looking for Women's Political Rights in History, and Feminism History and Theory. Your bloody receptionist—yes, I'm talking about your lazy arse—refuses to even speak to me."

I inwardly groan, even as a chuckle escapes at hearing Marlene try to defend herself in the background. "Give me a few minutes and I'll be right there," I tell her.

"Thank you, thank you, thank you," she cries out in joy.

Laughter spills out of me. "See you soon."

I race up the stairs to my bedroom, grabbing my dress for the wedding that's hanging on the bedroom door. I know I still have hours before I need to get dressed. I shouldn't risk getting something on it. But I also know from experience that I'm easily distracted, and I don't want to make us late by forgetting to get changed. Not after last night's argument. I want to make a good impression today and turn up on time and look the part.

With that in mind, I strip out of the pyjamas I have been lounging in and slide the dress over my head. The forest green ankle-length dress is more daring than any of my other dresses. I bought it a few years ago but once I put it on, it felt too revealing and every time I'd look in the mirror, I'd cringe. I felt like a little girl playing dress up. Now, as I stare in the mirror, I feel anything but. It's empowering and I feel sexy. There is a newfound confidence inside of me that pushes me out of my comfort zone.

The thin-strapped dress has a deep V cut down the middle, showcasing my cleavage. The bodice below clings to my waist like it was made perfectly to fit my figure. It hangs a little looser at the waist, but not by much, so it flares. It still clings to me but the wrap over style at the bottom gives me room since there is a spit up the middle that reaches the middle of my thighs. I slide on my matching shoes, the heels barely giving me any height. Which I don't mind. I'm practical over style and I know from experience that being drunk in high heels is never a good thing.

I grab my clutch from the side table, already having packed it earlier. I only need to put my phone and keys in there.

Snowball's reptile meow greets me when I reach the front door. I glance down, finding him and Katnip sitting there. I kneel in front of them, running my fingers through their fur. "You can't come to the library with me today."

Meow.

"I promise, you can come next time."

They have both been coming with me to work. The children who visit love it, as well as most of the people who enter. There are only a few grumpy people who don't and who swore to never return. I'm kind of happy about it. I don't have one of those policy's where I can refuse someone's entry. Legally I could, I just don't have one. Anyone is welcome at the library. All but people who don't think kittens are cute or don't like animals all together... Those people can't be trusted. In my opinion anyway.

Plus, Katnip only hissed at the woman because she blocked the sun from where he was sunbathing.

It was all a misunderstanding.

I give them one last scratch behind their ears before grabbing the keys off the side. I send a text to Drew, letting him know I'll be at the library and to meet me there.

Katnip distracts me, making me drop my phone. I pick it up, mindlessly throwing it in my bag. "Katnip. You need to be a good girl for Mummy. And look after Snowball."

She sniffs before waddling away, and something fouls hit me. Adorable and so mushily cute, Snowball glances up at me, his reptile meow quiet before he, too, walks away.

"For someone so cute, your farts are deadly," I call out.

I'm not sure if it's a male thing or a rag doll thing, but when that cat farts, I swear I can taste it in my mouth it's that bad. Before the rotten smell can cling to my clothes, I head outside, locking up behind me.

I dodge the potholes, not wanting to break a heel, and as quickly as I can, I head into the library, hearing raised voices as I get through the first door. An older gentleman, who I've spoken to a few times before, pushes past me, his face pale. "I'll come another day."

"Goodbye, Mr Wilkins," I call out.

He doesn't give me a reply. I head inside, finding Nora facing off with Marlene.

"It doesn't tell me I have to find the books for people in my contract," Marlene snaps. "It's not my fault you are too lazy to look."

"It's called customer care. Look it up," Nora snaps back, crossing her arms over her chest.

Rita hobbles over to me. I run my gaze down her khaki three-quarters, seeing no injury to her leg, but when I take a look at her ankle, I notice swelling. Her arthritis is playing up again. Before I can tell her to go home, she speaks up.

"Everyone bar the people in the café have left. Those two bickering for the past hour has driven them out. I'm going home, and if I were you, I'd close up early or you might risk losing visitors from coming inside ever again."

I wince. "That bad?"

She rolls her eyes. "No manners at all, that one."

"Rita, she's a child. Well, a young adult," I gently scold.

"Not the young'un. I'm on about that trollop you sit at the desk. Why she ever came back is anyone's guess. Then again, not many jobs let you watch Netflix on your phone whilst customers are waiting to be seen."

I nod, understanding the deeper meaning she's telling me.

I have to fire Marlene.

It will be sad seeing her go, but a lot easier without her. I spend a majority of my days fixing her screw ups.

I bite on my lip as I watch them squabble back and forth. Maybe I could invite Uncle Max here.

Or Hayden.

I won't need to fire her and hurt her feelings then.

Nora steps toward me. "You should fire her arse. I'd work here after school and on weekends if it meant saving the population and little kids from seeing her face." She bounces on the balls of her feet as she comes to a stop in front of me. "And I'll get to see you more."

"Fire me? She can't fire me. And if she does, I'm leaving right now, and with how you are dressed, and seeing that Rita has just left, you'll need me."

I sigh at the bite in her words. I was warned before going into this business or any business that there would be hard parts. And this is one of them.

For months now, I've been trying my hardest to help her fit into her role and with those around her. I've forgiven and let transgressions lie, knowing some people just need a chance. From her very first week I've had people tell me to let her go.

I should have listened.

I could have made it easy and invited my uncle or cousin to do it. They wouldn't even need to tell her she's fired. By the time they were finished, she'd beg me to let her leave.

"If you walk out before a shift ends or before your notice, I don't need to pay you your contracted hours. It's in the contract you signed."

I had it put there after my last receptionist walked out and then expected to be paid for it. When she received the wages for the hours she worked, she was livid and it went to a mediator. In the end, I paid for those hours but made sure I put it in the contract for when I hired the next receptionist.

"You need a reason to fire me."

"I have plenty. You sit at your desk doing nothing but looking at your phone, doing your nails, or reading magazines. I've tried for a long time to get you into the ropes of things around here but you've chosen to ignore them. Strike one," I tell her softly. I don't like upsetting people, don't like hurting their feelings or being hard on them. "Strike two is your lack of customer care. Last week a mother complained because her daughter got a pair of your nail scissors."

"That kid shouldn't have been messing with my shit."

"Your shit, as you eloquently put it, should be in the staff room in the back and not at your workstation."

"It's a bloody library."

"And whilst I've just heard you confirm that this indeed a library, then you should know not to leave unlidded drinks near books or near the computer. I've told you multiple times not to drink with them close by. Strike three."

She bares her teeth. "Then you can take this as my two-week notice."

I beam at her and clasp my hands together. "To make it official, I need it in writing."

She huffs, slamming down into her chair. She pulls herself closer to the desk and seconds later, she begins typing away.

Nora watches me with wide eyes. "Dude, you are a badarse."

I lift my shaky hand out of Marlene's view. "I'm trembling like a baby right now."

She chuckles. "You did good."

"I just hope I wasn't too hard on her."

Her lips twitch. "Nah." She waves me off before glancing over her shoulder, smirking at the curse coming from Marlene. When she turns back, her gaze holds excitement. "Does this mean you'll hire me? I could use the money since Dad won't let me work."

I bite my lip. "If your dad doesn't want you—"

"It's not that he doesn't want me to, it's just that he wants me to concentrate on school. And what better place than a library to do my schoolwork. I could do it here and still do everything you need me to. It's not like I have tons of stuff I have to do at home."

I think it over for a minute. "If your dad agrees, then you're more than welcome to work here."

She pumps her fist into the air. "Yes."

I glance over her shoulder at Marlene, and when she meets my gaze, I begin. "We are going to shut the library early today. Finish with whatever you're doing and then begin to close down."

"But you said—"

"You'll still be paid since it's me closing."

I don't want to admit she's right. With Rita gone, there is no way I can trust Marlene on her own. I had been surprised when she came back, especially since a body was found. But she didn't seem to mind and found it easy to speak to the press, who had come in to ask questions.

The press aren't the only ones who have come to the library. People have begun to use the place as a tourist location. We have mediums, ghost hunters and other forms of people checking the place out. After the first week of reopening, we told them unless they were here for books, they needed to leave. After that, our murder/mystery and true crime for sale section sold out. The café has thrived too, and we had to hire part-time staff to cover the traffic coming in and out.

A whistle followed by a cat call pulls my focus back to the present and I turn to Harriet and Olivia heading toward us. "Girl, you look hot."

I run my hand down the forest green dress. "Thank you."

For the first time, Nora takes in what I'm wearing and grimaces. "You have the wedding today. I forgot. I'm sorry."

"It's fine. And I've got plenty of time."

"That's not what I'm sorry for. I've met his family."

"Alison isn't so bad," I murmur, not wanting to speak bad of the others, even if they are mean.

"No, but the other one makes Lucifer seem sane."

I chuckle then turn to the girls. "This is Nora, Drew's sister. Nora, these are my friends, Harriet and Olivia." They exchange greetings and when they're done, I ask, "What brings you two here?"

Harriet's the one to answer. "I need some new books and was hoping to pick them up here while we were passing through."

I beam. "Well, you are in the right place. Let me just sort Nora out."

"We'll come with you. You can tell us what we've missed."

I snort. "Not much. The police still think I did it."

I duck my head, sadness filling my chest. They don't know me. Don't know my character. And although PC Megan Brown believes me, she can't go off that. They need proof. My alibi is solid. I was seen on CCTV outside the gym. I have my hospital records and the time of the phone call my mum and dad made before we left for the hospital. I just don't have anything from before or anyone to witness I left him in my doorway alive. Anyone could have moved the body for me whilst I was being seen to.

It's been hard having people accuse me of such a horrific thing. I meant what I said to Drew. I might have disliked him, but I would never wish harm upon him. I'm not sad that he's dead, only sad for those who will mourn him.

Harriet rubs her hand down my arm and leans in, giving me her warmth. "They'll find out who's done it. And even if it goes to court, one look at you, and they'll know you could never possibly be capable of it."

"I can get angry though," I whisper. "I was taken in, but never charged once, for being in an altercation."

"The guy with the cousin?" Harriet asks.

Olivia's lips twist. "Didn't that involve a stoned muffin?"

I throw my hands up. "It never had a stone in. It was just... hard."

Nora chuckles as we turn down another aisle of books. "I'm so glad my brother has you."

"Charlotte," Hayden screams.

I pause, all of us looking to where the sound came from. "What—" I stop, sniffing the air. "Hey, am I smelling things or can you guys smell petrol?"

"I can smell it," Nora replies, warily scanning the area.

"Charlotte, where are you?" Madison cries out.

"Here," I call out, racing for the front.

They meet us in one of the stacks, breathing heavily. Madison clutches the shelf for support as she points to me. It's Hayden who recovers first. "We know who his wife is and we think she's the one who has been sending you those notes and sending you the flowers," she rushes out in one whoosh.

"Who?"

Her lips part, the name on the tip of her tongue, when Marlene's yell has us all looking to the front of the library. "Hey, you can't do—"

Her yelp and grunt of pain has everyone pushing to the front, but I can't go, not yet. I don't have a good feeling about this and the churning in my gut intensifies as my friends and family disappeared from view. I grab Nora's arm as she rushes past me.

"What?" she whispers.

"Go and hide in the back. If you follow this as far back as you can, there are a hidden set of stairs behind some wheeled shelves. Use it and go up there."

"I'm not hiding."

"Yes, you are. Please. I don't know who this is but I know they're capable of hurting someone. I don't want you in the middle of it."

"Charlotte," she pleads, her gaze shooting to where the others have run off to. I can hear Hayden yelling, Madison pleading.

"Please."

She takes one more look at the front before nodding. "I'll call Drew."

I nod. "Go."

She runs off in the direction I told her to, and I take a lungful of air before rushing after my friends and family. I don't want anyone else getting hurt. They have already endured so much. They don't need this.

But as I come to a staggering stop, where Hayden is being held back by a crying Madison, and where Harriet clings to Olivia, blood pouring down her cheek and arm, my entire world falls apart around me.

Standing, red-faced, a knife in one hand and a lighter in the other, is someone I called a friend.

Someone I shared my secrets with, my inner thoughts.

None of it makes sense.

I slowly turn to Hayden and Madison, my lip trembling.

"Who is his wife?" I ask, afraid of their answer.

Hayden, who is glaring holes at the intruder, slowly turns to me.

"Charlotte, meet Sophia, Scott Parish's wife."

I step back, folding my arms across my chest to ward off the chill that has soaked through to my bones.

Her smile is no longer warm, it's cruel, the same with the shadows that lurk in her eyes and surround her. This isn't the woman I have come to know.

I want her to deny it, to tell them they have it all wrong, that this has been some misunderstanding.

She steps forward, and I can feel her hatred like it has been slammed into me. "I guess that's out of the bag."

"Rose," I breathe. "What have you done?"

FORTY-ONE

CHARLOTTE

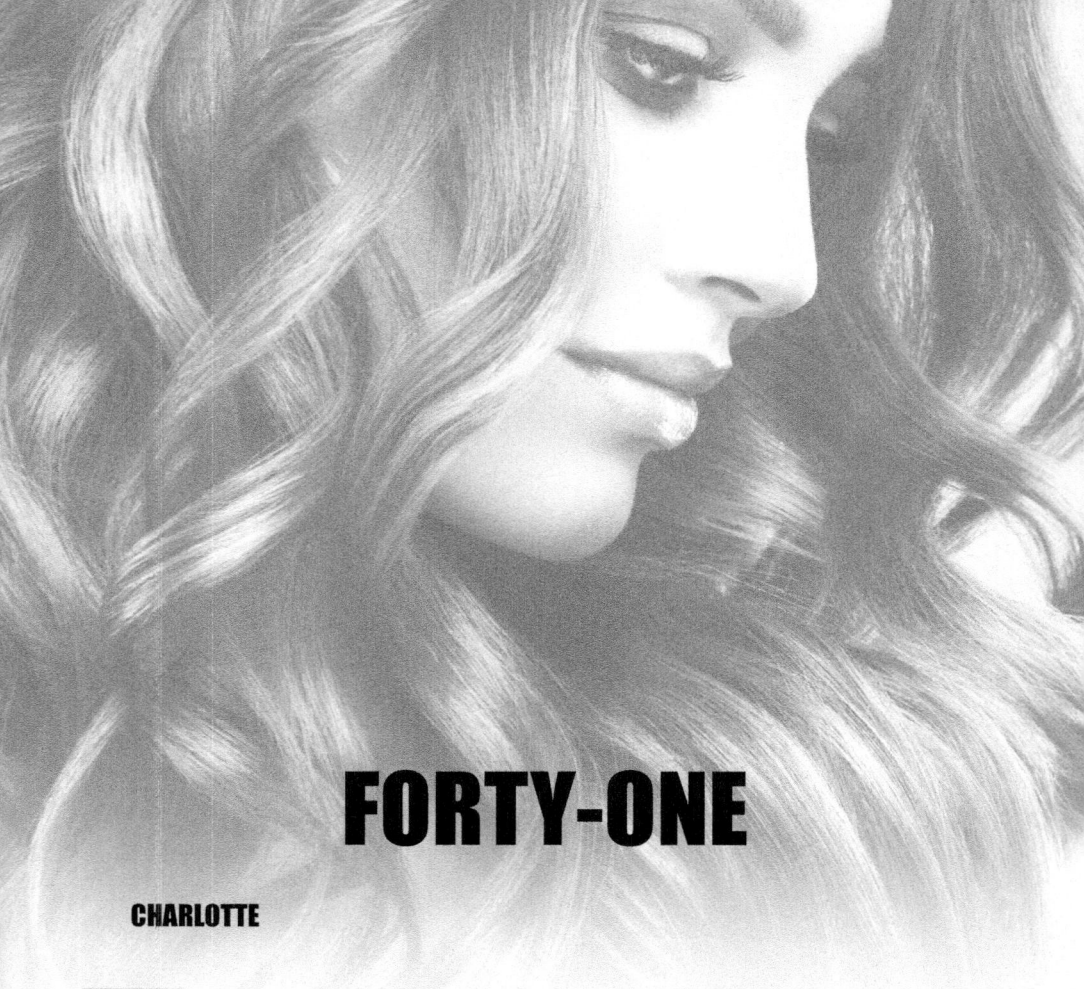

The deadbolt has been locked on the library door, and from my peripheral vision, I can see the entrance leading into the café has also been locked.

The question is: is she keeping people out, or keeping us inside?

The latter worries me the most. Because it was definitely petrol I smelled back there in the stacks, and it's petrol canisters which lay empty—aside from one that still has some dripping—near the door.

If she lights that lighter, we are as good as dead. We are surrounded by books and wood.

My hands shake so badly I can't hide the tremor. We're trapped in a death trap, and maybe we can get to the café door in time before the flames reach us, but would we escape the knife she wields in her hand? Our only hope of getting out of this is Nora getting through to Drew. He will come. The police will come. My family will come. I have no doubts about it.

It's whether they come before she does something irreversible.

"Why?" I whisper, wondering if there are any remnants of the person I had come to know.

Everything, all our time spent together, hits me like a lightning bolt. We first met the day after I first bumped into Scott. She had been here, wandering the aisles, looking lost so I went up to her and helped her. We hit it off and not once did I get a bad vibe from her.

I think about all the personal questions she asked that I answered, mistaking it for her wanting to get to know me. It didn't register until now that she never revealed anything about her life.

I think about the times she listened to family conversations by lurking around or being directly involved. It was all planned.

She knew who I was all along.

What he was doing behind her back.

And she did nothing.

There's a roaring in my ears and I lose track of what everyone is doing for a moment, my focus on her.

Another person who fooled me.

She sneers. "You really have no clue, do you?"

"Why the fuck don't you clue us in then, you psychopath," Hayden snaps.

"Why?" I whisper again, my voice broken and raw. "We were *friends*."

Or at least, I thought we were.

I don't even recognise the person standing before me. *Am I really that blind to those around me?*

You're an embarrassment.

You are so fucking clueless.

Are you blind?

They are laughing at you.

Your family wouldn't understand.

Why do you have to make my day harder?

You should try harder.

You aren't who I thought you were.

All the things Scott threw at me come rushing back, but then, like a hurricane wind, Drew's float inside, pushing the negative away.

You aren't a fool.

You are strong.

You are beautiful.

You are special.

You brighten up my days.

I love being with you.

I love being around you.

I love you.

Her laugh bounces off the library walls and a cold chill slivers down my spine. She must be able to see the conflict running over my expression. I was dumb in listening to Scott. I was a fool to believe Sophia's intentions.

"We were never friends, you silly bitch."

"Then what were we?"

"I wanted you to be the last."

"The last?"

"I wanted to show him girls like you are weak. That they break easily. He wouldn't listen. Every time he said it was the last time, but I knew him. Knew him better than he knew himself," she tells me, banging the fist holding the knife against her head. "I was meant for him. He was meant for me."

"Why didn't you ever tell me? Why did you let him keep cheating? I would have ended things," I assure her.

Her eyes glass over. "Because he would have just found another one. It had to end with you. He needed to see I was the only one for him."

"Another redhead?" Madison asks.

The look she gives Madison is enough to make me step in front of my cousin. Madison grips the back of Hayden's jacket when she goes for Rose—*Sophia*. I don't know what to call her now.

"Let me at the fucking bitch."

"Come near me and I'll slice you fucking open."

"Why are you doing this?" I blurt out. "Why are you here? Scott is dead."

She laughs without humour, reminding me of every witch I have ever witnessed laugh in Disney movies. "I know he's dead. I'm the reason he's fucking dead. He pushed me too far. He wanted to come back."

"Come back?" I whisper.

"To you," she sneers. "He wanted to make it right again, said he was going to leave me."

I take a step back, bumping into Madison's side. "No."

"You were easy to bend to his will. You, the person I was going to break, to show him how weak you were, and that you'd never understand him, was the person who broke *him*. *I* understood him. *I* loved him. *Me*. But you got in the way."

"He hurt me."

She spits, her face flaming red, and the veins in her neck bulge. "You know nothing about being hurt," she screams.

"You are a raging bitch," Hayden spits.

"Shush, you aren't helping," Madison hisses.

Hayden grunts. "I'll help in a minute. I'll help shove her face through that desk."

"Rose; *Sophia*, you don't want to do this—whatever this is. It's not worth it. *He's* not worth it."

"We were meant to be together," she tells me, more lucid than she was a moment ago.

I close my eyes, the anguish in her heart hitting my chest. A thought occurs to me. I'm not sure if it's something I read or something I watched, but I remember once learning to speak to your kidnapper, to keep them occupied until help arrived or let them get to know you enough that they let you go.

Sophia already knows me. I can't go down that route with her, but I can listen to her; I can keep her talking.

"I don't understand."

"We saved each other. Scott had strict parents. They would never leave him unsupervised, nor his little sister. He was sixteen, but you would never know since his parents sheltered him that much. They were religious too, and the only time he socialised was when they went to church functions. They left a babysitter to care for him and his sister. She abused him. Every day she babysat, she abused him. First, she made him touch her, then she touched him, and then she began to fuck him."

"Sophia," I whisper.

"I don't need your fucking pity. He doesn't either."

"He isn't fucking getting it," Hayden snaps.

"Stop antagonising the psycho," Harriet pleads.

"What happened after that?" I ask before Hayden can make a remark.

"He never felt clean. *Never*. It broke something in his mind. I would watch from my bedroom window, hearing his cries."

"You never helped him?"

"I saved him," she spits out. "He knew my uncle was beating me. He heard my cries too. We would sit at the bedroom window at night, just staring at each other. We both knew right then we were kindred spirits, lost souls who had found each other."

"*Touching*," Hayden spits out.

"One night my uncle went too far. He was going to do to me what Scott's babysitter was doing to him. Scott witnessed it and saved me. He came through the window, took the whip of the belt for me."

"So you repaid the favour?" I guess.

She nods, her expression turning blank. "The day she brought over one of her male friends, I helped him. He was lying face down on the bed when I walked in, bloody and soiled. The guy was grinning, bragging about having a virgin, saying nothing had ever felt that good."

I clutch my stomach as bile rises in my throat. "I—"

"We killed them. We killed them for hurting him. I hit the guy first, hit him over the head with the bat I grabbed from my uncle's shed, and something snapped in Scott that day. He gripped Bea by her red hair and slammed her into the window. It shattered, slicing through her perfect porcelain skin. We didn't stop; we butchered them long after they took their last breath."

"And you were never arrested?" Olivia asks, still holding pressure on Harriet's arm.

"No. We locked his sister in her bedroom so she wouldn't see them. We took a lot of money from his dad's safe box and took his spare bank cards. I did the same at my uncles, taking all the money I could find and pieces of jewellery I could sell along the way. We never looked back. Not once."

"How? How did you get away with it for this long? He hadn't just hurt Charlotte or those people who hurt him. There were loads of women."

"All of them fucking deserved it."

"No, they didn't," I reply, straightening my shoulders.

I didn't deserve it.

Amber didn't deserve it.

None of them did.

I didn't deserve it.

The thought knocks me back a step and my eyes clench shut as I let it really hit me.

I didn't deserve it.

I have spent so long now wondering if it was me, if it was something I did that made him do this. All the things he said, the snide comments or judgemental stares, had me believing it was me.

Did me saying yes give him consent to ignore my no?

All this time I questioned myself, but right now, in this moment, it finally sinks in.

I wasn't to blame.

I said 'no'.

A two lettered word that holds a far greater meaning.

"*Yes*, they did. He needed to feel clean. Virgins helped him feel clean."

"And you didn't make him feel like that?" Hayden argues.

"He loved me. He loved our children. And he promised; promised he would stop. We had run away as kids and survived years whilst making a life for ourselves. We reinvented ourselves. But he had his demons. I had mine."

"But why terrorise those women? Why let him hurt another living being when you knew how it felt?" I ask. "Why let him hurt me?"

"Because we were made for each other. We belonged together. I loved him and I couldn't let him leave me. I wanted him to be happy. We belonged together."

"Yeah, in a mental institution," Hayden barks.

"Hayden," Madison hisses.

She begins to pace, smacking the handle of the knife against her head. "I didn't mean to kill him. I just got so angry. He was going to leave me. For real this time. Leave our family. He nearly left me for the other one, the other redhead, until I hurt her and told him I'd keep hurting her until he left her alone. And he did after seeing what a weak fool she was." She laughs, throwing her head back. "So weak it didn't take much before she ended her own life."

Hayden gasps, like she knows something I don't.

"And with me?"

She stops, her nostrils flaring. "He was going to ruin everything. It only took one person to recognise him, to recognise me, and we were screwed. We never answered to killing those people, even if they did deserve it. And my uncle would have killed me after I stole all that money and stuff," she explains. "He left marks on you, marks we couldn't risk. We argued and he threatened to leave. He was done with women telling him what to do, with me telling him what to do, and he was going to make it up to you. Or have you make it up to him."

There was no making it up to me. What he had done—not just the cheating—was unforgiveable.

"So why put his body inside the library? Why not bury him and be done with it?" Madison asks.

"I wanted *her* to take the fall. You are to blame for his death. If you hadn't bewitched him, he would have moved on like he did with the rest. But he kept saying you were different, that you obeyed and listened," she explains, her words filled with venom. "Then I had to watch you strut around here playing the victim and then move on like he never existed. Like his death meant nothing."

My nails dig into the palms of my hands. "I didn't know he was dead."

"Are you listening to yourself?" Harriet bites out. "You have to know how crazy that sounds."

"Shut the fuck up, you whore. You strip for a living. You have no right to judge me."

"No, it's you who has no right to judge me, not after what you've put innocent women through."

Sophia does nothing but sneer at Harriet, and for a moment, I fear she'll go after her with that knife. Maybe we could stop her. Maybe not. But no one in this room is worth the risk of being injured. Not even Marlene.

I have to pull her attention away from them. "And now? What is your plan now? The police know who you are and other women have come forward."

The hatred shining back at me threatens to choke me. "I'd have killed them all. Thought I had killed them all—the ones who were a threat to us."

"You were the woman who hurt Amber, who ran us off the road." I say it as a fact, not as a question.

"And I would have ran over your body had it not been for the guy in the van," she sneers.

"And what now?"

I need to know what we're up against, what she plans to do.

"Now you are going to die. I'm not stupid. I know eventually the police will be knocking on my door. I had planned to draw out my revenge. The notes were just a taste of what was to come. However, my neighbours were starting to ask questions, wondering what the smell was. I had to do something. Do something with him. And I thought… I thought I could pin it on you, but that bitch of a policewoman… You pulled the wool over her eyes too. She didn't believe me and I could sense it."

"She was doing her job," Hayden sneers.

"Then you can blame her for what I'm about to do," she tells her, as her thumb rolls over the lighter, the flame bright as it flickers to life.

I can't look away.

Groaning from the floor pulls my attention away from Sophia, and my breath hitches as I watch Marlene roll to her side, her hand pressed to the back of her head. When her hand comes away, thick clots of blood cover her fingers.

"Marlene," I cry, taking a step toward her, but movement from Sophia stops me.

"Don't you dare fucking move."

Marlene turns to me, boiling with so much fury her teeth clench together. "I fucking quit. I'm done. Fucking done. Do you hear me? I've been poisoned, subjected to your family—"

"Hey," Hayden snarls.

"And now I've been hit over the head. I'm fucking done."

"It's going to be okay," I assure her, keeping my voice calm.

"It's not. I'm fucking insulted," Hayden argues.

"It's not going to be okay," Marlene explodes as sirens echo from outside.

"No," Olivia cries, and a cloud fogs inside my head as I slowly turn in their direction, my hair swinging over my shoulder.

The screams, the yells, the sirens, it all washes away as I watch her light the rag in her hand.

Setting light to my dream.

To one of the things that kept me up when I was down.

A split second. That's all it takes. A split second to realise we are most likely going to die.

I can rebuild what I have here. It's bricks, paper and wood.

But these people… Madison, Hayden, Olivia, Harriet and even Marlene; they aren't replaceable.

They don't deserve this.

Olivia barely reaches for Sophia before she swings the knife out, slicing the arm Olivia lifts to shield herself.

I'm not weak.

I'm not controlled.

I am my own person.

Taking a deep breath, the same way Drew taught me, I move, not letting this woman take one more thing away from me or anyone else.

FORTY-TWO

DREW

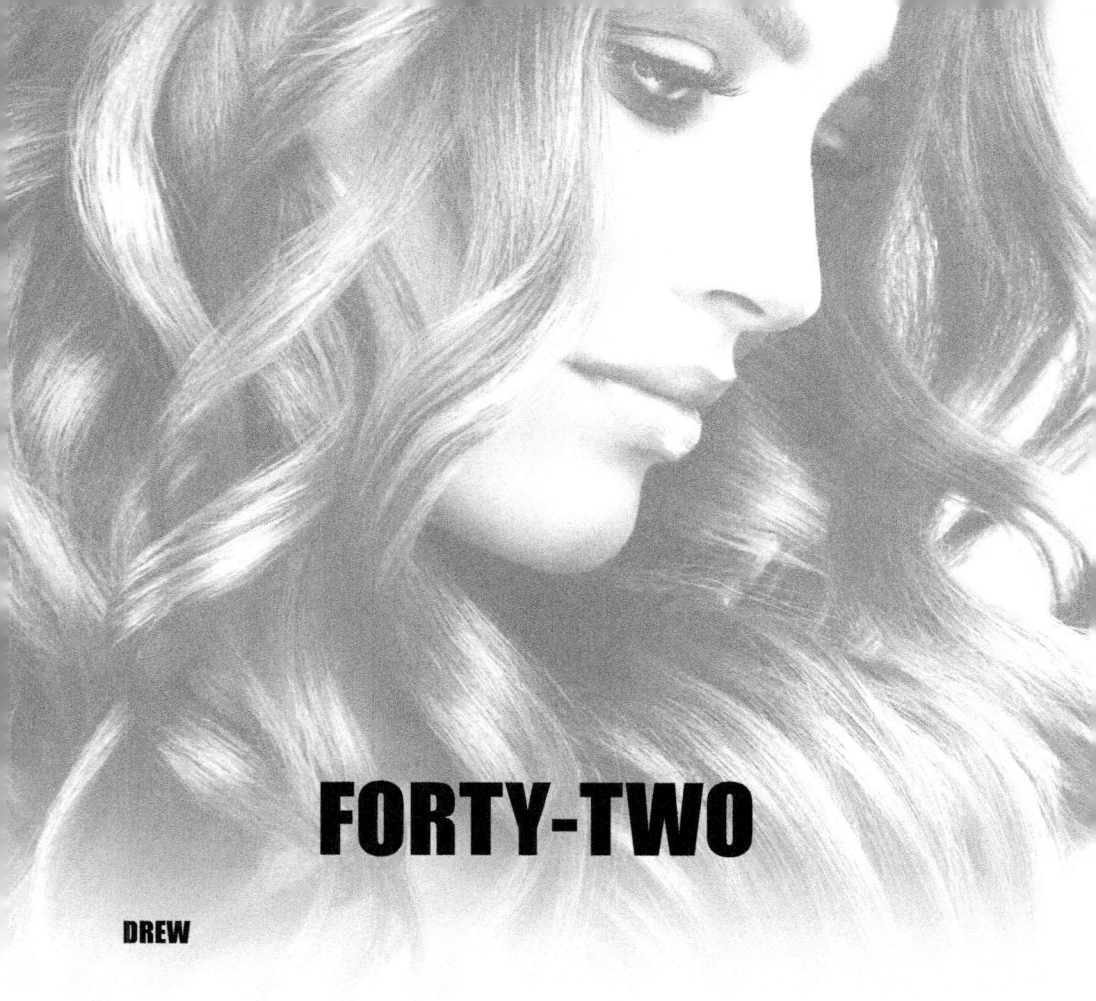

Landon barges through the office door, a primal growl tearing from his throat. It wasn't that long ago that he stormed through the doors in the same manner. It had been because he was frustrated and angry over not being able to find Scott. All his leads had come to a dead end and he had given up hope that he'd ever find him.

This time, we know where Scott is—rotting in some morgue where he deserves to be. Landon, however, isn't done chasing those leads. He wants every bit of evidence he can get to discredit Scott, to make sure they can't twist Charlotte's story any more than they have already tried to. He doesn't need to worry. You don't need to know Charlotte personally to know she wouldn't hurt anyone. Maybe in self-defence, but not life threatening, and most certainly not to end a life when she breathes so much of it into the world.

She breathes it into mine.

Last night was the first time someone other than my dad and Nora has ever stood up for me. People take one look at me, see someone tall, muscled and intimidating, and think I can handle myself. And I can. But that isn't the point. Those things don't contribute as to why I can. I had to learn myself after years of dealing with guys bigger than me wanting to brag about taking me down. I've had friends who thought the same, and left me to handle drunk dickheads. Strangers weren't innocent either. None of them step in when someone gets out of line with me.

It has been that way my entire life. Sometimes it did benefit me. Some guys who are out to cause trouble take one look at me and fuck off. However, that wasn't the situation I was in when it came to my family last night.

Charlotte knew I could handle the situation, and yet stood firm and strong as she put my family of vipers in their place because they hurt me. She didn't care that she could get stung. For the first time, I wasn't alone.

I wish she hadn't been put in that position, but I can't deny how proud I felt in that moment, witnessing her strength and courage. It was a moment I'll never forget, and I'll make sure she knows that the minute we get home and I get her under the sheets.

"I take it todays visit didn't go well?" I drawl, leaning back in my chair. He has been going to see the list of women my dad tracked down, and today, was the last girl on the list.

He throws himself down in his own chair, throwing his phone onto the desk. "Yes and no. It's the same story. The same manipulative story."

"Is that why you look like you're about to tear the roof down?"

The lethal stare he gives me doesn't faze me. I'm used to it and have faced down bigger men than him. Only, he has an advantage on them—none of them could fight like him.

"No, I want to tear the fucking roof down because for one single moment, I had a sick thought and blurted it out."

I sit up at seeing the revulsion in his expression. "What do you mean?"

He runs his fingers through his dark, shaggy hair. It has grown over the weeks. So much is monopolising his time that he hasn't even had time to get a haircut.

"I said: how didn't anyone see him for who he truly was."

I grit my teeth. "Mate, what the fuck?"

"I know. I didn't mean it like that. I didn't mean to imply they were stupid not to have known what he was like. But I couldn't stop the words from slipping out. Aunt Kayla ripped me a new one but she didn't need to. I'm doing it to myself."

"Tempers are flaring," I remind him.

"It doesn't make what I said okay."

"It doesn't. But you also know deep down it wasn't their fault. It was his."

"How is she doing? I've popped in a few times but she always pastes on a smile and tries to distract us by throwing baked goods at us."

I grin. "Good, right?" And they are. I don't know what went wrong with that cake she made me the first time, but my girl can bake. Sometimes. "And she's doing fine. It's on her mind but that's to be expected. She's strong though, and I think she just wants to prove that to you guys."

He nods, relaxing at my reply, but then his brows pinch together and the look of utter disgust shines back at me. "And no, they aren't good. They taste just as vile as before."

Huh. "Are you sure you're eating the same things as me, because the muffins she baked me to bring to work this morning tasted amazing."

"No," he huffs out. "But it seems its only you who she makes them good for."

I grin wider. "Nope. Lily had the other batch and was eating the last one when I left." He turns pale suddenly. "What?"

"Did you stay last night?"

"Yeah."

He shakes his head in disgust. "I'm going before I deck you."

"What?" I ask as my phone begins to ring. He's keeping me in the dark about… I chuckle at the realisation of where his thoughts were going.

Every time she's baked something good, we've spent the night together. It seems when Charlotte is truly *happy*, she can bake. I wonder if she has clicked on too and that's why she is insatiable in the bedroom. I would tease him but he looks ready to vomit all over our office and I'm not cleaning that shit up.

"Even if it tastes good next time, I'll never be able to stomach it, not knowing what gave her the *inspiration* for it."

I glance down at Nora's name and for a second, I think about ignoring it. I pick it up, still chuckling as Landon gathers his things. "Nora?"

"Drew," she trembles, a sob breaking out.

My entire body tenses. If her mother has done something to her, nothing will stop me from reporting her this time. "Nora, what's going on?"

Landon stops at the door at my tone, raising an eyebrow at me, but I can't answer him.

"I'm at the library. You need to get here. Right now," she whispers, her voice trembling, and I know she's struggling to remain strong. "T-there's a, there's a woman here. She's poured petrol all over the books downstairs and is having a stand-off with the others."

"Charlotte's library?" I ask, and Landon steps forward, his hands clenched into fists. "Are you okay? Is she okay?"

"Yes, Charlotte's library," she snaps. "And she's here. I called to ask her where a book was and she came over. I shouldn't have called her. I should have just laid into that receptionist and searched for the books myself. I—"

"Nora," I demand lightly, pulling her attention back to me before she truly loses it.

"This woman has a knife. The receptionist is unconscious," she whispers, her breath hitching. "And I don't know what to do. I don't know what to do."

I place the phone on loudspeaker as I grab my keys from my desk drawer. "It's going to be okay. I'm coming," I assure her. "Who else is there?"

"Harriet and Olivia, Marlene and two other girls showed up. They just told Charlotte they figured out who the wife is when everything happened."

"Madison and Hayden?" Landon asks as we rush out of the gym.

"Yes, I think that's what they are called. I think it's the girl Hayden who keeps mouthing off to her. I like her."

I pull open the door to my car, dropping the phone on the dashboard. "I'm coming. I'm on my way."

"Wait, if Nora's on the phone, where is she?"

Nora makes a noise in the back of her throat. "Having a cup of tea and eating popcorn whilst I watch it all unfold," she barks.

Landon's eyebrow arches. "She sounds like she's related to my sister."

It was a protective retort. She's scared out of her mind and is lashing out. "Nora, where are you?"

"I'm upstairs. Charlotte told me to run and hide. She told me before she knew what was even going to happen," she tells me and stops for a moment, choking back a sob. "Drew, I'm scared. I don't know what to do."

"You are doing everything you should be doing. Stay there and don't move until I come and get you."

"I'm going to mute the phone and be quiet. I don't want to risk her hearing me," she whispers.

"Good girl. I won't be long."

"Okay," she tells me, and I hear a button pressed on the other line.

I turn to Landon, who seems more angry than worried. "I'm surprised you didn't run there."

He shrugs. "Hayden's there."

"This woman might be the person who killed Scott."

"Hayden isn't an angel. And she's not stupid. She'll either piss whoever it is off so much they direct their anger to her, or she'll attack them."

"And you're okay with that?" I grit out. This is his sister. His triplet.

"Fuck no. But if anyone can take care of things, it's Hayden. She's a fighter. Had to be. Charlotte doesn't have the heart to kill spiders and she's petrified of them. She makes someone come and carry them outside—then checks to make sure it doesn't have family close by. She won't fight back."

Now that sounds like Charlotte.

I scrub a hand down my face as I weave through of traffic, not caring if the police are called. Speaking of. "Have you called the police?"

"I've messaged our family group chat and told them to. And if the library has been doused with petrol, they'll need a fire engine too. My family will sort it. I didn't want to speak over you and risk missing something your sister said or being heard over the other end."

"Who is doing this?" I ask.

His jaw clenches, the first sign of the Landon I have come to know. "We're about to find out."

Yeah, we are.

I SLAM THE breaks on outside the library, or as close to the library as I can get. Police cars and fire engines block most of the road.

I jump out, leaving the ignition on and don't bother to shut the door as I run to where Myles, his wife, and a few other members of her family are. Jaxon is pulling Lily away from the building, her grief echoing over the sirens.

My dad should be here any moment. Landon called him in the car and Dad was frantic and livid.

Kayla drops her head onto her husband's chest, tears streaming down her cheeks as her body shakes with her cries.

"What's happening?" I ask, motioning to all the police standing and chatting. "Why aren't they going in there?"

"The doors are blocked. No one can get in. At the moment, they are trying to call the library but it's ringing out," Myles answers.

"We can't hear the phone," Kayla chokes out.

"I'm going in," I tell them, moving toward the alleyway. It's where she keeps the bins but there has to be a way, some old door or window we can climb through.

"I'm coming," Landon declares.

"There's no way in," Myles interrupts, stopping us. "And the police won't let us get near it."

"They threatened to arrest us," Kayla bites out.

Max scoffs. "There's always a way in."

Yes, there is.

We jog toward the alley and two policemen step in front of us. "You can't go down there."

Screams that are more like pleas echo from inside, right before flames engulf the heavy duty curtains she has for show on the window near to us. We step back, the heat hitting us in the face as the glass shatters. "Fuck!" I hiss, my stomach bottoming out.

We stare at the flames, all of us knowing what it means. Police rush past with a yellow battering ram. It will be fruitless for them to even try. I have seen the bolts she has on the inside of the doors. They aren't getting in that way unless one of them manages to unlock it.

"Let us past," I grit out.

"Now," Landon demands.

"Sir, step back," the tall, lanky officer demands, placing his hands up.

"No," Max screams and the police officer's attention goes straight to him. "I need my book."

"It's my book," Myles yells.

"Charlotte," Kayla screams, Lake's following with her own daughter's name flowing from her lips.

Harlow, a woman I have only met a few times, collapses to her knees as she takes in the blazing fire. "No, Madison, no." Her husband lifts her to her feet, clutching her to his chest. Her face is pale, gaunt, and his looks no better.

They have so much to lose in that building.

But my future is in there.

My world.

I glance to the left in time to witness Myles shove Max away. Max hisses. "You can't even read a cereal box."

"You can't even read that," Myles fires back.

"Don't make me use big words."

"Do you even know any?"

"No," Max barks. "Because my fucking dictionary is in that building."

"It's not yours," Myles yells.

"I'm going in after it. I can't let it burn to ashes. Not my dictionary. Not today," he wails.

When he goes to make a move, the police officers blocking our way intervene. They have been so riveted by the act they are playing, they haven't even remembered us, and we manage to slip by without any other officer bumping into us.

We reach the place where she has the bins tucked against a wall, and Maddox jumps out from behind, scaring the fuck out of us. I'm glad Landon made a noise too. I'd never have lived it down if they thought they could get one up on me. Not that it matters right now.

"When did you get here?" Landon hisses, glancing up at the building.

"I've had a bad feeling in my chest for a while—"

"Probably heartburn again," Landon mutters, scanning the wall. There's one window, but even with the added height of the bin to stand on, it's too high—even for me.

"No, it's Madison. She messaged me saying she was on her way back earlier and was going to head to Charlotte's. After that, I had this feeling that wouldn't go away. So when she wouldn't answer, I started making my way over here. I received your message not long before I arrived. I've been trying to get in ever since."

Landon just stares, dumfounded for a moment. "Your twin thing freaks me out."

Maddox rolls his eyes. "Yes, because you, Liam and Hayden are so much better."

"Drag the bin to that window," I order. We don't have time to chit chat.

I watch as Landon does the calculations in his head. "It's still too high."

"Not with a little boost."

I quickly send a message to Nora, asking her if she can get to that window. She doesn't reply and that sinking feeling, that gut churning I have ignored since the fire began, erupts. What if she's hurt? What if the person has found her? What if she's caught in that fire?

Moments later, the window above smashes, glass raining down on all of us. "Help!" she screams.

All of us move at once, dragging the bin below. I jump up, the other two following. Landon grips his fingers together and I press my foot into his hands, and reach up, grabbing the pipe sticking out to hoist myself up. Glass keeps shattering above before Nora sticks her head out, placing her jacket over the edge of the window, covering the glass.

I grip the ledge, and using all my upper strength, I pull myself up into the window. My sister steps back, her shoulders dropping as she begins to cry. "I can't get down there. There's too much smoke. But I heard screams. You need to go and help them."

"And I will. It's going to be okay, Nor," I promise, jumping inside. I stick my head out, my gaze meeting Landon's. "Let me get Nora out and then I'll help you up."

He nods and my sister shakes as I turn to her. "You can't be serious. Go help them first."

"Let me get you out first. I don't want you stuck up here. Landon and Maddox are outside. They'll help you."

Her hand is clammy and hot when she takes mine. "Please don't drop me," she warns as she sits up on the ledge, swinging her legs over.

"I won't," I promise, helping her turn. Landon and Maddox are there, both reaching up as I dangle her down the wall. Once they grab her legs, supporting her weight and balance, I let go. She whimpers, but pushes them away.

"Go help the others," she orders, jumping down from the bin.

I go to reach for Landon but the sight of Kayla and Lake rushing up the side of the alley, has me freezing in place. They are carrying a three-storey ladder, their expressions filled with guilt, like they stole it.

"We stole it from a neighbour when we saw what you were doing," Kayla answers the silent question before glancing over her shoulder like she's worried about being chased.

Maddox and Landon grin. "Stay there. They'll need help getting down if we can't open the doors."

"Don't you dare get hurt, Landon Carter, because I'll kill you myself."

"Mum," Landon mutters, giving her a pointed look.

"Just please get your sister before she kills someone," she demands.

They nod, both gripping the ladder before ascending. I don't bother to wait for them. Something inside of me is pushing me to get to Charlotte.

I cover my mouth with my jacket and reach out with my hand until my fingers hit a shelf. I'm not sure which way to go. The smoke is thick, clouding every nook and cranny in this place as I navigate my way through it. It burns my nostrils, and the scent of scorched paper fills my mouth.

The smoke grows thicker and I know I'm heading in the right direction. My hand meets something metal and I grab it just as my foot meets air. I nearly topple down the stairs. The further down I get, the thinner the smoke gets.

Screams.

"Charlotte?" I roar, staggering to stop in the middle of chaos. I blink through the haze of smoke, wondering if what I'm seeing is real or my imagination.

"My books. You burnt my books," Charlotte screams from where she's perched.

On a woman's back.

While said woman spins, fighting to get her off and waving a knife in the air.

I can't believe what I'm witnessing. I'm not even sure who we are meant to be saving right now.

Landon staggers to a stop beside me, taking in his sister, bloody and covered in soot, to his cousin who's lying next to her, unconscious, and then to Charlotte, who is screaming about her books and for everyone to save them.

"Wouldn't fight back, huh?" I mutter.

"Okay, maybe she can get mad sometimes. She really does love her books."

"Get the books free," she cries.

Following her gaze, I notice Olivia, fighting to get the knife from the woman, and then Harriet, blood pouring down her arm as she uses her jacket uselessly to put the fire out.

Maddox lifts his mouth from his elbow. "Why am I not surprised," he mutters, shaking his head at the scene.

I peer closer through the fog, the fire long forgotten as I focus on the woman's face. "Is that a... a..."

"Yes," Landon replies, pinching the bridge of his nose.

FORTY-THREE

CHARLOTTE

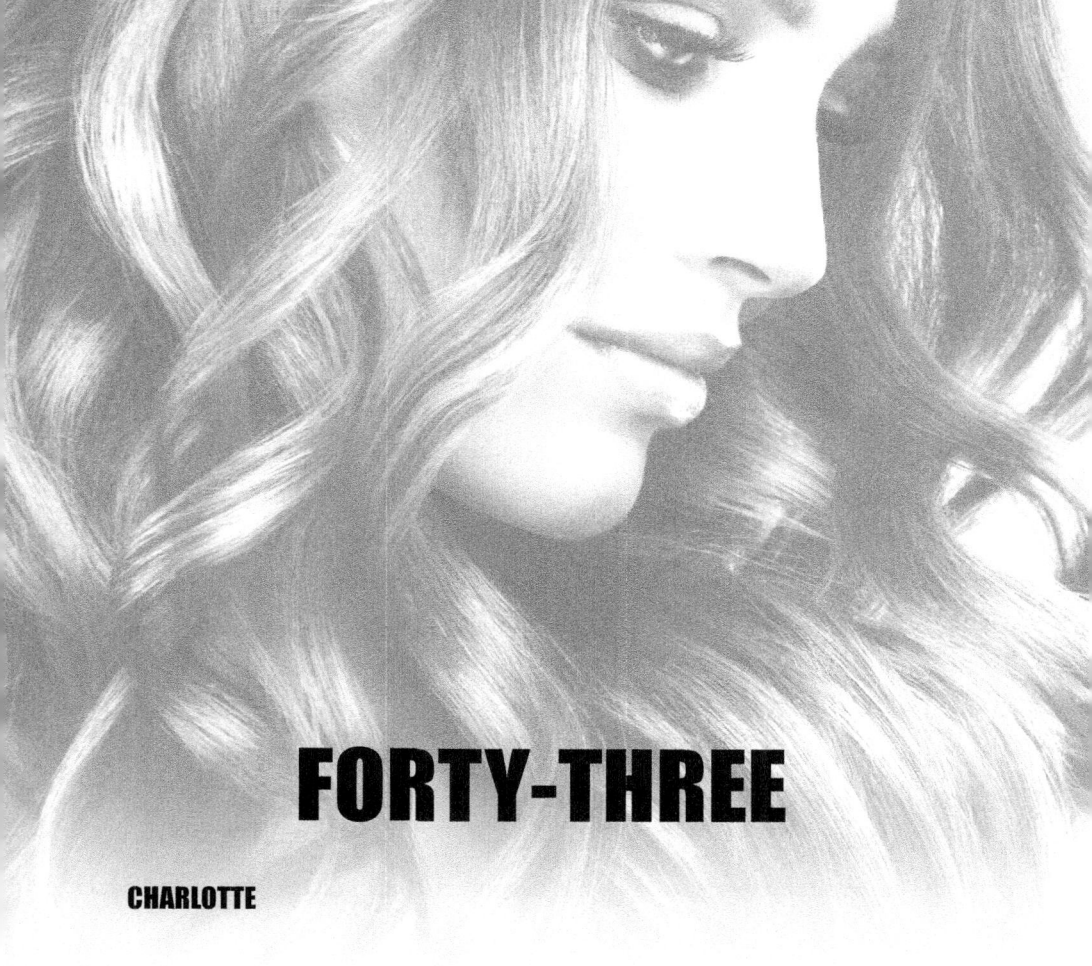

My fingers clench around the straps of the black leather ball gag Olivia threw at me after finding it in her bag. I have it wrapped around Sophia's mouth, pulling with all my strength to keep her from hurting one more person. It's the only weapon in our arsenal and one I will question Olivia about on another day.

Maybe.

Sophia's muffled cries behind the gag don't even register. She has said enough and none of it was from regret or remorse for what she has done.

I'm not present in my own body. I don't feel the same connection I do to all living beings. All I want to do is stop her.

There was a moment when I was leaping on her back that it felt like I was watching from the side-lines. I couldn't control my reaction at all. Yet, it was all I could do in that moment.

"You crazy bitch," Olivia yells at me, dodging the swinging knife Sophia still wields, and then points. "Get down from there right now."

She's speaking to me like a scolding mother would to her child. It's sweet of her to care, but I don't heed her warning. I don't let go.

"Save the books," I scream. "Save yourself."

"You need to save yourself. Fuck the books," she mutters sarcastically.

My library.

My sweet, peaceful library has done nothing to deserve this kind of hatred.

Madison had done nothing to deserve the glass bottle Sophia had pulled out of her bag and smashed over her head. She's unconscious; unmoving on the floor. It's only the steady beat of her chest rising and falling that lets us know she's okay. Hayden isn't faring well either. She had gotten caught in the middle of the attack to stop Sophia and smacked her head against the reception desk. After she went down, everything had become a haze.

No one messes with my family.

Nor my friends.

"Charlotte!"

The smoke must be getting to me because I could have sworn those were Drew's words, his fear palpable as I fight her to drop the knife.

"My books. You burnt my books," I scream, my throat burning from inhaling the smoke.

Olivia steps forward, once again trying to get to the knife. I want her to get the others and get out. And hopefully save at least some of my books.

My poor books.

"Get the books free," I yell at her.

She shakes her head as she struggles for breath. "I'm not leaving you with this crazy bitch."

My fingers slip from the strap and the ball gag drops to the floor. "I'm going to kill you," Sophia screams.

Drew suddenly steps in, pushing Olivia away when the knife gets too close to her. "Follow Landon," he demands, pointing to where my cousin is standing. "He's going to open the door."

"Drew," I breathe, beaming wide, and for a moment, I forget where I am, what I'm supposed to be doing. I get that flutter in my stomach, the jump in my heart from the sight of him. I drop to the floor as she manages to overthrow me, and land on my back, the breath getting knocked out of me.

Drew is here.

My eyes widen as the horror hits me.

Drew is here. The library is on fire and there's lunatic with a knife.

And my books are on fire.

"No," I whisper, my eyes wide as saucers.

Just as I go to warn him, to tell him to run, she faces him, her scream so loud it echoes over the walls, over the blazing cackling of the fire.

She charges at him and the breath in my lungs stills. The hand holding the knife rises into the air and I blink, the fear choking me. And in that blink, Drew moves, so lightning fast that I barely see it. He has the knife out of her hand and her arms wrapped around her back in a second.

"You need to teach me that move," I whisper in awe, and I'm not sure if he heard me.

"Go," he demands, jerking his head over my shoulder.

I shake my head. I can't leave him. I won't. Not while he's still in danger, not while he still has her in his clutches. He doesn't know what she has done, what she is capable of doing. I won't leave him alone with her.

She struggles in his arms, her face contorted with anger and disbelief. The room suddenly feels smaller, tighter, and just when I think I won't be able to take another breath, the place is swarming with people.

Firefighters rush in, and one reaches under my armpits, lifting me off the floor. My dress catches, tearing at the bottom on something as he drags me out.

I can't look away from Drew, from the destruction around him as he follows us out, dragging Sophia with him. He reminds me of a gladiator with his hair down, the fire burning around him.

Fresh air hits my face and I gasp in a lungful of it. My lashes flutter as the air stings my eyes.

It all hits me. Everything at once. Scott bumping into me. Scott manipulating and gaslighting me. The night he ripped me apart.

And *after*.

My eyes close as a wave of grief hits me. The flowers, the notes, Amber, and then our car crash.

Scott's body being found. Me being taken in for questioning.

My library.

Everyone has a story to tell. Everyone has a trauma of some kind to share. This is my story. My trauma.

And I found Drew and true love because of it.

This woman turned her nightmare into someone else's. She validated her actions because of it. And for that, I came face-to-face with true evil. A person who shows no remorse or sorrow for what she has done.

For the lives that were lost.

Even now, she fights to get out of the cuffs the police have smacked around her wrists, like she's the victim in all of this. And at one point, she was the victim in her story. But now she is the villain.

She twisted everything inside her head as if it somehow proved her narrative of the story was the right one. It didn't. All it had done was make it crumble.

And she nearly took us all with her.

I stagger forward, squinting to take it all in around me.

Madison is lying on a bed in the back of the ambulance, her mum and dad crowding the entrance, waiting for the paramedics to check her over.

I blink, my eyes watering.

Hayden is standing at the end of Lily's drive, arguing with her dad and brother whilst her mum shakes her head.

I blink through the haze, my attention going back to the library and the smoke bellowing from the windows.

My breath hitches and I keep going, finding Nora safe and sound, sobbing into her father's chest.

I stagger again, my gaze going to the other ambulance where Olivia and Harriet are being treated.

Then back to the woman who caused all of this.

I push through the crowd and rush toward her. Dad, who was already storming toward me, catches me around the waist, pulling me back when he figures out what I'm going to do.

"You crazy bitch," I scream, shocking not only my dad, but my mother.

"Charlotte," he whispers.

Drew snaps around at the sound of my voice, then says something to the police officer before rushing to my side. "She burnt my books."

"The firemen are dealing with it," Dad assures me.

Drew reaches for me, but when I once again go to make a move for her, he pulls me back. "Your head is bleeding. We need to get you looked at."

"She hurt my friends. My family. She burnt my books," I choke out.

"The crazy bitch did more than burn your books," Hayden retorts, blocking my view from the woman in question. "She murdered her husband and other people."

PC Brown—Megan—stops mid-conversation at Hayden's words. She scans us over before taking a step away from the other officer she was talking to nearby. "Do you have proof of this?"

Hayden curls her lip. "I won't need proof once I tell you the horror story of her youth. Fucking bitch thinks it's a licence to kill," she returns. "Or you could give me five minutes with the psycho and let me return the favour." She points to her head, still furious she got hurt. "After, she'll sing like a canary."

Megan scans the area, making sure no other officers can hear us. "You need to calm down. Watch what you are saying."

I struggle to get free from Drew, my chest rising and falling. I can hear my pulse beating wildly in my ears. "No. I won't calm down. My books. My books are gone. She hurt Madison. She hurt Hayden. She hurt my friends. She hurt Marlene. She—"

"Like we will lose sleep over that bitch," Hayden interrupts.

Drew tightens his grip on me. "Charlotte, babe, please, calm down."

"No," I scream. It's so loud, so raw, it feels like a thousand razor blades are slicing down my throat. "No."

I push him away again, and the hurt, the devastation on his expression as he goes to reach for me and I step back, threatens me to my knees.

"Charlotte, please," he pleads.

"Baby," Mum chokes out.

I step away from them and they surround me like I'm a wild animal they're about to capture. I can't take it. None of it.

It has all hit me.

"I've been fighting for as long as I can remember to live my dream," I whisper, then turn to my dad. "You told me to dream big." I turn to Mum. "And you told me to follow my dreams, no matter what they were."

"Baby," she whispers, stepping forward.

I hold my hand up, stopping her, my vision blurry with tears. "And I did. And he…" I gulp around the ball in my throat. "He turned it into a nightmare. She turned it into a nightmare. They twisted my dream and made me feel like I was selfish for reaching for it. But I wasn't being selfish."

"No, baby, you weren't," Dad replies.

I turn to Drew, my shoulders dropping, my heart soaring. "For so long I thought my dream was having everything picture perfect. It was a job I loved doing, owning my home and having a husband with children to raise. Then you came into my life."

A mask drops over his expression and I can't figure out what he's thinking. He scans the crowd watching me, watching the spectacle I'm making of myself, but I don't care. Each breath is sharp, heavy, and with it, so are my emotions. "Why don't we get you looked at by a paramedic?"

I close my eyes, savouring his voice. When I open them, more tears gather. "It hit me inside the library. It's not about the job you have, the house you own, or the car you drive. It's not even really about getting married and having children. Because thousands of people have those things and still aren't happy."

"I don't understand," he replies, taking a small step toward me. I don't stop him, not this time.

I meet his gaze, unblinking and steady. "I was wrong about my dream. It wasn't about the things I had, the possessions I held. It was the love of my family. The love from my friends. It was *you*. I can live without it all except for you and them. Never without you. It's you who I've been searching for, who I felt was missing inside of me."

Dad coughs into his hand, glancing away. "Wrong choice of words."

I shake my head. "No. It's not. I've felt like a part of me has always been missing. I didn't quite fit in anywhere," I begin, before turning my attention back to Drew. "But with you, with you, Drew, I felt whole. I fit.

"I love you. I know you told me to wait to say it. I know you probably think I'm saying this because I have a huge heart and my emotions are heightened. But that's not it. That's not the reason. I'm saying it because today, I watched as my library burnt."

"Let's not bring up the books again," Hayden mutters, glancing away when everyone sends her a silent warning to be quiet.

"And all that mattered was you. The life I have with you. I love you. I love everything about you. and I hope, so deeply hope, you love me back." I duck my head, panting heavily. When he doesn't speak, when my legs threaten to give out, I peek out through my lashes and lean in. I keep my voice low. "It's okay if you don't. I know that probably sounded way crazy and stalkerish and—"

"Charlotte," he croaks, before pausing, clearing his throat. I take in my surroundings and gulp. My entire family has congregated around us and are glaring at Drew, their stance ready to pounce if he doesn't say it back. It almost makes me smile.

"If it's the pink or glitter, I can change it," I ramble. "Or if the sex toys are embarrassing, we can totally give them back. I've never used them so I'm sure she will take them."

"Fucking hell," Max groans, stepping away from the group.

"There are some things a father doesn't need to hear."

"Or cousin," I hear muttered.

My gaze is pleading, my heart breaking. "I can learn to cook better. I won't practice with the poles or—"

In one long stride, he's standing in front of me, his fingers running through my hair until he's cupping the back of my neck. He drops his head down, his eyes blazing as he stares at me through those thick lashes. "Never change who you are."

"But—"

"I love you, Charlotte. I meant it the night under the stars and I mean it now."

"You do?" I whisper, my lip trembling.

His lips tug into a small smile. "I do."

A laugh slips free. I can't stop it. I don't want to. It's happiness bursting free. I turn to Mum and Dad. "He loves me."

Mum clutches Dad closer. "We heard."

My attention goes back to Drew as I lean up on my toes and wrap my hands around his neck. "You love me. All of me."

His eyes darken. "And you love me."

Our lips meet and he flicks his tongue against my bottom lip. White light flashes behind my eyes as everything that had hit me in full force, slowly evaporates, leaving only me and him.

"You love me," I whisper, the world around me spinning. My legs give out and he catches me, pulling me into his arms as we lower to the ground. "My library is or was on fire."

"I know."

My voice shakes as I continue. "She nearly killed us."

"I know."

"She killed Scott— not that it's a loss."

"I know."

A paramedic kneels in front of me, shining a light in my eyes, and I blink away the harsh light.

"Oh my God," I cry out, sitting up.

"What hurts?" the young paramedic asks.

I turn in horror to Drew. "We need to go. Your sister is getting married."

Megan Brown looms above us, a notepad in her hand. "We need to get your statement before you leave."

I pout. "Really?"

She chuckles, shaking her head. "Yes. You can run through it while the paramedic looks over that cut."

"Is it over after that? I mean, you still don't think I killed him?"

"I never did," she replies softly. "But hopefully, yes, it will be."

I glance up at Drew. "It's over. It's just me and you."

He grins, beautiful and sexy. "Just me and you."

We have a bigger challenge to face than Sophia Parish, something far greater than the ramblings and actions of a crazy person.

We have to deal with Drew's family.

It's hard to believe it was only last night that I stood up to them and everything unfolded.

Now we're late and we look a hot mess.

Neither of us had time to shower. My mum helped me fix my hair the best she could and reapplied some of my makeup. But with the soot and the smoke sinking into my skin and hair, there wasn't a lot we could do. I changed my forest green dress for a simple wrap around one, and all it has done is highlight the scrapes on my legs, the bruises on my arms.

PC Brown kept us longer than we anticipated, but I was more than happy to fill in the blanks that she had been missing. Missing pieces she needed to send Sophia to prison for a very long time. They even got word to us before we left that they found evidence of the notes and proof the flowers had come from Sophia. It was all clicking into place. *For me.* But not for the others. It's too late for some of them to get justice but I hope it doesn't stop their family from pressing charges.

It isn't something that will happen overnight though. We have time. Right now, it's time to heal, to get our strength back. It's a time for living.

Living for a future that holds no certainties. I don't need them. Not anymore. I don't need everything to be in order or to fit into a neat box. What I have with Drew, what we share, it surpasses all of that. He goes beyond my wildest dreams. This is just one chapter of our story. Tomorrow, the page will turn, and we'll start another.

And I'm excited to see what it will bring.

I can wait for children. I can wait for marriage. Just as long as we always feel like this toward each other while we wait.

"Are you sure you are up for this?"

I grip his hand over the gear stick and link our fingers together. "We've had a really bad day. I don't want to make it worse for you."

"Alison would understand," he assures me. He said the same thing outside the library.

"Maybe, but I don't want to be the reason you don't turn up to your sister's wedding."

"I love you," he tells me as he pulls up outside the church. "Remember that."

I gulp. "I love you too."

He puts the car into park and neither of us waste time gathering ourselves before we slide out, rushing up to the church. Alison steps out of a door located at the side of the entrance, her bridesmaids, Natalie and a girl I don't recognise, following behind her.

Her eyes widen as she takes us in. "Drew, what on earth?"

"We aren't late," I breathe, sagging with relief.

Her attention cuts to me, running her gaze over the cuts and bruises and probably the soot I couldn't wipe off my skin. "We had a delay," she murmurs.

Drew bends down, kissing her on the cheek. "You look so beautiful," he tells her. "We really are sorry. It's a long story, and one we will tell you after you've gotten hitched. We just couldn't miss your special day."

His mum steps out, and the anger radiates off her. In fact, I'm pretty sure every time I've had the *pleasure* of being in her presence, she's been angry over something.

"You know, masturbation is known to be one of the best stress relievers. It releases endorphins and—"

"Charlotte," Drew muses, pressing his fist over his mouth.

My eyes widen as I take in her flushed face. I was only trying to help. She might smile a little more.

"It's been a really long day," I rush out. "*Please*, forget you heard that."

Drew chuckles. "Charlotte."

"Actually, forget you even saw us."

"Or smelled you," Natalie sniggers.

"We will make it up to you," Drew promises.

His mother sighs. "Get inside before I have a mind to send you home."

He grins and slips his fingers through mine. We push through the first door, ignoring the stares from their guests. "Together," he whispers.

I beam, my heart beating rapidly. "Together."

EPILOGUE

CHARLOTTE
EIGHT WEEKS LATER

My life changed the night Scott hurt me. I had been a plate smashed into a wall and all that was left were all these tiny broken pieces. I observed and criticised every single one, every part of me, wondering if that was the piece that was needed or if it could be left and forgotten.

I had put it together without filling in the cracks, without healing the very fracture that made it shatter. And I did it because I needed everything to be okay. I wanted to be smiles and happiness once more.

Somewhere along the way, I became someone more. The fractured pieces of me healed, but what melded those pieces together gave me strength, courage and self-worth. It brought me into the real world with wide, open eyes. Instead of it being clouded by what happened, the skies opened, and what I felt was beautiful prior to Scott, blossomed and glowed in a way it hadn't before, in a way I could appreciate since I had tasted darkness and knew what that light truly meant.

Sophia will never again walk the streets. She is currently in a facility where she will be held until her sentencing. After her mental evaluation is done, they'll go forward with the sentencing. I'm not sure what happens to mentally unstable prisoners. Is there a place they currently go or are they thrown into a cell with everyone else? I don't know. A part of me doesn't care as long as she remains locked up.

My new security system my uncle Liam had installed at the library managed to record her confession. It helped cement our case against her and make it rock solid. She tried to claim she had done it under duress, that she wasn't well in herself. But watching that video play back in court, there was no way she could deny she was lucid during crucial moments. She knew exactly what she had done to me and to all those other women.

My only regret is Scott wasn't standing next to her. He should have been up there. His crimes were just as heinous as hers.

Her kids, a son, aged five, and a daughter, aged three, are now living with Scott's parents. All this time they had looked for him. They were beside themselves with grief when they learned what the babysitter had been doing to him, and more sickened to learn their son turned into a monster. I met his parents briefly outside the court. Both were apologetic on behalf of their son and wished me a full and happy life. I grieved for them. I grieved for what could have been and what they had lost. But they had their grandchildren to care for now, who, I was informed, are thriving and doing well thanks to my uncle who looked into it. Most monsters are made, not born. Scott was made, not by his parents' hand but by his own. His own choices wreaked havoc on those around him, those he came into contact with.

All of that is behind me.

For eight weeks since the fire I have trained. My library is due to reopen any day now, but I don't waste my time sitting around and dwelling. I use it to train. I don't want to be in a position like that again, where I can't protect my loved ones. Instead, I hung off her back using the only weapon at my disposal.

Not anymore.

Not now.

Hand in hand, Drew and I walk into the room where we are to teach our first self-defence class. Tears gather in my eyes as I take in the occupants of the room. Men and women stand before us, some looking ready to bolt, some wary and scared.

Drew looks as taken aback as I do, but he straightens his stance and expression, not losing focus on the task at hand.

Up front, standing strong and proud, are Madison, Hayden, Nora, Olivia, Harriet, Gabby and Emily. Beside them is April and Amber. I give them a smile and a wave, and the small gesture seems to make them relax.

I know from Landon—who told us before we came in—the women Drew's dad had located and Landon had gone to speak to, are inside this room. I'm not sure who is who or what their stories are, but it warms my heart to know they are here. I also know one of the women who stands amongst them is the sister of the girl who had killed herself because of Scott and his wife.

These people have had their own trauma, and their own story to tell.

They have fears and triggers.

However, the moment they walked through those doors, was a step they took to heal. It was the first step *I* took to heal.

My shoulders shake with silent tears. He did it. Drew really did it.

Hayden takes a step toward me but Drew blocks her view, standing in front of me. "If you can't do this, I can get someone else in to help me. It will be okay."

"You did it," I whisper hoarsely.

Realisation dawns and he runs his hands down my arms. "*We* did it."

I nod, stepping a little closer, close enough to feel the warmth radiating from him. "Together."

He leans down, kissing the tip of my nose. "Together."

When he turns to the class, his expression remains calm, soft, but there's an authority there that wasn't before. "Welcome, and thank you for joining us," he greets.

My eyes still glassy with tears, I watch as every single person in the room hangs on to his every word. They take it all in, all moved and touched by his wisdom. Some even stand straighter, stronger, and I can't control the storm of emotions within.

I turn and observe him, my stomach fluttering. He's like an avenging vigilante, someone who looks out for those who need it.

And he is mine.

I am his.

He didn't save me. He helped me save myself. And all these people are going to experience the same.

I don't need a dream to make things happen. Not any longer. Dreams are always good to make, fulfilling to achieve.

But I don't need to anymore. I don't need another wish or dream. I don't need to reach for one. For he is standing right next to me. Broad, tall, and powerful.

And his hand is wide open for me to take.

Sometimes, the reality is better than the dream.

Happiness and love weigh far greater when you aren't pushing for it. And my love for him outweighs us both, but it doesn't pin me down; it doesn't suffocate me.

Because I'm free-falling.

Free-falling into a life filled with much more than my dreams could ever have imagined.

And we have only just begun.

ACKNOWLEDGEMENT'S

Writing this book has felt like an obstacle I had to go through. It had been in the works since the very beginning, since the very first word I typed out during Faith. It has taken a long time to get to this book, to her story, and it was worth the wait.

Each word, every minute or hour that passed while writing Charlotte's story, felt like an achievement I never thought I'd reach—an obstacle I'd never complete.

But I did it.

And she's here, and I couldn't be prouder.

Although her story is in no way a reflection of mine, there are parts of Charlotte that *are* me, and writing her story became my dream.

For me, her character has always been this loving, funny, caring and naïve young woman. And I hope I gave that to you whilst building on her character. I hope I gave justice to a story so many women can identify with.

'No' is a two-lettered word.

Two.

But it has a far greater meaning. It's an entire sentence.

And when you say no, it means no.

Charlotte was written through grief, tears, laughter and through health issues I've been fighting. It's been a rollercoaster of emotions, but all were worth it to get to this. And I never could have done it without the constant support from my readers/ readers group. I wish I could name every single one of you.

All those who have private messaged me or even posted in the group. Whether you are new or have been there from the start, your support has kept me going. Even without mentioning names, I hope you know this applies to you. All of you.

This book is for you, and for every single one of you who continue to read this series, who make it thrive and keep going.

I'd like to say a special thank you to my beta readers. They have been so, so, so supportive whilst patiently waiting for me to finish this book. The constructive feedback has been nothing but welcome. Your praise and love have given me strength when I really needed it.

You guys are awesome, and it's been an honour working with you.

To my children, Paige, Ellie, and McKenzie, and to our new family members, Nadia and Lina: THANK YOU! Thank you for giving me the time to finish this book. For lifting me up when I felt like a failure for not being able to work. For not hating me when I was working and got lost in the story. I swear, I never purposely ignored you.

Thank you for all your uplifting support.

To Stephanie, my friend, my editor, and my alibi if I ever need one: Thank you. I know I have given you a lot of work this past year and you're probably cursing me to stop. LOL. Thank you for understanding my characters, my vision, and for being a rock when I needed it.

Working and learning from you never gets old. Or boring. *Never* boring. But I guess not everyone needs to hear about our random conversations.

Thank you for being you.

And once again to my readers: thank you for loving this series as much as I do writing it.

If you enjoyed Charlotte, please share your love and thoughts by sharing and reviewing on the appropriate platforms.

I love hearing from you, so please don't hesitate to get in touch.

And if you haven't guessed from Charlotte's story, a new series is coming.

One I think you are all going to enjoy.

To keep up to date with what's happening next,
please feel free to join my readers group:
Lisa's Luscious Readers.

BOOKS BY LISA HELEN GRAY

A Carter Brother Series

Malik – Book One (New edited version out now)
Mason – Book Two (Newly written and edited version, coming soon)
Myles – Book Three
Evan – Book 3.5
Max – Book Four
Maverick – Book Five

A Next Generation Carter Brother Novel

Faith – Book One
Aiden – Book Two
Landon – Book Three
(Read Soul of My Soul next)
Hayden – Book Four
(Read Eye for an Eye here)
Maddox – Book Five
Charlotte – Book Six

Take a Chance

Soul of My Soul – Book One
Eye for an Eye – Book Two

I Wish

If I Could I'd Wish it All Away
Wishing for a Happily Ever After

Forgotten Series

Better Left Forgotten – Book One
Obsession – Book Two
Forgiven – Book Three
(Newly written and edited versions coming soon)

Whithall University

Foul Play – Book One
Game Over – Book Two
Almost Free – Book Three

Kingsley Academy

Wrong Crowd – Book One
Crowd of Lies – Book Two

Printed in Great Britain
by Amazon